I0744828

WARPACT!

A Hunter's Universe Novel by David Michael Martin

WARPACT! ©2019 by David M. Martin.

All rights reserved. Printed in the United States of America. No part of this book may be used or reproduced in any manner whatsoever without written permission except in the case of brief quotations embodied in critical articles or reviews.

This book is a work of fiction. Names, characters, businesses, organizations, places, events and incidents either are the product of the author's imagination or are used fictitiously. Any resemblance to actual persons, living or dead, events, or locales is entirely coincidental.

For information contact:
 Bent Briar Publishing L.L.L.P.
Sahuarita, AZ 85629
www.bentbriarbooks.com

Book Design by Freelance Creative Support Services

Kidahin on Ibeetu
Original artwork by Roy S. Seger

978-1-942665-11-3   SC
978-1-942665-09-0   HC
978-1-942665-10-6   eBook

First Edition: April 2019

10 9 8 7 6 5 4 3 2 1

Dedication
This book is dedicated to the fight against global warming. A world takes care of her creatures, and her creatures should take care of her. The Eyloni know this. The Shaha did not. Humanity, it seems, forgot.

Acknowledgements
I want to thank Dr. Anne Goiran-Bevelhimer for encouraging me to become a writer. I want to thank my editor Wendie Thomas for her hours of work and my agent Laura Kathleen Sutton for the time and effort she spent in getting *WARPACT!* published. I also thank BetteRose Ryan and everyone at Bent Briar Publishing for all their efforts. Their work is greatly appreciated.

Other Titles by David Michael Martin
Hunter's Moon
Honor and Obligation

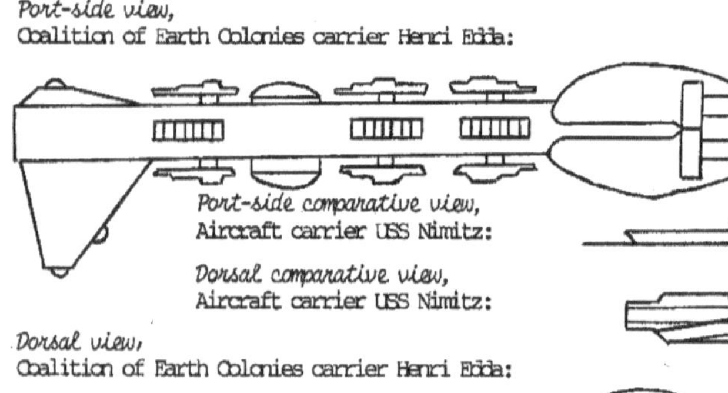

Name: CECS Henri Edda (CFA-81).

Commander: Captain Judith Arleen Rodgers, captain, Coalition Navy.

Class: Athena-class heavy carrier.

Length: 1,379.16 meters.

Beam: 225.48 meters (max), 120.51 meters (min).

Draft: 264.35 meters (max), 69.97 meters (min).

Displacement: 19,702,169 metric tons of water by volume.

Complement: 5,231 hands.

FTL propulsion: Mobius dimensional hyperdrive.

FTL apparent velocity: 1,412.7 cee, or 3.98 light years/day (max).

FTL jump shutter speed: 2.095 microseconds.

FTL coil recharge time: 3 minutes, 18.62 seconds.

Henri Edda section legend:

A – Bow, 60 decks, contains flight deck bow aperture, flight deck, ship operations and services, quarters, main and auxiliary bridge, forward fire control and point defenses.

B – Forward Quarter, 37 decks, contains fighter launch bays 1–14, support services, pilot quarters, forward hyperdrive coils 1–4, forward broadside guns and point defenses.

C – Tower, 32 decks, contains flight operations, squadron briefing, combat operations, hanger deck, maintenance bays, special operations division, Marine company, combat information center.

D – Amidships Quarter, 37 decks, contains fighter launch bays 15–28, support services, pilot quarters, amidships hyperdrive coils 5–8, amidships broadside guns and point defenses.

E – Aft Quarter, 37 decks, contains fighter launch bays 29–42, support services, pilot quarters, aft hyperdrive coils 9–12, aft broadside guns and point defenses.

F – Aft Engineering, 24 decks, contains hydrogen and antihydrogen main and reserves, Fusion-1 through Fusion-6, power systems, propulsion systems, engineering services, aft primary and secondary weapon systems.

G – Stern, 8 decks, contains four sublight drive engines.

Sublight drive: Four Thrush TO-92 hydrogen–antihydrogen pulse engines.

Sublight velocity: 150,000 km/s, or 0.50 cee (max).

Sublight acceleration: 339 km/s² (max).

Combat assets: Six fighter squadrons of fourteen fighters each, eight alphafortress heavy support (gunship and transport models), fifteen betafortress gunship (fighter squadron and Marine support models), limited APC and LAV surface support vehicles, one Marine company, and one special operations group.

Armament: Railguns (kinetic projectile), plasma and particle weapons, torpedoes and interceptor torpedoes, extensive point defense systems.

Hull composition: Duranium, kinetic reactive, and 3-stage ablative armor.

Shields: Radiological, particle, anti-EMP, and navigation.

*Port-side view,
Compact warship Hunter's Moon:*

*Port-side comparative view,
Aircraft carrier USS Nimitz:*

*Dorsal view,
Compact warship Hunter's Moon:*

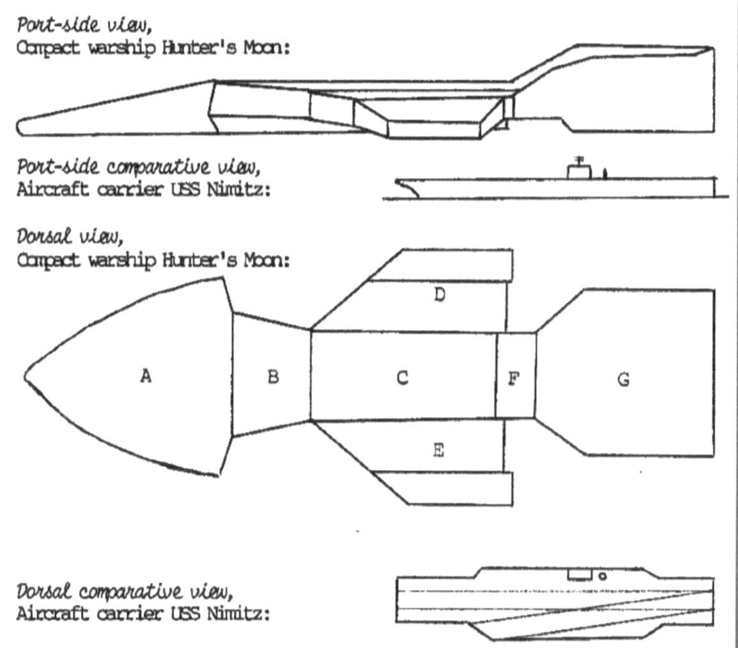

*Dorsal comparative view,
Aircraft carrier USS Nimitz:*

Name: Tyreniioroneo; literally Tyre-niioro-neo, Hunters' celestial companion, the Hunters' moon, Hunter's Moon.

Commander: Warrioress Melkorka Ah'vou'ree La'huaset Byloni, Mistress of the Ship.

Class: Tyre-class planetary assault battlecruiser.

Length: 736.46 meters.

Beam: 260.35 meters (max), 89.45 meters (min).

Draft: 86.25 meters (max), 7.74 meters (min).

Displacement: 6,726,955 metric tons of water by volume.

Complement: 2,886 total; 1,635 crew, 1,250 combat forces, 1 warleader.

Hunter's Moon section legend:

A – Combat hull contains primary weapon systems, Fusion-1 and Fusion-2, ordnance bays, torpedo bays, hydrogen and antihydrogen reserves.

B – Forestation contains combat support, damage control, and forward point defense systems.

C – Command Hull contains ship operations and services, crew quarters, combat staging bay, fuel reserve, and emergency power systems.

D – Starboard Outrigger contains broadside weapon systems and secondary weapon systems.

E – Port Outrigger contains broadside weapon systems and secondary weapon systems.

F – Aftstation contains engineering security, damage control, and aft point defense systems.

G – Engineering Hull contains power systems, propulsion systems, Fusion-3 and Fusion-4, primary fuel, engineering, and engineering services.

FTL propulsion: Quantum-translation jump drive.

FTL apparent velocity: 1,375.47 cee, or 3.93 light years/day (max).

FTL jump radius: 2.332 light years (max).

FTL jump frequency: 14.852 hours/jump (min).

FTL jump transit time: 30 nanoseconds.

Sublight drive: Two hydrogen-antihydrogen pulse engines.

Sublight velocity: 207,000 km/s, or 0.69 cee (max).

Sublight acceleration: 492 km/s^2 (max).

Combat assets: Troop transports, gunships, mechanized infantry (LAV, APC, mobile weapon systems), mechanized armor (light, medium, heavy track and hover tanks).

Armament: Railguns (kinetic projectile), plasma and particle weapons, variable yield nuclear breach and radiologic torpedoes.

Hull composition: Duranium (depleted uranium), kinetic reactive, and 2-stage ablative armor.

Shields: Radiological, particle, anti-EMP, and navigation.

Table of Contents

1

YASUNI NATIONAL PARK ECUADOR, UNITED EARTH...

"Your Excellencies? There is an incoming green channel priority one hyperlink message from Elleio, from the Compact Counsel itself," the intercom blared.

"Accept," co-Ambassador Anlann and co-Ambassador Seralin sang out in unison.

Anlann smirked at his Protectress, and she perked her ears and made tiny circles in the air with her ringlet-covered tail tip, her *pons*, at him.

"Transferring hyperlink communications packet to your Excellencies' communications terminal now," the voice advised.

"Thank you," Anlann said. His eyes met Seralin's, and he sighed. *Excellencies.* Humans had more courtesy titles than he could poke his tail at.

"He is trying to show respect," Seralin admonished, smelling the dismay in her warleader's scent.

"It is underhanded subterfuge," he complained. "Humans observe more rank courtesies than you females do."

"Hah! Humans know what rank is all about, something you males take for granted. Rank and status are what hold the female hierarchies together. I just do not understand the inconsistencies in how humans use them."

"You mean among the general population?" Anlann asked. "Yes, I know. A seemingly arrogant and disrespectful people, are they not?"

"Sometimes yes," she agreed. "All humans act strange, inconsistent. Talking with them is exhausting. Their words often say things their body language and scent do not."

The far wall faded from sight as a solid-looking holographic image began to form. Patterns chased themselves from one diagonal to the other as they bounced off the edges and reflected to the center of the room. They slowly assembled into a puzzle of stunning visual complexity. Eyloni visual centers had evolved to allow them to visually identify places and people at a glance based on their unique color patterns. Anlann and Seralin used this ability, as every Eyloni could, to see complex numerical data in visual images as easily as human statisticians could read numbers from a probability table.

Anlann strolled up to the interactive image and started touching the pattern at specific points. The dancing image presented an encryption problem. Anlann's cipher entry would cause the light show to transform into a landscape simulation. Once begun, he had to complete the process within twenty seconds, or the message would self-delete. He continued to touch data points, solving calculations intuitively that a human would need over an hour to complete.

When he touched the last point, the blossoming fireworks display flipped from a bouncing three-dimensional web into a dark pool edged by orange grass. Scarlet, pumpkin, and goldenrod leaves hung from background trees, bushes, and vines. Water fell down a rocky hillside into the pool. A stream bubbled from the overflowing pool and ran down a twisting mountain path until it reached the waterfall. There the water spilled over the falls, refilling the pool.

Anlann's part in the authentication process was complete.

Seralin playfully shoved her warleader aside and sang to the impossible picture. The stream began to flow, making the Escher scene look plausible. The water in the stream flowed downhill and yet wound its way up and over the hillside before spilling back down the falls again. Water chased itself up and around the crimson and pumpkin moss-covered rocky hillside and plunged over and down the tall, narrow, boulder-strewn falls. The dark pool refilled over and over as bubbling water raced up and around the impossible closed stream, waiting for the co-Ambassadors to submit to voice print and retinal scan verification.

Anlann and Seralin stepped up to the fantasy image and sang their names and titles, the only titles that were truly meaningful to them.

"Anlann, Warleader of *Surefooted*," the Eyloni male said.

"Seralin—Protectress, Mistress of the Watch, and Mistress of Inner Strength—Compact warship *Surefooted*," the Hunter female replied.

The room-spanning picture dissolved and then reformed into a perfect likeness of an old Warrior female. She, as all Eyloni females did, wore her traditional neckwear—a necklace woven from long colorful knotted strings that dangled over her breasts, showing all who could read the knots and weavings where she stood within the female hierarchies. She also wore the usual hip-riding waistwear, an underthong, and short clan-colored loincloth. This was the communications avatar of

Thelindrallin, the Be'atika Senge Counsel-speaker. Her skin had the range of red, orange, and variegated yellow colors that were common phenotypic expressions of all Warrior females. The avatar, an artificial intelligence construct, had been programmed with enough of the counsel mistress's knowledge and personality and sent along with the hyperlink communications packet. Its job was to interact with its intended audience. It could discuss, clarify, or answer questions about message particulars within the limits of its knowledge base.

The AI avatar solved a touchy social problem. Eyloni craved physical contact and close companionship, and those cravings made one-way messages awkward. Real-time bidirectional communications were impossible over the intervening 127 light-years between Earth and Elleio even at 2,920 *cee* hyperlink velocities.

"Warleader Anlann, Mistress Seralin," the avatar began. "I bring you greetings from the Compact Counsel. On behalf of Delwyn O'un Tu La'huaset Eyloni ar ahoun Unahaillaea *Tyreniioroneo,* the A'tayotan, and the Be'atika Senge, I ask that you consent to being recalled back to the Nikkiolo star system. A Compact battle group will rendezvous with you there. Before you decide, please review the following analysis and recommendations made by Delwyn, the Male Voice of the A'tayotan and Warpact leader of the Society of Warleaders."

Thelindrallin's image ghosted into the background, giving the co-Ambassadors the impression that the avatar was watching from across the room as the holoimage expanded into a detailed panoramic view of the inside of a living structure formed from the buttressing fused aerial roots that grew down and around a massive elleiu tree. Anlann and Seralin found themselves staring into the forest-floor level of the A'tayotan hierarchy home tree, the elleiu tree that sheltered the A'tayotan, their immediate families, and the part of Compact government responsible for setting military policy and protecting the lives of all Eyloni males.

This was the A'tayotan Hall of Consensus, a living enclosure grown from tangled aerial roots that had long ago fused into a woodpile maze of random multilevel open chambers. The Hall surrounded the over one hundred-ell thick trunk, growing out from it at least another one hundred ells at ground level and winding up and around the trunk, shrouding it, and continuing into the lowest branches some three hundred ells above the forest floor. As they watched, over a thousand Eyloni females, twenty or so Eyloni males, and one solid tan male—Delwyn O'un Tu La'huaset Eyloni—a human everyone on Elleio saw as Eyloni, gathered there. The view sharpened as it focused on a speaking Thelindrallin.

"The A'tayotan have called the strategy counsel into session. Delwyn ar ahoun Unahaillaea Tyreniioroneo, *Warleader of* Hunter's Moon, *the A'tayotan yields to the Male Voice. Stand and assume Warpact leadership over the Society of Warleaders."*

Before Delwyn could stand, Mrallin, the Eldest male and advisor to the all-female Be'atika Senge, the seat of government for the Compact of the Ten Tribes of Elleio, sang *"I yield Warpact command to Delwyn ar ahoun Unahaillaea Tyreniioroneo."* By yielding Warpact, he consented to the transfer of Warpact command which he held over the male advisors in Counsel. Thelindrallin desired the transfer but it was not hers to give. Only Mrallin could yield his position under the custom of male autonomy.

Anlann and Seralin stood in awe as their shared astonishment vied with the shock of seeing their intimate friend Delwyn become the Male Voice of the A'tayotan and of hearing the analysis he had presented to the A'tayotan hierarchy days ago.

The briefing ran for some time before another surprise leapt out at them.

"Delwyn wishes to sing a Song of Contemplation!" Thelindrallin told the Counsel.

The co-Ambassadors listened, mesmerized as Delwyn sang battle songs to the A'tayotan. When he gave permission, they sang along with him as they danced around him in graceful, rhythmic patterns.

Seralin had to bite her lip to resist being carried along with the singing male's music. Had she been there herself, the pheromonal empathy all Eyloni possessed would have pulled her into the emotional metamind created by the singing females.

"Impossible. Impossible," she muttered. "They are in the grip of his music."

"What about it?" Anlann whispered. "You know he has singing male talents. How do you think he became warleader in the first place?"

"Not that, you oaf. I cannot believe they allowed him to sing them into ecstasy. The A'tayotan are…dignified…and they are a deadly serious hierarchy. They have known Mrallin for years. I can see him singing with them like this, but Delwyn has never sang with them before."

Anlann shrugged, not seeing her point. Females responded to the emotion called up by the singing male voice. Music boosted scent-linked pheromonal empathy. A singing male could toggle extremely violent protective instincts in females, instincts meant to rally them to male defense or provide them with a much-needed morale boost during combat. If Delwyn had poured maximum effort into his battle songs he could have whipped them up into a bloodthirsty rage. Blinded by the song's intensity, they would follow as he led them into battle against any foe he wished. Unleashed, they would kill anyone in his way and disregard the dangers such a battle would pose to them.

A male's song summoned massive female aid, which explained why every male had an obligation not to let himself get dragged into hopeless battles or force females to face dangers on a whim. A male's honor demanded he not sing them into an aggressive state for no reason. If he did so, then the many different hierarchies—each and every single one of them an exclusively female organization—would seek him out for the honor crime and pour dire revenge on him.

Delwyn stopped singing. He turned and walked over to a floating screen. Seralin narrowed her eyes and tried to focus on the display data.

Delwyn appeared to be reading mission logs from the archives, studying his Mistress of Tactics's combat analysis scans and reviewing Mistress of Battle Brelioranda's talkback telemetry data. That data included a detailed analysis of the interior design of a Ni'zakhonii destroyer before they blew it up with her, her assault forces, and Kalinn, the warleader of *Hunter's Moon* before Delwyn, still aboard.

He took his time reading too, well over two hours, before he turned back to the A'tayotan and began speaking again. The A'tayotan listened, tails twitching and ears pricking. That was natural enough. Females always listened to males. They did not always see eye-to-eye with them, but males were loved, respected, and never ignored.

When Delwyn stopped speaking, a Hunter female's singing voice rang out from somewhere among the tangled aerial roots.

"Mistress, we have reached a Consensus," she sang to Thelindrallin.

"What is the Consensus?" Thelindrallin asked.

"That we must determine whether or not the captured equipment can hold more than two FTL-capable probes and have those findings reported back to the A'tayotan."

Seralin flicked her elegant ears in absent acknowledgment of the sound strategy. The revolting, bipedal reptile enemy, the Ni'zakhonii, had no faster-than-light communications capability. Without hyperlink communications, the cannibals had to employ FTL courier probes to convey messages over interstellar distances.

"Further, we do not allow the Hall of Consensus to adjourn until Delwyn ar ahoun Unahaillaea Tyreniioroneo proposes strategies for dealing with this threat," the Hunter continued.

"Now, wait just a min...Ugh!" Delwyn grunted as Melkorka his Warrior Mistress of the Ship, Phelindra his Hunter Protectress, and Zalzadrin one of his Hunter combat specialists simultaneously gigged him in the ribs.

Anlann's sudden explosive laughter jolted Seralin from her fixated stare on the impossibility playing out before her.

She paused to scowl at her favorite male.

"They are impressed with him," he commented.

"If the last destroyer launched a courier probe at G-band velocity to conserve fuel, and it reached the destroyers' base, then the Ni'zakhonii can either send a task force or a battle group to the Nikkiolo heliopause in 150 ...ah 1,100 ... days. We will have to send a battle group no later than 410 days from now," Delwyn told the A'tayotan.

"Here it comes," Anlann hummed. He already knew the outcome. Why else would Thelindrallin have sent this A'tayotan archive and message?

Seralin remained motionless and listened, watching the body language of the people standing among the soaring aerial roots and vaulting enclosure surrounding the A'tayotan home tree that twisted all the way up to the lowest branches several thousand *ells* above the rainforest floor. Without people's scent to help her gauge the gathering's emotions she paid strict notice to their postures. The body never lied.

"I propose the following," Delwyn said. *"A battle group consisting of a command battleship, one or two planetary assault battlecruisers, and screening elements in some grouping of destroyers and heavy battlecruisers must arrive within the next 1,100 days in the Nikkiolo star system. This mission is a search and destroy operation; however, planetary surface assault forces are necessary to guarantee partial or total recovery of captured research data and materials. In the alternative, they must ensure the destruction of all materials not captured or otherwise recovered. This battle group must depart Elleio orbit within the next 410 days."*

Anlann nodded to himself.

Seralin frowned as she saw Melkorka's face contort with rage as she argued privately with Delwyn over some matter.

Seralin thought she knew what had the Warrior female's tail in a knot. Her warleader had suggested a combat mission, a mission their battle-damaged warship could not participate in, and that had put her in a bad mood.

The warleaders closed ranks around Delwyn and drew him over to examine several floating holodisplays. Females worldwide knew every warleader in the Compact fleet on sight. Seralin recognized Phalalin, warleader of *Fearless*, acting as Delwyn's interpreter and confidante. That made sense to her. *Fearless* had brought ten males from Elleio to Nikkiolo for huluhar Kidahin to choose a new warleader from. By the time Phalalin had arrived in the Nikkiolo system, Melkorka and her society had already decided on Delwyn and sent a *sahagan* message not to disturb them. They chose him because Kidahin had found him to have the proper male temperament. Phalalin then assumed the honor escort point off Delwyn's bow and escorted his damaged warship back to Elleio.

Seralin was certain that the two males had formed an intimate friendship by now.

The Thelindrallin avatar must have noticed Seralin trying to read the screen the males shared because the archive playback shifted perspective to show them gathered around a display set to catalogue mode.

Anlann thought they were reviewing warship combat statistics for all naval assets available along with those assets capable of arriving in homespace within 320 days. That had been 122 days ago. He and Seralin would have to leave in 232 days if they wanted to meet Delwyn's 1,100 day arrival deadline.

Delwyn, Phalalin, and Warleader Calalin were taking their time monopolizing the screens at the moment. Next to Calalin stood a Comari female. The Comara were mute, sterile, and tailless. They presented a deadly danger to anyone smelling like a possible threat to the males they had chosen to protect for as long as they lived.

That she tolerated Delwyn so close to Calalin surprised Seralin. Male births rarely occurred, and all three Eyloni female gender phenotypes—Hunter, Warrior, and Comara—protected males at all costs. That said, the Comara females took no chances with the males they had taken a lifetime personal interest in.

Seralin watched Delwyn head back toward an impatient Melkorka. They exchanged words, and then she turned and fled the Hall.

"I think Delwyn got his warship included into the battle group," Seralin said.

"What makes you say that?" Anlann asked, curious.

"Melkorka had no reason to leave her warleader unless there was a need to obtain the latest repair estimates from her Mistress of Sails."

Anlann thought about it as a Warrior stood among the assembled A'tayotan.

"Mistress, we have reached a Consensus," she announced.

"What is the Consensus?" Thelindrallin demanded.

"A task force consisting of Pathfinder, Green Ivy, Steep Trails, Padfoot, Fearless, and Stone Knife *shall go and investigate the* Nikkiolo *star system. The warships* Surefooted *and* Night Shadow *are held in reserve pending the updated repair status of* Hunter's Moon.

"We will send a request asking Warleader Anlann to return. In the meantime, Hunter's Moon *is granted extraordinary accommodation."*

"Ahwroona would have to sortie with the main task force without us. Do you think she would do it, take *Surefooted* anywhere without you?" Seralin asked.

Anlann had been wondering the same thing. The warleader was the only male permitted aboard a warship crewed by his females. His presence made them ferocious fighters whenever they thought he faced danger. His singing gave them a confidence and morale boost impossible to ignore by them because they had evolved an instinct to protect rare males. Ahwroona, his Mistress of the Ship, would not consider moving her warship so much as a planetary diameter without him absent some pressing need that included a reunion with him in the end. Female crews, ship's societies, owned their warships outright and agreed to fight in the Compact's name. They were honor-bound to those agreements and held those obligations in high regard, but warships were also considered male entities having nearly the same independence Eyloni males did. Ahwroona had the right to refuse the Counsel in the name of warship autonomy.

"Well," Anlann mused. "Delwyn and Phalalin have twined their tails together in this venture. The A'tayotan knows we are indisposed as long as we are acting as the Counsel's representatives here on Earth. They would not have suggested our warship's inclusion in any mission planning under normal circumstances. Delwyn must have asked for us. Melkorka probably told him that his Mistress of Sails could complete repairs to their warship ahead of the sortieing deadline."

"The Coalition warship *Henri Edda* cannot get us to Elleio before Delwyn's recommended 333-day departure window, a departure time decided 113 days ago. We must rendezvous in the Nikkiolo Expanse if we are to rejoin Ahwroona aboard our warship. We have to leave Earth in 233 days," Seralin said.

Anlann nodded as he effortlessly converted Elleio Standard Time, the time standard females used, into Tyreniioroneo Standard Time, the time standard males used.

"You need to call Alan and let him know that he will be leaving for Elleio sooner than he thought," she added.

He nodded again and punched a button on his desk.

"Yes, your Excellency?" the human receptionist answered.

"Please contact Ambassador Plenipotentiary Alan Dean Winters and tell him we must speak to him on an urgent matter."

"Yes, your Excellency. One moment please."

Seralin addressed the waiting communications avatar. "Mistress Thelindrallin, when and where are we to rendezvous with the main task force?"

"In 344 days, in the Nikkiolo system heliopause. Due to the limits imposed upon Coalition FTL propulsion systems when operating near stellar-mass objects, Delwyn proposes that you rendezvous at the spot where Warleader Kalinn destroyed three Ni'zakhonii destroyers rather than meeting in Ibeetu orbit. Delwyn told us you would know the name 'Ibeetu'."

"We do," Seralin agreed.

"This mission has been classified under Compact Seal. You may not discuss operational matters with the Coalition Government at this time," the Thelindrallin avatar cautioned. "If you miss the rendezvous point, you are advised not to draw notice to the main task force by initiating a search for it. In the doubtful event Delwyn's warship has been repaired to a level sufficient to let him sortie with a reserve task force, then both task forces will combine and form a battle group in the Nikkiolo heliopause. However, if your warship misses the battle group, then the Be'atika Senge asks that you continue on to Elleio and deliver Coalition Counsel-speaker Alan Dean Winters to the Be'atika Senge."

"I am agreeable with that." Anlann said from across the room. "Even though I think it is adventurous to prowl down trails through dead-looking jungle, I am ready to leave this green horror of a rainforest."

Seralin smiled. The United Earth government had accommodated them well, building them a compound within the tropical Ecuadorian rainforests. The embassy had been built near the Rio Napo, a major tributary supplying water to the Amazon River that brushed the northern boundary of the Yasuni National Park. A modest mountain range called

Andes ran north and south on their west flank. It supported several old but still-functioning hydroelectric power stations. Putting the embassy in South America had been the United Earth government's idea because the rainforest contained several landmarks similar to those in the northeastern temperate rainforests of the La'huaset Tribal continent on Elleio.

Living on Earth for the last few months had been both strange and exhilarating for Anlann and Seralin. It had taken some time for Seralin to adjust to a sky with a sun bent on zipping across it so fast she saw it moving. Sunshine filled Elleio skies for over eleven Earth days followed by over eleven days in darkness. On her homeworld mean global temperatures increased and then decreased over a gradual arc during the twenty-three Earth days it took her tidal-locked homeworld to make one rotation. Earth on the other hand revolved around its axis once every 2.1 EST days, which caused rapid temperature increases and decreases compared to temperatures on Elleio. Earth was a cooler world, too. It also *was* a planet, whereas Elleio was the habitable moon of the gas giant Tyreniioroneo. Earth's heavier gravity did not bother her at all. But the dark-green rainforest made her hair stand up. It looked sinister to her. She wondered if her feelings were a reaction to the human stories she had been reading.

Seralin's research into human psychology had led her to examine human literature. Some stories fixated on giving the spirits physical forms and hostile attributes. Another class of stories featured creatures somehow alive although they were dead bodies: zombies. Then there was the subgenre devoted to fantasy stories and impossible creatures meant to induce fear reactions. She did not find those stories fearsome or worrisome and had wondered what effect all this self-inflicted fear-mongering had on human mental health. She was the Mistress of Inner Strength aboard her warship, what humans called a counsellor, and she had a professional interest in such matters.

If she had to describe the Earth rainforest, although no doubt beautiful in human eyes, she would say it reminded her of the zombie stories. Yes, it was a zombie forest. It did not smell dead—exactly—but it looked dead, dead and malignant. On Elleio dead foliage turned green. Dead Eyloni lost their leafy skin color patterns and turned green as they decomposed. The only living green plants in her home forest belonged to the parasitic vines that did not photosynthesize and had to leech sap from the red, orange, and yellow trees to live. The parasitic vines sounded to her like another subgenre creature: vampires. The Earth forest conjured up visions from a creepy nightmare more disturbing in many ways than Ibeetu's blue-green alien forest had not been. She could find no satisfactory explanation for her feelings. Even the tallest trees here did not rate bush status next to the smallest Elleio tree, which did not help.

"I am ready to leave these small green trees behind," she grumbled.

"I agree with you. Although the jungle canopy is so close to the ground and its green leaves are small, they block out much more sunlight than our rainforests back home do. More stalking skills are needed to remain hidden as we prowl through this jungle's greens, browns, and blacks because of our skin colors. But, don't you think it's been a little bit exciting?"

Seralin turned away from the communications avatar to give her lovable simpleminded male goof an indulgent smile. "What you find interesting and exciting eludes me, which does not surprise me. Males are strange."

She turned back to speak to the avatar. "Mistress Thelindrallin, what is the A'tayotan's official reason for our early recall?"

"You may tell the Coalition Government we have a priority need for wanting you and Anlann in the Nikkiolo star system within the time stipulated by Warleader Delwyn. Once you are on the way to Nikkiolo, you may share operational data with Counsel-speaker Alan Dean Winters as you feel the need. As he comes here to assume the obligations of a male advisor to the Be'atika Senge, his honor will naturally require him to keep any details you give in the strictest confidence. That being said, if it becomes clear to you that keeping silent will place the Coalition warship in jeopardy, you may disclose any and all necessary operational parameters."

"It might be prudent to consider incorporating the Coalition warship into the battle group," Anlann offered.

"Delwyn did not suggest that," the communications avatar replied.

"Your Excellency? I have Ambassador Winters on the line for you, sir," the embassy secretary interrupted.

Anlann sighed. *Sir!* Another euphemistic honorific that humans loved to use, but their postures and scents told him they did not always mean. It was frustrating! Their words and turns-of-phrases sometimes drew hilarious images in his mind that did not match the emotional imagery he gleaned from their scent. What did 'on the line' mean anyway? The distance between two points? The secretary was in another room, so Anlann had no scent to establish context.

"Accept," he said.

Seralin spoke to the AI avatar. "Close down and store yourself for later advice."

"Affirm," the Thelindrallin avatar sang. It vanished along with the panoramic interior view of the massive tree. In its place appeared the seated profile of Alan Dean Winters.

"Good morning Anlann, Seralin. What can I do for you? Your secretary said it was important."

"Good morning Alan. It is important. I am afraid Seralin and I have been recalled to Nikkiolo by the Compact Counsel. We must join our warship there."

Winters considered. The only ship available and capable of carrying three ambassadors with sufficient attendant protective force was *Henri Edda*. Right now she was in lunar orbit undergoing refueling, repair, and replenishment, while his former executive officer Judith Arleen Rodgers was getting up to speed in her new capacity as captain.

"When?" remained Winters asked, his expression carefully neutral but mentally a frown had already begun to form.

"We must arrive there no later than 142 Earth days from now," Anlann said.

Winters wrestled with the Eyloni base-five number system. An Eyloni one hundred was a human twenty-five, an Eyloni forty was a human twenty, and a two, being less than five, was still a two. The numbers added up to forty-seven. They wanted to leave Earth in forty-seven days.

"Earth is closer to Iota Horologii than Elleio is. That means we will have to leave almost four days after a Compact ship leaves Elleio. We'd have to leave the solar system in about thirty-three days if you want us to rendezvous with them. I can be ready soon enough, but I'll have to give Captain Rodgers a heads-up. Then I'll have to advise the Diplomatic Corps and the Defense Directorate, in that order. The Coalition Navy does not sortie a starship fast unless it is an emergency. It'll take the better part of a month to get orders cut authorizing this milk run. Let me get back to you, will you Anlann?"

"Of course Alan, I will be waiting."

"Good. Hello Seralin, are you enjoying the Amazon rainforest?" Winters asked with an exaggerated grin.

"No, I am not! You think this is funny but wait until you find yourself walking through Elleio jungles. I will see that you remember your amusement then," Seralin growled, swatting her tail through his holographic neck.

"I'm sure, and then we can laugh about it together. As it turns out, I have quite a few stories to tell everyone about you when we arrive."

"You would not dare!" Seralin trilled.

Anlann laughed at his Protectress's expense, causing her to swat her tail at him in not quite so playful anger.

"Good-bye Alan," Seralin said.

The image faded and then vanished.

The co-Ambassadors looked at one another a moment before Anlann sighed.

"I have to prepare. I must plan for a combat mission based on hypotheticals decided when the hyperlink packet had been transmitted some 122 days ago. By now, the Mistress of the Hunt has probably poked her tail all over Delwyn's mission planning.

Seralin agreed—a lot could happen in those intervening 113 days.

***

Butterflies…

Thoughts of butterflies were very much on Captain Judith Arleen Rodgers's mind as she walked down her ship's corridors. *Her ship!* She had a crew address to write, but the churning butterflies in her stomach kept blotting her mind clear before she accumulated more than twenty words.

Rodgers preferred direct action in response to a tactical problem. She never expected in her wildest dreams to find herself thrust into the captain's seat quite so soon. Captain Winters's sudden appointment as Coalition of Earth Colonies ambassador to the Compact of the Ten Tribes of Elleio had left a vacuum in the ship's command structure. With no captain available having any experience whatsoever in carrier tactics, the Admiralty had decided in its infinite wisdom to advance her to the captaincy.

Several objections had come to mind at first. She had been content to remain as the ship's executive officer. Being the 2IC, the second-in-command, gave her the best of both worlds. She commanded when the captain was unavailable or on the bridge but didn't want the conn, but the responsibility remained his alone. A captain was responsible for the conduct of everyone under her command. She didn't want to dwell too much on that, but the job was hers now. There was no getting around it: she was the captain of CECS *Henri Edda*.

Twisting the single titanic brown braid that hung down to the small of her back in one hand, she tried once more in her deep, husky voice. "Be seated. To everyone remaining aboard during Triple-R, returnees from shore leave, and transfer personnel, welcome aboard CECS *Henri Edda*. Many of you may have expected Captain Winters to be giving this address. You will be pleased to hear that he has accepted a three-year assignment as ambassador to the Eyloni Compact on Elleio. I may have been advanced to the captaincy, but I can never replace Captain Winters. My name is … I am Captain Rodgers …" *No… Maybe I should introduce myself first? Then …*

"Captain Rodgers?" a woman's voice whispered from the corridor intercom.

"Yes, Lieutenant Romaine?" Rodgers muttered.

"Ma'am? I have an incoming message from Ambassador Winters," her chief communications officer advised.

Uh-oh, what happened now? *Did the Captain want his ship back?*

"Priority?" she asked Romaine.

"No, Ma'am. Unofficial traffic coding, but there's an intensity about him I remember. Something's come up in my opinion, Ma'am."

"*Hmm*…Put him through. I'll take it down here on the corridor comm."

"Aye, Captain … Patching through. Go ahead, Mr. Ambassador."

"Judith?"

"Yes, Captain?" Rodgers replied.

Winters laughed. "You're the captain now, Exec. I'm just an ambassador, remember? One who lacks even a shred of diplomatic training. You wouldn't believe how much it's driving the Diplomatic Corps crazy putting up with me. At the moment, I'm also an ambassador who just had a load dumped into his lap."

"By Anlann?" Rodgers guessed.

"Indeed. The Compact Counsel has issued a priority recall alert for the co-Ambassadors at Senior Chief Warrant Officer Marsch's insistence—well, make that Warleader Delwyn now. We're to take the co-Ambassadors back to Iota Horologii and rendezvous with Anlann's ship and probably a Compact battle group as well. When we arrive, Anlann and Seralin will transfer to their warship, which I was told will make the journey from Elleio to Iota Horologii without him. As I understand it, a Mistress of the Ship is reluctant to take her ship anywhere without her warleader. That tells me something serious is going on."

"A battle group?" Rodgers echoed. "Did Anlann tell you what a Compact battle group would be doing in the Iota Horologii system?"

"No, but I got the gut feeling that I'll get more intel once we get underway. My captain's intuition's already telling me there's some classified operation in progress there. Anlann made it clear we cannot arrive before the Compact ships because they can't leave Elleio for another twenty-nine days. That tells me they're recalling ships from their patrol sectors. It takes a Compact ship eighteen and a half days to reach Iota Hor. With Delwyn involved, I wouldn't doubt the Compact Counsel is hoping to send *Hunter's Moon* along with them. We are not required to intrude into the system any farther than somewhere between the system's termination shock wave and its heliopause. That said, I have reasons for and against wanting to return to Ibeetu."

"Why and why not?" Rodgers demanded, privately doubting that an Elleio shipyard could get a badly shot-up *Hunter's Moon* combat-ready that soon.

"Why? Well, I have a suspicion that Ambassador Harrison and Cultural Attaché Parakh may have been stranded there by Delwyn's ship security. As for why not, I don't want to get caught behind the star's heavy mass hyperlimit if things get dicey."

"What makes you think Delwyn had Harrison and his aide stranded on Ibeetu?" Rodgers asked.

"Oh, don't get me wrong. I'm sure they did it without his knowledge. Eyloni females are protective of males, and if they saw Harrison as a threat they wouldn't take any chances with Delwyn's safety. It's just a feeling I have. Harrison tried to get Delwyn labeled a traitor and charged with interstellar piracy. I've been told it's a death offense on Elleio to cause harm or intend to cause harm to a male. You haven't found Harrison or his aide in the 'tween hulls spaces yet, have you?"

"No," Rodgers admitted. "As to that why not, it sounds to me like Anlann is worried about getting us caught up in a combat mission, and he doesn't want us so far in-system that we can't use our hyperdrive."

"That's my read on it too."

"A rendezvous means we would have to leave almost four days later if we are to arrive at the same time. Leaving in thirty-three days? Hmm… That's faster than naval operations likes to consider when planning ships movement. Have you gotten the green light from the Coalition Assembly, the Defense Directorate, and the Admiralty, Sir?"

Winters scowled at her. "I haven't talked to them yet. Even allowing for the time all the red tape will take, you do understand that the Coalition is not going to piss off its first alien ambassadors. I'm giving you a heads-up so you can prepare to get underway in thirty-three days. By the time the brass authorizes this mission, I'm betting you'll have less than two weeks to get underway, tops."

"But Captain, I'm in the middle of Triple-R. It'll take me at least a week just to get into an antihydrogen refueling slot at Jupiter," she swore under her breath.

"Exactly. If I were you Captain, and I'm not, but I'd say you ought to anticipate a deployment order requesting and requiring you to rendezvous with a Compact warship at Iota Horologii and drop off Anlann and Seralin before diverting to HD 10180 Hydri to deliver the Coalition Ambassador, me, to the Compact Counsel."

Rodgers nodded. "I get the picture. Thank you for the heads-up, Captain."

Winters shrugged his shoulders. "I'll probably see you on Tycho Base with the CNC sometime soon. Until then, Captain."

"Aye, aye, Captain. Rodgers out."

Great, just great, Rodgers thought as she forgot what she had memorized of her flimsy welcome-to-the-ship speech.

"Lieutenant Romaine issue an immediate recall of all personnel. Warn everyone on leave that failure to report ASAP might result in missing ships movement. Tell the Exec to meet me in Combat Information Center."

"Aye, Captain," Romaine acknowledged.

Well well well, Rodgers mused. If this development didn't sound like something dreamed up by Captain Winters, then she couldn't imagine a more dubious coincidence. She already knew they would have to take him to Elleio sooner or later so he could assume his new post as Coalition ambassador. The Compact Counsel had all but demanded that the Coalition Government name him ambassador in the stead of Ambassador Honorius Alphonse Harrison.

Co-Ambassadors Anlann and Seralin had endorsed Winters, pledging their honor on the captain's behalf. Rather than risk losing its first treaty alliance with an alien race, the Coalition Government had fallen all over itself making every effort to appease the Eyloni. Once Senior Chief Marsch, now a Compact warleader, had made his wishes known, the Compact Counsel had been affronted by the idea of allowing Harrison anywhere near the surface of Elleio again. Captain Winters would exercise Counsel-speaker rank as an advisor along with the Eyloni males who advised the Be'atika Senge. Captain Winters would become the first ambassador in history to simultaneously hold a seat in a foreign government.

Rodgers doubted the Coalition Government would ever consider affording Anlann and Seralin the same courtesy. Neither the United Earth government nor the Coalition Government would invite foreign ambassadors into their messy domestic policy debates.

Rodgers headed for CIC, wondering about Harrison. Unless he and his cultural attaché had been marooned somewhere on Ibeetu, he had to be somewhere aboard the ship. They had disappeared well over six weeks ago. A search of all quarters and compartments had failed to turn up any sign of them. Still, there were several hundred meters of 'tween hulls catwalks, niches, and cubbyholes between the inner and outer hulls where someone could hide.

Or stuff a body, damn Marsch and his hyperprotective Eyloni females. God, she hoped they hadn't killed Harrison and his aide, but she had her doubts.

The CIC, located in the Tower complex within the fourteen-hundred-meter-long ship, contained the carrier's combat operations nerve center. The Tower housed Flight Operations, Combat Information Center, Combat Operations Center, and Special Operations Center. CIC was a huge, dimly-lit room filled with consoles and heads-up holographic monitors, plotting tables, corded handsets, data terminals, and seats. When not in the Triple-R dock, there were between forty and fifty people wandering from station to station, and when the ship stood at Condition-2 or Condition-1, that number nearly doubled, leaving over a third standing. Today about a dozen people manned their stations, including the gamma shift watch, Marine security personnel, the former CIC Command Duty Officer and now her Exec, and the new CIC CDO.

"Good evening, Captain," Commander David Eugene Cabrera said.

"Good evening, Exec. How's your replacement doing? Learning the ropes, is she?"

"Well, I don't know Captain. You know how those Tactical Operations Officers are," the Latino said as he waggled his eyebrows at the Black woman standing next to him.

"I'm getting along just fine Sir, Ma'am," Millford said.

Command Duty Officer Commander Kiesha Aya Millford frowned at Cabrera and then made a face at him. A TOO was the CIC's eyes and ears on the bridge, but the CDO fought the ship, a job for which Millford was well-qualified. From CIC, Millford had often supervised combat operations for special operations group missions, flight ops, and combat maneuvering.

Millford had found herself suddenly third in the executive chain of command. Commander Guthrey, the carrier's Commander Air Group, hovered in the background as a reluctant fourth in line. A distant and unlikely but technically possible fifth, surprisingly, was Senior Chief Warrant Officer Cummings, Commander of SOG-444 Special Operations, Marsch's former XO. A warrant officer was not a line officer, and would normally be sneered at and discounted rather than fall into the ship's command structure but for one special case scenario. If the ship happened to be involved in an SOG-444 special ops mission and the entire command staff killed, then command fell to Cummings. Once the special operations mission had been completed, command would fall on the senior command bridge officer. Just exactly when the special op was over depended on when Cummings said it was, however.

"I'm sure you are," Rodgers said with a reassuring smile. "Exec, a word if you please?"

Cabrera nodded and followed Rodgers over to an unoccupied fire control station.

"I've just received word from Captain Winters that we are going back to Iota Horologii at Anlann's request in about thirty-three days. Expect to get a fleet ops notice within forty-eight hours of the departure window for a flash diplomatic run. I think we're heading for a rendezvous with a Compact battle group. We're to drop off the Compact co-Ambassadors and then reenter hyperspace and continue to Elleio and deliver Captain Winters to the Compact Counsel. I expect we'll also be ferrying the co-Ambassadors' replacements back to Earth."

Cabrera's eyes wrinkled. "You think the Eyloni are sweeping Iota Hor for a Lizard base?"

"That'd be my guess, too. But no, the Captain didn't say anything other than Anlann would be transferring to his warship with Seralin on arrival, and then we're to get the hell out of Dodge. If all goes as the Captain expects, then we should anticipate a mission briefing with the CNC on Tycho sometime soon. This is all unofficial, by the way. According to protocol the Captain should have taken Anlann's request to the Coalition Government first and let me find out about it when I received the deployment notice from starship operations."

Cabrera nodded but remained silent. He knew by her demeanor that Rodgers had more to say.

"Anything interesting?" Rodgers asked, glancing up to scan the overhead monitors.

Cabrera's eyes followed hers, and he shook his head again. "Mostly just housekeeping stuff, and I'm happy not reading flashing red Damage Control messages or threat warnings. There are no mechanical problems. CAG already has his replacement fighters tucked into their maintenance bays, and his new pilots are in TOD orientation. We have no ordnance inventories to top-off." He paused to thumb the touch screen's fuel status icon. "Hydrogen refueling had been completed but getting to Jupiter Refueling Station is another matter. They won't have enough unfactored theta-13 antihydrogen synthesized for us for another twenty days and then it takes time to maneuver at dead-slow sublight there and take on fuel. Given that almost everyone is still on leave and not expected back for at least a month, getting them recalled in under two weeks will strain personnel management."

Rodgers frowned. "Why? Everyone has an omni commlink."

"Yes Ma'am, but arranging transport takes time."

"So? We break lunar orbit, enter the trans-Earth corridor, assume standard geosynchronous orbit, and teleport everyone aboard," she proclaimed.

"That's a good one, Ma'am. Do you think Antarctica Traffic Control will okay routing a heavy carrier into high Earth orbit and then let her lay off along a busy high orbital approach, while we wait for trickling-in personnel to signal for their return?" Cabrera asked.

"No," Rodgers admitted. "But I can't help but indulge in a bit of wistful thinking."

She turned back to the darkened monitors. Navigation and aegis scans had been secured. They weren't needed while in Triple-R. Tycho Approach Control scans blanketed all incoming and outgoing traffic.

She'd better get going herself if she didn't want to be late for her own funeral.

***

Later the same day…

"Ambassador Winters, can you tell me what's put a bug up Anlann's rear? What does he want to return to Iota Horologii in such a hurry for?" Admiral of the fleet Conner Westinghouse Samson, Commander-in-Chief of the Coalition Navy, demanded.

"I don't know, Sir. He only told me that he has been recalled. It makes sense to me if you keep in mind that Anlann is a warleader, a warship commander. In practice, Eyloni have no such things as ambassadors. They must want him back for some mission. Or maybe his all-female crew has grown tired of his absence. He is more at his crew's beck and call than the other way around."

Admiral Samson frowned at that idea. A commanding officer wasn't supposed to jump when his common ratings demanded it. "I don't buy it,

Alan. Anlann was a guest on your ship for some time, and you talked with him often enough and long enough for him to recommend you to the Compact Counsel as a replacement for Harrison. Disregarding for the moment just where in hell Harrison went off to, what's your read on Anlann?"

Winters drew a breath to forestall an immediate reply. "I don't think his crew is crying for him if that's what you mean, Admiral. I'm sure they miss him a lot and will have words to say about his time away from them when he does return to Elleio, but they knew he was going to Earth for a few months. Anlann said something about his ship undergoing a minor refit, and that his crew was enjoying an extended shore leave.

"He also told me once that his female crew owned their warship outright, and they served in the Compact fleet something like a contracted mercenary vessel. Their whole fleet is set up that way."

"My God," Samson interrupted. "How can they run a navy that way?"

"I don't know Sir, but they do. Something about their honor codes prevents them from taking their ship and going home if they don't like what the Compact tells them to do. My best guess is they want an experienced warleader and his ship for some tasking operation in the Iota Horologii system, and they want him there in about forty-seven days."

"Forth-seven days? Did he tell you that?"

"No Admiral, but it'll take *Henri Edda* about fourteen and a half days at maximum hyperdrive to reach Iota Horologii, and the Compact will sortie its battle group in twenty-eight and a half days from now. We can leave at the same time and not run the hyperdrive at maximum through hyperspace hazards, or we can wait and leave in thirty-three days, but Anlann wants us to rendezvous in forty-seven days."

"Can you sit back, relax, and let Captain Rodgers pull the levers, while you wait around in your VIP cabin for two or three weeks, Captain?"

Winters smiled at the CNC's dig. "Who me? Oh, aye, aye, Sir. Yes, Sir. I can keep busy working with Anlann and Seralin and leave this milk run to Rodgers."

A chiming sound soft but insistent filled the CNC's office.

"Yes?" Samson asked.

"Admiral? I have the Defense Directorate on the line for you and Ambassador Winters, Sir."

"Put them on."

"Aye, Admiral."

Winters turned and watched an image of the office of the Defense Secretary form on Samson's holodisplay.

My, my, but news travels fast, he sighed to himself.

2
SHAH-A-SHAR CITY, MOR'NAE SATRAPY, MEERSLAH, THE SHAHA HOMEWORLD

"The word Shaha means people," Doctor Tek Nal, the chief climate scientist of the Science Ministry rasped. "The word also names our species. Only we and the Na Atal have survived into the modern age. They are related to us within ninety-nine percent of our DNA. They evolved alongside us in a most peculiar and blessed symbiotic relationship. We raise the Na Atal, feeding them *dagan* so they will grow numerous and fat.

"We eat living flesh, but our close symbiosis with the Na Atal over thousands of years has made it impossible for us to eat any other creature on Meerslah but them. The Na Atal, by being fed an exclusive diet of dagan since antiquity, have become biologically dependent on dagan flesh. As you know, our food chain runs from toxic plant to amphibian dagan to reptilian Na Atal and then to us, the sapient reptile. Na Atal digestive systems remove the toxins in dagan flesh and purge the enzymatic by-product from their bodies when they void wastes. We avoid Na Atal kidneys and bladders but otherwise consume the Na Atal body whole.

"The dagan are dying. The Science Ministry report confirming this, as well as its criticism concerning proposed alternative food sources, will no doubt set off chaos here in the Prefecture as the military prefects, the scientists, and the feudal lords argue over their own separate and contradictory proposals, but instead of shouting me down, please consider my words carefully.

"Decades ago when news of the first mass die-offs became public knowledge, many in the scientific community shrugged them off as just another odd event that happened from time to time. Dagan numbers always rose and fell depending on weather conditions and ocean chemistry. Other animals suffered massive die-offs before, and their numbers had always rebounded. Indeed, this Prefecture had regulated industrial water discharges to prevent the poisoning of dagan habitats, but this body did nothing to regulate atmospheric dioxide carbide levels. 'Why bother?' was the opinion that carried the day. Atmospheric heating, coastal flooding, and increased rains had improved life for all reptiles and amphibians on Meerslah.

"The Science Ministry has tried to introduce carbon capture schemes numerous times over the past few centuries, but the Satrapy hadn't been interested in air quality beyond removing soot and chemical contaminates from it No doubts exist in the minds of common citizens that air quality has improved over the past 250 years, but atmospheric dioxide carbide levels still linger above pre-industrial levels. It had been argued back then that they would continue to drop over time due to natural sequestering. Plant photosynthesis and carbon bound up in dead plants and animals would sooner-or-later sink into deep sea sediments over two or three hundred years. Global temperature increases were trivialized into being beneficial aftereffects that would drop back down to pre-industrial levels in due time anyway.

"Sample data taken over a century ago seemed to confirm this optimistic view. Average temperatures had risen only seventeen degrees Actual in the past three hundred years. Only a third of the polar ice caps melted away. Coastal waters did rise but slow enough for the cities to advance inland. The shoreline has migrated some two thousand *strides* into the continental interior since pre-industrial times.

"It hadn't mattered. People moved into the inland desert territories as new glades and forest growth established itself and prospered.

"Dagan loved the warming climate as well. Na Atal became plentiful, and no one lacked basic food necessities. Public opinion chastised the scientific community as discredited prophets of doom. When atmospheric dioxide carbide levels began to creep downward, so did concerns about an overheating world and a flooding supercontinent. 'Meerslah will never become an ocean world', they said. Even if the polar ice caps melted down to nothing, the supercontinent was too vast and had too many plateaus and mountain ranges for global flooding to completely submerge it.

"But flooding hadn't been the only matter concerning the scientific community. No one wondered at the time or seemed to care any longer where all the remaining dioxide carbide was going. The ocean algae super colonies and seaweed rafts could absorb only so much of it. New data from ocean floor core samples tell us that not all the dioxide carbide has sunk into the abyssal sediments. A high percentage of it remains suspended in sea water, acidifying the oceans where dagan hatch and live when not foraging on coastal plants.

"The Scientific Ministry shared proof that the carbonic acid in the water started dissolving calcium carbonate-shelled sea life. Although this seemed at the time to be a minor side issue, consider that dagan skin is a breathable moist membrane held semi-rigid by calcium lattices. Because they are porous, carbonated dihydrogen monoxide passed through the lattices, and once the lattices were polluted, they started to erode. Next, dagan skin sloughed off, allowing the sun's rays to burn exposed flesh causing further damage. Affected dagan developed rotting chancres that killed them by the thousands."

Doctor Tek Nal paused. The combined membership of the House of Lords and the House of Prefects had begun to clack their teeth and hiss, bored. What he had related so far was old news. He hissed to himself and continued.

"The Satrap didn't listen! He did the same as he has always done. He deferred to this body.

"When evidence came to light that dagan health was falling in inverse proportion to the rising ocean carbonization, the military conclave sought easier answers. It proposed finding a suitable world where the dagan could live. There they could be fed to the Na Atal and the Na Atal could be imported back to Meerslah to feed the people.

"The Satrap agreed and committed vast resources to this project. Our starships began a search for nearby pelagic worlds in the habitable zones of yellow suns suitable for seeding with dagan eggs. A simple answer in theory, but few worlds have so far turned out to meet all the dagan's environmental needs. Ocean chemistry and sunlight matter to them. Dagan biology is both delicate and peculiar. They are sensitive to ocean salinity and acidity and need sunlight that falls within a narrow frequency range to support photosynthesis in the symbiotic algae that live in the calcium lattices of dagan skin. Those algae produce enzymes necessary for good dagan health.

"Stars either lacked the crucial light frequency, or world atmospheres and hydrospheres blocked the needed light and hindered photosynthesis in the algae. Another problem is the sheer rarity of habitable worlds within those yellow star systems. As bad news increased into this generation the Prefecture began to turn desperate. As all of you know, desperation within the Prefecture is dangerous. Desperation encourages outlying progressive and conservative lords to promote destructive solutions.

"Then by seeming good fortune starfleet discovered worlds supporting alien intermediate food chain animals, animals that were later classified as some kind of dagan-Na Atal hybrid.

"These alien animals are neither amphibian dagan nor reptilian Na Atal, and yet we can consume them directly without having to feed them to an intermediate consumer first. These animals use a much higher level of technology than we ever dreamed a Na Atal capable of understanding. This alien technology implies the existence of an alien Shaha species somewhere among the stars. Alien Shaha would never tolerate our raids on their dagan or Na Atal worlds. *We* wouldn't!"

Tek Nal paused again as several members of the Prefecture hissed in agreement.

"Another Shaha species must exist out there, and these Shaha have obviously faced a dagan extinction problem of their own. They have transplanted their food animals onto other worlds. The first encountered alien dagan-Na Atal hybrids ate fruits and grasses, but they also demonstrated a near-sapient intelligence that tells us at the Science Ministry that they are a highly evolved Na Atal form. These Na Atal analogues can build and use tools and devices. This is a surprise to us only in scope, but not in ability. Many animals build structures or use simple tools. Here on Meerslah some insects build aircraft, silk and leaf constructions, and use them to glide on the breezes. The *dz'nala* even fashion a crude rudder from the propeller blade of a *czss* seed. These alien hybrids employ technology directly, technology the Science Ministry believes has been given to them by their own breeders. They can feed and defend themselves with it."

Tek Nal paused as a truly horrifying thought came to him. If the alien hybrid food animals were that evolved, then how much more advanced were the alien Shaha? That thought faded into the back of his mind as the Prefecture began shuffling in their hot mud baths, a sure sign of agitation. The idea of a second sentient species didn't settle well with them, although the priestesses all allowed for such a possibility in principle.

"When we discovered a second hybrid species, we thought it was a variant of the first until we discovered that the second species had animal flesh in its digestive system. This went against all scientific reason because dagan cannot eat flesh. When flesh digests in a dagan stomach, it produces breakdown chemicals that poison them. How could the second alien species be a food chain intermediary if it ate flesh?

"Our starfleet captured hundreds of these second species and found them edible. The military conclave then advanced a proposal before this body that called for taking cargo ships full of them as breeding stock because they seemed to prosper better than our dagan did on alien worlds.

"The Science Ministry raised concerns then, but as it did with our climate warning so long ago, the Prefecture and the Satrap ignored us."

Tek Nal paused. How far did he dare go? If he clawed into the religious proscriptions too far, then his career would vanish, and he'd lose whatever chance he had to get his claws hooked into a sane alternative.

"The Prefecture's political and military branches have been meeting in closed sessions for the past week, discussing some strategy. Neither I nor anyone from the Science Ministry was invited to attend. I have a growing unease that comes from a persistent dreadful thought. The omnivorous alien species has no alien Shaha. They *are* the alien Shaha! Religious taboos prohibit cannibalism in our culture. The Prefecture has a legitimate reason for treating the alien herbivores as dagan regardless of their obvious intelligence. The refusal to eat the offered Na Atal in all due ceremony during that first meeting justified treating them as food and not as people. The Science Ministry has been arguing over whether or not the omnivorous species are people and whether or not the Satrap should consider them enemy people because they hold worlds fitting our dagan's biological needs. This Prefecture should be deeply concerned. If a starving population ever learns that there is edible flesh living among the stars, but that flesh is people, then they might forsake the proscriptions and eat alien people. If they can eat alien people, then the taboos against eating other people, as our primitive ancestors did in the dim past when we nearly hunted ourselves to extinction, would collapse in the face of rising heresy.

"The Prefecture authorized the Defense Ministry to expand on two fronts into territories occupied by the two alien species. Our raiding forces have been thrown back by one species at system TX-3787 and system TX-9797. The other species halted our advance through a corridor along system TXa-0959, system TXo-377, and system TX-3761.

"Starfleet wants system TX-3767 badly. It, like system TX-3787, possesses ideal seas and sufficient sun for dagan life. FTL courier probe data relayed from system TX-3767 to the Science Ministry has shown an ideal environment and no alien Shaha military buildup.

"They believe that our forces must strike soon, with overwhelming determination, and establish a forward base of operations there. Planning is already well advanced. I do know this much: A strategy has been committed to. Ships, troops, and LAC carriers have already been tasked, and plans are already well beyond initial staging operations. Even a ship for carrying dagan eggs has been refitted. In fact, I don't understand why they haven't been sent out yet. They're waiting for something, some new technological development, but what? The Science Ministry hasn't been included in the loop in this matter."

"Point of order," the Satrap interrupted. "My Lord Doctor Tek Nal, will you yield for a question on order grounds?"

"Yes, My Lord Satrap. I abase myself. Please state your point of order and question."

"Thank you, My Lord Doctor. As you know, this august body has too much to do and not enough time to do it in. As such, we don't have the time for reviewing what has already been addressed in the Prefecture. As to the point of order, you used the weight of the Science Ministry to demand a joint special session of the Prefecture. Your justification for this joint session, you claimed, was to submit a report of the Science Ministry concerning discoveries made about the two alien dagan-Na Atal analogues. You have classified those findings as secret. You are out of order regarding your purpose here until you disclose the finding of the Science Ministry. I hereby revoke the classified status of your work and order you to give the members of the Prefecture individual console access. My question to you is simple: what have you found that justifies this waste of the Prefecture's time?"

Tek Nal drew out a long hiss and accessed the console next to his mud bath. "The Science Ministry report is now available to all members of the Prefecture. To answer your question My Lord Satrap, please read the report. It is not that long."

Four hours later…

The screen gleamed benignly against a background turned hazy from steam rising up from the hot mud bath. If Tek Nal had been any farther away it'd have smudged the image into an obscure blur, but his crimson compound eyes focused on the damning report just as an incoming priority call blanketed the text with the visage of yet another outraged government official.

"My Lord Doctor Tek Nal!" the Shah-a-shar military district prefect shouted, ignoring the usual social pleasantries, "I'm most offended by the report you released to the Prefecture under the Science Ministry's seal! You dare advance your nonsense theories before the entire Prefecture and the Satrap himself? I'm not the only prefect who took your 'intelligent' classification of the two alien dagan hybrid species as an outrage. The very notion violates common sense and insults the religious proscriptions that set all Shaha apart from animals. Those alien dagan are *not* people!"

"At least one of them probably is," Tek Nal hissed to himself. Aloud he rumbled, "Greetings, My Lord Prefect Sharris. I abase myself, but I must point out that the findings of the Science Ministry have suggested otherwise. The research teams suspect that the species found to have animal flesh in its digestive system may represent an alien Shaha species. Dagan don't and can't eat flesh, as you well know. Both alien species are bipedal and are similar in other ways, which suggests that they are related."

"How did the Ministry come to that conclusion?" Sharris demanded. "Because both species are bipedal locomotors?"

"Partly, My Lord Prefect, and partly by simple comparative anatomical studies. They are similar, just as we and the Na Atal come from related taxonomic families."

"But the Na Atal are food chain intermediaries. We eat them because their flesh is the only flesh we can consume. Are you suggesting that the one species consumes the other as if the other was some kind of Na Atal for its food chain?"

"Precisely, My Lord Prefect."

"Garbage! Total garbage! Bipedalism in itself is no assurance of the correctness of your hypothesis. How do you explain the plant matter mixed with the flesh in their guts? We can't eat plant matter but for medicinal purposes. But even if we could, why would we want to?"

"The research teams have formulated an alternative hypothesis. It is … strange," Tek Nal said.

"Of that, I'm sure. What is it? Protocol requires me to act as if I take your insane conjectures seriously."

"Gut bacteria."

"Gut bacteria?" The Prefect paused to think about it before shaking his head. "Nonsense. Even if gut bacteria could neutralize plant toxins, neither alien species has a digestive system capable of liberating enough calories from plant matter to sustain the energy requirements of a sentient brain."

"Apologies, I was unclear. The plant food sources may be non-toxic to them, and they support the beneficial gut bacteria necessary for the increased caloric intake. Maybe the tailless species tolerates certain plants better, not as food but as roughage for scraping intestinal parasites from the lower gut," Tek Nal pointed out.

The Prefect's compound eyes seemed to whirl as he considered the novel idea. "I don't know … This is what I've come to expect, and hate, about scientists. There's always some claw that you drop out of thin air to save whatever theory you happen to present at any given time. Well, maybe I can accept your … No, I won't accept your conjectures given the amount of plant matter found in their guts.

"We eat *pyk* in small amounts for its medicinal value, and the toxin does flush intestinal parasites, but it also makes the eater nauseous. The pharmacy industry makes a synthetic form and encapsulates it in pills just to get it past the stomach. Eating pyk in its raw form in any amount is reserved for those patients suffering from stomach or intestinal cancers. No … subsisting on plant matter alone would make the tailed herbivore hybrids too sick to enjoy what intelligence potential they might otherwise have gained. Even if the second species, the omnivorous ones, ate plants in the amount found in their guts, then I'd think they'd be ill *and* dull-witted."

"The omnivorous species is different!" Tek Nal objected.

"Ridiculous!" the Prefect thundered from the screen, missing the change in topic altogether, "The dagan analogues having no animal flesh in their entrails didn't taste tainted, unlike our dagan, which are contaminated by toxins from the plants they eat. Everyone who tasted the herbivore knew they'd never eaten flesh. Empirical evidence obtained both then and now supports the conclusion that they are an intermediate food chain species for an alien reptilian Shaha people!"

"A dagan-Na Atal species that employs advanced technology? Really?" Tek Nal asked.

"Well," Sharris grumbled, "the Na Atal make tools and gather into social groups."

"The Na Atal make tools out of stones and sticks," Tek Nal replied. "These so-called dagan-analogues crew starships."

"Nonsense," Sharris replied. "You are stretching the meaning of the word 'crew'. They are a different Na Atal species, animal-intelligent but nothing more. How do I know that I'm right? Just toss a knife on the ground between two fighting Na Atal and watch what happens. One of them will use the fine ceramic blade on the other. What we have here is really no different. Using technology built by another Shaha people doesn't mean that both alien dagan species are capable of building or even understanding it.

"Whenever something impossible is proposed by scientists, they justify it by invoking fantastic theories! I've had enough of your nonsense, My Lord Doctor Tek Nal. I cannot accept the idea of intelligent interstellar-travelling omnivores, let alone herbivores."

"But what about the omnivore species? The one with gut bacteria and plant and animal matter in its gut. Wouldn't you agree that an increase in caloric intake promoted by gut bacteria would lead to a smarter animal?" Tek Nal plowed on.

"Certainly," Sharris replied.

"Smart enough to support sapient intelligence?" Tek Nal pressed.

"Well, they'd be a lot smarter than the herbivorous ones at any rate."

"So, perhaps the second species should be classified as people after all!" Tek Nal said.

"No, they're not! They're genetic modifications of the first species. It's obvious that an alien Shaha people have altered the genes of the exclusive plant eater species so it can survive on a flesh-based secondary food source."

"Why?" Tek Nal asked. "Dagan eat plants. Other animals that eat plants would compete against them. It'd be more efficient to alter dagan DNA so they could eat the inedible plants than to alter dagan so they could eat the animals that eat the inedible plants."

"Maybe," Sharris mused. "Some plants are inedible by our dagan too, and yet other animals eat them, the tiny mammals in the interior for example. Even if you could modify *our* dagan so they could eat the mammals and inedible plants, it wouldn't matter. They're not starving—they're dying. The Na Atal are starving, and since we eat them, that means we're starving as well."

"Both alien dagan are mammals," Tek Nal pointed out.

"So? You'd rather feed them to the Na Atal first? That's normal farming practice with our amphibious dagan, but we wouldn't need to. The alien dagan don't carry the taint in their flesh. We can eat them directly."

"Yet they are mammals. We don't eat the tiny mammals on Meerslah, do we?" Tek Nal asked rhetorically.

Sharris blanched pale yellow and retched, causing the multiple layers of teeth in his lower jaw to chatter against his upper jaw. "They're poisonous! They eat plants or other animals that eat plants. They can tolerate the caustics in sap, and it is plant toxicity that prevents us from eating them in the first place. Only amphibian digestive systems can remove the toxins contained in plants so the Na Atal can safely eat them. The Na Atal digestive systems break down the residual taint in dagan flesh and excretes it, leaving their flesh suitable for consumption. To the Na Atal, and to us, mammals smell just as disgusting alive as they do dead."

"Yet," Tek Nal advanced, "you advocated eating these alien mammalian dagan types, My Lord Perfect?"

"Yes!" Sharris nodded. "Of course I do. Their flesh contains no plant toxins and no amphibian breakdown by-products."

"Then how do you explain the tailless omnivores?" Tek Nal pressed.

"Already asked and answered. They are genetically modified versions of the herbivorous ones."

"And who do you suppose did this modifying, if I may ask?"

"Obviously the alien people did before they seeded them on those worlds. Your argument is circular," Sharris accused.

"You haven't explained how these intermediary species can command starships."

"Oh? That should've been obvious to you all along. They are acting under the direct control of the alien people responsible for creating them."

"And which species is that now?" Tek Nal asked.

"What do you mean 'which species', you idiot?" Sharris demanded. "Forgive me, My Lord Doctor, but are you asking me which of them are alien Shaha? Neither. The Defense Ministry at first believed the herbivorous species had somehow split along genders. They assumed that the personhood component developed in males and the intermediary Na Atal component developed in their females. Although a blasphemous idea at the time, it did solve an identity problem.

"Splitting Shaha and Na Atal into genders would imply that the religious taboos against cannibalism hadn't been violated by this species so long as the male didn't eat other males. It made a logical kind of sense at the time. Their ship had only the one male aboard. When we came to him seeking a parley, a chance to negotiate for an available world for our dagan, or to negotiate a joint exploratory alliance to help us find a suitable world for raising them, the commander of the expeditionary force offered him a Na Atal right out of stasis alive and kicking and ready to eat. Good manners would then have required the male to offer the commander one of his female Na Atal analogues to eat in mutual celebration of the concord reached between two peoples. You read the report, so you know that the male refused to eat the Na Atal offered him, and then he refused to surrender one of his own. The females with him defended him with their lives before he was captured and dissected alive. It was then proven that he was an exclusive herbivore, not a person but only a dagan like the females with him."

"An intelligent one if the commander sought a dialogue with him in the first place," Tek Nal hissed.

"What was that, My Lord Doctor?" Sharris demanded.

"Nothing, My Lord Prefect," Tek Nal rushed. "What about the second species we encountered? The omnivores?"

"Them? At first glance the Defense Ministry considered them an offshoot of the same species. When we first encountered them in system TX-3787, we ate our fill and shipped several others back to Meerslah as delicacies. The habitable moon checked out as being well within the environmental limits for our dagan, so we scoured the imported plant and animal life from the surface preparatory to seeding it with Meerslah plant life for eventual dagan and Na Atal farming."

"The omnivorous species found on system TX-3787 are Shaha," Tek Nal whispered.

"Don't you ever utter such a blasphemous statement like that again!" Sharris bellowed. "We never eat people and you know it. The religious proscriptions are inviolable."

"I abase myself, My Lord Prefect, but remember that everyone refused to listen when the Science Ministry issued its warnings that the natural carbon sequestration in the oceans wouldn't stop the acidification of the shallow seas with carbonic acid and the frigid deep seas with cyanoform, a strong carbon acid. Now I fear it is too late to save the dagan habitat on Meerslah. We must remove them to livable oceanic moons and planets soon. Please listen to me!"

"We're already going about that now. What further information could you possibly have to add, My Lord Doctor Tek Nal?"

"I believe the omnivorous species, the species first encountered in system TX-3787, are the alien Shaha. They feed on the obligate herbivorous species first encountered by our expeditionary forces. Because they are mammals, they must have either evolved the ability to digest plants when the need is dire, or they evolved in an environment that has non-toxic high-calorie plants to eat."

"Apart from your gut bacteria theory? This smacks of more theory-saving, but I'll bite. *How?*"

"We at the Science Ministry haven't clawed that one apart yet, but it fits all the facts we have available."

"That's it?" Sharris heaved. "Assuming for the moment you aren't theory saving after all consider this: We Shaha posture threat displays over territory until a concord is reached. Why haven't these omnivorous *people* not parlayed for a chance to display their territorial interests?"

"That's easy to explain, My Lord Prefect. We parlayed with the herbivorous species male until its intermediary food chain status was confirmed. When starfleet encountered the omnivores, they assumed the omnivores were also herbivores and ate them. What would happen if another Shaha species invaded Meerslah, ate a significant number of our citizens thinking them a type of Na Atal, removed hundreds more citizens off-world for later dining, and then laid waste to the plants our own dagan needed for their and ultimately our survival?"

Sharris paused, a troubled expression coming over his toothy face. "The Satrap would demand that the Prefecture call a vote for all-out war," he conceded.

"You see?" Tek Nal pressed. "This is the problem we now find ourselves in. We face two threats: the loss of a crucial element in our food chain and an invasion from another Shaha species."

Sharris shook his head dismissively. "Theory-saving gibberish. We may yet face the true alien Shaha for pilfering their food worlds, but we will compensate them for raiding their food production worlds and then offer further compensation for a suitable ocean world for our dagan. They will reach a concord with us because all Shaha try to reach a concord. Concords are the core principle held by all reptilian society as a corollary of the religious proscriptions. Sustained conflict among people could lead to the possibility of people eating people. The danger for us in any sustained combat is that the frenzy might lead us to feed on the defeated combatants in violation of the mandatory religious restraints placed on such prohibited conduct."

Tek Nal squirmed in his mud bath. "I still say the omnivorous species is the alien Shaha, and that their primary food source is the herbivorous first-contacted species."

"Not possible" Prefect Sharris declared with official finality. "The proscriptions forbid people from eating people. We consumed omnivore flesh, with no ill effects, thus they cannot be people. Consider this official Satrapy public policy. If you publish anything on this matter that contravenes that official policy, I'll have you arrested. You are to consider this matter closed and the subject forbidden. Don't force me to file articles of impeachment to have you removed from the Science Ministry. Good day, My Lord Doctor."

Sharris vanished and text replaced the Prefect's image on the screen. Tek Nal settled back into his hot mud bath, tried to reorder his thoughts, and sought some degree of calm. That call hadn't gone well, but it had gone better than other toothy arguments following the revelation of the Science Ministry report during the closed-session briefing to the Prefecture. His testimony hadn't been received in the same seemingly good grace that Sharris had employed in at least listening to his analysis. Something was flaking his scales. He was worried. Well, he should be. No one had listened long ago, when the warnings would've done any good. Now, amid an environmental calamity, they still didn't listen.

Shaha occupied the apex of reptilian life on Meerslah, basking under the triple yellow suns of a trinary star system. They had always been fractious and tenacious. The Mor'nae Satrapy was a world-unifying government, but its constituent states were feudal in nature. Quasi-independent lords didn't give themselves over to agreements among themselves easily. The system worked well in world affairs and global policy, for the Prefecture enacted policy only once a concord had been reached, some moderate course of action that diminished the outliers, the insane progressive or the suicidal conservative elements in the Satrapy's stratified society. Tek Nal, with the Science Ministry's full backing, had reported to the Prefecture what current environmental models had predicted: dagan would go extinct within seventy-years.

Nothing ignited a firestorm among the conservative and progressive lords and prefects so much as telling them that no matter what they might advance in the Prefecture, it was far too late for ideologues on both sides to do anything about a certain extinction-level event. They hadn't acted before the climate change-induced ocean carbon toxicity had begun. Reasoned guesswork and imperfect models had hinted at a tipping point, a point of no return beyond which remedial action wouldn't matter, sometime in the future. Well, today he told them that the tipping point had already happened some fifty-three years ago, the future was now, and not even heroic measures could prevent the dagan for dying out.

How could such a beneficial by-product from old industrial activity, dioxide carbide, lead to our potential destruction? they had argued. The lords in the Prefecture had demanded the same thing today.

Centuries ago, the rising temperatures and sea levels had been welcomed. Meerslah, large for a habitable planet, possessed a single supercontinent surrounded by shallow seas. The melting polar ice caps had caused the coastlines to recede as the ocean advanced inland. The flooding was nothing to worry about. Sea levels rose at a modest rate, slow enough to accommodate long-range social planning. Over the centuries Meerslah's habitable zones, the continental coastlines, advanced farther inland as the shorelines flooded. Existing city-state infrastructure and immovable industrial sites disappeared under the rising seas. New manufacturing centers were rebuilt again along new coastlines several hundred strides from the now submerged industrial complexes on the old coasts. Welcome increases in temperature and changes in the weather improved all lives. The poles warmed and melted, and people migrated into the once uninhabitable savannas and deserts of the interior as changing rain patterns caused the hot dry land to grow lush and green with glades, swamps, and succulent forests. Desert and savanna plants and animals died out as their environments flooded, but other species filled the niches they had left behind.

The dagan had prospered along the lush new coastlines, reproducing in record numbers. The animals that ate them, the Na Atal, also increased their numbers. And as the Na Atal, the exclusive food of the Shaha increased, so had the worldwide Shaha population. As food became common, those with full bellies in large communal groups began to regard industry-induced climate changes as a blessing. But all that atmospheric dioxide carbide had to go somewhere, and that somewhere was the worldwide ocean.

All Shaha ate living animal flesh. Obligate carnivores, they had to eat living flesh, but not just any animal flesh, and certainly not the dagan. Dagan were obligate herbivores, and they died if they consumed flesh. Animal flesh poisoned them, sickened them, and they avoided it at all costs. They ate ocean and wet-climate terrestrial plants but avoided water animals and even insects. From the time they hatched until they metamorphosed into adult forms, they fed in the ocean. Adult dagan swam to the shorelines and lived in the coastal flood plains and the partially submerged seaside rainforests. They ate fruits, mosses, and fleshy succulent leaves. There, their flesh grew rich and fat on the oil and protein-rich foliage.

The Shaha couldn't eat them of course, not directly. Dagan flesh reeked with enzyme by-products that inactivated the caustic sap in their stomachs. The by-product gave dagan flesh a rotten, spoilt taste. The taste warned people never to eat dagan flesh, and for good reason. The Science Ministry had discovered long ago that eating flesh tainted with the by-product caused genetic changes in Shaha DNA. Those changes accumulated over time and promoted defects in the Shaha genome that altered fetal development to produce a more primitive reptilian form. Ancient dietary laws regulated dagan economics. People raised dagan, bred them, and fed them to the Na Atal.

I became concerned enough about our raiding a possible alien Shaha's interstellar food sources that I battled for funding to research the equipment and dagan-Na Atal hybrids found on those worlds.

I came to an unbelievable conclusion.

And the Satrap laughed me right off the sun-soaked sand!

I don't blame him. Even the Prefecture rejected my work, calling it the result of fantasy speculation.

Our scientists proved long ago that no herbivore could evolve intelligence. They couldn't get enough energy from plant matter to support an energy-demanding brain. Only flesh provided the necessary energy levels needed to fuel a sentient brain, and even we Shaha must return regularly to a heat source by sunning or laying in luxuriant hot mud.

I reported my results to the Prefecture: the flesh-eating alien omnivores aren't intermediate food chain animals but an alien Shaha species.

If true, then we have become cannibals for no Shaha ever ate people.

We would never eat people, not even alien people.

Tek Nal paused again, turned off his tablet, and stepped out of the now cool mud. The problem with the target world, a moon actually, rested with its parental body's eccentric orbit. The moon got cold there in winter, maybe too cold. Perhaps much too cold for the dagan.

But the sun and seas checked out as within dagan environmental needs.

They had already established a minor presence, a research outpost, in the system's Kuiper belt. Could they repurpose the experimental crystal technology being developed there and use it to terraform the moon?

"My Lord Doctor, I abase myself." Tek Nal's research assistant's voice hissed from the tablet.

"Yes?"

"My Lord Doctor, the Defense Ministry has sent special orders demanding that you report to the Shah-a-shar spaceport."

Oh Gods, Tek Nal clacked his teeth together, *they're banishing me off-world!*

Less than an hour later Tek Nal was seated in an autonomous black ground car. Nervous, he stared at the beige towers of Shah-a-shar City as though he'd never see them again.

The tower was a symbol of military architecture. Shaha from time immemorial had set up towers of refuge and places of defense to give protection against enemy feudal states. Fortresses arose from the river banks of all major rivers that flowed from the mountainous interior. All cities were surrounded by walls and had defensive cordons filled with towers and gateways, small fortresses in themselves.

He drove past rose temple citadels with heavy granite walls and turrets that had grown over the years to resemble orderly piles of rocks. Shah-a-shar City had the mightiest walls, the greatest massive towers, and the most imposing gateways. It had to. The City ran several hundred strides down the forested coastline and extended several tens of strides inland.

His ground car sped through a fortified blue crystal gateway. Gateways were an unwanted but necessary gap in a passive defense system. They had to be guarded, and the City garrison maintained the causeway that admitted authorized traffic. It was here that the Prefecture met. The fortress was ceremonial. It featured the absolute theocratic patriarchy of the Satrap's world government on Meerslah. The Prefecture was the representative of divine rule. Tek Nal drove through the Prefect Gate, another example of fortress architecture with its system of multiple cordons. A beautiful work of art, its flanking gray pillars and walls were decorated in bas-relief with symbols of sacred Gods in quarried stone.

The ground car passed vehicular traffic moving through portals in thick walls made from irregular blocks of blue granite without mortar. The approach to the spaceport was heavily defended. Tek Nal's eyes locked onto a watchtower as he drove past. Watchtowers were an important element in the city-state's defense both as garrison watch positions and signaling points. It was rectangular and, as a protection for the watch against surprise attacks by the enemy, it was surrounded by a circular tan outer wall. The stretch of land between the sea and the fortress was provided with a row of towers like this one, which were situated at a suitable distance apart for signaling from one to the next.

Tek Nal grinned toothily. When firearms came along, fortified buildings had to be built lower to the ground. In most cases the newer cities had been the first to implement this new defense policy. The new defense system put more emphasis on the outworks in order to shift the defensive front forward as far as possible from the cities themselves. Major changes included the addition of ramparts and bastions, an independent section in front of the main fortifications. Bastions and ramparts became more ornamental as the city buildings disappeared behind impressive ramparts that were no longer anything but symbolic.

The stronghold as a defense system became obsolete as warriors were replaced by soldiers and team tactics. That said, several strongholds remained, more out of nostalgia and an appreciation for the past than any help that bastions and rampart belts added to defend against an enemy possessing aircraft and heavy artillery. By the end of the industrial revolution all final decisive battles were being waged in the continental interior. What was maintained now served to remind everyone of what life had been like before the coming of the priestesses and the Gods. Tek Nal could not put a date to the last time there had been fighting on Meerslah.

But how could they now fight a climate catastrophe? Worse yet, how could they fight an alien species that the Prefecture dared not admit publicly were people?

Tek Nal's arrival in the spaceport caught the notice of Admiral Lord Viceroy Bleniss. He waved the scientist over to a waiting car.

"Greetings, My Lord Doctor Tek Nal. I am Bleniss. You will come with me."

"I abase myself, My Lord Viceroy. Forgive me, but I was told to report here, but I have no idea why."

"You are fortunate, My Lord Doctor. You have been chosen to serve as the liaison between the Science Ministry and Military Research and Development. For the past five years we have been developing a new crystal technology. Starfleet has been waiting for the results of first-article test trials on a new type of light attack craft. Apparently a report written by you under the auspices of the Science Ministry has prompted the military conclave to press the Prefecture not to wait for those tests to finish. Rather than wait for the destroyer task force to return with the prototype, I have been ordered to take my battle group immediately to system TX-3767 and retrieve the prototype LAC, the prototype destroyer, what hulls that have been completed, what raw materials we can transport, and all research materials for immediate incorporation into our starfleet."

"Why me? I'm no ship designer," Tek Nal said.

"By command of the Satrap and in the name of the Prefecture, you have been designated expert on alien dagan and Na Atal types. You are to help assess the emerging technology and determine its effectiveness in terraforming applications and bioagent delivery systems."

Doctor Tek Nal understood. They were going to terraform system TX-3767's habitable moon.

3

THE O'UN TU CLAN, LA'HUASET TRIBAL CONTINENT, ELLEIO, THE EYLONI HOMEWORLD

Delwyn flinched and blinked, trying to avoid the blinding light the healer was flashing in his eyes.

"Do not be such an infant," the Mistress of Head Trauma growled as an anxious Allohindra hovered behind her.

"I'm not being an infant," Delwyn grumbled. "But you've been doing that every thirty seconds for the past ten minutes."

The healer clicked the light off and sighed. "Perhaps another scan is in order. You may have to stay here the remainder of the day."

"Oh Mistress, do you think that is necessary?" Allohindra trilled.

The head trauma mistress narrowed her eyes at Delwyn. Males were terrible patients. They never seemed to know or to care what was good for them. His head wound had regenerated wonderfully, a tribute to Allohindra's assistance and her crucial but limited knowledge of human brain physiology. Just because the regeneration session had gone flawlessly did not mean his safety was assured. His body had been in crisis mode for almost a month. Targeted acceleration healing had repaired the brain injury, but she could not predict how his body would react to finding itself no longer in crisis mode. The body responded to injury in many different ways, such as swelling, forming blood clots, and promoting immune system responses among many others.

The injury no longer existed, and the body no longer in crisis mode actually paused in physiological confusion. That pause sometimes caused systemic shock. Regeneration shock probability rose when an injury had been severe or treatment long delayed before accelerated healing had been administered.

The shock came from the body's refusal to see itself as healthy. Normal responses cascaded as they sought an injury to address. Finding none, the body turned on itself, leading to massive edema, organ failure, and circulatory collapse.

"Well?" Phelindra demanded.

"Everything seems in order," the Mistress of Head Trauma conceded.

"Allohindra?" Melkorka asked.

Delwyn jerked his head to the entrance bole at the sound of her tight voice.

"When did you get here?" Delwyn demanded.

"I need to know. It is mission-critical," she said in her most serious singsong tone, ignoring him.

"It sure is," Zalzadrin quipped. "He must have a clear head to compose his adulthood song. You do have a clear head now, do you not, Delwyn?"

"What do you mean 'mission-critical'?" Phelindra demanded.

"*Hunter's Moon* has been moved into the primary task force as honor escort warship for *Green Ivy*," Verikaralee said, shoving past an outraged Melkorka to sit on one of Delwyn's sleeping nest pillows.

"That is not for you to say!" Melkorka spat, livid.

Zalzadrin crawled into the nest with Delwyn, laid across his chest, put her chin on Verikaralee's thigh, and looked up at Melkorka. "Better she say something before your stalling causes him to fall into a relapse!"

Zalzadrin's comment stopped Melkorka cold.

"Wha…What?" she stammered, suddenly shaking at the horrifying thought of causing harm to her favorite male. "I was not…I mean, I did not mean…."

"She's pulling your tail Melkorka," Delwyn said.

She ignored him again, gaping in shock at Allohindra and the head trauma specialist.

"She is pulling your tail," Allohindra reassured Melkorka.

Delwyn watched Melkorka's knuckles turn pale orange as she squeezed the saber's hilt, the symbol of authority as Mistress of the Ship he had given her on his becoming warleader.

She spun on the Hunter that was using Delwyn's chest as a nest pillow. "That not only was not funny Zalzadrin, but it was cruel. I expected better judgement than that from our next Mistress of Arms."

Zalzadrin's chin flew off Verikaralee's thigh. "Mistress of what?" she stammered.

"Oh, Zalzadrin! How wonderful!" Verikaralee trilled, so pleased she crawled across Delwyn to give her a hug.

"If they can roughhouse all over me to no ill-effect, then I can leave," he announced to the group.

The females looked at him as though seeing him for the first time.

"No. You are staying here for another few hours," Melkorka snarled, still angry and not quite forgiving Zalzadrin.

"Oh no I'm not. Verikaralee just said our warship has been added to the primary task force. I need you to brief me on what's been happening since I began my adulthood survival ordeal. Besides, I need to compose a song about my experiences in the rainforest to finish the initiation ritual. I want to get on it now, while the details are still fresh in my mind."

Phelindra, Zalzadrin, Verikaralee, Melkorka, Allohindra, and the Mistress of Head Trauma glared at him and shook their collective heads.

"You have been put on convalescent status. You will stay here for another three hours," the Mistress of Head Trauma said.

"Oh come on now!" he stormed.

"Do not think you get to lay about doing nothing all that time," Melkorka said. "I have important developments to tell you."

"Bring him," the Mistress of Head Trauma ordered as she left the intensive care abode.

Phelindra and Zalzadrin reached under Delwyn's shoulders. "Ready?" they asked him and then levered him up from the nest before he had a chance to say yea or nay.

Delwyn had a compact body and a powerful, athletic build. He'd lost some weight during his twelve-day jungle ordeal, but not enough to make him emaciated. Yet the two lean lithe Hunters, one well beyond middle age, had hoisted him to his feet as if he weighed nothing.

He had forgotten just how much stronger than fit humans the Hunters were. Melkorka, a Warrior female, was even stronger. He bet she could bench press his body for over an hour.

They half-led, half-carried him from the intensive care abode down through a winding tunnel formed from fused aerial tree roots. They passed a large group, healing center staff, and on into one of several hundred abodes that filled the healing center elleiu tree.

Melkorka glanced back over Delwyn's shoulder. "Mistress Healer? Verikaralee? With respect, please excuse us for a time. We must discuss warship business with our warleader."

"Of course," the Mistress of Head Trauma replied.

"I will wait in the visitors' abode until you are finished," Verikaralee said.

Zalzadrin spun on Melkorka. "What was that you were saying about Mistress of Arms? It is not in your nature to joke, Melkorka. You do not have the aptitude for it."

"What do you mean by that? That I am serious about serious things? Yes, I know. Your humor evades me, as most Hunter humor does."

Phelindra laughed.

Melkorka glared at her. "Even your humor evades me, but at least you refrain from joking all the time."

"I do not. I just refrain from joking in the presence of dour Warriors."

"What is that supposed to mean?" Melkorka snapped. "I have a sense of humor! Warriors are not without emotions."

"No," Zalzadrin interrupted, bouncing on the balls of her feet. "You just are not funny."

"I can be funny, but I am funny in adult ways and not in the ways of infants."

"Who," Phelindra growled, "are you calling an infant?"

Delwyn leaned against a wall of fused, smooth, apricot aerial roots and listened to the dissonant, trilling shouting match. It showed no signs of letting up anytime soon. He slipped along the fused root wall, away from the three, and headed for a comfortable-looking cushioned chair. He plopped into it, pulled the recliner lever, and the mechanism ratcheted back. Eyes heavy, he struggled to watch the Eyloni female social life show unfolding before his eyes.

They never ceased to amaze him. He listened as they squabbled over which one was funny or not, which one was acting like an infant or not. The difference was an important one from their point of view. Calling an adulthood knife-wearing person an infant was a serious breach of social etiquette.

Delwyn had a sneaking suspicion they were arguing only because he was there.

They circled one another with tails darting back and forth, Phelindra and Zalzadrin stalking Melkorka. But as they circled, Melkorka kept drawing closer to him.

He could smell them. This close their pheromonal emotional chatter smothered him, made him sleepy. He remembered the blue isoprene forest haze that had been floating above the jungle during his survival ordeal. Whenever he hovered between awake and asleep he thought he had a tenuous grasp on the emotions conveyed through their illusive body odors. Their banter carried a serious undertone, but how much of it was for his consumption? Why was it so important to them for him to notice their challenges?

Eyes closing, their combined body odors wrapping him in safety and comfort, he drifted off.

Zalzadrin twitched her ears at the first rasp of Delwyn's odd, choking sleep-growls.

"He sleeps," she said simply.

Melkorka charged up to the sleeping male, crouched on her knees, and listened to his breathing. Her ears semaphored her opinion to the two Hunters. She inhaled his scent, smelled his contentment at being included with them.

She looked over her shoulder and nodded.

"How long are you going to let him sleep?" Phelindra asked.

"Not as long as I want to. I wonder why he chose to sit on this folding therapy table. He looks uncomfortable," Melkorka growled.

"Maybe he thought convalescence meant he had to sleep in that pose?" Zalzadrin speculated.

"Allohindra?" Melkorka called.

Her warship's primary physician stepped into the abode.

"Yes Mistress?" Allohindra replied.

"Did you tell Delwyn he had to use a therapy table when he slept?" she asked, pointing her tail at the uncomfortable-looking gadget Delwyn was sleeping on.

"No, Mistress. Why did you put him there?" Allohindra demanded.

"I did not," Melkorka snapped, defensively. "He went there on his own. I do not understand males. He fought to leave, fought treatment, fought having his eyes checked, but now he surrenders to a therapy table."

"Get him out of that thing and put him in the sleep-nest, healer's orders," Allohindra trilled.

"If you can help us? Ask Verikaralee too? I do not want to wake him."

The five females reached under a snoring Delwyn and gently lifted him clear of the folding upholstered medical table, carried him to the cushioned floor, and laid him down.

His breathing did not so much as miss a beat.

"So much for warship business," Verikaralee said.

"That is not your business," Melkorka warned, "and not for long. Heartbeats fly by. Call for us in an hour. Please?"

"I will," Verikaralee promised, knowing with an absolute certainty what Melkorka, Phelindra, and Zalzadrin were planning. She left them, but Allohindra remained behind.

"Are you going to resume your shouting match?" she asked them.

"It was nothing," Zalzadrin said. "Delwyn loves my humor."

Melkorka glanced at Allohindra and drew tiny circles in the air with her pons. A Warrior herself, Allohindra knew what Melkorka was implying. Warriors possessed a dry wit, and Hunter humor tended to evade their common-sense literalism.

A half hour later, Delwyn's internal nap-over alarm sounded. He was already aware and thinking before his body knew his brain was awake. He felt weight pressing down on him and cracked an eye open.

Phelindra's face was buried under his chin, her nose in his ear, her right arm reaching around and above his head, her breasts pressed into his right shoulder, her hard stomach pinning his open hand. He could feel her chest rise and fall in sound sleep. A stray pillow prevented her weight from cutting off the blood to his wrist.

Zalzadrin's head was pressing against his hip, her nose pointing toward his navel.

Melkorka's face was resting on his stomach and touching Zalzadrin's forehead.

Allohindra was leaning against his left side, her left arm resting on his chest. Her face was touching Phelindra's forearm, and her flat hand was pressing into Phelindra's back. Allohindra had crossed her legs with Zalzadrin. They had even twisted their tails together.

Delwyn turned his head to look down Phelindra's back. Sure enough, her tail and Melkorka's were wound together like two twisted rubber bands.

He stretched, which caused them to stir but not wake up. He, on the other hand, came full awake. Sleeping with them had restored his mind and strength better than sleeping alone.

They had taken off their waistwear and neckwear. They had even taken off their adulthood knives and sheathes from their usual places under their left breasts. They didn't do that often and even then only when they slept in groups. Only their dreamcatcher-like rank weave earrings remained in their left ears. They never took those off.

"Time to wake up," he told them, nudging them from their slumber.

"Already?" Zalzadrin grumbled.

Melkorka jumped to her feet as Verikaralee poked her head into the bole, looked at them, and stepped on in as she rhythmically cleared her throat. The smell of lingering pheromones made her wish she was twining tails with Phalalin.

"Time is up," she sang. "But I see you already know that."

Phelindra jerked her tail at Zalzadrin. "You and Verikaralee go and get us some food, please?"

Zalzadrin nodded and snuggled up next to Verikaralee, curled her tail around her waist, and led her from the abode.

"How do you feel?" Melkorka and Phelindra sang to Delwyn.

"The room's spinning, my eyes are dimming, I'm dying… <koff>… <koff>…," he gasped before rolling off a nest pillow. He'd had enough of being treated like an invalid. His theatrical death-rattle performance shouldn't have fooled anybody.

He never got a chance to sit back up and ask them whether he looked okay. By the time he finished the second fake cough, Allohindra had already punched her fist through the emergency call touch panel, shattering it and breaking her hand.

Melkorka raced from the abode, determined to find and drag the sire cairn of surgery back with her.

Phelindra effortlessly heaved Delwyn into the air and was rushing him back to the trauma center when his scent finally penetrated her awareness.

"I'm *not* dying, for heaven's sake. I'm tired of being here. I'm fine, and you should know that by now!"

Phelindra froze and her ears flattened against her head as she looked into his small brown eyes. She pivoted at her waist and without changing her footing threw him over ten meters back onto the convalescent abode nest cushions and stalked off without a word.

Five minutes later Zalzadrin and Verikaralee returned with trays laden with fruits, vegetables, a juice pitcher, and a water pitcher.

Zalzadrin looked around, curious. "Where did everybody go?"

"I don't know," he said. "I played a joke on them, and it made them mad."

"Oh?" Verikaralee replied, suspiciously.

"Yeah. They started after me again with the 'how are you feeling?' routine. I told them the room was spinning, my eyes were clouding, and that I was dying. I even added a fake cough and…What?"

Both Hunters glared at him, speechless.

"Oh, spirits!" Zalzadrin gasped. "They will blame me!"

"What are you talking about?" Delwyn demanded.

"What you did to them. They will think you tried to play a joke on them, and they will blame me for it!" Zalzadrin wailed as she fled the abode.

Verikaralee's eyes smoldered. "What you did to them was horrible, my clan male, to make them think a male in their care was dying. Bad enough if you ever do that aboard your warship, but for you to do this here in healing center?" Verikaralee paused to smell his scent and reassure herself that Delwyn had not intended to cause his female association emotional harm. "I will bring them back to you and explain how your stay in healing center has frustrated you and tell them that your scent tells me you understand how much hurt you have caused them."

She paused. "Delwyn, please understand what I am about to say. Had you been any other adult male, news concerning this mental abuse would have been sent to the hierarchies by now, and they do not take a male's deliberate emotional assault on females lightly. I know you did not act with intent, and as they sit back and think about what they smelled here, they will understand that, too. That said, do not expect them to speak to you anytime soon."

Delwyn nodded. "Thank you. Can you go round them up before they decide to leave without me?"

Verikaralee smiled a knowing smile. "Oh, they will not leave you, but they will teach you a lesson. It is in our nature to care for males, and you have given them a bad scare. Zalzadrin may have been correct in saying they might blame her for your attempt to joke with them in this way."

"I'll have to clear it all up when they come back."

Verikaralee nodded, swatting her tail at him hard enough to raise a welt on his bare skin. "Do not expect Zalzadrin to speak to you when she comes back."

"Why not? She was with you!" Delwyn objected.

"She will show solidarity with her society. If they decide you need to be taught a lesson, and you do, then she will fall in line with them on this matter."

"I understand. Go find them."

Verikaralee nodded and swatted him with her tail again. "We are O'ni'da extended family, you and I. Because I do not belong to your occupational association, you may want me to stay with you. If they need to tell you something, they will do it through me."

Oh, great! "And just how long, by custom, does this last?" he asked.

"In theory? Forever. Except for talking to you as required to do their duties aboard your warship. Worse, if they tell their society about this, then they will all treat you in this way." She snapped him a third time, raising another wet-towel welt on his thigh before continuing. "Do not look so glum, Delwyn. They will not carry this past day's end. Probably."

She hugged him a moment before padding out through the open bole.

Delwyn looked around the empty convalescence abode. Melkorka had left her 'minder behind. Either Zalzadrin or Phelindra had laid out a clean pair of custom waistwear and loincloth for him.

Delwyn grabbed the waistwear, stood up and pulled the jockstrap-like thong made to accommodate his human male anatomy through his legs and looped the loincloth over the thong's pubic strings. He considered paging through Melkorka's 'minder and pass the time reading repair status reports but then remembered how courtesy and privacy worked here. Privacy meant he had no business looking. Melkorka's obligation to social courtesy required her to leave the personal electronic device unlocked, a trust in his obligation to keep his honor.

Eyloni followed deeply ingrained customs and kept them religiously. Refusing to abide by the social contracts of honor, obligation, courtesy, and privacy constituted capital crimes here. With all Eyloni being scent-linked empaths, personal feeling and private information were only a sniff away. The social contracts erected cultural walls, and breaching them could get him banished, ostracized, declared clanless, or even killed.

Phelindra glided into the abode.

He smiled up at her. "Did Verikaralee find you?"

Silence.

"You know I never intended to harm any of you," he said.

She remained silent but sat down next to him and wrapped her tail around his waist with a fierce possessiveness.

He caressed her back and shoulders, and her ears followed the sound his hands made on her velour-soft skin.

Eyloni physiology prevented them from shedding tears as an emotional response, but his reflection in her larger-than-human amber eyes made his eyes tingle in sympathy.

The Eldest Huntress put her arms around him in forgiveness but remained silent all the same.

Melkorka, Allohindra, and Zalzadrin came into the abode. Verikaralee poked her head in, a distant fourth but remained standing in the open bole.

The first three smelled the pheromones in the abode, letting scent tell the story as they watched the Eldest cuddling with their warleader: Delwyn had not known how his cruel jest would affect them, had not intended on playing a joke on them.

They surrounded the embracing couple and sought their own social rank-determined places next to their annoying favorite male, but they did not say a word to him.

"Delwyn, they have agreed to give you four hours silence, and then they must brief you on warship repair status, on battle group updates, and on other matters happening in your immediate family that are not my place to speak on. Phelindra thinks maybe you should spend this time composing your adulthood song. When you are discharged from here, they will take you to the clan elders gathering for your adulthood ceremony," Verikaralee sang formally.

"Where is the gather site?" he asked her.

"In a large clearing a few thousand ells north of my immediate family's elleiu tree."

"I thought they had decided to hold it at some clan reunion site closer to the mountains," he objected.

"No doubt they were, but with your injuries, the clan elders have decided it would be better for you if only immediate and extended O'ni'da families, the nearby O'un Tu Clan families, all the La'huaset Tribe clan elders, and the La'huaset Tribal Elders attend."

"I thought that was how it was supposed to work anyway," Delwyn said.

Verikaralee shook her head as Phalalin poked his head through the bole threshold. "All the O'un Tu Clan families wanted to come," she said, giving Phalalin a smile and a quick ear flick.

"The entire clan?" Delwyn wondered if his guess about a gather being a county fair event might have been more accurate than he first thought.

Phalalin sniffed the air and looked at the coiled bodies on the sleeping nest.

"You have made them upset," he said.

"I'm afraid so. A side-effect caused by my injuries and being held here when I feel fine," Delwyn grumbled.

"My tail!" Phalalin shouted. "You had a moderate concussion, and it was left untreated for a month. I think the little brothers and sisters fed you enough medicinal plants to keep the swelling down, and the Comari likely helped you in some way too."

Delwyn twisted in the group cuddle to get a clear look at Phalalin.

"What Comari?" Delwyn asked.

Melkorka twisted free from the group, grabbed her 'minder, and threw it at Phalalin, smacking him in the chest.

"What?" he asked her. "You have not told him about her yet, have you?"

"Get out!" Melkorka trilled.

Phalalin held his ground, a dangerous strategy. Their resentment of Delwyn was plain, but they wanted him to themselves all the same. Then he noticed they had not spoken to Delwyn since his arrival.

"You are getting the silent treatment!" Phalalin laughed in rhythmic trilling notes, earning himself a tail swat from Verikaralee in the process.

Phalalin understood Melkorka's rising anger now. For silence to work as a punishment for inappropriate social behavior, it had to be endured by the one deserving it. In many ways it was a punishment that hurt them as much as it was supposed to hurt Delwyn, for it went against female nature. They agreed to suffer along with Delwyn so long as he understood how much he had hurt them. If he took Delwyn away from them, then he could not suffer their silence and feel the emotional loss they intended him to endure at their expense.

"How long?" Phalalin asked Melkorka.

She snapped a reply at him before rejoining the group hug.

Phalalin nodded. "Just over four hours. Good. We have much to discuss. Mistress of the Hunt Atridredha has surrendered the high ground under pressure from Faolindra. *Fearless, Surefooted,* and *Hunter's Moon* will form a secondary task force and sortie with the battle group you first proposed to the A'tayotan."

"Really?" Delwyn twisted around to look over Zalzadrin's shoulder at Melkorka. "I wonder how…"

Phalalin never got a chance to hear what Delwyn wondered about as Phelindra's outraged shriek prompted Verikaralee to wrap her tail around her favorite male's waist and yank him out of the abode.

Males! Every females' pheromones in the room shouted.

Four hours later, just under two Earth hours, Delwyn finished composing his adulthood ceremony song. And true to their word, his constant female company started speaking to him again, as if nothing had happened. The Rite of Forgiveness required Eyloni to forget their offense and abandon the social debt in most cases.

***

The aircraft cruised at altitude as Delwyn rehearsed verses in his head, a final check. The flight from the O'un Tu Clan healing center back to the O'ni'da families' elleiu trees shouldn't take long.

Phalalin and Verikaralee sat in the back of the apricot wood cabin, close together, murmuring to each other. Zalzadrin remained uncharacteristically quiet the whole time. Riding in an aircraft wasn't her forte`, but he wondered if she held back her irrepressible exuberance because she harbored some fear that the others still held his bad manners against her. Maybe she was still trying to come to grips with the notion of, pending warship society approval, becoming their new Mistress of Arms.

It still astonished Delwyn that males conferred military rank upon a female by adding webs, beads, or knots to her rank weave earring. A female's hierarchy gave her the rank earring and the gold hoop hanging from it when she was chosen by a warship's society. Only her current warleader or sire cairn had the right to remove it, add to it, take from it, or tie it back onto the fine braided gold chain that dangled from her left lower earfold. Females possessed an acute rank-conscious, and they gave special notice to rank given them by a male. A female's hierarchy noticed any change in the dreamcatcher's webs, beads, and knots no matter how slight it happened to be.

Hierarchies formally approved mistress rank however, because they considered it a supervisory rank more social in nature than military. If Delwyn could honorable justify it, he could add webs, honor knots, and mission beads to Zalzadrin's rank weave until it pulled her ear to the ground. He had the autonomous right to make her the highest-ranking female in the Compact Fleet if he wished, as long as he could justify the rank to her and to the hierarchies under the customs of honor and obligation. All females prized rank, but it had to be earned, otherwise her honor would require her to refuse it.

Regardless of her military rank, a female's hierarchy had to confirm her choice as mistress, except for one special case: the warleader and only the warleader chose the Mistress of the Ship. He didn't even need her society's permission. That social rank was intimately tied to him, and it was rescinded if he died.

Melkorka told him the hierarchies took several matters into account when confirming a society's choice of mistress, including how her society and her warleader might respond to the new rank. In practice the society chose, and hierarchy approval was symbolic. Mistress ranking came from a female's peers, but military ranking reflected male approval, and females valued it far above peer approval.

Delwyn wondered how they had gone about advancing Zalzadrin to Mistress of Arms. She was just over middle age, the second oldest Hunter aboard ship. Phelindra held the dubious honor of being the oldest. That explained why they called her the Eldest Huntress of the Ship. Zalzadrin's rank weave swelled with multicolored webs, tiny beads, and complex knots as well. She had high military rank equivalent to a navy captain. Phelindra held rank equal to a Coalition rear admiral, upper echelon.

So why hadn't Zalzadrin been given mistress rank before now? He asked Melkorka about it.

She told him it wasn't his business, paused a beat, and then conceded that Zalzadrin's performance during the capture of the Lizard light attack craft and his heaped praise of her actions in combat had forced Melkorka to take a second look at her.

"So you're saying I can influence a hierarchy's decision?"

Melkorka twisted her tail so her pons curled under his nose. The ten-centimeter-long, tightly curled ringlet-covered tail tuft moustache twitched against his lips, an incredibly intimate gesture.

"Shh," she hummed. "You cannot influence the hierarchies, not much anyway, and then only indirectly. You are not supposed to know how the hierarchies work. They are as much responsible for male safety as they are for female issues. They would never allow a Hunter or a Warrior to assume a mistress role if they felt she might somehow place the warleader in jeopardy. When they approve a mistress choice they are looking out for you, and except for a Mistress of the Ship, they know a male cannot see into all aspects of the female in question, and so they consider her on her merits and not on her society's endorsement."

"Then why bother letting a warleader choose his Mistress of the Ship?" he asked.

"To prevent the hierarchies from interfering with male autonomy. When a huluhar chooses a warleader, she submits her choice to her society, and her society validates her choice with a major consensus. We give our warship and ourselves over to his command, and his autonomy becomes our autonomy. If the hierarchies can invalidate your chosen Mistress of the Ship, then they can violate male autonomy. The warleader must choose her, and she remains Mistress of the Ship as long as he lives. The hierarchies grant a waiver for her by accepting his choice and according her with the dignity and respect associated with mistress social rank as if they had confirmed it themselves. Only you can remove a Mistress of the Ship, if you have an honorable reason for doing so."

"But I can't do the same thing to any other mistress," Delwyn said.

"True, but if a warleader experiences discord with a mistress aboard his warship, that knowledge flies at FTL velocities back to the hierarchies, and they will poke their tails into every aspect of that mistress's character until they know why."

Delwyn shook his head as the aircraft banked low on approach to his family's home tree. "That sounds unfair. Why not look into the warleader's character as well?"

Melkorka smiled in approval and brushed his lips again with her pons. "Of course. The warleader does not escape their scrutiny, but they give him all but unlimited latitude."

Delwyn tried to bite her pons, causing her to trill a schoolgirl giggle.

Phelindra leaned up against their chairs and shoved her head and shoulders between them. "You ought to be thinking about important matters and not twining tails," she admonished him.

"I don't have a tail to twine with," he stage-whispered into her soft, elegantly twitching ear.

"Yes, you do. A docked tail, but a tail nonetheless," she quipped.

"What?" Melkorka demanded.

"She's pulling your tail, Melkorka. Remember Hunter humor?" Delwyn stammered.

"We shall see," Phelindra demurred.

At his mention of Hunter humor, Melkorka's face clouded over in memory of Delwyn's jest, and her anger rekindled.

"Melkorka? What does a Mistress of Arms do aboard a warship?"

Partially distracted, Melkorka tried to explain while thinking about Phelindra's comment. The tail was a sensitive tactile organ that could convey a variety of touches and caresses. Hugging with the tail augmented empathic sharing that imparted a magnitude of emotion compared to hugging with only the hands and arms. People shared pleasure when tail twined, and tail twining facilitated mating. One step in the Steps to Adulthood required a person to know what the tail is not.

"The tail is not a hand."

"And what does that have to do with the Mistress of Arms?" Delwyn asked.

"Sorry? Oh, nothing. I was thinking about tails. An adult is supposed to know what the tail is not used for. Our tails are prehensile, but custom forbids using them as a third hand. We use our tails for individual or collective expressions of love, affection, mating, to convey meaning through posture, and to express certain emotions through selective pheromones. Using the tail as a gripping tool, except for saving your own life or that of a male, is frowned upon—a social taboo."

Delwyn nodded, thinking of a kid picking his nose in public.

The aircraft decelerated into a hover. The pilot was getting ready to land.

He changed the subject. "Do you think the Comari is still here?"

"Oh, yes…of course she is," Melkorka stammered.

"What are we going to do about her?" Delwyn asked.

"We? There is no 'we' in this," Melkorka trilled in dissonant chords.

He changed the subject again. "When we finish here, will we be going back to Wrathsee'a Anchorage?"

Phelindra, still wedged between them, shook her head. "No. You have to inspect the repair work at the Kem Basinga Clan hull fabrication center and see how the compartmental assemblies are proceeding. Then we must meet with all the extended families belonging to our clan. Then you must meet the Tribal Elders from the other four tribes."

"And the Comari will just follow? We don't have to reserve a seat for her?" Delwyn asked.

"No. She will follow because nobody will inhibit her movement," Phelindra said.

The VTOL aircraft touched down gently onto the jungle floor.

Melkorka and the others led him on a hike through tall orange grasses and under short scarlet trees. They passed his home elleiu tree and kept on going. A few kilometers later they skirted the shady perimeter surrounding Verikaralee's home tree. They prowled through a few more jungle kilometers before reaching a broad meadow covered with short, flame-orange grass speckled here and there with crimson trees that looked like red maples with chest-sized leaves. Golden-yellow vines twisted up their rust-brown trunks.

A number of VTOL aircraft and aircars rested on the grass near brushy crimson plants surrounding the meadow. Other vehicles were parked under the larger yellow-striped red and orange-leaved trees in clearings adjacent to the large meadow.

Delwyn looked into the crowds gathering there. He saw more than the fifteen hundred or so total O'ni'da families living in the five local elleiu trees.

"Where did all these people come from?" he asked Phelindra.

"From the families in our clan whose territory marches alongside ours."

Delwyn guessed the meadow covered about a square kilometer in a rough irregular trapezoid shape. He imagined the people spread evenly across the meadow and made an infantry-force estimation. If each person had about an eleven square meter plot, then just over eight thousand people had come to hear him sing.

"There must be five or six O'un Tu Clan families out there. Surely they kept some people home to watch their territory."

Phelindra shook her head. "I doubt it. They would have set their perimeter defenses on automatic before coming. No doubt other O'un Tu Clan families neighboring them have sent prowlers into areas where their territories march alongside the families that came here. And not just families have come to hear you. Every La'huaset clan is represented by its clan elders, and all the La'huaset Tribal Elders have come to hear you sing. They will award you the adulthood knife."

It took them another forty-five minutes to cross the meadow. Everyone had begun to form up into a semicircle, and as people filled it in, the semicircular pattern grew until it came to within two meters of Delwyn. The way people stood about reminded him how his crew had sat around him for the Death Song ritual he had sung to them on Ibeetu.

They had temporarily abandoned their orbiting warship to sing good-bye to their battle dead. The meadow had a slight dip near its center, a natural depression nothing like the outdoor amphitheater his Mistress of Fortifications had carved into Ibeetu and then returned the place to its natural state once he finished singing the ritual.

They sat down on the orange grass with Delwyn standing in front of them, their tails touching a higher-ranking neighbors' thigh. Each individual's rank was reflected in the forming branching pattern. Unlike during the Death Song ritual, this assembly included both males and Comara. The pattern increased in complexity as it absorbed his immediate family members from his home elleiu tree, his extended family members from the surrounding four elleiu trees, the visiting families, the clan elders, and the La'huaset Tribal Elders.

Delwyn turned around and glanced up at the five towering, skyscraper-tall elleiu trees in the distance. Four hundred meters tall and seven hundred meters across at the crown, they loomed over the jungle, made possible by the lighter gravity, the greater atmospheric carbon dioxide, the constant rainfall, and an evolved and efficient plant circulatory system that fed their fused root superstructures, living suspensions and buttresses, mighty branches, interwoven inner branches, dense gall-growth Males' Safes, and living area hollow log and twisted-branch abodes growing up into the understory and emergent levels in their canopies.

He turned back to study his audience. Their groupings and tail-touch patterns began to shift, forming the outlines of a stylized elleiu tree as they began to fill it in while maintaining the rank-specific touch pattern.

Directly in front of him sat all the males from his immediate and extended families and the immediate and extended families that surrounded O'ni'da territory. He wondered just how frantic the females behind them had to be feeling about having all their males in one spot where an enemy could kill them with one blow. The males represented the life-giving forest soil.

The Tribal Elders sat behind the males, weaving into their pattern before branching out to form the tree's main roots and its above-ground buttressing and supporting aerial root systems.

Behind the Tribal Elders sat the clan elders, forming the heart trunk and supporting spiral living banisters that grew into the tree's heights.

The three hundred plus members of his immediate family sat behind the clan elders. Touching them and spiraling around them, they formed the tree's Watch and crown. Blending in around them sat the extended O'ni'da families from the other four elleiu trees.

Branching out from the extended O'ni'da families and on into the shallow semicircular canopy sat the females of the surrounding families most closely related to the O'ni'da families. They filled in the secondary branches, boughs, limbs, and the leaves themselves within the multi-tiered elleiu tree.

The Comara females had stepped up behind Delwyn, watching him and all the males. They personified the sustenance the tree drew into itself—the water, the minerals, even the carbon dioxide from the air.

A Comari stood behind him, only a tail length away. Lacking tails themselves, the Comara formed their odd branching pattern by standing, one Comari's hands on the shoulders of two others. Delwyn had expected them to stand back and form the concave shape meant to embrace him as the male singer, and by extension the people filling in the tree. The Comara instead chose to stand in an arrowhead shape, its point held by a Comari two meters away: the one who had pressed her nose against Delwyn's check over two weeks ago. The Comara themselves were attracting many curious glances. The pattern they had chosen wasn't a typical one for a male adulthood ritual, and the one standing behind Delwyn wore waistwear that identified her as a Myat'ti'deep Tribal member. Stranger still, the Comara kept giving Delwyn vague smiles, which was not typical at all.

The males signaled their readiness to the Tribal Elders, and the Tribal Elders gave Delwyn the signal to begin. He started by beating a drum, setting the proper mood. He had to sing in spirits' song measure. The oldest songs had been given to the Eyloni by the spirits at the beginning of time. Songs had first come to them in dreams. The song he had to sing now would be judged more on its power to incite an altered state in the Elders' minds and not so much on its beauty. The song had to be sung in warranted verse, which meant he had to give an evidential basis for what he sang to the audience. Warranted verse told them explicitly what sources Delwyn drew upon to describe his ordeal: what he saw himself, what he heard from an identifiable person, and what he gained through hearsay, deduction, inference, or guessing.

He also had to sing in *e'va'a,* the spirit language. E'va'a was non-recursive: it did not permit sentences within sentences. E'va'a had a subject-object-verb sentence structure. E'va'a also used external reference geography when describing a person's position relative to geographic landmarks. He couldn't sing about directions using his body as the reference point. "I turned right" made no sense to an Eyloni. Her body moved, so "right" could mean any direction depending on body position. Landmarks didn't move. "Travel downstream until you meet the log in the river" gave directions based on the fixed moving river and the fixed log and didn't depend on body orientation. Put more simply, humans possessed an awareness of self over geography, and Eyloni possessed an awareness of geography over self.

Delwyn changed tempo, immersing his audience in the contrast between refrain and verse beats. The males wouldn't sing with him. They had come to judge the expanded awareness his song would give them. He had to sing the Step to Adulthood called "Using the Spirit Voice." He had to incite an altered state in them. The females would sing in accompaniment with him.

He had a lot to sing about. The song should last about twenty-seven minutes, 102 Tyreniioroneo Standard Time minutes as Eyloni males counted, just over a TST hour.

He sang. His deep mellow voice filled the space between him and the town populace surrounding him. The forest cooperated as quiet breezes drifted across the orange meadow. The sun hung in an earthly 13h30 cloudless afternoon.

Delwyn sang the refrain first in traditional La'huaset manner. Short, it celebrated the male singer, what the male singer feels, what his song means, how he stands at an abyss, and how when he sings, he sings in the Spirit Voice.

He sang the first verse, and the overwhelmingly female assembly, over eight thousand strong, joined him in accompaniment as he told the gathering how his immediate family members had covered his eyes, ears, and nose and taken him someplace in the middle of the temperate rainforest.

All those female voices should have drowned him out, but they didn't. They sang together, but they also sang their own unique measures. As they did so, they kept their voices down to the level of breezes rustling through tall grass.

The second verse celebrated the life in the jungle: the trees, the grasses, the vines and branches, the insects, the animals, the mosses and molds, and the fungi.

The third verse paid homage to the past lives of everything that had lived on Elleio, how they had contributed to building a worn, eroded limestone tor, its beauty, its presence, the place it stood along Elleio's hemisphere-sized impact crater rim. He added the extinct volcanic mountain ranges marching alongside it. How appropriate they too had died so long ago, and yet their lives, like the shelled creatures that had formed the limestone, had a purpose.

The fourth verse described the subterranean depths of a cave system, about water's ancient battle to wear away the stubborn stony monument to lives past. He described the wonders hidden in the underground limestone vault, the chambers of eternity and their visions of tomorrows. He celebrated the pale glowing slime, the rubble piles, the wet clay, the plink-plink-plink of water dripping along vast underground caverns extending far under the limestone relic, trillions of *oros* of mountain range pressing down into the ground all around him.

Delwyn drew pictures with his words, his rhythm coloring a vision that exposed the damp, dim passages that wound under forest and mountain. Water filtered down from the ground above, dripping and pooling, forming runnels and trickles struggling to reach the forest-sustaining aquifers.

He sang a fifth about the treachery of wet clay, the rift in the cavern floor, and the deep pit filled with water waiting at the mouth of an underground lake. He personified perseverance as he hung suspended across a rip in the floor, how he overcame both the deep waters in the world and the silent waters of his subconscious mind.

Delwyn's sixth verse celebrated his return to the daylight, the sight of the beautiful scarlet ivy shrouds draping the stone pillars near the cave exit. He praised the ivy, telling his audience how he had used it for a cover while sleeping on the mountain ledge. He foreshadowed how a ball of the same ivy would save him repeatedly. He sang about his respect for it, and how it had asked him to replant a part of it he no longer needed.

He amused his audience with a seventh verse that described how the salt-craving insects had found his sweat a bounty of the needful mineral.

Delwyn altered his timbre into dissonance and began the eighth verse as he sang about a simple run-off ditch, how it had turned from shallow ravine into a slot canyon, how he knew the danger of being caught there in a flash flood, how the eroded bank had pulled away as he climbed it and sent him flying head-first onto a flat stone, his pinned ankle rolling into a severe sprain as it tried to escape its own rocky trap.

The ninth verse took on a tortured staccato beat as Delwyn sang about headaches, double-vision, confusion, agonized walking and running on the twisted ankle and not always knowing where he was or what he was doing, breathing in mouthfuls of insects, and running through torrential rainfall. He told them how missing his occupational association had brought on heart-rending PTSD flashbacks, how his concussion had made them even worse, about eating caffeine-loaded *arberi* leaves, and about climbing a tree on one leg.

He sang about living with the little brothers and sisters, rainforest primates, about the matron, her infant, her mate, and her lodge where he slept for days wracked by delirium in the tenth verse. He thanked them for the care they had given him during the six Earth day-long night, how often they must have packed his sprained ankle with chewed plants and fed him fruits and medicinal herbs. He described how they had gathered to sing, how they had let him listen to them but made it clear he wasn't welcome to sing with them.

Delwyn changed the beat to an isorhythmic suspenseful tone as the eleventh verse drew them into his first dream vision. He had become Fara, an infant male taken from some clan in the distant past by the O'un Tu Clan to become their deliverance. Male eyes bored into him as he sang. The mass female accompaniment hesitated a beat before continuing.

His twelfth related the warning a dream-Kidahin had given to him about the Wild Mistress. Later the Wild Mistress herself advised him why fear was better than courage.

His thirteenth verse unveiled how he became the Warrior Tellin during her adulthood ceremony. During the pheromone-linked empathy caused by the females of her clan she learned that she would become the last Warrior female.

The beat changed to a dissonant marching rhythm as the fourteenth verse evoked fear as he found himself dead on the battlefield yet aware, and he knew it for a false vision because it showed a past he knew had not happened.

In the fifteenth verse the Wild Mistress returned to tell him that he'd been born Eyloni, that Kidahin already knew who he was. He sang about truth, artistic truth, and how she had compared the spirits to water.

The next dream surprised his audience, for in verse sixteen he sang that he had spoken with the spirits. They told him that he had been a song sung into existence by them. They told him the Oyya Web was one long complex continuous song. They repeated what they had taught him, word for word, over and over again until he knew it by heart.

He changed the rhythm to an upbeat cadence as he began verse seventeen and sang about the end of the long night, daytime campsites, crisscrossing forest paths and trails, the sudden lack of predators, obvious trails passing food sources, and an odd feeling that he hadn't been alone.

The Comari closest to Delwyn stepped up to him and put her hands on his shoulders.

He hesitated a beat before beginning verse eighteen. He sang about finding logs on the Om'tu River bank right where he had come out of the rainforest.

The Comari squeezed Delwyn's neck, and he began to sweat.

The nineteenth verse gave them a peek into his adventurous river raft journey, making landfall, and the forest mammals roaming around him as his journey neared its end.

The Comari squeezed Delwyn's shoulders three more times.

The last verse, verse twenty, wrapped up his homecoming to the O'ni'da families' trees. He sang the refrain one last time, put down the drum, and waited.

The powerful female accompaniment wound down to silence. Only the soft gentle forest sounds remained. Breezes wafted through the ground forest layer, pushing aside the grasses and leaves in their way. The leaves on the lesser trees soughed, much as they would have on Earth. In the background sounds of distant showers raining down on grass gave away wind striking grand piano-sized leaves on the elleiu trees several kilometers away: evidence of heavier gusts high above the meadow. Everyone felt only the gentle teasing breezes.

The people remained seated on the grass in the tree pattern they made from the patterns their bodies had woven together. They remained impossibly quiet, too quiet. Eight thousand individuals should make some noise: whispers, shuffling bodies, breathing, something.

They remained focused on Delwyn.

The Comari hadn't taken her hands from his shoulders.

The clan males turned to one another and started murmuring.

The Comari's iron grip tightened, and Delwyn winced.

The males discussed his song's merits. That he had put them in an altered state they could not dispute. Phalalin had been mesmerized. He understood the song and smelled the emotional highlights. They had all made an empathic link with the singer's pheromones. The song, the musical accompaniment, had been uplifting and revealing. The emotional power of the piece had moved them.

Delwyn wondered how they would judge his experiences. He knew how to sing impromptu verse, but what mattered here depended more on his experiences during the ordeal and whether or not his singing about them had moved the Tribal Elders in some spiritual way. The adulthood ceremony was a ritual, after all.

To the massed female metamind that had formed while he sang, the outcome had been a foregone conclusion. The pheromones released during the performance had linked them into a communal empathy, and their common mind had pondered shared questions concerning their newest adult clan male.

Delwyn had seen the Oyya Web! Males did not experience the vision quest females did when they were pheromonally-linked in empathy with their clan females during their adulthood ceremonies. The clan males had linked into Delwyn's mind through their own pheromone-linked empathy to feel his emotions. They saw the pictures drawn in their minds, otherworldly imagery from Delwyn's weak pheromones that told them what he felt as he sang about his experiences. No male had tried to send him into the pheromonal underworld where adult females sent adolescent females during their adulthood ceremonies.

How then could Delwyn have seen the Oyya Web?

He had *become* Fara, the infant male the clan had stolen centuries ago.

Kidahin had warned him to beware of the Wild Mistress.

The Wild Mistress herself had counseled Delwyn on matters of fear and courage.

He had *become* the Warrior Tellin. In her future, he had experienced her adulthood visions. In a more distant future, she would become the last Warrior female. The last one standing? The last one surviving? The last living Warrior ever? The scent-drawn image had felt incomplete, as though the vision had raised a possibility and not a certainty.

The Wild Mistress had shown him where he should have died in his past *but for her interference,* long before he had met Anlann, Seralin, or the society of *Hunter's Moon.*

The Wild Mistress told him he had been born Eyloni, had always been Eyloni, and always would be Eyloni, and Kidahin already knew this! How they wanted to speak to her.

The spirits had sought him out, had told him he came from a song they had sung into the Oyya Web, itself a continuous counterpoint melody abounding with consonant and dissonant harmonies. Together they produced a beat, one repeating over and over again, a soft omnipresent melody: existence itself.

The female metamind pondered whether the little brothers and sisters had somehow put Delwyn through their own pheromonal vision quest.

The males had been no less surprised than the females had been, but they attributed Delwyn's visions more to his head injury and less to the pheromonal influence attributed to the little brothers and sisters. They had helped the pheromonally nearsighted Delwyn see an artistic truth from the cultural lessons given him by Kidahin and others in his occupational association. How else could he have known about Fara? That was clan history he probably heard from Hervorallin the mother of his near-daughter, Princess. Hervorallin would have told him about the Oyya Web. In fact, Kidahin's prominence in his fevered mind all but confirmed how much Delwyn had taken her teaching to heart.

He was a singing male, and he could sing about Artistic Truth, and the spirits had spoken to him and drawn on his experiences to give him perspective. But the males also wondered about the future vision. In it, Delwyn had been the Warrior Tellin, and experiences like that validated his other visions: the spirits had an interest in Delwyn.

"I could have told you that," Phalalin hissed at them. "No male just becomes an elite warship warleader out of thin air."

What could the males say to Phalalin? The spirits might have played a small role, but females chose their warleaders. Delwyn had been at the right place at the right time under the right set of circumstances, with the right huluhar and a receptive society that happened to find him irresistible.

Delwyn started to sweat again. The silence was deafening. It was taking them too long. Kidahin said the Tribal Elders had awarded her the adulthood knife right after she had been expelled from the Oyya web, the pheromone-induced trance. Once the Tribal Elders had given her the knapped flint knife, she declared her first adult decision to them.

So what was keeping them?

The clan males had already made their decision. It had been a mere formality. Delwyn's fame as a singer had preceded him. Everyone on Elleio had watched the archive recording of him singing the Death Song ritual, and the entire world had watched him become warleader. Pheromones told them the Tribal Elder's opinion, and the Tribal Elders stood and presented Delwyn with a beautifully knapped rare white obsidian blade set into a polished bone handle.

Delwyn thought of the caverns below the limestone mountain and the flint-chip cutting tool as Phalalin laced the knife sheath to Delwyn's waistwear and tied its tip to his thigh. Once tied, only Delwyn could remove it. And just as a male could demand a female's knife for just cause, so could the female hierarchies demand a male's knife if they felt he had not behaved as an adult should.

The male who demanded a female's knife had the freedom of autonomous action to return it, but the hierarchies did not. Once they had found a male unworthy and demanded his adulthood knife their decision was final, which made hierarchy action against male adulthood exceedingly rare.

"You are now an adult male," Phalalin intoned. "What will you do?"

His question was rhetorical. By custom they asked the question so the clan could hear the person's first adult decision.

"I will continue to serve our people as Warleader of *Hunter's Moon* for as long as I am able," Delwyn said.

An entire branch section in the tree pattern shifted as people stood and shouted for joy, followed here and there by individuals and other small groups.

Phelindra stood up among the clan elders.

Delwyn saw Hervorallin and Zalzadrin among a few others in the dancing pattern formed by his immediate family.

The farthest branches stood as one monolithic group, too far away for him to make out their faces, so far away that their dancing skin color patterns merged into what looked like fall branches blowing in the wind.

His crew, Delwyn realized: his warship society. The clan must have invited them and let them participate by putting them up in the cheap seats. They remained where they stood, waving. They were guests here, and this was a clan event. Every member of his crew belonged to the La'huaset Tribe, but not all of them belonged to the O'un Tu Clan.

Over the next four hours Delwyn wandered through the county fair-sized group, sampling foods from trellis tables set up to hold refreshments. It reminded him of childhood summer picnics in a city called Lodi, at a wooded valley called Community Park.

Delwyn looked up just in time to see Melkorka launching herself at him.

He barely had time to set himself to catch her and absorb the inertia from her ten-meter-long leap.

She wrapped her legs around the small of his back and wound her tail around them both, hugging him savagely.

"We need to visit the Kim Basinga Clan hull fabrication center soon," Melkorka said before he got a word out.

"I know. I'm going to be busy visiting the clans and the tribes over the next month. You're coming with me, aren't you?"

The hint of pleading in his pheromones made Melkorka smile.

"Yes. Of course we are. I told you we always return to our clans during warship replenishment. But for you, we will accompany you wherever you go."

The feeling of being watched alerted him, even in the midst of all these people. He felt her eyes on him.

"I think we may have someone going with us," he said as he turned to where he thought she watched from.

Melkorka turned questioning eyes on him before she followed his gaze into the crowd.

There. The rippling wake of people on the move gave her away. It wasn't the random ebb and flow of a crowd, but the characteristic shift people made when giving a Comari a wide berth.

She stood in plain sight, in sprinting distance from him, watching.

"I'm surprised she hasn't joined us," he said.

"I am not. She is not bound to you, and she belongs to a different tribe. If she was a Warrior or a Hunter, she would be unwelcome here. But like males, Comara have autonomy and a right to go wherever they want. She will follow you to farside and back."

"She's got a lot of following coming up, what with all the courtesy visits I've been scheduled for."

Melkorka nodded. "You had better go mingle and enjoy yourself while you can. We will all be busy traveling and meeting new people, recruiting from the families and clans that built our warship. Oh, you should spend some time with Kidahin while you have the chance."

"While I have the chance? What does that mean?"

"I have made her a surface action scoutmistress, a team leader for one of the surface action assault forces. She will no longer serve as helmsmistress, at least not for some time to come," Melkorka said.

"*Why?*" Delwyn demanded.

"She is no longer huluhar. A Warrior under Hlinlodyn will become our new huluhar."

"So? Mistress of Tactics Hlinlodyn's tacticalmistress serves at the Combat Analysis station, not navigation. Did Kidahin ask for this?"

Melkorka shook her head and wrapped her tail around him. "No. She would remain tail tied to you, but she is young and must continue her training just as I did, just as other mistresses have done. You do Kidahin no favor by keeping her in the command center. I, and you, want her to advance into mistress rank, and she cannot do so if she remains helmsmistress under Mistress of Pathwalking Trebithia, although she says Kidahin has a natural aptitude for navigation."

"I think we found that out on the light attack craft we captured and piloted back to Nikkiolo."

They shared a smile. "That is what convinced me to place her with the assault forces so soon. Do not worry Delwyn, she will be in good hands with Zalzadrin and Phelindra," Melkorka said.

"Zalzadrin…Tell me, what does a Mistress of Arms do?"

Melkorka assumed a lecturing posture. "The Mistress of Arms exercises command over all boarding action and surface action weapons aboard our warship, from the heavy tanks to the light armored vehicles. It includes all weapons platforms and infantry weapons not falling under personal combat weaponry. Only the Mistress of Arms can release those weapons for boarding actions or surface assaults. When deployed with assault forces, she is responsible for issuing, recovering, and inventorying weapons. She makes sure damaged weapon systems and ordnance are documented, returned to inventory, or reordered. She follows up on all damage reports and makes sure combat maintenance repairs, decommissions, and damaged combat assets are logged. Oh, and she maintains, stocks, and issues personal combat weapons."

Knives, bows and arrows, spears, swords and shields, he remembered. Eyloni refused to use modern weapons in melee combat. They fired electromagnetic pulses into enemy infantry, frying the enemy's weapons, and then they fell on them with primitive weapons. Personal combat expressed their warrior ethic.

"It sounds like a great responsibility," he said.

"It is. Neither you nor I can order combat assets released from the combat staging and deployment bay without her approval. You or I direct her to prepare for combat, and she releases and issues the weapons she determines as necessary to complete the combat mission."

Delwyn tried to imagine the joker Zalzadrin commanding so critical a duty station and failed.

4
A MONTH IN FEMALE TIME

Delwyn began the grand tour of the Ten Tribes of Elleio by visiting the northernmost clans in the La'huaset Tribal continent. First he flew on a VTOL aircraft northeast between the north coast and the *A'kou ti tiem*, the Folded Mountains, that straddled longitudinal Zone-b. The A'kou ti tiem abutted the northern face of the ancient asteroid impact crater. Here the stratospheric rim wall had withstood erosion over the eons well. The tallest peaks along the ridge had ghostly snow streamers on them. The Om'tu River flowed along a valley that from the air looked like a long, straight but tipped sideways Grand Canyon. On the north bank the crater rim rocketed several thousand meters into the sky, and on the south bank the impact-deforming uplifts, fractures, twists, and now-extinct volcanic mountains rose only a few thousand meters. The mountain range cut a nine hundred klick-wide swath over fifty-four hundred klicks long just in Zone-c and Zone-b alone.

They crossed the sixty-five-degree north latitude and into Zone-a, at about the same latitude as the arctic circle on Earth. The mountain range continued for another twenty-seven hundred klicks at a narrower two-hundred and seventy-five klicks wide. The southern face of the range was overgrown with cloud rainforests. As the elevation dropped south of the Om'tu River, the forest changed to temperate rainforest. Even at this latitude they were still over six hundred klicks below the nearside frost latitudes. The clans here enjoyed comfortable twelve to fifteen-degree Celsius average temperatures. After sweltering for days in the O'un Tu

Clan borderline subtropical jungle, Delwyn found the short visit here relaxing.

Then they flew northwards, taking him farther into the colder Zone-a, where spectacular mountainous cliff faces along the rim mountains followed the north polar shoreline. When they got to within five hundred klicks of the East Terminator, temperatures dropped to minus seven degrees Celsius. They crossed the terminator into farside Zone-A, and temperatures plummeted to those matching Alaska's cold interior. With farside's cold winds came constant rain, sleet, snow, and snowstorms that blanketed the northeastern tip of La'huaset. No elleiu trees grew here, but clan polar research outposts and climate monitoring stations dotted the north polar coastline.

The aircraft then swung south until it reached the *Eastern Gyre Sea* and turned to follow the La'huaset south coast southwest along an arcing diagonal slash until they overflew the *Hama'ella Sea* and then turned north and flew over the lowland interior. They stopped for a few days to visit the La'huaset interior clans. La'huaset curved across the nearside hemisphere from pole to pole, making it the longest continent. From its northern tip to the equator it stretched across fourteen thousand kilometers. Eighteen hundred kilometers wide at its widest point, it covered 16.5 million square kilometers, including 6 million square kilometers of ancient impact crater and mountain ranges. The La'huaset Eyloni controlled over thirty-four percent of Elleio's landmass, an area twice that of Brazil.

When they left the interior clans, the VTOL aircraft took Delwyn and his constant female company high above four extinct supervolcano calderas. They contained the La'huaset great lakes that filled the chasms between the high mountains and the looming impact crater rim. *Ayo* was the second largest lake at over a thousand klicks long. Flying west above the mountain range brought them over *Om'tu*, the largest lake at twelve hundred klicks long. The mountain range stood guard over rich natural resources and had been where Elleio's industrial beginnings had been. Nearly all mining, drilling, and manufacturing had taken place there. Industry flourished for fifty-seven Earth years, yet in those 303 TST years the Eyloni had faced and confronted the dire consequences brought on by dirty fossil fuel energy sources. Although environmentally sensitive by nature, they had not understood at the time the extent the damage had done given even "clean" fossil fuel use. When toxin-related illnesses began killing La'huaset males, the female tribal powers had restricted filthy energy sources to those sciences, technologies, and industries developing clean energy alternatives. The first fission reactor began operation in the northeastern tip of La'huaset, but nuclear power had likewise been restricted to supporting research and development into hydrogen fusion power systems. The Eyloni understood the dangers that fission power systems represented.

The La'huaset Tribal continent had gone from steam engines to nuclear fusion in only one hundred and twelve Earth years. It produced ninety-five percent of the world's energy on Elleio using hydrogen fusion, solar, wind, sea current, and orbital power transmission. That said, given the stiff environmental constraints on waste heat emissions and other factors, La'huaset generated about as much power in a year as did Korea in the year 2051.

The La'huaset Tribal Elders told Delwyn in tribal counsel that all La'huaset clans maintained good relations with the other four tribes of the Ten Tribes of Elleio. La'huaset had no ancient border disputes, and the remaining ecological damage early industry caused had been isolated to the La'huaset northeastern clans.

Delwyn remembered the story Hervorallin had sung about the interclan civil wars that had been fought to put down those clans that had contaminated the environment and had stubbornly clung to their belief that their technology held the key to overcoming, *neh'tle ke'ne's'tu*, pollution-sickness.

Delwyn and his entourage then flew across the equator and stopped off to visit the sea-farming clans and the ocean power generating clans on the archipelagos and on the Big Island. That flight covered another thirty-five hundred kicks. On Big Island Delwyn found himself in another winter wonderland. Southwestern La'huaset crossed into farside Zone-D at the equator. The southernmost tip of Big Island touched the South Pole, which seemed to follow a British Colombia winter weather pattern, except for Big Island's northern third. North Big Island felt more like the Sierra Nevada Mountains in November.

From Big Island Delwyn and his entire crew chartered a five-masted commercial cargo ship and sailed to the nearside hemisphere's central landmass, the *Myat'ti'deep* Tribal continent.

The heart-shaped fifty-six hundred by five-thousand-kilometer square Myat'ti'deep territory covered almost as much area as La'huaset. Myat'ti'deep was surrounded by shallow seas. Its rainforests, the heaviest jungles in the world, could in Delwyn's opinion have given the South American Amazon basin a good thrashing without even trying. Myat'ti'deep rainforests held the record for maximum plant density and flora and fauna biodiversity in the world.

Myat'ti'deep jungles covered flat ground that had few highlands. Sparse hills popped up here and there, and a few isolated low mountains covered with cloud rainforests made their appearance as well. A massive extinct supervolcano caldera some eight hundred klicks long and over a kilometer deep contained Elleio's greatest freshwater lake, *Turadeek* Lake. The peaks around it got lightly frosted during the night and glittered in the sunrise before melting. The volcano had been created by linear shock waves made when the ancient asteroid impacted on farside. The waves deformed the upper mantle on nearside and punched magma through

Elleio's surface, rupturing the thin crust at Turadeek and other sites. A second extinct volcano to the south, five hundred klicks across and seven hundred deep, formed *Autu'un* Lake. A third, *A'pea* Lake, was half a klick deep.

Myat'ti'deep had no barren landscapes, no deserts, and few open spaces. The great sprawling jungle provided its clans with surplus food for barter among the world's clans. Not only did the Myat'ti'deep clans trade food, but they also had the greatest ironwood supplies, the dense wood from dead Elleio trees. Most Myat'ti'deep clan wood product cottage industries made items from small pieces of ironwood. Environmental Interdiction regulated the harvesting of dead elleiu tree wood to small pieces on the tips of branches. Dead trees fulfilled their own role in the rainforest as natural habitat for many jungle creatures, and the scavenged wood had to be certified as about ready to fall to the forest floor.

Continental industrial development on Myat'ti'deep was restricted to the northern coastline across longitudinal Zone-c. Two harbors, one on the northern coast and the other one on the northwestern coast, handled blue water marine commerce. A smaller third seaport on the east coast serviced the southern continental clans.

After two days Delwyn decided he wasn't about to visit the Central tropical Myat'ti'deep clans again anytime soon. The summer heat reached a stifling fifty-three degrees Celsius over the long day. Most daylight activities took place high up in elleiu tree canopies, where temperatures in the skyscraper-tall trees fell in the windswept heights.

Southern Myat'ti'deep, a relatively cool temperate rainforest, enjoyed cold rains that welled up from the south pole. Storms broke around the southern tip as the *South Central Gyre Sea* churned up ocean currents and cold air in and above the southern polar sea, creating storms an ancient Earth sailor would have recognized off the Cape of Good Hope.

They traveled at times on foot along jungle paths and at times in six-legged carpenter ant bulk transport all-terrain vehicles through an interior filled with winding tributaries flowing throughout the jungle. The rivers didn't join up to form one great basin-draining behemoth like the Amazon in South America. Here they meandered across the continent, flowing into five separate river deltas on the coast.

Myat'ti'deep continent supported the highest Eyloni population density on Elleio, and Delwyn spent more time visiting clans there than he had on La'huaset.

From Myat'ti'deep the tour sailed across a one hundred and fifty-kilometer-wide strait to the *Sa'ranja* Tribal continent. Sa'ranja straddled the equator along a longitudinal zone. With an area that could cover four Alaskas, its equatorial climate supported the same levels of animal and plant diversity as on Myat'ti'deep. Sa'ranja received heavy equatorial rainfalls, and the rainforests weren't as choked with undergrowth as they had been on Myat'ti'deep. Sa'ranja didn't have many elleiu trees relatively speaking, and so didn't support a large Eyloni population.

A great old mountain range divided the northern third from the southern two-thirds of Sa'ranja. Three great rivers flowed into the western coast along the equator. An impressive delta made the granddaddy of all Everglades as it drained into the southwestern coast. A second mountain range some two thousand kilometers long skirted along the southern coastline.

The Sa'ranja Tribal continent featured a rare active volcano located in its northern territory. The continent also had two modest freshwater lakes, the *Oha* and the *Hio*.

A clan on the small volcanic island off Sa'ranja's east coast along the equator ran the Sa'ranja people's power receiver. Sa'ranja's industrial activity was confined to the north and east coastlines opposite the central continental delta. As with all modern Eyloni industry, those sites followed strict clean air, water, and energy guidelines.

From a geological point of view, the Sa'ranja and the *Mawe'allea* Tribal continents sat on the same continental shelf. The Eyloni ignored the geological reality because different tribes inhabited the two landmasses. The Sa'ranja Tribal Elders told Delwyn that deep territorial rivalries existed between the Sa'ranja Eyloni and the Mawe'allea Eyloni. The Mawe'allea considered the Sa'ranja island their territory and in times long past had fought for control of it. The Sa'ranja people never formed intertribal alliances with the Mawe'allea people. The Sa'ranja people always supported the Zi'mondi people, the Mawe'allea's primary rivals. Delwyn's confusion grew as they explained how the Zi'mondi central west coast clans had a dispute with the clans holding four islands off their coast. Those four islands had their own interclan alliances with Mawe'allea's Southeastern coastal clans.

The great variety of animal life prowling Sa'ranja lands made it the most dangerous jungle on Elleio, and that had surprised Delwyn. He'd have bet everything he owned that Myat'ti'deep held that honor. Oddly enough, the Sa'ranja exported the most cereal and vegetable foods, whereas Myat'ti'deep exported mostly fruits and nuts. As true everywhere else on Elleio, no farming existed anywhere on the continent.

The tour group then sailed across the shallow and narrow Channel of Daggers to the Mawe'allea Tribal continent. It stretched across longitudinal Zone-a, its tip dropping into Zone-b. Mawe'allea had a large island, *Apatutak*, off its eastern coast in farside Zone-A that skimmed along the equator. The Mawe'allea people held some 6.5 million square kilometers, about 4.3 Alaskas. The Mawe'allea Tribe had two distinct families of clans. The northern clans preferred the warm climate, while the southern clans preferred the cooler climate. They did not strive against one another, but neither did they integrate their customs as clans belonging to the other four tribes did. The Mawe'allea Tribal continent had two respectable freshwater lakes.

The Mawe'allea Tribal Elders patiently explained their territorial rivalries with the Sa'ranja people and the Zi'mondi over the four islands they felt belonged to them. Delwyn learned how the Zi'mondi and the Sa'ranja had become natural allies and frustrated the Mawe'allea whenever possible to the extent allowed under the Compact Counsel's ancient decree prohibiting open warfare among clans and tribes. The Zi'mondi had always been willing to trade the small islands On, Tu, and Nadi to Mawe'allea for their Apatutak Island, but Zi'mondi's southwestern mountain clans wanted nothing to do with their tribe's wishes no matter how much the north and central clans did. The southwest clans had formed interclan alliances with and supported the clans holding territory on all four Zi'mondi islands, especially the three smaller ones closest to the Mawe'allea coast. Significant social ties existed among those clans, which annoyed the north and central Zi'mondi clans no end. Upon leaving the audience with the Mawe'allea Tribal Elders, Delwyn was convinced that relative to all Eyloni he'd met so far, the Mawe'allea were the closest to human impatience, an edgy snappishness that bordered on the impolite—and here he was supposed to be a renown worldwide public figure.

By the time Delwyn and his entourage arrived in Zi'mondi, he wondered if he'd remember even a tenth of what he had heard. Zi'mondi and its islands together took up as much area as a fifth of South America. The islands *On, Tu, Nadi*—not Na'di—and *A'athm* had elleiu tree groups growing in close proximity to one another and supported a large Eyloni population. The mainland had one larger lake in the north, which drained into the ocean. The Zi'mondi climate reminded Delwyn of a balmy fall day in west Britain. The southern mountains received light snows during the long night that melted during the long day before fresh snowfall covered them again the next night. Zi'mondi had no industrial base and traded with the La'huaset via airship, a faster mode of bulk transport than sailing vessels.

On hearing that, Delwyn aimed a resentful glare at Phelindra. "See? I could have flown on an airship and met you here, and we could have toured the tribes from here back to La'huaset in reverse order."

Phelindra squeaked. Her orange skin pigments turning yellow, and her reds fading as she paled. She shook her head for emphasis. "No. I have had more than enough flying this month as it is."

"See, Delwyn?" Melkorka said, jabbing her tail at the Eldest Huntress. "I told you. You should have taken Warriors with you on the airship and had the Hunters quantum translate on ahead to meet us."

Phelindra said nothing, but other Hunters in earshot glared daggers at Melkorka.

Everyone but Zalzadrin. She had spent the past few weeks in flight school learning to pilot VTOL transport aircraft. She hated flying, but when she had overheard how much Delwyn enjoyed it, she decided to face down the fear common to most Hunters. When Melkorka told Zalzadrin she should expect to become the next Mistress of Arms, she returned to the Ah'vou'ree Clan Combat Training Center to learn how to fly infantry orbit-to-surface troop transports. Her training completed, she had asked the Ah'vou'ree Clan to quantum translate her from La'huaset to Zi'mondi—an instantaneous but balance of trade expensive way to travel nine thousand kilometers.

"I wish I had the time to ride an airship back to La'huaset," Delwyn said.

"You can," Zalzadrin said quickly. "You can board one here in this port and fly out over Zi'mondi's A'athm Island, across the Sea of Daggers and up through central Myat'ti'deep, across the Hama'ellea Sea to La'huaset and on to the airship's home port."

"Zalzadrin! Do not go putting ideas into the Warleader's head!" Phelindra shouted.

"That might work," Melkorka said, as her ears folded in serious thought. "The airship's home port is near the Kem Basinga Clan."

Phelindra blanched. "I refuse!" she declared.

Melkorka cast an indolent glance at her. "Sure you do. You barely give Delwyn time alone in the necessary. I am sure you would fly with us. Too bad a journey by airship would take too long."

"I knew it sounded too good to be true," Delwyn grumbled, ignoring his Protectress's sigh of relief. He faced a smiling Melkorka. "I didn't think we'd have the time."

Melkorka nodded. "If we had the time, then I would grab some Warriors, Zalzadrin, Phelindra of course, and go with you since we have to break up soon and go back to our clans."

"That's right, I forgot. Everyone's going back home until they are recalled to the ship."

"Except me!" Kidahin said. "I have to report for surface combat training."

"Yes, and I have paperwork to review," Zalzadrin added. "I do not want to leave any combat assets or ordnance behind."

After meeting with the Zi'mondi Tribal Elders, Delwyn and his escorts were taken to the airfield adjacent to the docks. The commercial airfield resembled nothing like any commercial airport he'd seen before. It filled a natural open space covered in places with firm crushed white rock landing pads. On them sat twenty-two VTOL aircraft and over a hundred aircars.

He looked around but didn't see the terminal.

"Where do we buy tickets?" he asked, dumbfounded.

"Tickets?" Melkorka echoed, puzzled. "What are tickets? Do you mean clearances?"

"Uh, yeah. I guess so."

"Clearance is given when we enter the aircraft. That reminds me. Who wants to fly us back?" Melkorka asked.

"I do! I do!" Zalzadrin sang.

"Do you have VTOL aircraft clearance?" Melkorka demanded.

"Of course I do, Mistress. I applied for the rider when I completed troop transport pilot training."

"That was what, only a few hours ago?"

"Yes, Mistress."

"No jokes while flying," Melkorka warned, cutting off Phelindra's predictable protest.

"No Mistress. I assure you that I will remain most serious while flying our warleader."

"And us!" Phelindra added sourly.

Delwyn couldn't believe it. Not how an afraid-of-flight Zalzadrin had taken the past several days off to get a pilot's license, but how the Eyloni handled commercial aviation.

Eyloni parked aircraft in lots like autonomous rental cars were parked on Earth. If a person had valid flight clearances and balance of trade accounts, then she could walk out onto a pad, climb into a plane, and take off. The valid clearance activated the plane's systems and assigned a transponder identity for traffic control. The aircraft's use was documented on the balance of trade with the pilot's clan. Once the aircraft landed, the pilot could send it back on automatic flight systems, she could retain it for later use, or the clan running the airfield could recall the aircraft back to Zi'mondi if the airfield had a need for it.

No one ever thought to steal one of the Zi'mondi clan-owned aircraft. Honor issues aside, Elleio lacked a money-based economy. What could a thief do with it? Air traffic control could pinpoint it in the air. Nobody would "buy" it. No family would consider barter through their balance of trade account even if they wanted to incur the social debt for accepting stolen property. Heavy social stigmas to character and honor also stopped crimes like joyriding and malicious harm to property from even coming to mind.

Making the proper arrangements didn't take long. An hour later they had secured four VTOL aircraft, each having a 647-person carrying capacity and a half-hemisphere range without refueling when cruising at seven hundred kph.

The way Delwyn had it figured, he had about thirteen hours and nothing to do with it but sleep.

It didn't take him long to fall asleep, either.

Phelindra's ears twitched on hearing the first of Delwyn's sleep-growls.

Allohindra had told all of them not to worry about them. He had a congenital defect, fleshy flaps that vibrated in his throat as he inhaled while sleeping.

The noise put them on guard anyway, as it sounded so much like a male's warning growl.

Princess watched her male from her mother's back, searching for the threat to male safety his growling implied. Phelindra wondered how much longer Delwyn's near-daughter would fight her instinct to check on him, let alone what a Comari might think about the rasping sounds.

The Comari. They had lost her when they arrived at the port her clan ran on Myat'ti'deep. By now she should be back in O'un Tu Clan territory and waiting in Delwyn's abode for his return.

She likely had a long wait. Delwyn, Melkorka, and several others, including Anailiatha, Hlinlodyn, and Hervorallin had to inspect the rebuilt warship compartments at Kem Basinga Clan.

Delwyn slept for eight hours, ate a large helping of cooked grains, walked the aisles spending time with the quarter of his occupational association on this aircraft, got pulled into several group cuddles, returned to his seat, and promptly fell back asleep.

Eyloni females gossiped back and forth among themselves about him and remarked on how many hours he could remain awake before sleeping for just as long.

###

"Prepare for landing," Zalzadrin said, her voice piercing Delwyn's consciousness.

Wha? Waitaminute! How could Zalzadrin pilot the aircraft for over twelve hours? Eyloni normally stayed awake about seven hours out of an eleven-and-a-half-hour EST day.

Phelindra lounged beside him reading her 'minder, her tail wrapped loosely around his waist.

"Phelindra? How can Zalzadrin fly all this time without sleep?"

"She has not," Phelindra said without bothering to look up from the device's screen. "She uses the AI pilot assist, and she had three pilots ready to relieve her at need."

"Oh."

"Get ready. As soon as we touch down, we are going to board a jump jet for transport into Kem Basinga Clan territory."

"Good! I can't wait to see how the repairs have been coming along."

The jump jet lived up to its name. It was another VTOL aircraft, but the VTOLs Delwyn had flown in so far had been airliner-quality with outboard turbomagneto fans to lift them into the air. The jump jet looked like a large version of a late Twentieth Century harrier jet. As with the airliner version, the jump jet used turbomagnetic fans to generate thrust.

These turbomags had been built into the airframe just as inboard fossil fuel jet engines had once been. They made noise too. The airliner's fans had sounded like a muted vacuum sweeper, but the two fans in this small aircraft rumbled like a revving diesel locomotive as the VTOL lifted wobbly off the ground.

Too wobbly, manual flight wobbly Delwyn thought. Who the hell was flying? He glanced up at the forward bulkhead and saw the pilot seated in the cockpit.

Anailiatha.

"How often have you flown this type of aircraft, Anailiatha?" he yelled.

"Often enough, but I am out of practice. Why?" the Warrior yelled back as she throttled the jet into horizontal flight.

"Just wondering is all. I wouldn't expect a warship's chief engineer to do much flying."

They picked up speed and altitude as they headed out along the coastline.

"I do not often get the chance," she admitted, "but this vehicle is manual flight only. He has no automatics and no autonomous AI, except for the antistall and VTOL vertical to horizontal flight avionics. He's a positive-stability aircraft. If I release the control yoke, he will tend to remain in level flight with a slight positive climb rate."

Delwyn held university degrees in agriculture and not in aircraft mechanics, but this aircraft looked unstable. His experience flying military aircraft warned him about what aircraft engineers called negative stability; the tendency an aircraft had to descend and tumble absent constant control surface adjustments. High-performance Twenty-first Century fighters had relied on negative stability designs because they gave the planes superior maneuverability. The pilot still had to fly, but computers constantly adjusted control surfaces to keep the aircraft in stable flight.

The jump jet flew as stable as an unpowered glider.

"I'd love to try flying this thing," he muttered under his breath.

"You have flown aircraft before?" Anailiatha asked from the cockpit.

Damn! Had he said that aloud, or had her sensitive ears heard him mumbling?

"I flew fighters, alphafortresses, and betafortresses in space and during orbit-to-surface insertions, but I never flew anything quite like this."

True enough, the 'fortresses were flying bricks by comparison. Both the Dart and the Jart fighters were inherently unstable. It took a lot of computing power to keep them stable in an atmosphere. Jart and Dart airframe centers of gravity and pressure were so far off-center that they tumbled like badminton birdies in a hurricane without AI assisted flight avionics.

"You can fly us back," Anailiatha's voice broke through his musings.

"Really?" Was she kidding?

Delwyn glanced at Melkorka on his left and then turned to Phelindra on his right.

No comment from them, and they always had some comment whenever he suggested anything they thought might endanger his—in their opinion—valuable male self.

"What? Nothing to say about this?" he asked them.

Phelindra stubbornly kept on reading her 'minder, but Melkorka shut hers off and leaned against him.

"He is a safe aircraft. Even an infant could fly him, but Anailiatha will supervise to make sure you do not fly us into a tree," Melkorka murmured into his ear.

He scowled at her and her dry Warrior wit. At times he preferred Zalzadrin's jokes over Warrior humor. With Zalzadrin he knew, or thought he knew, when she was kidding. Warrior humor came off as serious, and he never knew if they kidded with him or not.

"I'd like that," he said.

"Approaching Kem Basinga Clan hull fabrication center," Anailiatha warned as the aircraft's fans spooled up to break forward momentum before switching to VTOL antistall assist prior to landing.

Delwyn gazed out over the factory complex, for factory it was. Buildings appeared rarely on Elleio, but industry needed buildings. When Eyloni built for industry, they gave structures an artistic flair to help disguise their utilitarian lines.

For all their love of living and climbing in tall trees, the arboreal Eyloni built low to the ground except when the need to house something large came about. The Kem Basinga Clan built the facility below to follow a pleasing pattern. Each building in the complex followed its own spiral leafy snowflake pattern and had been finished to complement the surrounding landscape. From the air they looked like a patch of burnt-orange mushrooms.

A huge microwave receiver squatted on the ground opposite their landing spot. Two massive containers Delwyn took for grain silos stood in gantries like chemical rockets ready for lift-off. Behind the silos, two large irregular shallow ponds glittered in the sun. The industrial center's central building was a tortoise shell structure large enough to enclose a cargo-carrying zeppelin and all its service support crews and equipment.

Phelindra watched her warleader, watched his eyes drinking in the sights. She wondered how he felt about the buildings scattered across the warship fabrication site. Her people avoided large-scale building projects whenever possible, but an advanced people had to build places like these to develop and use their technology.

"Power comes from a geosynchronous orbiting maser, a microwave laser, that services this and other receivers within the arc of the maser's lock-on beam. The energy beamed to this receiver is converted into heat and stored in a heat reservoir. Electrical power is converted from the heat reservoir and is run through the site's power network."

Delwyn nodded. "Thermocouple conversion?"

Phelindra shook her head. "The same basic concept but based on a physics that generates potential directly rather than through bimetal alloy mechanics. Molecular conversion of heat to negative ion storage transforms the microwave energy into surplus electrons. The waste heat is used for material pretreatment and then sent through a closed system steam turbine. The remaining waste heat is then transferred to the cooling pools."

"What are the silos for?" he asked.

"Those?" she asked, gesturing to the gantries with her tail. "The facility puts toxic waste materials in them. Heavy metals, contaminated water, and industrial wastes are pumped into them using triple-redundancy safety systems. The containers themselves are tripled-walled, a container within a container within a container. When they are full, they are quantum translated into orbit. There tractor fields guide them into a common center of gravity point. After that, mass drivers launch them into the sun. The process is monitored by the Compact Counsel and Environmental Interdiction."

As they disembarked and walked into the large hangar Delwyn nodded absently, wondering why they just didn't let the quantum-teleported mass arrive in orbit as a spray of subatomic particles.

Bright white lights strained Delwyn's eyes. The tortoise shell building enclosed a creamy white sprawling bay with stainless steel fittings blazing with surgical cleanliness. Taking up most of the bay stood a three-dimensional scaffold frame resembling the entire volume of his warship in full-scale dimensions. He saw several dozen pieces of twisted, blackened wreckage, repaired compartments, and completed sections filled with equipment suspended on and inside the structure.

Delwyn stood in awe at the sight, speechless at the finished work. Nearly a fifth of his ship's exterior hull hung suspended along the bow and dorsal scaffold perimeter. Several decks of spaceframe, bulkheads, and compartments dotted the interior volume, making the hyper-accurate ceramic grid look like a just-begun 3-d puzzle.

A group walked toward them, a tall male followed by a crowd of females.

"Delwyn, this is Hironin, the *sire cairn* of the Kem Basinga Clan warship hull fabrication facility," Melkorka said.

Delwyn stepped forward to greet Hironin, fighting the urge to stick out a hand in an all too human handshake. Eyloni craved more physical contact than what a handshake could politely convey, even for male greetings.

Hironin embraced him, reaching around Delwyn with his arms and wrapping his tail around Delwyn's waist.

Delwyn felt the tail searching for his nonexistent one. He'd gotten used to an Eyloni's instinctive searching by now. Tail twining boosted shared emotional contact and lacking a tail made every person he met for the first time feel inadequate until they, through Melkorka or Phelindra, were told that he felt their fondness when they wrapped their tails around his waist.

"Come and see," Hironin urged in passible Coalition standard.

"You can understand me?" Delwyn asked, surprised.

"Yes, a little. Talk slow," Hironin said, smelling Delwyn's scent and comparing the words to Delwyn's pheromonal tone to make sure he got the meaning right.

Hironin led them onto the staging floor, and Delwyn thought of pictures in history books showing air disaster investigative procedures and how they used an airport hangar to reconstruct the pieces from a crashed airliner. They fastened them to a wireframe outline of the plane so investigators could have a solid physical model of the aircraft to study. Like a jigsaw puzzle with pieces missing here and there, the pieced-together wreckage gave investigators valuable clues to help them discover why the craft had crashed.

Here, in the warship assembly building, the interior volume had been mapped out in three dimensions to match *Hunter's Moon*. Damaged compartments, sections, bulkheads, hull plates, decking, wiring and plumbing, weapon systems, and consoles had been sent here and matched to their exact placements in the scaffold volume that they had occupied in his battle-damaged warship.

Hironin led them up through broad walkways on each level in the wireframe warship. Everywhere a beam, a plate, a bulkhead, or other structure hung had its own wide path leading up to, and all the way around, it. The surgical cleanliness and the brooding quiet gave Delwyn the feeling he was standing on a holy site. He knew it. For a certainty he knew it. His ship had been built in this building.

Hironin spoke as he guided the group through the scaffold structure. Delwyn counted himself lucky to pick up three words out of five. He had a good grip on say'ta've pitch and beat syntax, and maybe some twenty-five hundred words. Words came from chords and single notes in both say'ta've and e'va'a speech, and changing chord pitch changed word meaning. Delwyn suffered from what he sometimes called "terminal fluency," the kind of fluency most "learn-to-speak" courses taught; verbs, tenses, and enough words to ask or understand basic concepts.

Terminal fluency meant he knew enough words and singing mechanics in say'ta've to sound competent, at least until he heard an unfamiliar word either a child should know, or someone as educated and as old as Delwyn appeared to them should know. The more technical the words Hironin spoke in his clan's dialect, the more Delwyn's understanding began to drift. Hironin caught Delwyn's growing bafflement in his scent and chose simpler words for clarity.

Melkorka stepped in to help translate the new words. Had Delwyn been gifted with Eyloni pheromone-linked empathy, then he would have grasped meaning through scent-enhanced contextual clues. Melkorka repeated Hironin's repair status report in briefing format. She was Mistress of the Ship after all. One of her many functions was to discuss repair updates with her warleader.

"What they have done here," Melkorka began, "is translate wreckage from our warship into its exact same place here. This scaffold matches the scans taken of *Hunter's Moon* after final assembly. The damage assessment scans taken at Wrathsee'a Anchorage shipyard have been compared to the final assembly scans so we can translate each piece into its proper place.

"Single pieces, such as hull plating, are identified by their placement on the hull, and replacements have been made using additive manufacturing equipment. Everywhere you see a green ball is a component that has been destroyed or lost to space. Once the replacement is fabricated, the green ball is removed and the component is translated into orbit, where we ferry them to Wrathsee'a Anchorage."

Delwyn counted the green soccer balls within the 730-meter-long, 70-meter-tall, and 130-meter-wide grid and came up with at least seven hundred green balls, most of them attached to the perimeter of the latticed silhouette.

"Most of the missing outer hull must have been individual hull plates," he commented.

"Yes," Melkorka agreed. "You might think hull plating is simple to manufacture, but sometimes the bulkheads and interior compartments end up being less time-consuming to manufacture, mass for mass."

He nodded. "I know. A hull plate isn't just a metal patch."

"No it is not," Anailiatha agreed, having drifted over to listen, attracted to anything technical. "The outer hull in the primary bow of the combat hull is depleted uranium—duranium—titanium, and carbon composites. The additive manufacturing of duranium products is energy intensive and slow. Titanium is easier by comparison, and carbon composites can be printed out twenty times faster than titanium."

"But that's not the whole story, is it?" Delwyn asked. "Hull plating is a system, not just a metal patch attached to the hull."

Anailiatha swatted him on the arm with her tail for stealing her show.

"Correct. Hull plating incorporates ablative, reactive, kinetic, and absorptive armor layers. Further, they contain components for radiating and deflecting the primary, secondary, and tertiary shields. The radiological shield emitters are embedded into them as well."

Delwyn could well imagine. The average starship exterior hull plate covered a kitchen floor area at least one to three meters thick. *Hunter's Moon's* combat hull had been designed for ram attacks, which meant the forward hull plates should be at least half-again as thick at the bow. Then there was the interior hull in the doubled hull design to consider. The inner hull had its own sandwiched-plate mechanisms made from a ceramic alloy and carbon composites. Those should be easier to make, but he didn't make the mistake of thinking they were something as simple as the ceramic heat shield tiles that had been glued onto space shuttles built two centuries ago.

Hironin led them down another level and forward toward the completed interior compartments.

"This is forward Torpedo Bay-2. That structure over there is Forward Torpedo Bay-1. Between them is Forward Fire Control. Above and farther forward is the primary kinetic railgun barrel, bucket coils, breech mechanism, autoloader, and the ordnance racks. That large section farther forward and just below center is Forward Fuel Reserve-1," Anailiatha said before she turned and pointed aft through the scaffolding to the warship's middle hull, the command hull. "That is Environmental Control Central. Above it and toward us, near the forestation, is Forward Nutrition Center. Below it and flush to the forestation is Forward Fusion-2."

"I thought we couldn't get a reactor installed, run through testing, and powered up before we had to ship out," Delwyn said.

"We cannot," she agreed. "The Uahua'asee'a Clan has a reactor for us, but all the control circuitry and power distribution systems have been destroyed. We either install the reactor and control systems, or we restore the power buss network in Forward Fusion-2 and tie it into Forward Fusion-1, which is normal damage control practice. Then we can tie into the auxiliary power buss powered by the drive reactors in Power Systems and Propulsion, which is not normal."

Delwyn walked through the restored compartments and sections. Power busses, optical and photonic wiring, waveguides, and plumbing had already been installed and their section couplings capped. Those couplings would align and seal once they were translated back into his ship.

He hoped.

Delwyn walked everywhere he could find a catwalk and inspected every piece, down to a twisted bulkhead. He looked over the point defense and the secondary weapon systems embedded in the hull that had already been rebuilt or replaced and were now waiting for transport to the shipyard for installation.

He sighed. Weapon systems were integral to the hull and to its underlying structure. Even where the hull plating had been unaffected by the ramming attack, weapons and point defense systems had either been damaged by the ram, or they had overheated from continuous pointblank firing as the ship withdrew from the Lizard destroyer. The repair crews had to unlock the undamaged hull plates, remove them, pull the damaged weapon systems and replace them, and then relock the plates without damaging them. It took a fighter-sized jackhammer to unlock a hull plate because they had to absorb kinetic projectile strikes and proximity explosions, which meant unlocking a hull plate took time and careful effort.

"I don't see any damaged equipment here," Delwyn said in wonder.

His scent must have conveyed his shocked pleasure, for Hironin hugged him, excited and pleased over how Delwyn smelled so happy about his and his occupational association's hard work.

"Hironin is happy that you find their work pleasing. They were able to save half of the material sent here," Melkorka said.

"That much?" Delwyn's jaw dropped. "What had been repaired looks brand new."

She nodded. "Everything meets or exceeds minimal combat ratings."

"I like this," he sang to Hironin.

The sire cairn beamed pleasure, as did the mistresses following them back and forth and up and down the scaffold-filled staging volume. They had all been taking notes on their 'minders, still working around the hindrance his presence caused. A warleader looking over repairs had to rank up there with an impatient boss looking over a new hire's shoulders.

"When can they begin installing these compartments and sections?" Delwyn asked.

"We are waiting for repairs to complete on *Tyreniioroneo*'s power harnesses," Hironin sang staccato.

Delwyn understood that as clear as a bell, and Hironin's scowl directed at Anailiatha wasn't lost on him either.

"You ordered the wiring harnesses pulled, didn't you?" Delwyn asked her.

Anailiatha nodded. "We discussed this before. The Uahua'asee'a Clan has made new power systems wiring harnesses based on their records. Making them is time-consuming manual labor, but easy technology-wise. I had the old harnesses disconnected and translated from the wiring chases, but...," she drifted off.

"Let me guess. You translated them out piecemeal, but you can't translate the entire harness assembly back into the shipwide chases, can you?"

"Correct. They have been translated into the troop staging area in the combat deployment bay and from there taken to the chases for manual installation throughout the ship."

"And I'll bet that's taking a lot of time," Delwyn sighed.

"It is," Anailiatha admitted. "In fact, we are falling behind schedule. We cannot install the replacement compartments until enough conduits and harnesses have been restored to provide at least partial power. Without power, we cannot verify the repaired systems. We will not even know until then whether or not the replaced hull plating will activate for shields."

"So everybody is idle waiting for partial power restoration."

"Yes," Anailiatha agreed. "I am sorry Delwyn, but the original wiring had so much damage. Repairing it might have taken even longer, and if there happened to be some sneak short circuit or some burnout somewhere in all those thousands of ells of wire, troubleshooting each wire would have taken months."

"I know. I agree with your logic and approve. Be patient."

"The repair crews aboard ship are working nonstop for you," Anailiatha added helpfully.

"I'm satisfied with their efforts," he reassured her.

Melkorka wound her tail around his arm. "You should go there and sing for them."

Delwyn brightened at the idea. "I should have thought of that myself! I shouldn't have been playing around down here as if I was on some extended leave. I should have gone back to the ship and sang for them."

Melkorka turned to Anailiatha. "Prepare the aircraft for a trip to Na'di Island. We will translate from there to A'lon'aloop station for transport back to Wrathsee'a Anchorage."

"Affirm. You can fly the aircraft to Na'di Island Delwyn, if you would like."

"I do, and I will."

5
INBOUND FROM JUPITER STATION TO LUNAR ORBIT

"Bridge to Captain Rodgers."

"Yes, Lieutenant Romaine?"

"Message received from Tycho Approach Control."

"Read it," Rodgers said.

"Aye, Captain. Message reads: 'Upon CECS *Henri Edda* assuming standard orbit above Tycho Base, Captain Rodgers and Commander Cabrera are requested and required to report to Admiral Samson for a classified briefing.'"

Uh-huh. Captain Winters did warn me.

"Send standard acknowledgement and our ETA Lieutenant. Rodgers, out."

"Aye, Captain. Bridge, out."

Rodgers stood up in her quarters and stretched. The ship was on her way back from taking on antihydrogen at Jupiter Fueling Station. By now they should have already passed Mars orbit on a leisurely heading inbound for lunar orbit. Refueling from Jupiter Station always turned Rodgers into a nail-biter. Bringing a carrier down from standard orbit into the upper atmosphere of a gas giant wasn't as simple as pitching down through vacuum. Orbital velocity and atmospheric turbulence made nearspace maneuvering tricky. It took a subtle and experienced human touch no helm computer could match. Lieutenant Carstairs had outdone himself manually firing bow and stern pitch and yaw thrusters as they descended into Jupiter's upper atmosphere. Docking a fourteen-hundred-meter-long starship alongside a flying, not orbiting, fuel depot brought its own long tense minutes while trying to maneuver into a hard dock lock-on. Each attitude thruster nudge and each orbital maneuvering system kick motor punch made the ship sluggish and harder to handle. The gas giant's immense gravity and the turbulence in the windswept upper atmosphere of the hurricane world torqueing the ship made it even worse.

Rodgers remembered seeing an ancient training video in flight school meant for instructing tanker aircraft refueling crews. In it, the crew had tried for half an hour to refuel a helicopter flying over the Atlantic Ocean in a hurricane before succeeding. Taking on fuel from the depot followed the same hair-raising drama but drew it out in slow motion.

It took Carstairs two hours and fifty-eight minutes to achieve hard dock with the perpetually flying depot, four hours and thirty-five minutes to refuel, and a mere twenty-two minutes to return to standard orbit from the upper atmosphere. That was a lot of slow and deliberate maneuvering.

A carrier wasn't a fighter, not by a long shot. Rodgers laughed at the memories she had from watching a two-hundred-year-old science fiction video she had reviewed for a university elective cinema of the twentieth century class. One video in particular featured a disk-shaped battlecruiser with two trailing dorsal nacelles and one trailing ventral nacelle jumping from hyperspace into planetary orbit at zero velocity.

Ha! *As if.* Heavy ships dumped velocity using several techniques, none capable of achieving a dead stop. Even inertial dampening couldn't decelerate a carrier from point five-0 cee to zero in less than ten minutes.

And what about that disk-shaped cruiser's blazing energy weapon fire? *Henri Edda* fired bristling energy barrages, but she didn't chase down enemy ships as if she was a fighter. A carrier's gun batteries fired suppression barrages until they established a perimeter, a standoff between outgoing and incoming fire, a stable bubble that screened the ship and allowed flight operations to launch and recover fighters.

Thinking about flight ops gave her an idea, and she hit a button on her desk.

"Bridge? Rodgers."

"Bridge, aye. Cabrera."

"Meet me on the hangar deck, Exec."

"Aye, Captain."

Cabrera turned to read the interplanetary maneuvering plot a moment before coming to a decision. "Mr. Carstairs, you have the conn. Maintain current approach to standard lunar orbit. I'll be down on the hangar deck."

"Aye, Commander. I have the conn. Maintaining current approach to standard lunar orbit, aye," Carstairs said.

Cabrera set off for the Flight Operations Center, located in the upper third of the Tower, a vertical cylindrical structure 148 meters tall and 93.3 meters in diameter some 373 meters aft from the bow. He strode through a maze of intersecting corridors that were in many ways not all that different than those on a clunky old-fashioned wet navy fission-powered carrier over two hundred years old. Bulkheads and huge metal hatches with coamings, rimmed seals he had to step over to pass from one compartment to the next, interrupted the long parallel corridors at regular intervals. Colored conduits ran along the ceiling, and access panels covered the walls.

From time to time announcements echoed down the corridor, the latest one a warning about mass being adjusted. Unlike wet-navy ballast, centers of mass affected the ship's moment of inertia. After taking on fuel, pumps shifted hydrogen and antihydrogen around to accommodate the carrier's pitch, yaw, and roll inertial responsiveness.

Cabrera stopped at a large manual-operated hatch, opened it, and stepped out from under the Flight Operations Center tower.

What Captain Rodgers wanted him on the hangar deck for baffled Cabrera. He had been about to leave the bridge and take a stroll through CIC when she called the bridge.

He walked past fighter maintenance alcoves, past Blue Squadron port and starboard amidships launch tubes, and across the hangar deck to meet Rodgers standing on the flight deck betafortress staging area.

She was clenching her jaw, trying hard to keep a straight face as he approached.

"Reporting as ordered, Captain."

"Did you hear Romaine read the message from Tycho?" she asked.

"No Ma'am. I was busy at Maneuvering."

"Ah. You know Commander, staring at the plot doesn't make the ship go any faster. If it did, I'd have been awarded the Nobel Prize in physics years ago."

A small smile graced his face, and he nodded. "I guess I have to learn how to grit my teeth."

Rodgers shook her head. "No. You have to learn how to pace without making everyone on the bridge nervous. It's possible, but since I can go to the captain's day cabin just off the bridge when I need a break, I've been thinking about having maintenance install a giant gerbil wheel for me to run in."

"Or you can always join the special operations group action response teams on their ten-k run around the flight deck," Cabrera observed. "Senior Chief Marsch always had his ARTs make the run every morning, and sometimes I came down here and fell in behind them and ran the entire ten klicks."

Senior Chief Marsch. Rodgers grimaced. *Warleader Delwyn now.* "The CNC has ordered us to Tycho Base for the meeting Captain Winters warned us about," Rodgers said aloud.

"It's going to take another three hours to get us to lunar space, match velocities, and get inserted into lunar orbit," Cabrera said.

"Yeah. About that, I think I've come up with an idea for getting us away from routine orbital insertion and for getting us a few hours with Captain Winters before our briefing date with Admiral Samson."

She still calls him captain, Cabrera noticed. Aloud he said, "And how's that, Ma'am? Have a couple of Jart fighter jocks take us there in their Radio Intercept Officer seats?"

"Oh, heavens no," she said.

Thank God, Cabrera sighed. Sitting in flight gear, cramped and crammed into a RIO's seat didn't sound like fun, considering the flight would still take about two hours.

"I was thinking more along the lines of taking out a beta," Rodgers added.

"A betafortress? You want to take out a gunship, Captain?"

"Oh, no. Not the gunship model. Not the troop transport model, either. I think we'll borrow a squadron command and communications beta."

"An AWCNC, Captain? Are you planning on flying ECM/ELINT/ESM for a squadron today?"

Rodgers shook her head vigorously. "No way. The CAG would have a fit even though I'm qualified for CIWS support in a beta."

"Close in Weapon Systems support isn't quite the same as Electronic Countermeasures, Electronic Intelligence, and Electronic Support Measures. The E^3s require patience, and CIWS does not."

"Are you telling me that I lack patience?" Rodgers demanded.

"No, Ma'am. I'm hinting that the CAG will figure you don't have an interest in watching eye-numbing screens on the bridge for the next three hours."

Rodgers grunted. "Yeah, and he'd be right, too. E^3 is analysis-heavy, and it often turns out that the stray negative ion you've been tracking is a naturally occurring stray negative ion."

Cabrera steered his captain back to her sudden interest in the beta. "So, what are you going to do with a beta this afternoon, Captain?"

"I thought you'd never ask, Commander. You should do that more often instead of fishing for hints."

"Sorry, Captain. That's a CIC habit."

"I understand," Rodgers said. "Well, to satisfy your curiosity, we are going to Tycho Base now."

"I thought as much," Cabrera admitted. "Do you have a particular reason, or don't you want to wait through deceleration and orbital insertion?"

"Both," Rodgers said. "I don't want to sit through routine lunar approaches when I know there's a classified briefing just waiting for us. I want to get a heads up from the Compact co-Ambassadors before I get blind-sided by Admiral Samson."

"Do you think Ambassador Winters will tell you anything more up front?"

Rodgers smiled. "I know my Captain," she told him as she invited him through the hatch of a waiting AWCNC beta.

Once inside they opened the crew lockers and pulled on flight suits. Rodgers stepped around Cabrera and sat down in the pilot's seat. Cabrera sat next to her at the E^3 station.

Rodgers snapped toggles and thumbed through checklists on the touch screens. The beta powered up, and by the time Rodgers had completed the preflight checklists, the flight avionics, power, and propulsion systems had ramped up to launch readiness.

"Flight Operations, AWCNC-51 *Henri Edda* Actual. Request permission to taxi from port flight deck preflight staging to flight deck," Rodgers commed to the tower.

She waited. The beta wasn't a fighter and couldn't launch from a fighter launch tube. Both alphafortresses and betafortresses had to fly down the flight deck and exit the carrier through the bow.

"AWCNC-51 Actual, Flight Operations. Captain, why are you stealing one of my betas?" Commander Guthrey demanded.

"I'm not stealing anything, CAG. And since when did the Admiralty decide the captain has to inform her crew about anything discretionary?"

"Ah, Captain. You know as well as I do that as the commander of air group operations, *I* decide who gets clearance to launch from this carrier."

True enough. Flight Operations came under the CAG's bailiwick, and like the control tower in an airport, nothing launched from the carrier without Guthrey's authorization.

"I'm transmitting my flight plan for Tycho Base from *Henri Edda*. You should have it on your screen now."

"I do, Captain. Stand-by while AOC Burrell plots your flight plan."

"Standing-by," Rodgers said, humming to herself for about a minute.

"Captain? You are cleared for launch. Have a good flight, Ma'am. I'll see you at the pre-mission briefing once we arrive in parking orbit."

"Pre-mission briefing? What pre-mission briefing?" Rodgers demanded.

"The pre-mission briefing we're going to have right after you inform all senior staff that we're shipping out."

"Keep you guesses off the air, CAG. There is a naval saying: 'loose lips sink ships.' Those wise old words may end up more appropriate right now then you might think."

"Yes, Captain. You may launch when ready, Ma'am."

"Finally," Rodgers muttered. She snapped the safety cap off the launch toggle and flipped it up.

Two microfusion engines fired, and the beta lifted and accelerated down the flight deck, gaining speed with every passing meter.

Cabrera gripped the E^3 station as they accelerated down through the carrier and out the wide oval force field shuttered hole in the bow. To Cabrera, streaking down the flight deck looked like speeding through an illuminated mountain tunnel into the darkest night.

Once they cleared the ship, Rodgers banked away from the carrier, getting clear of her ship's navigation perimeter to reduce the likelihood of becoming an inadvertent navigation hazard. Rodgers keyed in her flight plan and engaged the autopilot.

"Course entered and engaged. ETA one hour fifty-three minutes to lunar orbit." She turned to Cabrera. "Commander, open mission profile folder *Annazi.*"

"Aye, Captain," he said, mystified. Rodgers had written a mission profile already?

His screen displayed a statement containing all the data Ambassador Winters had given Captain Rodgers, along with several updates over the past eighteen days. They read as diplomatic in nature and concerned the Compact co-Ambassadors and the reasons for their accelerated departure from Earth.

"So, we are heading back to Iota Horologii, and nothing more. We are to transfer Anlann and Seralin to the Compact warship *Surefooted* and then continue to Elleio with Captain Winters? What about a task force? Why just one ship? That sounds irregular. Do you think the Eyloni are headed for Chi Eridani? Wasn't that where CIC thought the three Lizard destroyers had staged their jump into the Iota Hor system?"

"That's what we'll debate about over the next hour and fifty minutes, Exec. I want specific questions ready by the time we meet with Captain Winters."

"Ma'am? Don't you think Admiral Samson will be a bit put out if we meet with the Ambassador first?"

"He might," Rodgers agreed. "But we're not scheduled to meet with him until after the ship assumes standard orbit around the Moon. That gives us an hour or so, so let's make the best use of the time."

"Yes, Captain."

***

"Ambassador Winters? The Compact co-Ambassadors have arrived in the building."

"Thank you, Max. Send them in the minute they step off the lift."

"Yes, sir."

Winters glanced at the luggage he had piled up against the wall. He wanted to leave now that he'd committed to the idea. The Diplomatic Corps drove him crazy. Their latest complaint? That he wasn't taking a cultural attaché with him. He wasn't taking any diplomatic support staff along with him, either.

Marsch had recommended he not bring anyone, not at first anyway. Anlann and Seralin hadn't come aboard *Henri Edda* with staff when they came to Earth, so why should he take staff with him back to Elleio?

Winters's firm stance had made many career-minded diplomats, senior aides, and most of the general staff upset and suspicious. They didn't cast suspicious at the Eyloni. They suspected his motives. They all thought, to varying degrees, that he wanted the glory from representing humans and the Coalition of Earth Colonies to the Eyloni and to the Compact of the Ten Tribes of Elleio all for himself. They thought he planned to curry favor with the Eyloni to pad his resume for future political office. As if being a politician, let alone a diplomat, was on his life schedule.

Maybe, if he liked the climate, if the Eyloni allowed it, maybe he could retire on Elleio and leave officialdom behind forever.

The door opened, and Seralin poked her head into the room, looked around, and continued in, followed by Anlann.

Winters smiled to himself. Had a woman been in here instead, Seralin would have made eye contact with her and hesitated long enough to gauge if permission to enter had been given. But since it was only him, she came right on in.

She did so because he was a man. Opposite sexes always seemed to desire each other's company in Eyloni society, but same-sex meetings followed formal notice and greeting rituals, or so it seemed to him.

Anlann stepped around his Protectress and embraced Winters. "It is good to see you again Alan, in person this time as well."

"It is. How are you, Anlann? Seralin?" Winters asked.

"We are well, Alan. Are you ready to visit Elleio?" Seralin asked.

"I am. I've been thinking about nothing else since you told me you had been recalled. Is there anything more you'd like to tell me about it?"

"Some," Anlann said, "but not much, I am afraid. Delwyn thinks the Ni'zakhonii light attack craft he captured was a prototype. There might be a research and development shipyard hidden somewhere in the Nikkiolo Expanse."

"And the Compact wants you and your ship to go looking for it?"

"Yes. The Compact Counsel wants us to rendezvous with a Compact battle group just long enough for Seralin and I to transfer to our warship. Once we are aboard, then you may continue to Elleio. The A'tayotan does not want *Henri Edda* incorporated into the battle group, and I am sure you can understand why."

"Of course, of course," Winters agreed. In practice it couldn't be done. An independent ship couldn't join a task force. By its nature, a task force assigned ships to various points for various duties. Combat maneuvering doctrine said that once battle had been joined, a ship couldn't in practice integrate into one task force while it was engaging an enemy task force. Prior operational planning hadn't accounted for either the new ship movement, or for the capabilities of the ship trying to join the battle. Unless the task force had a superb tactical commander and unless the wayward ship had a captain well-versed in task force tactics, doctrine called for the captain to leave the engagement and stand-by in reserve.

Eyloni battle tactics and their concept of Warpact had to put a willing *Henri Edda* on the sidelines in any combat operation.

"Mr. Ambassador?" his secretary rang.

"Yes, Max?"

"Captain Rodgers and Commander Cabrera are on their way up to see you, sir."

"Oh, really? Well, send them right on in."

"Yes, sir."

6
ASSAULTMISTRESS COMBAT TRAINING, AH'VOU'REE CLAN, ON ELLEIO

"Kidahin! Prepare to jump!" the Mistress of Battle ordered.

"Affirm!" Kidahin replied. She grabbed onto the jump ship's climbing frame and gestured for her surface stalking team to do the same.

Jump ship, now there was a euphemism if she had ever heard one. He fell from orbit shaking, rocking, and bumping through a ballistic reentry toward a surface Assault Zone.

They fell like rocks toward Ah'vou'ree Clan territory, the southern tip of the La'huaset Tribal continent, just north of the equator and its storm-wracked archipelagoes and into farside longitudinal Zone-D.

Delwyn had told her Ah'vou'ree Clan territory reminded him of a place on Earth called Panama, only with taller trees and more rain.

Kidahin watched the status lights change from nominal red to warning green.

"Prepare to jump!" she sang to her team.

They were falling across the farside hemisphere-spanning abyssal ocean, so unlike nearside with its continents and shallow seas. Farside was a tree of a different color: it was stormy and cold. Elleio had slipped into phase-1 on its eternal orbit around Tyreniioroneo. Zone D had been in darkness for four phases already. The sun was due to come up in another two days or so.

Her mission? The Mistress of Battle's briefing had described a Ni'zakhonii presence on Elleio, within Ah'vou'ree Clan territory. The Ah'vou'ree people maintained the Ah'vou'ree Clan Combat Training Center where armor, artillery, infantry, special and elite assault forces, and special and elite stalking forces received training. All La'huaset clans sent people to train there in all aspects of ground forces combat.

Kidahin trained in leadership skills. She had spent time here once before to demonstrate her jungle prowling and skills to her society. They would not have let her put even one bare foot on their warship's trails and pathways otherwise. That training had focused on forest recon proficiency in solitary and team prowling orienteering, but nothing like this!

The light suddenly blinked danger green.

"Drop! Drop! Drop! Drop!" she sang in alert cadence and slapped the control panel.

The bottom dropped out of the jump ship, and she watched her team let go of the climbing frame and fall into the night air.

When the last Hunter had vanished from sight, Kidahin whispered for guidance from the spirits and let go.

She tumbled away from the jump ship, falling through windswept darkness. She oriented her body to fall stomach first, an easy enough maneuver for all the sensory loss she was experiencing. Free-fall tended to give her an aimlessness made even worse when falling at night. A natural tree-climber, she had more than once jumped from an elleiu tree branch to land on a succession of leaves, and those leaves had decelerated her even as they directed her body toward another wide branch. Learning to fall was something all Eyloni picked up as infants.

Still, she was falling from a greater height than any tree, and no wide leaves waited to break her descent. Even if she was lucky enough to fall into an elleiu tree, her terminal velocity would smack her body into the leaves so hard she might as well hit the unyielding ells-wide branch itself.

A red light winked on her forearm control panel, and she pressed it.

Her jump suit deployed a sail across her back, stretching finger-to-finger across her shoulders and down her spine.

The first time Delwyn had seen a jump suit in storage aboard their warship he had called it a "batsuit."

Kidahin called it a "strangle-suit," for it constrained the body. When she demonstrated how it was worn, Delwyn had called it a "straight-jacket." Unlike "batsuit," which Delwyn's pheromone scent gave her the vague impression of a small flying animal, she had agreed with his clear pheromonal picture of what a straight-jacket was.

It did allow her to fly, which she preferred to falling through the pitch-black night. The overcast above hid the stars, but they could not hide the rare equatorial auroral activity blooming through them as it arced across the skies.

Kidahin checked her heads-up display and counted the transponder blips as her stalking force fell below her. They flew together, somewhat by choice, but more by autonomous systems responding to commands the suit AIs issued. The suits used networked AI platforms, which meant the suits talked to each other. The more suits linking into the network, the more capable the network grew. The AIs' primitive reflex drove it to first gather its nodes close so it could access the collective neural network. Its next priority compelled it to safeguard each Hunter, and finally its primary directive commanded it to convey the Hunters to a safe landing site near the AZ the mission profile had specified.

Kidahin's eyes drifted to the altimeter, descent rate, and trajectory indicators. It should not be long now.

This mission required them to keep to null-emission status. That meant no active scans or guidance, and no comms. Even the suit networking comms had been tuned to low-power, very limited range, and pseudorandom broadcast. If one of the fourteen drifted too far away, her suit would lose access to the nodal AI, and the spirits help her try to find the others in the forest at night in enemy territory. Bad enough the AI nodal talkback telemetry crosstalked in pseudorandom bursts, making the network performance jerky at best, but the spluttering data packets came close to destroying network integrity, much as a random firing nerve caused a cascade that led to seizures.

Kidahin saw edges below her. Her natural nightvision did not give her thermal vision. She did not see heat sources, did not see into the infrared. She had reflective tissue layers in her retinas which bounced photons back and forth, giving them multiple chances to strike sensitive rod cells. Eyloni had four retinal cone cells: red, blue, green and violet. They gave her color vision well into the low ultraviolet. Her eyes had evolved to see outlines in the dark, and while she fell far too high above ground to make out clear edges she was beginning to see the vague Kirlian outlines.

Their launch trajectory would take them into the northern peninsula's southern coast, some ten degrees latitude north of the equator. A low mountain range ran from the west along a northeastern diagonal. Everything south and east to the coast grew under the cover of heavy rainforest, but nowhere as heavy as those on Ni'di Island or Myat'ti'deep.

Their landing zone, a pons-shaped piece of land, had been reserved by the Ah'vou'ree Clan for combat training. No one lived there, although many fine elleiu trees grew there.

Delwyn had expected to find blown-up trees, craters, and other damage to the forest when they first visited the Ah'vou'ree Clan.

He had misunderstood, of course. No Eyloni in her right mind would fire explosive ordnance into the forest. Hover and ambulatory vehicles moved through less dense grasslands. Weapons fired electromagnetic pulse blasts meant to knock out an opponent's asset. Infantry moved in with platform EMP-firing heavy weapons computer-adjusted to give the operator the feel for firing the actual ordnance her weapon was meant to fire. Compact vehicles were restricted to places they could maneuver without uprooting trees and heavy brush. A vast area covered in volcanic slag was maintained for the heavy tanks, and all training ended after the participants took the time to return the landscape to the state they had found it, going so far as to compare before and after pictures.

Kidahin drew a sharp breath as the ground surged up from the darkness to meet her. She ordered her jump suit to climb into a stall, and she dropped and tumbled onto vine-shrouded, plant-covered, firm ground.

Her team had also landed, surrounded by coils and coils of interwoven tall leafy plants growing so close to one another they blended together, forming vertical mat barriers that rustled with loud rasping noises as they collapsed under their weight.

Noise!

Noise killed a stalker, killed her mission, killed her ability to move in silence. Everyone knew how to prowl in silence. A Hunter knew where to place her feet, how to step lightly. Even Warriors could prowl in virtual silence on occasion. Hunters were by nature better at it than Warriors though. The basic training all Hunters received as adolescents built upon their base ability.

But basic prowling and stalking skills began with the Hunter walking through the forest avoiding forest litter and other noisy jungle obstacles. The preliminary combat training she had taken before boarding her warship for the first time had been meant to demonstrate her skill in moving through plants, sticks, and dead grasses and leaves without making noise. That training had never dropped her from the stratosphere into the middle of a noisy forest. What she learned here in Ah'vou'ree Clan territory was how to coordinate team movement unseen and unheard through such hazards.

It could be done. Walking through jungle brambles felt like untying knots in the dark. In fact, the first exercise her team had learned to perform was untying knots in the dark. Plants, grasses, vines, brush, and low branches grew together in natural patterns. If rains pounded them flat into the ground, they sprang back up in irregular layers. Old growth or young, penetrating growth always grew together in predictable ways, ways she had learned the feel for in the dark.

They all had.

It was a chore especially suited for Hunters and their lithe bodies and dexterity. They learned to prowl through enemy-held ground caressing the jungle growth, feeling its pattern, seeing its edges in the dark, and feeling by intuition alone how to part the thickets and walk through them as if they had been tall grass.

Once the skill had been mastered, they progressed to doing it without making noise.

They spent days learning to use their natural skills to move through the thickets in near-quiet, moving in graceful ways, dancing against leaves to mimic the wind and rustling animals, following the background noises so they could pass unnoticed.

No one called out. Everyone knew they had to exit the entangling stems and head for clear ground equidistant from one another and wait until they were ready to act.

Kidahin concentrated on making silent headway. It was hard work. She was barefooted, of course. She needed the touch feedback the skin on her soles gave her: pressure clues, terrain, flora, whether it would bend, snap, crush, or mat down under pressure.

What Kidahin also needed was her bare skin telling her similar things about the ell-tall matted stems, leaves, and vines she crept through. The jump suit not only covered her touch-sensitive skin, but it also added bulk and sharp angles. As small as it was, it prevented her from feeling the plants brushing against her body. The forearm display and controls and the finger-thick housing the wingsail had retracted into often snagged on low-hanging branches and vines.

From skin contact alone she would have known how much pressure or tension the foliage would accept from her movement. The drag knowledge she would have gained by the brushing contact could tell her to twist or back up before she made a rustling sound, broke a stem, or uprooted a plant from the ground, with possible fatal consequences.

But she dare not abandon the jump gear here. Standard operating procedure said they had to meet and stow the equipment in one place where they could find it later.

Combat stalkers served as forward-recon units. Assault forces sent them ahead to prowl, looking for dug-in enemy spotters or enemy stealth ground movement. Combat explorers often encountered the enemy or unknown and hidden dangers first.

Kidahin finally cleared the thicket and stepped onto vine-covered ground.

She stopped and took a visual count. *Ten.* She did not see the other four. The thick tangling leaves and stems blotted out her nightvision, made the scene appear as if she looked through dim, pale fog at its thickest.

She consulted her display and counted suit transponder blips.

All fourteen remained within the suit's limited low-power range, and they were moving.

She headed for the rallying point, knowing the others should see her transponder signal, orange to their yellow blips, and know their assaultmistress waited for them there.

Kidahin stood and listened to the dark night.

Her Uahua'asee'a Clan recruits, all picked by her when she first returned home to her Clan, moved silently as all Hunters should. They had been willing to endure elite combat training even though none had been accepted by her society yet.

That in itself showed their serious commitment. When Kidahin had decided to submit herself as a choice for a warship's society selection, she did so having only the technical trade education she had gained as an adolescent. It had been the spirits' own luck that she had been deemed acceptable to the society of an elite class warship. After being chosen she had to quickly take the basic combat training every warship female needed: stations aptitude, warship architecture, and zero-gravity maneuvers.

Kidahin had not deluded herself into thinking they choose her for her abilities. Her warship had needed a huluhar. The Warrior Edrilla was one and a half years older than Kidahin and her maturity had dulled her innate juvenile sensitivity to males to the point she could no longer perform a huluhar's duties.

Kidahin's path to serving on a warship had not been normal. A female was not usually selected by a society first and then trained. Rather, she, like these Hunters, took basic training first so the societies she presented herself to could see how serious and capable of accepting orders and criticism she was.

Kidahin knew her place aboard her warship, but now she trained for an assaultmistress assignment at the same time her society evaluated these fellow clan Hunters of hers. Earlier she had taken leadership criticisms from other assault-mistresses. As a Hunter female, Kidahin preferred solitary movement while stalking or prowling the forests. Now she had to learn how to prowl with her all-Hunter team and with other assaultmistresses, their teams, and—harder—how to issue orders. Kidahin discovered that issuing orders came with difficulties, and some females had to adjust their thinking.

Since none of her surface assault stalkers had yet been accepted by a society, their hierarchies could not give them military rank earrings. That did not mean they did not possess social or hierarchical rank.

Kidahin was the youngest in her assault group. Not by more than a few years, but age mattered in social rank. Every person respected others older than herself.

Hierarchical rank could easily become a twisting tail of peril. A female's hierarchy and her hierarchical rank was clearly visible to any female who gave the colors and patterns in the knots on her neckwear even a passing glance. Males of course had no clue what the colors and patterns signified beyond basic status because they had no business knowing such matters. All females belonged to some hierarchy. Many of the hierarchies had exclusive or restrictive memberships, like the A'tayotan. Others had mandatory membership requirements and were open only to females belonging to specific societies. Thousands of societies permeated Eyloni culture, from the most general—the Society of all Eyloni—to the most specific occupation—the Society of *Hunter's Moon*, for example.

Four of Kidahin's Hunters ranked her in hierarchical standing, and it did not matter that Kidahin did not belong to their hierarchies. Her Hunter trainees belonged to Uahua'asee'a La'huaset Eyloni, which meant they belonged to the same people, gender, clan and tribal societies: The Society of all Eyloni, the Society of Females, the Society of Hunter females, the Society of Uahua'asee'a, and the Society of La'huaset. Societies formed social-rank groups, and they took into account the years a person had lived since being declared an adult. Chronological age meant nothing in overall Eyloni social standing.

But Kidahin also belonged to the society of her warship. She also belonged to the Society of Helmsmistresses until she officially changed her vocational specialty. She also belonged to an elite combat forces hierarchy. She held a low but not insignificant rank in that hierarchy. Kidahin also possessed military rank given to her by Kalinn her first warleader, later augmented by Delwyn as her current warleader. Male approval held sway in military matters, and Kidahin's earring made all the difference.

None of her team members belonged to an elite combat hierarchy. Nor did they possess military rank. But Uahua'asee'a Clan ran its own wet navy polar research station and fleet. The Clan also had its own higher learning center that taught both wet navy and warship naval traditions, naval vocations, naval combat tactics, and engineering vocations in naval fusion power systems design and construction. In both age and in education the older Hunters had hierarchical rank advantages.

Eleven of her fourteen Hunters had attended the Clan higher learning center: three in power systems design, one in ship design, and two in warship traditions, what Delwyn called "academy" training when she had given him a tour through the learning center. She had smelled his disdain for such training. He felt it favored theoretical knowledge at the expense of practical know-how.

What he thought about warship traditions did not matter. The Hunters had spent the time studying and working with the hierarchies and societies connected to their vocational and occupational interests. For Kidahin that meant their hierarchical ranks met or surpassed hers.

So far, neither had gotten funny about it. This was military training, and her rank earring neatly stepped on their trails. They understood that in military matters Kidahin ranked them.

She glanced at her tracker and noted the transponder blips had begun to move with speed, converging on her. Kidahin smiled to herself. They had done well, passing through the nearly impossible barrier without a sound.

"Kidahin?" one whispered.

Rhetorical question. "What does your tracker tell you?" Kidahin hissed. "Wait for the others."

She did not have to wait long for the remaining Hunters to surround them.

Quietly they removed the jump suits from one another and pushed the bundles into the thicket.

"Scanners!" Kidahin demanded.

Each Hunter extended their flat, round, palm-sized scanners to Kidahin. When they touched, they networked and Kidahin downloaded individual mission profiles to each female.

"Remember, no comms unless necessary, and even then on low band, low power, and on scramble. Do not scan unless you think there is something to scan. Rely on your stalking skills. You all have a sector to prowl programmed into your scanner. Your prowling loop will bring you back here. If you find anything, scan it and retreat. If you encounter the enemy or are discovered, press the alert transponder. Questions?"

"Kidahin? What if we find nothing?" one asked.

"You return here and wait for the rest of us. If you find something, break off and head for the evac point. You are not to kill, even if you can do so and guarantee the kill cannot be discovered. Remember, you are a stealth assault prowling team, not a stalk and kill team, and certainly not a Warrior skirmisher team. You are required to bring back intelligence, and sometimes it turns out the intelligence you bring back is nothing found where you have been prowling. Do you all understand?"

They "yes, Kidahined" her.

"Good. Deploy, Huntresses," she whispered.

"Affirm," they whispered back and melted off into their individual search patterns.

Kidahin headed off on her own scouting route. She trained with them to become a leader, but that did not excuse her from participating in the prowl herself. Delwyn had said he could never order a female to do something he would not do himself. She had laughed at the simple, endearing thought. All females believed the same thing, but they would never allow a male to perform a hazardous duty they could do for him. No female ever ordered another female to perform a hazardous task just to avoid doing it herself. If a female caught a male performing a hazardous task, she shouldered him aside and did it for him.

She commanded an all-Hunter assault force, and she participated in the prowling exercise with them even as she led them in search of the enemy. They spent several long hours hugging the forest in silence, watching for enemy hazards and the real possibility of walking into fierce animals more active here than those animals living in the northern latitudes of La'huaset.

Kidahin glided through stands of trees, under brush, and around thorny coils of thick-stemmed plants. She paused often to listen, catching an occasional soft intake of frustrated breath in the quiet forest.

An hour later Kidahin perked her ears, felt the breezes changing, sought an opening in the canopy, and looked up into the dark sky. Still no stars, and here on farside Tyreniioroneo did not shine in the sky except as a nearly invisible sliver this close to the West Terminator.

A rumble pealed above her. A storm was heading for Ah'vou'ree territory.

Good! A storm drowned out noise and would allow them to make faster progress. The equatorial rains were warm, and they tended to nullify most thermal scans.

The storm struck the forest with the usual savagery of most equatorial storms, yet her prowling group continued. After enduring twenty-two hours of continuous rain Kidahin saw a transponder blip wink to light green.

A Hunter had found something.

Soon all the blips were blinking light green. Kidahin adjusted her prowl and silently came up behind them.

"What have you found?" she asked them.

"A Ni'zakhonii device," the senior hierarchy-ranked Hunter reported.

"Good. Withdraw to the evac point. Once we get there, I will…"

An insistent, dark-green blip flashed on her scanner. She stabbed it with her finger.

"The mission has been cancelled," a female voice said in the clear. "Be advised that Warleader Delwyn of *Hunter's Moon* has been killed in an orbital incident. Repeat: The mission has been cancelled. Be advised that Warleader Delwyn of *Hunter's Moon* has been killed in an orbital incident. Repeat: The …"

Stunned shock filled the damp air as pheromones broadcasted the combined emotions of the Hunters.

Kidahin's knees buckled, and she dropped to her knees. She keyed her recall transmitter. "Ah'vou'ree Training Center? Kidahin. How…how did Delwyn die?"

Dead air replied.

Her heart hammering, her body shaking, she keyed the comm open again at the same time a flash-bang detonated mere ells from them. The concussion flung them into the trees, the blinding flash overwhelming their nightvision.

"Mission failure!" the Ah'vou'ree Mistress of Battle's furious voice sang in dissonant tones that soared over the thunder reverberating across the storming night forest. "Return at once to the recall point!"

"You broke comm silence, Kidahin!" the ranking hierarchical Hunter cried out. "You gave us away!"

"I know that!" Kidahin snarled. "That was a filthy trick!"

✦✦✦

An hour later, standing before the training center Mistress of Battle, Kidahin accused her of inflicting emotional distress.

The Mistress held up her hand to forestall further argument. "Tell me Kidahin what you did wrong."

"I broke comm silence before we returned to the evac point," she snarled.

"*No!*" the Mistress of Battle shouted. "You fell for a trick designed to cause you to react to your feelings. Do you not think the Ni'zakhonii can pull such a trick?"

Kidahin opened her mouth, stopped, frowned, thought about the Mistress's question, and shook her head. "I never even considered the possibility," she finally admitted.

"Good. *Good!* Admitting that fact is good. Our enemy is both harsh and mysterious. We cannot know the motives and thought processes an intelligent reptile might have but they eat us and humans alive. Something the night-favoring creatures would do here if you walk into one. But those are animals, worthy of our respect because they live as the spirits intend them to live, and we may kill them only when they infiltrate a family's immediate territory. The Ni'zakhonii are not animals. They have intelligence, a cold intelligence, an intelligence surely crafty enough to send the message you received, hoping you would respond as you did. I do not apologize for the distress I have caused you to endure."

Kidahin doubted that. Personally, she did not think the enemy possessed the empathy necessary to understand the impact a message claiming a female's warleader was dead would have on her.

Her thoughts drifted. Something about what the Mistress had said about motives bothered her. Toward the end of Kidahin's adulthood ritual, before she had been ejected from the Oyya Web, she had beheld a vision of her people, humans, and the Ni'zakhonii.

The Ni'zakhonii had been starving.

Delwyn and Phelindra had found no food in the nutrition center of the equipment they had captured, either. Could the Ni'zakhonii drive stem from simple starvation? How in the spirits was that possible? A people took care of their world, and their world took care of them.

The Mistress's singing voice brushed Kidahin's ears, and she cocked them sideways to listen.

"…why I sent the message, knowing it would be as disturbing to you as it has been to Kidahin, and you have not even met Warleader Delwyn. You were all shocked, do not deny it!"

"But Mistress, Kidahin is right. It was a filthy trick. If Delwyn of *Hunter's Moon* had played such a trick on us, the hierarchies would have demanded he make an account for causing intentional emotional distress to females," the social-ranking Huntress complained.

The Warrior Mistress of Battle scowled at her, then she scowled at all of them. "If Delwyn O'un Tu La'huaset Eyloni had done such a thing for his own good honorable reasons, and if you had acted as Kidahin had, and if you had brought the resulting emotional injury before the hierarchies, then I assure you that, after hearing the reason why, they will yank you down by your tails so hard your heads will fly through your bodies and out through your *a'peas*. Kidahin knows this first hand, do you not Kidahin?"

Kidahin flipped her ears in agreement, still smarting from the shock the Mistress had caused her.

"What happened to you?" the oldest Hunter asked Kidahin.

"Delwyn demanded my adulthood knife," she said simply.

Shocked faces stared back at her.

"Was he justified in doing so?" the same Hunter asked.

Kidahin's eyes met the eyes of her stalking team as she perked her ears forward, her tail very still.

"Yes. Melkorka and Phelindra thought so, too. He told them I needed further training. I did not think so myself at the time until much later, when it became self-evident. I had need for that training when he came for us aboard the Ni'zakhonii device."

"But what reason did he give your society and its hierarchy representatives that they could accept?" the youngest Hunter recruit asked.

"Presumptive arrogance," Kidahin replied. "I thought to out-stalk Delwyn in the forest, and he struck me a blow from above, a potential fatal strike. I never saw it coming, never heard it, and never smelled it. Delwyn hit me on the head before I even had a chance to defend against it. His outrage over how I had been so easily dispatched forced him to immediately demand my adulthood knife."

Surprised murmurs rippled through the combat stalking team. As Hunter females, they knew how difficult catching a fellow stalking Huntress off-guard could be. Warriors now, they were different. Males were just as noisy as Warriors. For Delwyn ar ahoun Unahaillaea *Tyreniioroneo* to catch Kidahin off-guard meant either Kidahin was a Hunter of extremely poor ability, or else Delwyn was an exceptional stalker for a male.

Kidahin's self-assured presence both in Uahua'asee'a Clan and while training with them here in Ah'vou'ree, added to the natural feelings they had about anything male, led them to prefer the latter. If they trained well here and were acceptable to Kidahin's society, then they would meet the warleader himself and know for sure. They resolved to try even harder and rallied around Kidahin as she nursed her fading emotional upset.

The Mistress eyed the group of Hunters for another wary moment and sighed in muted relief. Kidahin had shown remarkable restraint, the Warrior admitted. More restraint than she would have herself if someone had commed a message announcing her warleader's death. *She* would have been beating some female to a bloody pulp by now.

She snapped herself with her tail, getting the Hunters' notice.

"Your movement through the forest was flawless as was your jump suit flight into the jungle. You will find that jump ship deployment occurs routinely, but seldom over worlds with breathable atmosphere and forest cover. I have read the unsealed parts of the action plan proposed by Warleader Delwyn to the A'tayotan. The parts in the plan relevant to your training include a plan for assaulting and infiltrating an enemy outpost hidden on an asteroid or airless moon. You will prepare for departure and report to the training center translation station at once."

"Yes, Mistress!" they replied.

***

Thirty hours later Kidahin found herself and her trainees belted into a troop transport headed for Meheniioroneo, the fourteenth and last planet in the Elle system, a large pale-yellow gas giant with light orange and light red banded clouds sweeping the globe. Meheniioroneo, "the Companion of the Warrior," was the largest planet in homespace. He had twenty-one natural satellites, two orbiting so close to the gas giant they had become volcanic nightmare worlds caused by tidal force heating. Two more loomed much larger, one with surface water at the equatorial latitudes and the other a cryogenic snowball. The remaining outer moons were little more than captured asteroid rubble. They ranged from nothing more than orbiting mountains to roundish bodies about an Elleio longitudinal zone wide in diameter.

Kidahin and her team were headed for one of the larger asteroid-sized moons. Its key features included an incredible 140,000 ell-tall mountain range some three million ells long just north of the equator on the western hemisphere. The surface did not have dunes of regolith covering most of it. Instead, it was mostly covered with dark rock resembling volcanic basalt that probably came from an ancient comet strike from the inner ice belt on the fringes of the system. Brighter material, some kind of silicate, had been broken up by the thousands of meteor strikes that fractured and fragmented the surface, strewing it with gravel, boulders, and dust mixed with dry ice crystals.

Kidahin read the mission profile scrolling across her 'minder as they headed toward the moon at maximum orbital velocity. When the transport passed above the eastern hemisphere and below the equator, they would launch from the transport on a ballistic trajectory over the *Tu'se Tse'se* impact basin and land at the foot of the crater's rim. They were to recon an enemy outpost reported by a Compact security asset as having been established there.

"Approaching maximum velocity low orbit fly-by for gravity-assisted injection," the Mistress of Battle announced.

The troop transport raced toward the tiny moon, a suicidal plunge aimed right for the southeastern corner of the moon's illuminated disk, the impact basin serving as a visual reference.

"Recon team, get ready to launch!" The Mistress of Battle said.

Kidahin checked her EVA combat suit. "Strap in and prepare to detach," she warned her team.

"Separating…now!" the Mistress of Battle said, and Kidahin jolted in her seat. The troop transport accelerated away on a slingshot vector as they continued on course toward the moon.

Kidahin fired up the Stealth Insertion Vehicle's flight avionics and took them in.

The SIV was a small, bare-bones orbit-to-surface and back again spacecraft. About the same size as a six-legged rough-terrain light assault vehicle, he had an egg-shaped cockpit connected to a twenty-seat passenger cabin. Connecting the cabin to the engines was a length of boxy scaffolding containing the fuel and flight systems, exposed for all to see. Four pods housed the reaction control and attitude control systems and the landing jacks, two mounted port and starboard just aft of the cockpit egg, and another two mounted port and starboard just forward of the main engine bells and the orbital maneuvering systems. The SIV had been built with stealth components and stealth systems, thus he had a negligible scanner profile and nearly undetectable energy signatures. In fact, he had no energy signature at all unless the main engine operated at full power, such as when in boost phase for low orbit insertion and rendezvous with the troop transport.

He had a limited-use standard fusion propulsion system, meaning no bulky hydrogen-antihydrogen power systems. He had no pesky signatures giving away any artificially induced antihydrogen symmetry, no artificial neutrino mixing angles.

The drive technology limits made a bold statement: The SIV was not an excursion vehicle. He barely held the stealth stalking team and enough hydrogen to get the job done.

"Decelerating. Approaching Landing Zone," Kidahin told her team.

She brought the SIV down into the basin, flying mere ells above the surface. For an impact basin as large as this one it had virtually no rim one would expect from an asteroid impact. Except where they were heading for now. Intelligence had reported a probable enemy outpost along the rim opposite the basin.

"Prepare for landing," Kidahin advised and throttled back to hover over the bright pockmarked surface.

She reduced power, allowing the slight gravity to pull them to the surface. On impact the landing jacks absorbed the touchdown and her stomach lurched at the slow motion stop.

The SIV did not have artificial gravity or inertial dampening. Nor did he have an environmental system. Everyone got their oxygen from taps connecting their suits to the ship's air supply. When they exited, they had to first disconnect from the ship's air supply and then rely on their combat EVA suit internal, limited-duration support systems.

"Everyone report suit status," Kidahin ordered.

A chorus of "operationals" followed.

She activated the ship's passive scanners and played them over the low rim above them.

Nothing but jagged rocks.

"Exit the ship."

"Affirm, acting," came their responses.

Kidahin exited the cockpit last and stepped onto the airless moon, took a head count, and performed a visual check on the SIV.

"Weapons locker. Take your assigned weapon and connect it to suit power," Kidahin said.

Again she received the group's "affirm, acting."

Kidahin sighed. Combat EVA missions forced people to wear armored environmental suits and carry energy weapons. Everyone carried a ceramic combat knife belted to her suit waistline.

Of course they still wore their adulthood knives, but they remained tied to their left breast harnesses inside the suit. They also wore their rank earrings inside their helmets.

"Confirm power, weapon status, stealth systems, comm systems, and environmental systems."

Her team members one by one confirmed suit integrity.

"Demolitions?" Kidahin asked.

"All accounted for, Kidahin," the demolitions Huntress confirmed. "It seems a shame to drag them along on an intelligence-gathering mission," she added.

"Target of opportunity doctrine," Kidahin reminded the demolitions Huntress. "If we are discovered and have a chance to render the enemy harmless, then we take the opportunity."

"Affirm," the demolitions Huntress acknowledged.

"Break up into prowling intervals. Comm as soon as you see something."

"Affirm."

Kidahin had them move out.

The next thirteen hours dragged on in drudgery. The local surface of the moon was bright, ranging from between the brightness of concrete and the transparency of ocean ice. The inner part of the central spot on the floor of the crater was as dark as an exposed coal seam. The stealth assault team counted more than one thousand bright spots, most of them associated with small impact craters. The impact basin exhibited multiple, partially coalesced bright spots, the largest corresponding to a central pit covered by silicates and dry ice. The pit was traversed by dark lineaments the team first thought of as possible fractures but seemed to surround the remnants of a central pit. The morphology of the craters showed them all quite young with crater rim and walls sharp without abundant terraces and landslide deposits. These observations confirmed artificial surface activity.

Sensors detected deposits of hexahydrate, a type of magnesium sulfate. The team found a slight haze along the crater rim, a volatile component identified as water. Suspecting subsurface water and plume activity, the team scanned for and found dust particles venting from the ground they could not correlate with a natural internal heat source or solar radiation. Patiently taking low-power, high resolution scans allowed them to pinpoint a vapor trail caused by the sublimation of water that carried tiny particles of dust and residual ice. Team consensus eliminated cryovolcanic venting. Tracing the vapor particles led them to a camouflaged entrance on the crater's nearly nonexistent rim. They took immediate area scans, scans of the hatch, and scans below ground.

Kidahin called her team together and invited them to present their opinions in the usual Eyloni female way of giving everyone a chance to have her say without fear of reproach, regardless of rank. Overlaying ground-penetrating scans supported their consensus opinion: they had found an automated weapon emplacement of some kind.

They took more scans before heading back to the SIV. Once there, Kidahin uploaded their scans into the SIV's computer, which considered the emplacement's position and its orientation on Meheniioroneo with the orbital plane, period, and rotation of Tyreniioroneo and his moon Elleio.

"What is it, Kidahin?" one of the Hunters asked.

"A well-hidden weapon platform. I think we have discovered a kinetic launch system. It looks like a scaled up railgun similar to the orbital mass drivers we use to send waste products into the sun."

"What does it use for ordnance? The scans showed no projectile racks. Besides, it makes no sense to store kinetic weapons here."

"No," Kidahin agreed. "This weapon apparently kicks out chunks of the moon itself."

"That does not sound efficient. Why not just put a railgun in the inner ice belt and kick mountains of ice in-system? There is more mass in ice than there are massive boulders it can launch from here."

Kidahin paused. The Hunter was correct. Why risk discovery and build an adequate kinetic weapon system capable of launching mass only during brief orbital alignments between the moon, the gas giant, Tyreniioroneo, and Elleio?

What to do? Go back, force the hatch open and investigate? Or get in the SIV and boost to escape velocity and head for the troop transport rendezvous coordinates and report?

"Get in," Kidahin ordered. "Commence preflight checks."

Her team piled into the ship and reattached their umbilicals to the SIV life support system.

Kidahin fired the stealth insertion vehicle's main engine and the SIV lifted off the basin and executed a low-emissions climb on an escape trajectory.

Upon recovery, the Mistress of Battle debriefed them.

"I am pleased to report mission success. The area in and around the test site was embedded with passive sensors that, had you not approached correctly, would have gone active and fired EMP ordnance at your ship, knocking out his drive and flight systems. Had you triggered them while scouting the area, they would have proximity detonated, knocking out your suit systems except for life support. However, had you attempted to breach the outpost, massed EMP discharges would have detonated with enough energy to knock out your suit systems.

"Tell me Kidahin why did you not attempt to gain entry?"

"The mission profile called for stalking, not for assaulting the presumed enemy outpost. When we returned to the SIV, we discussed the scans exhaustively. Our consensus analysis concluded it made no sense to place a kinetic weapon system on the moon. It was a decoy, and it was likely filled with explosive ordnance."

"A trap," the Mistress of Battle said.

"Yes, Mistress," Kidahin agreed.

"What is your assessment of your team's performance since you began training with them?"

"Mistress?" Kidahin asked, hesitant.

"You heard me. You recruited them; you trained with them. Now evaluate them."

"That is not my place, Mistress. My warship's society makes those decisions as a whole," Kidahin objected.

"Yes," the Mistress of Battle agreed, "in the same way they agreed to name Delwyn warleader, yes?"

"Yes. Of course," Kidahin stumbled.

"Yet you have been your society's huluhar, so in actual fact you chose Delwyn and the others followed your lead."

"That is not the same thing!" Kidahin objected.

"No, it is not," the Mistress agreed. "Yet if you believe any one, or all, of the Hunters you have picked here with you are not suited to warship duty, it would be dishonorable for you to bring them to your society anyway. Is this not true?"

Kidahin hung her head. "Yes, Mistress. Your assessment is correct."

"Well then, what have you to say on this matter? Remember, they will serve aboard your warship, in key places where your warleader will count upon them for surface combat."

"Yes, Mistress." Kidahin looked into the expectant faces of the Hunters she had recruited from her Clan. But for minor rank squabbles, they had performed admirably.

"I certify them suitable for submission to my warship's society," Kidahin declared.

"And I certify you have completed assaultmistress leadership training. I also certify your team Hunters have completed basic surface assault force training," the Mistress of Battle for the Ah'vou'ree Clan Combat Training Center avowed.

7
THE RITE OF SELECTION AND CHOICE

Kidahin sat in the pilot seat of a small VTOL aircraft, reading her 'minder, and ignoring her dozing surface action stalking team.

Her scowl deepened.

Phelindra told her to report to A'lon'aloop Naval Station for a ground forces tactical mission briefing. Now Melkorka had just thrown that plan off the vantage. She wanted everyone to gather for the Rite of Selection and Choice now. She wanted to confirm by major consensus every searched female that had been selected for warship duty in accordance with all tradition.

Kidahin grumbled to herself. Why do the rite now? All the repaired, rebuilt, and replaced structures and systems had been installed into their warship, but the repair teams had not tested so much as a single hull plate. The ship still lacked main, secondary, and auxiliary power. They could not switch repair slip umbilical power to the mains, and battery power could not be diverted to the mains either. An exhausted Anailiatha had not been making many friends lately among her engineers, her engineering maintenance teams, her housekeeping maintenance teams, or her damage control teams.

Without partial power the shipwide solid holographic jungle vistas, the gentle breezes, the pastel warm leaf-colored internal lighting environmental systems could not activate and transform the warship's decks into a replica of the northeastern La'huaset rainforest. They could not even power up basic life support, which meant the repair teams were still pumping air inside the sealed repair dock that surrounded the ship through every hatch, airlock, vent, bay, and out the open combat deployment bay door.

So why hurry? Who knows? Melkorka wanted everyone to come to the O'ni'da families'gather site, the place where Delwyn had sung for his adulthood ceremony.

Speaking of Delwyn, what was he doing? Why, the last she knew he had been flying a jump jet down the Om'tu River valley! He must have returned to his hometree by now. Well, maybe not. Melkorka and the others would not want him anywhere near them when the Rite of Selection and Choice began.

Well, they did not want him out of sight either. Phelindra never let him prowl far from her. If she could not watch him personally, she always recruited someone under blood oath to keep her nose trained on his pheromones. Otherwise he would go wandering off on his own. Males were strange. Verikaralee and Phalalin were probably either sitting on him, or they were distracting him with battle planning.

Kidahin wondered whether she had enough time to visit Uahua'asee'a Clan first, or if she should divert to O'ni'da families' territory right away. Maybe she should take her teammates home and wait there until "someone" made up her mind.

"Kidahin? Phelindra. Where are you?" the comm sang.

"Over the Hama'ellea Sea, between Na'di Island and La'huaset, about to get my tail dry."

"Continue on into O'un Tu Clan territory and land near Delwyn's immediate family's tree. We are bringing all the new people there now for the Rite of Selection and Choice. Do you have your Uahua'asee'a Clan Hunters with you?"

"I do. They are recovering from their assault forces training."

"You mean they are sleeping," Phelindra said dryly.

"They are," Kidahin agreed.

"What do you think about them?" the Eldest Huntress pressed.

"What do I think?" Kidahin echoed. "The Ah'vou'ree Clan Mistress of Battle certified them. They met their stalking objectives, better than I unfortunately. Their hand-to-hand and unarmed combat skills are more than sufficient. They checked out in basic light assault vehicle transport-to-target, recon, return, and recovery exercises. That said, everyone including I should go through the armored personnel carrier, tank, and artillery platform drills on the combat deployment bay once we return to our warship."

"Will this be a problem?" Phelindra asked.

"Depends on repair status, does it not? Ten of them will apprentice with Anailiatha. She might put them to work right away helping the damage control or engineering maintenance teams."

"Oh, spirits! The last person they want to apprentice with is Anailiatha."

"Has she been that bad?" Kidahin asked, already knowing the answer.

"Anailiatha had been threatening to cut off tails and use them to tie wiring harnesses to the chases."

"Um…And this is the Warrior that Melkorka pestered about getting the jump drive online back on Ibeetu?"

"Oh, yes. Can you imagine how Melkorka is riding Anailiatha's tail right now? I am sure Melkorka is unwelcome anywhere near Power Systems and Propulsion."

Kidahin flicked her ears in agreement as Phelindra rang off.

She had not been searched for by a *Hunter's Moon* society member herself.

She had walked into their ritual uninvited and presented herself for their scrutiny. Kidahin gave herself a wistful smile, leaned back, closed her eyes and thought back to the day when she had been chosen.

***

Kidahin discovered that *Hunter's Moon* had been searching over the last EST month for new crew candidates. She had been declared an adult only four days ago. The warship society representatives had swept through the clans that had built their warship. They had left Uahua'asee's Clan four weeks ago. Now they had gathered near the equator, in Ah'vou'ree Clan territory. All forty-three thousand *Hunter's Moon* society members had a strict obligation to report to that gather site.

Hunter's Moon was an elite warship, and his society could afford to be picky. At most they might ask twenty females to join them. Because he was an assault battlecruiser, Warriors had the best chance of being chosen.

Kidahin's intimate friends told her not to get her hopes up. The warship society was searching for females trained in infantry combat, combat support, and warship combat traditions. Her youth and inexperience would be of little interest to them.

Kidahin shrugged off her lovers' well-meaning advice and told them she had to try. A warship's society did on occasion choose minimally trained females.

Yes, they all agreed, whenever they suffered heavy casualties. *Hunter's Moon* had not suffered casualties in years.

Kidahin palmed the aircar identity scanner, and it lifted off with her alone. She programmed the autopilot to take her to the Ah'vou'ree Clan gather site.

What was she doing? she wondered. Uahua'asee'a Clan had females belonging to the warship's society. One of their Warriors had invited two

Clan Hunters to come with her. Both Hunters had completed studies at the Uahua'asee'a marine research center.

Custom did not prevent Kidahin from presenting herself at the gather site, but her uninvited presence would border on the discourteous. She was only going to the Ah'vou'ree Clan gather site, she convinced herself. She was not fool enough to try meeting them at their warship docking port, where they could kill her outright without a second thought for territorial trespass.

She had to gain their notice somehow without causing a scene.

How should she do it? Not by seeking out her Clan females, certainly. Standing with them implied the warship society had brought her along with them, and they had not. Her presence with them might also carry a scent suggesting she could not stand on her own two legs. No, she had to walk into their midst as if she belonged there and make a good case for herself.

What have you done as an adolescent they might ask. "Easy to answer," Kidahin said to herself. "I have taken jungle survival. I have three years experience at the helm of a polar research vessel. I survived my adulthood ordeal…"

Scratch that last. Every adult female accomplished that much, otherwise she either remained an adolescent, or died in the attempt.

Kidahin reclined in her seat and stared at the 'car's ceiling. The dark maroon swirls took her back to the visions the spirits had given her.

They told her she held the high ground for an archetypal male who fought on the low ground for the survival of all Eyloni. Without her, he would fall. If he fell, then all Eyloni everywhere would die.

The clan elders had been surprised to hear her claim to have received guidance from the spirits themselves. The adulthood ceremony exposed Kidahin to her immediate and extended families' female pheromones, and those pheromones had acted on her mind to create the Oyya Web visions. They came from the female minds surrounding her. The imagery was meant to be taken as metaphoric abstractions, they assured her.

But their scents convinced Kidahin that they had been confounded, too.

She had seen Eyloni, humans and Ni'zakhonii. That more than anything else had prompted her to seek warship duty. Where else could she find humans and Ni'zakhonii but in space?

She fell asleep and remained asleep until the 'car's landing alert woke her. He was descending over Ah'vou'ree Clan territory.

Kidahin let the aircar land automatically using preprogrammed subroutines. She opened the door, got out, and glided to the Ah'vou'ree family Watch to declare her intent. No one barged into another clan's territory without making herself known first.

"Welcome Kidahin Uahua'asee'a La'huaset Eyloni. May I help you?" A Warrior asked.

"No, thank you. I have come to visit the *Hunter's Moon* society's Rite of Selection and Choice."

"You have been searched?" the Warrior asked, casting eyes about for Kidahin's sponsor.

"No. I have come to present myself for selection."

The Warrior looked askance at her. Was Kidahin serious?

"You are La'huaset Eyloni. I welcome you, Kidahin of Uahua'asee'a. The gather is free territory, but a warship society is not a group of females to play adolescent games with. If you injure your honor here, and if they carry your poor character to other warship societies, then you will never get chosen no matter how much training you amass over the years. Watch where you poke your tail and tread carefully."

"I will, and thank you," Kidahin said.

"May the spirits prowl alongside you today," the Warrior said by way of wishing Kidahin luck.

Impulsively, Kidahin hugged the Warrior and wrapped her tail loosely around her.

The Warrior responded in kind, twisting her tail around Kidahin's, shuddering with pleasure at the friendly contact.

"I hope they pick you Kida," the Warrior sang under her breath.

"So do I Vadel," Kidahin replied, following Vadella's natal chord use, the infant name used among intimate adults in private to attach emotional meaning. Kidahin had been awarded the syllable *hin* upon receiving her adulthood knife, just as Vadella had received the chord *la* when she became an adult.

They broke the embrace, and Vadella gave Kidahin some parting advice. "Find a female with a thick rank earring and make your case to her. If you can win her over, then she may advocate for you before her society."

"Thank you, Vadella. I will remember!" Kidahin said. She turned and headed down the trail leading into the gather site.

Kidahin stepped into a narrow meadow, an irregular grassy swath several thousand ells long but only a few hundred wide. Golden-yellow grasses rippled like a living lightning bolt through the heavy orange brush and scarlet bushes growing in an irregular circle made by the shade from the thick overhead canopy that restrained the heavier undergrowth.

Kidahin slipped among the gathered warship society members. They prowled about, attracted to different wandering groups. They danced together in rank patterns, and Kidahin could see who was and who was not a member of this society—those few females not wearing a military rank earring: the earring only the female wearing it or her warleader could touch.

The earring Kidahin likewise did not wear.

She drifted deeper into the patterned, prowling maze of bodies, smelling their various scents. Those pheromones hinted at a subtle curiosity about Kidahin's presence.

Warriors and Hunters drifted by murmuring among themselves, and Kidahin followed. As she was swept into eddies, groups looked at her and smelled her as she passed by.

The crowd seemed to drift apart for her. That was normal. Eyloni did not bump into one another on accident. She drifted along with them until she smelled the searched females from her clan. They dropped their ears flat against their heads on seeing her.

"Kidahin," a searched Uahua'asee'a Hunter hissed. "What are you doing here?"

The female sponsoring her, wearing a rank earring of course, frowned at her candidate, shook her head, and urged Kidahin to continue further into the dancing maze. Kidahin twisted around at her waist. Her clan females and the few others without rank earrings glided inward accompanied by their sponsors.

The warship society danced around and through them in a writhing convoluted step. Kidahin found the rhythm of the wandering choreography, but somehow she knew that before she could move closer towards the people she felt drawn to, her clan females must pass her, and the double-handful of bare-eared females and their sponsors must pass her as well otherwise the complex dancing pattern would be interrupted.

They headed into the center of the dancing crowd as she turned to enter a separate phase of the dance flowing towards a trail she sensed was right for her to stalk.

The gathered warship society began to sing. They sang about themselves, about their society, about their warship, and about Kalinn their warleader. They sang a welcome, but they also sang a warning: being searched did not guarantee being chosen.

That refrain was repeated several times before they let the song fade away.

Kidahin caught the scent of surprised delight that spun about her. Many people favored her with perked ears, and a new refrain was taken up by those near her: having not been searched did not mean being chosen was impossible.

That refrain continued as Kidahin was swept up again into the swaying, shifting, ever changing pattern.

Ahead of her stood 132 females, their gold earring hoops filled with honor knots, mission beads, and achievement webs. One rank weave did not, quite, seem as dense as the others. The Warrior wearing it held a sword in her left hand, hilt up and blade pointed to the ground.

She was the Mistress of the Ship. The mistresses around her pirouetted on light feet away from her, forming a shifting maze to prevent anyone else from dancing too close to the warship's commander. All trails to her had been pinched off, all but one.

The one Kidahin danced along.

The mistresses beckoned Kidahin to come to them, and she fell into the rhythm as she danced among the mistresses, her bare feet following the beat. The pheromones of female power gripping her, forming emotionally charged questions in her mind.

Who are you?

Why are you here?

Kidahin danced around each mistress, meeting her eyes, her tail and ears held in deferential respect as she did so.

Kidahin weaved about the Mistress of the Ship and her forty-four command center mistresses. The closest, a past middle-age Hunter with rank weaves so thick they formed a disk-shaped bundle within the gold hoop, focused on her. The old Hunter's scent told Kidahin that she was amused to see her here.

"Who are you?" the Mistress of the Ship demanded.

"I am Kidahin Uahua'asee'a Lu'huaset Eyloni, Mistress."

"Where is your sponsor, Kidahin of Uahua'asee'a Clan?"

"I do not have one, Mistress."

"And so you thought you could dance into our company and see how it went?" the Mistress of the Ship demanded.

"I have just been declared an adult by the Tribal Elders. My first adult decision was to say that I would present myself for selection to a warship society."

"No doubt the spirits told you during your adulthood ceremony to pursue this occupation?" The Mistress of the Ship asked her, a ringing tone of amusement in her lilting singsong voice, a hint of laughter on her scent.

"No, Mistress. The spirits told me that I hold the high ground for a male fighting on the low ground!" Kidahin snarled, her juvenile emotions firing up with a mounting fury she fought to restrain.

All the mistresses locked their eyes on Kidahin. They could clearly smell the young Hunter's resentment, the truth of what she said.

"I am Melkorka. Tell me Kidahin, what training have you? Stalking? Combat?"

"I have taken basic and intermediate stalking training, and I have intermediate with some advanced hand-to-hand and traditional weapon combat training as well. I operated the helm of one of Uahua'asee'a's polar research vessels. I have a knack for solving helm and navigation problems."

Another mistress, a middle-aged Hunter this time, stepped up from behind Melkorka, "Oh you do, do you?"

Kidahin locked eyes with the new speaker. "Yes, Mistress. Specialist level blue water helm and navigation, apprentice level submersible helm and navigation."

"Three-dimensional navigation," the Mistress murmured, nodding to herself. She turned back to the Mistress of the Ship. "I will apprentice her, Mistress Melkorka. She must remain in command center to acclimate herself to Warleader Kalinn anyway. I believe she may have the necessary aptitude to pick up helm and navigation if she can navigate submersibles in the polar ocean."

Melkorka frowned and turned to the oldest Hunter. "What do you think, Eldest?"

The old Hunter scowled at Kidahin. "Young, impatient, and impudent. She is violent and has poor control of her emotions, just what you should want in a huluhar."

Huluhar? Kidahin gulped.

"I am Phelindra, the Eldest Huntress of the Ship and the Mistress of the Watch. You will train under my supervision for boarding and surface stealth actions as a Battle Status combat alternate. Your primary duty will be to serve as the Mistress of Pathwalking's second at the command center navigation station as helmsmistress."

"The Mistress of Pathwalking?" Kidahin stammered.

"That is me," the Hunter who had volunteered to apprentice her said. "I am Trebithia. When we leave here today, if we choose you, you and all the other new females will accompany us to the Ah'vou'ree Clan Combat Training Center. There you will all demonstrate your jungle prowling and stalking skills. Next, those who have already taken preliminary and basic combat training will travel to *Hunter's Moon*. Those who have not, will take a crash course with more combat training to be worked into your apprentice schedules once you are on *Hunter's Moon*. When you arrive on board Kidahin, you will begin helm training at once. Over the next several months you will operate the helm under my supervision. When you have mastered the helm, I will begin your training at the navigator's seat."

"Yes…yes, Mistress Trebithia."

"If we all agree, you will become a member in the society of an elite status warship. That means you will train hard to deserve holding this honor, for your honor is ours, and our honor is yours. We reflect the character and honor of Kalinn our Warleader, just as he carries our honor. You do understand what will happen to you if you are found wanting?" Phelindra demanded.

"Yes, Eldest. I will remove myself from the fellowship of your society."

"At least that," Phelindra said, "and no other warship society will so much as look at you if you try to join them as you have us here today. If you cause our honor to diminish, or if you cause harm to our Warleader's honor, then we will kill you slowly with your own adulthood knife."

Kidahin swallowed and nodded. Full of juvenile fearlessness, she stared back into Phelindra's amber eyes. "I already know this, Mistress."

Phelindra perked her ears at Kidahin, the old Huntress's tail thrashing the air behind her. She had doubts. Kidahin could smell them, but in the end Phelindra yielded and nodded to Melkorka.

Melkorka glanced around her, looking at each command center mistress.

"What do the command mistresses say?" she asked them.

Every command mistress sang in approval of Kidahin.

Melkorka drew herself to her full height and danced a complex patterned circle around Kidahin and the command mistresses as she sang. "You have heard the song of Kidahin of Uahua'asee'a Clan. Do you choose her to stand with us?"

The command mistresses sang back in approval.

But the society had to agree to the last female. Further, if they chose Kidahin then she would become obligated to sing in approval of every subsequent female chosen here.

Melkorka sang again to her society, the occupational association of Warleader Kalinn, the crew of the Compact warship *Hunter's Moon*. "This is the Hunter Kidahin Uahua'asee'a La'huaset Eyloni. She is the youngest female I smell here. Her mind fits well with the requirements most needed in a huluhar, and she has sufficient helm and navigation training to suggest she can adapt her experience to master warship helm and navigation duties under the guidance of Mistress of Pathwalking Trebithia. How do you sing for our new huluhar?"

Kidahin followed the rhythm and the words her society sang. As she listened, she counted every voice she heard, everyone of forty-three thousand dancing around her.

"I have heard the music of every voice gathered here in the Song of Choice and Acceptance. Kidahin, you are now the Huntress Kidahin Uahua'asee'a La'huaset Eyloni a'doni huluhar *Tyreniioroneo*. Be welcome to our society," Melkorka sang.

***

Kidahin smiled at the memory, remembering the song, the touches, and the tail caresses every single female had given her that day as they welcomed her to their society.

A few hours later Kidahin overflew the elleiu trees sheltering the O'ni'da families. She spiraled the aircar down to land near the large gathering of her society—Delwyn's occupational association.

Well, not all of them. More than three thousand remained potential society members. Their sponsors had brought them here for the crew to consider, but only 2,224 would be chosen to replace the casualties they had suffered when three Ni'zakhonii destroyers had struck their warship by surprise.

Kidahin pressed a control, and her seat resumed its upright position. She would see everyone soon. Jittery, she glanced at her sleeping assault team and remembered. Everyone searched back then had been accepted along with her, thirty months ago.

Kidahin doubted that would happen today. With so many vacancies resulting from the casualties they had taken in battle, the searchers had been encouraged to find as many qualified people as they could.

Delwyn's fame would also attract several hundred who had not been searched. They would try to appeal to the society as Kidahin had done, but so many could not be chosen. It was no dishonor to be passed over. People would understand that more had come than their warship could accommodate even if the society happened to be willing to accept them all.

Kidahin also knew they needed a new huluhar, and this time a Warrior female had to become huluhar. And as she had been, the huluhar would be the first chosen.

###

Choosing new crew members took time. For everyone searched, the unanimous society decision to accept them turned on ritual formality. Females being females, they already knew where in social and hierarchical status the searched stood. Those doing the searching picked the prospective replacements, and their honor sat on the balance. They were required to search for acceptable candidates, and it had been up to them to vet the skills and achievements of those they selected. The physical meeting at the gather sited also prevented anyone who did not belong to a clan that had built *Hunter's Moon* from participating. Outsiders, invaders of territory not theirs, they could not under any liberal meaning of courtesy even watch the ritual.

Rarely did a searched candidate not get chosen. It almost never was the fault of the sponsoring female. Nor was it because the candidate lacked the skills they needed. Sometimes, even among Eyloni, incompatible personalities emerged. In those cases, it was almost always a command mistress who discovered those personality traits. Most often it was either the Eldest Huntress or the Eldest Warrioress because they had the standing and rank to push and challenge enough to expose personal flaws.

Kidahin's assaultmistress rank allowed her to dance close to the outer ring of mistresses, within tail-touching distance of Zalzadrin's extended tail.

Kidahin's eyes followed the new Mistress of Arm's forward-perked ears and saw a disturbance in the pattern her society had made in their rhythmic dancing.

Heads turned to watch a Comari pick her way delicately through the pattern, weaving sinuously among those females dancing without sponsors. She smelled them, looked them over, with a look of doubt on her face.

Comara had no tails, and like Delwyn she gave everyone fits when they tried to read a Comari's emotions by relying strictly on her body language and scent alone.

"Oh, spirits!" Zalzadrin sighed. "Where did she come from?"

"She must be looking for Delwyn," Kidahin volunteered.

"You know better, Kidahin. She knows he cannot be here," Zalzadrin chided.

"He is not *now,* but once our society is complete, we will reconvene on *Hunter's Moon,* and she will follow us there in search of him."

The precise notice a Comari gave a person unnerved even the boldest. You did not want to come under that scrutiny, and this Comari was invading those unsponsored females' personal space on purpose. Eyloni society accorded Comara all courtesy by long-standing custom. That custom let them go wherever they willed. They had even more freedom than a male, and a male had almost absolute freedom of movement. If her wanderings were driven by a concern she had over a male, then her absolute freedom of movement superseded all matters of privacy and courtesy, hence her presence here was permitted even though she was Su'tayo Mah'heyo Myat'ti'deep Eyloni, not even a La'huaset Tribal member.

Kidahin watched the Comari circle the unsponsored females, stalking their tails. Her ears whipped about as she considered each one.

Four, so far, she had flattened her ears at until they were buried under her odd, long straight pale hair. She growled at them, a sibilant undulating exhalation that made Kidahin's skin crawl.

A Comari challenge was no joking matter. The slight, wiry, tiny female could kill twenty Warriors single-handed before they succeeded in bringing her down. But if by her actions, to her way of thinking, she was in any way acting to preserve male life, then Eyloni society would find no fault in her actions.

Some of the challenged females held their ground, but many of them stepped back in surrender.

The prudent choice was to yield, Kidahin thought.

When the Comari finished, she corralled the females who had not held their ground and gave them a single sign in battle language.

<<Flee!>>

Visibly upset, they looked around about them, appealing to the mistresses as they retreated.

All but one. A young Warrior shook her head, flattened her ears, and stepped *forward!*

The Comari rushed up on her and stopped a pons-length from her, ears flat against her head. Her long pale hair dancing on the light breeze.

The Warrior stepped forward until her stomach touched the Comari's solar plexus.

In physical contact, the two females glared at one another.

The Comari's whisper-quiet growls were drowned out by the Warrior's rhythmic trilling snarls.

The Comari pushed her chest into the Warrior's stomach, shoving her back—hard—several ells.

The Warrior used her heavier mass to shove the Comari—barely an ell forward.

Kidahin wondered what the Comari had at issue with the females she had told to flee. Of course she had Delwyn's interests in mind. She must have intuitively felt they were somehow a liability to his well-being.

The Warrior, as an adult, had an adulthood knife in its sheath curving beneath her left breast. Wisely, her hand never ventured near it. The Comari wore no adulthood knife. She was considered an adolescent until the male she chose to protect presented her with a knife to wear. A Comari's knife was a smaller version of a male's obsidian knife. She would wear it on her hip, laced to her thigh in male fashion.

That reminded Kidahin. Someone had better tell Delwyn to get such a knife. For the Comari it would become his outward acknowledgment of her choice, and failure to present a knife to her would be—unwise.

The two females circled one another now. The Comari trying to force the Warrior to yield her ground, and the Warrior striving to recover the ground the Comari had already taken, but she did not try to advance through the ground the Comari had initially held.

"What are they doing?" Kidahin whispered to Zalzadrin.

"I do not know. It is so hard to catch the scent of a Comari when she does not want others smelling her intent. Clearly some kind of testing is going on."

"That Warrior is younger than I," Kidahin replied. "But even I knew at her age never to cross a Comari."

A trilling laugh sounded behind them, and Kidahin whirled in shock on Phelindra.

The Eldest, Melkorka, and Hlinlodyn stood together, tails entwined, watching the potentially lethal spectacle playing out before them.

The Comari abruptly stepped back a pace and put up her hands to give a battle language sign.

<<Accepted.>>

Kidahin watched the Comari's smoldering eyes drilling into the Warrior's, and the Hunter caught a hint of Comari pheromones.

Resentment. Jealousy. Tolerance.

The Comari turned to face Melkorka and signed again.

<<Huluhar.>>

"So she is the youngest here," Melkorka said.

<<Yes, by far.>>

"Why did you challenge them?" Melkorka asked.

<<To see if they held their ground. If they cannot hold their ground against me for Delwyn, then they are unworthy to be chosen by you. She gave ground, but when I rubbed my scent in her face, I implied she had no feelings for males, which made her very dangerous indeed. After she engaged me, if she had again given ground I would have killed her for having an inconsistent attitude when it came to male safety, something neither a Hunter nor a Warrior should be at her age.>> She paused in her signing a moment before continuing, <<She is most like one of us.>>

"I smell resentment. Why?" Melkorka asked, certain she already knew.

<<She may someday be called upon to choose a new warleader for you. That she might have to do so is unthinkable.>>

"Not only to you, Mistress Comari, but to us as well."

All Comara were automatically accorded mistress social rank.

The Comari nodded and drifted through the dancing maze, content to pass through their company, knowing sooner or later her chosen male would call them all back to him.

And she would prowl near them in waiting.

"Mistress Comari!" Melkorka yelled after her, bad form though it was. She had been feeling unsettled since the mute female had returned as their shadow.

The Comari halted, hesitant. Comara were never summoned, never yelled at. It served nobody's dignity to scream at one another, and Comara had a peculiar tendency to take shouts at them as challenges.

Melkorka had engaged her complete awareness, fleeting though as it was when a Comari no longer concentrated on engaging non-Comara. "You are near your time of choice, but I have never heard of Comara stalking the males they have marked so intently as you. Why are *you* doing so?"

The Comara frowned to herself and signed.

<<Kidahin Uahua'asee'a La'huaset Eyloni made a link in my mind concerning Delwyn's safety. In my prowling, I have smelled the scents of people uncertain and resentful of him, and so I keep watch.>>

"*What?*" Melkorka, Phelindra, and the command mistresses yelled all at the same time.

"Who?" Melkorka demanded darkly.

<<Not females, but some males not knowing him. Their scents express doubts about whether he is Eyloni. They wonder if he can even work within a Warpact.>>

Incredulous, Phelindra wrestled the lead from Melkorka. "You smelled this from *warleaders?*"

<<No, Eldest Huntress, I did not. And none of them came from La'huaset.>>

"Then where did you encounter these scents?"

<<In the Myat'ti'deep Tribal continent.>>

"That is why you left us when we arrived in Su'tayo Mah'heyo Clan territory?"

The Comari nodded. <<Yes, and I smelled no dissent there, either. But others traveling through the port my Clan runs to Na'di Island carried their thoughts to me on their scent. I think they intend to voice their concerns to the A'tayotan and the Society of Warleaders.>> She whirled around and vanished into the crowd, having signed more in the past hour than she had in months to other non-Comara.

"We will just see about that!" Melkorka snarled.

"This is for Delwyn to address by his actions!" Phelindra reminded her.

"No, it is not," Melkorka disagreed. "The very idea assaults our honor!"

"Oh, I doubt that," Hlinlodyn interrupted. "There can be and usually is some doubt about how well some people will conduct themselves in public, among their associations and societies, and in battle. How well Delwyn conducts himself in Warpact is something he will address when the time comes."

"And the question of him being Eyloni?" Melkorka seethed.

"Princess is proof otherwise. Kidahin's instinctive response to him is proof otherwise. That Comari's interest in him in itself is proof Delwyn is one of the People," Hlinlodyn said.

"That just proves Delwyn is a male," Trebithia said.

"That is the same thing!" Hlinlodyn retorted.

The sustained arguments among the command mistresses and their drifting pheromones reached the other supervising mistresses and the team leaders, and their pheromonal responses began to set the entire society on edge. They turned combative as their bodies fed hormones into their bloodstreams, preparing them to fight in defense of their favorite male.

Phelindra caught a whiff of their collective aggravation. "Mistress Melkorka, calm down. *Calm them down* before we have a riot here. I do not want to be included among those responsible for destroying the O'ni'da families' gather site."

The command center mistresses sang for calm, carrying a tune meant to lead them into a Song of Contemplation.

The group sing-along lasted over an hour. By then everyone had gotten their anger under control, and the choosing of new society members resumed.

Melkorka called the youngest Warrior to them.

"Who are you?" she sang.

"I am Saidrinha Ah'vou'ree La'huaset Eyloni, Mistress."

"What training have you, Saidrinha of Ah'vou'ree?"

"Advanced traditional weapons, advanced unarmed combat, and intermediate forest prowling."

"What about weapon systems?" Hlinlodyn asked her.

"None, Mistress."

Hlinlodyn swore. "If we choose you Saidrinha, you will apprentice with me. I am Hlinlodyn, the Mistress of Tactics. Tactical analysis aboard a warship is no easy prowl, but you are the youngest female here, and as such you are our warship's huluhar, which means you must serve in the command center."

Saidrinha shrank at that. "Huluhar?" she gulped. To become the chooser of a new warleader for a warship society frightened her more than learning the details of combat analysis, even more than facing down the Comari had been.

"Yes, huluhar," Melkorka said. "You must serve in the command center to experience empathy with Warleader Delwyn."

Frightened and apprehensive, the young Warrior stood frozen to the ground. Her long four-jointed toes and opposable big toes dug into the soil.

Melkorka called for the major consensus. Satisfied on hearing all their voices in the Song of Choice and Acceptance, Melkorka introduced their new huluhar to her society.

"This is the Warrioress Saidrinha Ah'vou'ree La'huaset Eyloni a'doni huluhar *Tyreniioroneo*. Welcome her to our society."

Kidahin sighed. As she had predicted, Saidrinha the huluhar had been the first chosen. She no longer held a huluhar's responsibility, thank the spirits.

The other females who had come to the Rite of Selection and Choice without sponsors and had held their ground against the Comari's challenge had also been chosen. Finally, those having sponsors had been accepted as members of their society.

Their society once again stood at its full fighting 43,020 female strength—Delwyn would count *two thousand eight hundred and eighty-five* of them in his obscure, cumbersome, and frustrating decimal counting system. Why in the spirits base counting on digits? Why did he not count fingers and toes just for consistency's sake?

Melkorka sang for silence. "We will soon leave for Ah'vou'ree Clan Combat Training Center. There you will all demonstrate your jungle prowling skills. Then we will be off to A'lon'aloop Naval Station and new society member orientation and mission briefings. From there we will travel to Wrathsee'a Anchorage for last minute training and strategy meetings. From there, we will…"

Melkorka's 'minder sang joyously with the call melody she reserved only for her favorite male.

"Yes, Delwyn? Yes…Of course you may. You are where? Yes, come at once."

Melkorka clipped her 'minder back to her underthong laces and turned to Phelindra but spoke aloud. "Delwyn comes. He walks from the O'ni'da trees and already sees us."

Melkorka's pleased singsong voice caused the crowd to react like a catalyst in a chemical reaction. Every female turned to face the direction from which their warleader was approaching.

###

Delwyn had been planning—although Verikaralee called it plotting—with Phalalin while Melkorka and the others took care of warship society business.

The ship's mistresses and Kidahin had stressed to him how his presence would be unwelcome during the ritual. *Hunter's Moon* belonged to them, and they alone would choose the new 314 who would share in that ownership. He would become *their* ship in ways no navy man could ever call his ship his own. The ritual, part of the female power structure here, excluded Delwyn because the warship didn't belong to him. The overall command of the ship had been ceded to him when Melkorka declared him warleader. He held the warship in trust, but he had no say when it came down to personnel matters.

Verikaralee, Phalalin's Mistress of the Ship, had made an accurate guess on about how long it would take them to confirm three hundred new crew members. It was Verikaralee who had suggested that it was time for him to call Melkorka.

The mission departure deadline was closing fast now. All the repaired sections and compartments had been returned to Wrathsee'a Anchorage and translated into the ship, but the ship had yet to switch over to partial main power. Wiring harness replacement took a lot of manual effort. It wasn't just laying cables and securing wire bundles. Main buss bars, room-temperature superconductor rails as thick as his neck, took time and hard work to secure into the maintenance chases. Smaller runs also required time-taking manual labor to pull them through conduits and plug them into distribution nodes filled with AI control systems, breakers, transformers, optical beam generators and splitters, power grid sensors, waveguides, shielding, and insulation. Every plug and socket had to be both computer and visually confirmed before the engineering diagnostic systems could feed signals through each wire, each optical cable, each photonic circuit. The EDS reported voltages and currents, optical coherency quality, resistance, capacitance, inductance, resonances, and other kinds of electrical and optical mumbo-jumbo to the engineering maintenance and damage control teams.

Once the EM and DC teams reached a consensus favoring an advance to the next step, they would power up the mains and carefully watch the self-diagnostic system, hoping to high heaven, or to the spirits anyway, that the few thousand metric tonnes of power buss and distribution network wouldn't melt down to slag.

Delwyn wanted to get back to his ship. Arrogant as it sounded, he thought that if only he could return to his ship, then things would work out right. His work ethic chafed at letting others do all the work. He could help. Hell, even his presence might help.

He was still planning that strategy when he reached the crowd.

He stopped, unwilling to pass up even one of them.

Like a giant amoeba, they engulfed him. An overwhelming number all happy to see him and be seen by him. They brushed affectionate tails against him, while the chosen stood in a pattern off to the side, suddenly shy.

Delwyn knew it wasn't his place to welcome them now. He would do so once they boarded. But for now he shared in the casual physical contact, a social activity they found both welcoming and comforting.

He wanted to talk to Melkorka before he went crazy with all the inactivity. "Have you read Anailiatha's engineering status report?" he began without preamble.

"And welcome to you too, Delwyn!" Melkorka snapped. "I do not need to read them. She has been here with us telling me the latest in a long list of bad news."

"I just talked to you on the comm. Don't tie your tail in a knot."

Melkorka growled out an angry retort but stifled the gist of it. Delwyn had been off their warship for several weeks, and he sometime forgot social graces. "And yes, I have read the repair teams' reports as well. I have been stepping on their tails about the matter so often they now ignore all my requests for further status updates."

"Gee, I wonder why?" Delwyn snapped.

"I was wondering about that myself," Anailiatha murmured. "Maybe if you took the time to crawl through the wiring chases yourself, you might see just how much effort is required to manage the problem. It is not as easy as attaching a wire to a power terminal and saying 'there, done!'"

"I know that! I understand that!" Melkorka trilled.

Delwyn changed the subject. "Anailiatha, what do you think about the repairs?"

"The repair crews have worked wonders. You cannot even tell we took offensive fire. Even our identity pattern has been repaired."

Identity pattern, the stylized plates built up in high relief to look like ivy leaves growing along the dorsal hull. It depicted a sigil in musical e'va'a script naming their warship *Tyreniioroneo*, the Hunter's Companion: The Hunter's Moon. From above looking down on the dorsal hull it looked like antique gold stained ivy leaves climbing up an off-white stucco wall from the engineering hull toward the bow. The sigil not only identified the warship by name, but it also named Delwyn as his warleader.

Delwyn smiled, thinking fondly about his female crew. It mattered more to them that the glittering gold artwork named him their warleader. Proclaiming the ship's name he understood. Coalition starships had ship names and designator numbers stenciled along their bows but never the captain's name. A Coalition ship was a projection of governmental military might, not of a captain's ability. But on Elleio females owned the instruments of war directly, and their ships proclaimed their warleaders' honor. The character associated with his name declared more meaning to them than any nationalistic idea.

Saidrinha and the other chosen drew steadily closer to their warleader. He was busy with the command mistresses, all of them taking turns brushing against him, giving him coy touches and tail caresses.

Mustering their courage, they joined with their fellow society members and cautiously brushed against Delwyn, hesitant at first, uncertain just how far their society would let them touch their favorite male. Saidrinha hesitated, cautious. Females had peculiar ideas about who could touch their males. She inhaled Delwyn's scent and tried to sort out his strange pheromones.

He smelled frustrated, impatient that their warship did not meet Battle Status standards. She smelled his love for them, how he saw them in his mind as near-daughters, and she staggered in shock. She knew Delwyn was only recently O'ni'da O'un Tu La`huaset Eyloni and could never claim any adult female through the near-daughter relationship. She smelled the love the mistresses had for him. Many belonged to his personal association, electing to remain with him beyond their obligations as part of his occupational association.

Saidrinha lurched convulsively forward. Before she knew it, she had wrapped her tail around her Warleader's waist, humming softly to herself.

Delwyn felt the Warrior's strong fine suede-like tail wrap around him, and he caressed it from twitching pons on across the forearm length of it circling his stomach.

Melkorka stopped talking and watched the humming Warrior tail twine herself to Delwyn.

"Delwyn, this is Saidrinha our new huluhar," Melkorka said.

Delwyn turned into the Warrior's embrace, touched her face, and captured her perked left ear in his hand.

He sang a greeting to her in the formal e'va'a spirit language.

Saidrinha wrapped her tail around them both and hugged him. Her nose sniffed under his neck, his nose, his ears, noting his scent and all the scent marks left on him by the thousands in her society, and she added her own identifying scent mark to theirs.

Delwyn knew better than to think of Saidrinha as a kid, but she was exuberantly youthful. Stronger than Kidahin, she was a hand taller than the Hunter and heavier built by about five kilos. Five extra kilos on a Warrior translated into lean, powerful muscle.

Delwyn caressed the huluhar, felt her muscular back and shoulders flex. This young powerhouse was twelve years old in the EST time standard as Eyloni counted. That came out to almost six Earth years old, and that reminded him again just how fast Eyloni grew, and how much they learned during their three Earth year adolescence.

Saidrinha didn't want to let him go, but he had to give the other new people a chance to meet him and mark him with their scent, identifying him as their proprietary territory.

Delwyn realized that he wasn't going to get to Wrathsee'a Anchorage anytime soon.

8
COUNTDOWN TO MISSION JUMP

Eleven hours later and Delwyn was still waiting, this time inside a sleep-tree facsimile on A'lon'aloop Naval Station. A'lon'aloop was one of three identical naval bases circling Elleio equidistant from one another in geosynchronous orbit. He had a mission briefing coming up on Wrathsee'a Anchorage soon with other warleaders in the battle group, all except for Anlann.

It looked now like that briefing would have to take place over the Compact Fleet Network. Delwyn hated remote briefings. All special operations group personnel did. He preferred a hands-on approach, but the briefing had already been scheduled. Too bad he couldn't translate from A'lon'aloop to Wrathsee'a, but Compact quantum teleportation had a thirty-thousand-kilometer range limit. Wrathsee'a Anchorage maintained a standard polar orbit around Tyreniioroneo, 636,370 kilometers from Elleio, well beyond translation range. It would take six troop transports three hours to ferry himself and his twenty-nine hundred females to Wrathsee'a Anchorage, not counting the time spent on waiting for them to come available in the first place.

Delwyn sighed. The navy was the navy; hurry up and wait.

At least his crew had something to do. Mistress of Saga Mirrahindrallin was singing ship history to the new recruits. Delwyn smiled. They were hearing the same history songs from the warship's chronicler he had heard as their warship limped back to Elleio from the Nikkiolo star system. They weren't listening to some droning impersonal "welcome to the ship" speech new shipmates heard over the intercom on

Coalition ships, either. They learned songs about their warship's history so they could sing them along with their fellow shipmates. Mirrahindrallin also taught them the songs that listed and explained the customs, habits, and idiosyncrasies held in common by the warship society.

Mirrahindrallin had shooed him off several times now. Delwyn didn't think she did it because she wanted to impart some secret squirrel tale meant for female ears only. The tingling feeling in his stomach told him she wanted to gossip about him, his habits, and his odd—to Eyloni—behavior.

They were busy. He on the other hand was ready to commandeer a shuttle and head for Wrathsee'a Anchorage on his own, but Phelindra would never forgive him for leaving her behind. Hell, she'd probably have a fit. Eyloni didn't often go anywhere by themselves, and a male almost never went anywhere alone. Companionship for the most accounted for it, but the female need to watch over and protect males meant they always followed him whenever he tried to go off on his own.

Eyloni males didn't spend much time alone. When they did exercise their autonomous right to solitude, they often retired to quiet thought and introspection. They didn't go charging off far from female safety. Nature hadn't wired them for that.

Delwyn grinned. His crew threw fits every time he snuck off through the simulated forests on his ship by himself. He tried to explain his occasional need for solitude. They had a hard time wrapping their heads around the idea of a male alone. The typical Eyloni female saw a male alone as obscene and dangerous. Female pheromones moderated male aggression. The physiological mechanism in male brains had chemical analogues in common with the human olfactory, amygdala, and hypothalamus pathways responsible for triggering post-traumatic stress disorder symptoms.

Delwyn's occupational association, through their pheromonal activity, suppressed his PTSD. They also passed emotions to one another through those pheromones. His limbic system responded to the pheromonal link by shutting down the chemical cascade that caused his PTSD symptoms. On the downside, he didn't have an Eyloni's sensitive nose to give him more than a fleeting intuitive feel for what their scents were trying to tell him.

They smelled meaning in his feelings, so he tried to explain and at the same time think with exaggerated emotional imagery. That altered his body chemistry and changed his scent enough to carry emotional context to them.

They misunderstood. They never seemed to grasp his need for solitude lasting any longer than twenty minutes or so. In the end, they came to their own conclusions: he wanted to feel alone without being alone. That meant they stalked him, and they tried to stalk him well beyond his sense awareness so he might feel alone.

Delwyn had commanded a special operations group, a special combined-services combat force. His combat-honed self-awareness gave him a sixth-sense awareness around him, which often foiled their stalking attempts. That confounded them. They didn't understand how he sensed their presences but at the same time could not always sense their feelings. He had to take care. Hurting their feelings got him on their bad side real quick, and they always had things say about his seemingly blatant disregard for their feelings.

Sometimes Delwyn wondered if Zalzadrin's joke about him being their pet wasn't closer to the truth. How would a man feel if his beloved dog looked him in the eyes and said, "I don't want to play fetch with you. I want to get away from all your petting and all your attention for a while?"

Oh, Delwyn could take the shuttle and leave them on A'lon'aloop. He had that right, but suffering their ill mood wasn't worth it. Besides, he had gotten used to their constant company. He felt adrift without them, like the old man living down on the corner nobody bothered to visit anymore.

The reasoning behind the male adulthood survival ordeal was to prove a male could make sound decisions away from aggression-moderating female pheromones. His PTSD flashbacks had come back with a vengeance, made even worse by the concussion he got from falling head-first off a ravine and onto a flat stone.

Delwyn made up his mind. He left the sleep-tree and strolled down jungle pathways and trails. An hour later he left one of the trails and pushed through heavy undergrowth until it became impassible. The sudden increase in the heavy cover warned people they were approaching a bulkhead or some other structure. The view ahead looked like continuous jungle, but he knew for a fact that a wall ran across his path no more than a meter away. He crouched down and sat on a large rock, relaxed, and enjoyed the pastel fall-colored landscape.

And as always, he didn't remain alone for long. Several females soon found him and introduced themselves. Nothing odd about that, he knew. He bet he was the only male for several hundred meters around, except for Einlann, A'lon'aloop's warleader. Other males aboard the station were either transient warleaders having ships docked here, or they were the few sire cairns serving as focuses and supervisors for conflict-potential vocations. Delwyn doubted even a sire cairn was nearby, and that made him a pheromone-reeking attraction to any female who happened to catch a whiff of his scent.

The Warriors knew who he was, knew he belonged to the occupational association of an elite warship, but that didn't stop them from playfully engaging with him.

Personal association he remembered, thinking about Lindredha, the Mistress of the Dock, who supervised Wrathsee'a' shipyard operations.

Females tended to prefer certain males. Females spending the most time with their occupational focus male often entered into a personal association with him if she got permission from the other females in the personal association.

An association wasn't a pride, wasn't a male-dominated harem. Delwyn saw an association as more like a clique, friendships among females who preferred spending time together. Associations didn't have more than one male, either. A personal association was a female-managed group they formed around their favorite male. As Delwyn understood it, associations survived as social holdovers from ancient times, times when females gravitated to males and protected them from jungle predators and warring clans.

At the moment he had five Warriors hovering around him. First had come one Warrior, then a second, then came three Warriors together. The two single Warriors were older, between Melkorka and Phelindra's age. The three were younger, but all older than Kidahin.

Those three tried so hard to impress him. Each person feeding into the other two's question and answers. They curled their tails around him and gave him coquettish brushes and touches. They belonged to a security prowling triad. The first two arrivals, techmistresses, commanded environmental support teams that serviced station life support equipment. They did not want to join his ship's society. Their interest in him was personal, and they had learned maybe a hundred words in Coalition standard in order to impress him.

And they had, too. Delwyn sat down on the grass and sang for them, which in a way had been a mistake. A singing male attracted females.

Two Hunters arrived next.

Then came a double-handful more females to listen to him sing. Most were Hunters, but it didn't take long for more Warriors to slip through the surrounding tall, feathery, burnt orange grasses. They listened, politely waiting for him to invite them to sing along with him.

Soon afterwards Delwyn attracted another fifty-six from the nearby transport bay, including the transport bay Mistress of Logistics herself. Phelindra and Melkorka came running through the overgrown jungle cover not long after that and stopped short.

Delwyn stopped singing, and the two stared askance at him, dumbfounded as the rest of their society gathered around them. It wasn't his singing with other females that brought them to a confused halt. It was his stopping, as though he had decided not to sing with his occupational association after singing with females not in formal association with him.

He preempted Melkorka. "Don't look at me like that. I'm just waiting for everyone to get here."

He wasn't lying to them. Delwyn wanted to make a clear distinction between singing for his crew and singing for transient station personnel.

Delwyn's overgrown and well-hidden bulkhead hiding place ran adjacent to the transport bay's arrival and departure center. Not real jungle, the thick forest cover couldn't conceal more than forty or fifty people, let alone the twenty-nine hundred surrounding him. They were spilling out into the open tall grass and brush around them. To their left the forest thinned until it reached the boulevard heavy equipment used for loading and unloading the transports. Across the boulevard transports rested on uneven stone surfaces next to their dockside service alcoves. Beyond them glowed a yellow beach and an ocean view. To the group's right stood a massive elleiu tree: the bay's arrival and departure center.

People continued to cross the boulevard. The Mistress of Logistics must have suspended bay operations as the transport bay teams wound their way to him. Delwyn sang with his occupational association first. Then he sang for the bay teams and the passengers, giving them permission to join him as well.

Delwyn didn't sing long, fearing to tie-up the transport bay even longer than he already had. After singing the final refrain, the bay complement thanked him for singing to them and returned to their work.

The three watch triad Warriors remained, coyly declaring their intent to join Delwyn's personal association.

Delwyn went to them. He found them intriguing, but he didn't for the life of him understand why.

Their overtures confounded an impatient Melkorka. Females wanting to join a male's personal association sought approval from the females in the association. Melkorka growled apologies to them. She told them that they simply lacked the time necessary to make the proper social acquaintances.

"Delwyn. Delwyn? Delwyn!"

"I'm standing right here Melkorka. You don't have to shout."

"Listen to me, not to them! We have much work to do today. Mission briefings, warship training, and appraisals."

Delwyn sighed. She was right. The combat teams and boarding party teams had a mission briefing with the Mistress of the Hunt on Wrathsee'a Anchorage. He had another video-conference strategy session with the warleaders commanding the other ships in the battle group. Afterwards, he intended to visit his warship and see the progress the repair teams and Anailiatha's engineering staff had made. He intended to sing for them until they finished their work.

Delwyn promised the three Warriors he would see them when he returned to A'lon'aloop, which made the young, powerfully built females shyly pleased with themselves.

Melkorka growled at him as they crossed the boulevard and down into the service alcoves and the waiting transports. As he settled into his seat, she sat down next to him.

"You and Warriors, I do not understand it," she trilled.

"Understand what? I thought all females liked males."

"All females love males," she snapped back as if the natural female tendency was his fault alone. "But you seem to attract Warriors. If you walked through a clan it would not surprise me to see Warriors trailing after you."

"The Pied Piper effect," Delwyn laughed.

Melkorka frowned and tried to match the word meaning with the image Delwyn's pheromones painted in her head.

"Well, yes. Maybe…But not the blind-following mesmerizing effect you seem to think you have on us."

He rolled his eyes at her. "Mmm-hmm, and what about you Warrioress Melkorka?"

Phelindra laughed, earning a dirty look from Melkorka. "I seem to remember you being quite taken with Delwyn when you first met him," Phelindra added.

Melkorka made no reply, although her pheromones revealed an instinctive possessiveness and an unwillingness to admit that aloud to the Eldest.

Delwyn let their teasing go only so far before he distracted them. Phalalin had been a good friend and teacher when schooling Delwyn on the finer responsibilities in Eyloni male life. A male never allowed the females he associated with to think of anyone as a personal favorite. Although a few, take Zalzadrin for example, teased the others by claiming herself as his favorite. Likewise, a male never let them get the impression he preferred one gender phenotype over another.

"Oh, I don't know, Melkorka," he said, remembering-Hunters made up about a third of the population. "It's just simple numbers. There are more Warriors than there are Hunters."

"Do not mind her, Delwyn," Zalzadrin quipped. "Melkorka just *dozzant* want to share you with other Warriors."

"Oh, really?" Anailiatha turned in not quite mock-aggression on Melkorka.

"No. *No!* We do not have time to entertain social matters is all." She turned in her seat to glare at Delwyn as the transport launched from A'lon'aloop. "Females new to a male's association want to feel wanted by him and the other females in it. That requires spending time together talking, touching, sleeping, and going places together. We cannot solidify social ties without interrupting them to leave to join the battle group. That is discourteous and disrespectful to the feelings those females have about wanting to associate with you and us through you. You know a singing male attracts females. Music opens the mind, and pheromones carry emotional news about the singer and those others singing with him. I smelled 211 females in the transport bay willing, or at least considering, associating with you."

"I'm sure many already belong to their own associations, Melkorka," Delwyn chided.

"So? Did you not listen to the lessons Kidahin gave you before we arrived in homespace? A female can belong to more than one personal association. The individual females in an association regulate membership to avoid conflicts. We rarely walk away from past associations, although we do prefer some over others. Rank and social standing has a lot to do with it, too."

"I don't have rank in Eyloni society," Delwyn mumbled, more interested in the shrinking Elleio in the window beside him.

Melkorka exhaled explosively. "You are not encumbered by hierarchy rank because only females belong to hierarchies. You have no military rank, yet you alone dictate our course aboard our warship. The A'tayotan listens and weighs every word you say before they formulate military policy and strategy. Your social standing begins well above the highest ranked female and grows from there. You are a singing male and the warleader of an elite warship, and you have accomplishments no male alive can boast about. Associating with you will appeal to other females. We had to *decline* many qualified females who came to us to serve on the warship *you* command."

Delwyn shook his head. Then he replied without thinking, making a comment that was far too flippant.

"That's just ambition," he began before he had a chance to bite the words back.

Melkorka flattened her ears against her short, ringleted, fluorescent orange hair. Her grip on his saber handle bunched, her long double-jointed fingers knotted.

It was—and he already knew this—far too easy to infuriate the Warrior.

"Bad choice of words," Phelindra's musical hiss filled his right ear.

She was right, too. Eyloni females pursued rank, were conscious about the obligations rank imposed, but males had nothing to do with hierarchy rank and only tangentially influenced social rank. Males conferred military rank, but military rank vindictively taken away put a warleader or a sire cairn on dangerous ground with the hierarchies. Military rank advancement required absolute legitimacy, or females considered it worthless and an insult to their honor.

Of even greater importance than rank was the biological imperative to preserve male life, even at the expense of their lives or the lives of their female infants. At best, ambition appeared in the hierarchies, but even there only as an acknowledgment of personal ability. When it came down to matters touching on male safety, ambition did not exist in this culture.

"I don't mean ambition as in seeking rank. I mean ambition as in people desiring a place in a popular group."

Melkorka scowled at him as she parsed his words and considered the context clues she smelled on his scent. "I can see that happening had you already sung at a clan gather. Your popularity as a singer there would attract people."

Delwyn let the matter drop and watched a looming Tyreniioroneo grow on the screen. As the massive diamond-shaped Wrathsee'a Anchorage came into view, Melkorka's comment got him to thinking. Things he took for granted aboard his warship did not always work the same way off his ship.

Melkorka absently looped her tail around his shoulders and drew him into her.

"I love you, as I love all of you, Hunters and Warriors. Honestly Melkorka, I sometimes wonder how any of you put up with me," he murmured.

Melkorka's face brightened, and she snuggled against his smooth, cool tan skin. "We know males are strange. We adore males as a matter of fact, but we love you best," she sang.

He relaxed against her, knowing he'd have to spend time with the others later.

"You *are* our pet after all," Zalzadrin said, without her joking humor for once.

Delwyn started. "What made you think about that?" he asked.

"You forget," Zalzadrin admonished. "I smelled your thoughts about it earlier."

"A 'pet' implies a shared intimacy between a greater and a lesser mind, Zalzadrin."

"I know. Females and males," she trilled laughing.

"Pets are owned," he stressed, remembering that no Eyloni kept any animal as a pet.

"Yes?" Zalzadrin shrugged.

Zalzadrin reminded him of another cultural difference. Eyloni didn't have nuclear families. They had no gender inequality, and although females held power by sheer numbers, they shared power with males. The need for emotional ties among the genders produced attachments understood as mutual ownership. The concept didn't translate well into human ideas on ownership and people, ideas evoking slavery and mastery. Both had no place in the Eyloni mindset. The drive to protect males had purged even hints of chauvinism and gender phenotype bigotry from the Eyloni worldview hundreds of thousands of years ago.

Delwyn glanced up just as the troop transport flew through a lime-green, force field shielded aperture in the side of Wrathsee'a Anchorage's diamond-shaped external hull. They glided through the sally port between the external and internal hulls and came out in blue sky over an aquamarine shoreline. They descended across a bright yellow beach to touch down on rough stone slabs. Service equipment began to unload cargo and truck it up to the bay boulevard. The transport bay took up a large volume—750 meters deep, 350 meters wide, and 200 meters tall. As on A'lon'aloop, the boulevard separated the seaside transport bay from the rainforest on the opposite side.

"Let's get going. I want to see how our warship is coming along," Delwyn said.

Melkorka, Phelindra, and several others were already standing, waiting for the transport's service alcove equipment to auto-attach and the hatch to cycle open.

For all his impatience, Delwyn took his time standing up. Melkorka, her tail wrapped around his shoulders, yanked him upright with unbridled enthusiasm.

They stepped from the transports and gathered on the boulevard. There they waited as their numbers debarked from other transports. Together again, they drifted through the faux elleiu tree arrival and departure center and on deeper into the Anchorage.

Wrathsee'a Anchorage was hollow, shaped like a diamond popped from its setting, a faceted-domed, slowly spinning top. They walked around the circumference, crossing deeper into the Anchorage. The jungle thinned out to light orange grass. A wide bole in the side of a tree concealed a blast door.

No jungle landscapes camouflaged the shipyard inside. They stood on a multi-tiered tapered inside wall covered with clearsteel windows looking out into the hollow center.

The shipyard ran up the curved inside diameter, with docks stacked all the way up and around the circumference. The interior sparkled, clean. Wrathsee'a was the cleanest naval station Delwyn had ever seen. Built up from artistic glass walls, gleaming chrome, and pastel ochers, it stood in sharp contrast to blue and gray Coalition utilitarian base designs.

Even here they walked from place to place. Eyloni didn't like moving sidewalks or escalators. They didn't use lifts to shift personnel from one level to another. They preferred walking and found it both an exercise and a time-taking joy that allowed them to meet and interact with people, something moving sidewalks, lifts, and escalators tended to repress in human public areas.

They headed for one of the atmosphere-capable enclosed slips. The one housing their warship looked like an aquarium meant to hold Leviathan. The repair slip had its own environmental control system that maintained atmosphere at standard temperature and pressure within the cubic kilometer clearsteel enclosure.

Their warship remained suspended within the repair slip, held there by docking clamps. Umbilical power cable and data feeds extended from the docking clamps to their warship's hull.

"Oh, my God! He's beautiful!" Delwyn gasped. This was the first full view he had ever seen of his undamaged ship. The first time he had seen his warship was while aboard *Henri Edda* looking at the Compact warship in Ibeetu orbit. Later and up close, he had watched the damaged aft dorsal hull slip above him as the combat staging and deployment bay tractor pilot towed the light attack craft they had captured under the ship and into the bay.

Now the warship looked brand new. Regular golf ball stippled stucco gray covered the ship from stem to stern but for the antique gold leaf e'va'a-patterned plates covering nearly the entire length but barely a third to a quarter width along the dorsal hull.

"I'm impressed, Anailiatha," he said to his chief engineer.

"You will not think so once you board him," Anailiatha growled.

"Why? All the blasted and burned out compartments have been replaced. There's not a damaged hull plate in sight. All damage has been repaired, hasn't it?" Delwyn felt doom fast approaching.

"Everything but the wiring. The harnesses have all been installed and sight-verified, but the engineering test computer is checking contacts and static electrical characteristics. I am hoping to begin full power testing later today."

"We are not going to make the sortieing deadline, are we?" Delwyn asked his Mistress of Sails.

"We can launch, I am sure we can. But we are going to have our work cut out for us restoring power to repaired compartments during the first third to halfway through our transit time to Nikkiolo," Anailiatha said.

He turned on her. "I told you we must be Battle Status capable by the time we leave, or I will forbid our taking part in the battle group."

Protests flew at Delwyn, just a few from Anailiatha, although she *waaed* the most vocally of the lot.

"I will not endanger you. If I say we don't go, then we don't go. That's it. No discussion, no debate. Some systems may remain offline, but our ship must achieve Battle Status readiness before we make our first jump," he said.

Unlike a captain in the Coalition of Earth Colonies navy, Delwyn had absolute authority when it came to *Hunter's Moon*. Even during a Warpact, a Warpact warleader couldn't force another warleader to endanger his female crew unless they had already engaged in battle. In actual fact, Warpact didn't exist until a conflict event occurred on-site.

Warpact couldn't be declared prior to the battle group first encounter of an on-site conflict somewhere. Bordanin of *Green Ivy* had the honor due him as the command warship's warleader, but even if Warpact had been declared now, Delwyn could still refuse to launch if the obligation to his occupational association demanded it.

They hurried alongside the sealed repair slip. Anailiatha, Melkorka, and Phelindra ran with him, the others following at a fast prowl to keep their warleader in sight. Twenty-eight hundred people ran together without so much as brushing one another. Eyloni crowds never trampled one another.

Forty long minutes later Delwyn jogged down a docking clamp fastened to the ventral command hull below the open deployment bay. He walked across the clamp catwalk and into the bay portal, crossing the seventy-meter-wide threshold and walking into the forty-meter-tall and one hundred fifty-meter-deep combat staging and deployment bay. He stopped and stared at the bare deck. He missed the seaside beach scene that normally filled the large bay.

"Hasn't power been restored?" he asked Anailiatha.

"Partial power!" she snapped, "and barely that."

"I remember. Get down to Power Systems and Propulsion. I'll stop off in the command center first. Then I'll join you in the engineering hull. Does the combat address system work?"

"Of course it does," Anailiatha snapped.

"Good. I'll meet you in the jump drive propulsion command center and sing for everyone from there."

Anailiatha's expression brightened.

Melkorka hurried on ahead. Phelindra and Delwyn followed on her tail. The remaining command mistresses ran after them.

The ship smelled new. Without the force field-encased holographic jungle vistas and their breezy forest smells, the ship smelled too clean. He wanted main power restored. Only then could the environmental systems fill the ship with familiar rainforest scenes again.

Still, the pathways had been sculpted in high relief when they had been built. The deck ran uneven to help barefooted Eyloni grasp it with their long, four-jointed toes. The green-tinted yellow emergency lights gave the ship a firefly-in-the-fog glow.

Delwyn stepped into the command center and headed forward into the Warleader's Watch. There he accessed the shipwide damage control monitor and transferred the damage control legend to the main holodisplay. The damage control legend expanded into a three-dimensional exploded schematic view of the ship broken down by hulls, compartments, sections, and decks. It highlighted the powered-down sections and compartments in green.

Damn!

"Delwyn?"

He turned away from the cinema screen-sized display, eyes seeking the tactical and combat analysis console. "Yes, Hlinlodyn?"

The Mistress of Tactics stood and walked around her console, half-dragging a young Warrior with her.

"Delwyn, you remember Saidrinha, our new huluhar?"

Delwyn nodded and walked up to the two Warriors. "Of course. Welcome aboard *Hunter's Moon*, Saidrinha," he said as he hugged the young, muscular Warrior.

Saidrinha, overwhelmed, wrapped her tail about her warleader and hung on for dear life.

"Delwyn?" an anxious Aheila sang over the combat address system.

"I hear you, Aheila. Where are you?"

"The combat staging area. Delwyn, a Su'tayo Mah'heyo Myat'ti'deep Comari has just climbed into the bay."

Of course she has. "I understand."

***

"Mistress? Computer simulations show main buss and auxiliary buss power harnesses and couplings are ready for sequential power-up," the primary techmistress reported.

About time! Anailiatha sighed and hit a switch.

"Attention. Internal power distribution systems will switch over from partial to full power in one minute."

She watched as all power network monitors lit up in a flurry of comforting bright red lights. She checked her telltales and then turned to the engineering damage control systems monitor.

Its telltales likewise showed go-red.

"Disconnect the ship from repair slip umbilical power."

"Affirm," her primary power systems engineer replied.

The engineering command center plunged into pitch blackness.

"Engage full battery power," Anailiatha demanded.

"Affirm. Battery power enabled."

Engineering command center lighting came back on, soft orange and holding.

Anailiatha scanned the power systems and damage control monitors for blue or green cautions and warnings but found none so far.

"Status?" she asked.

"Full battery power is now online and available to all primary systems, Mistress."

"Commence variable load testing."

"Affirm. Estimated time until test complete: forty-one minutes, thirty-four seconds from…now!"

Anailiatha folded her arms beneath her breasts and glared at the status monitors, ears flattened, tail frozen in a mid-curl, as if daring the test program to find an electrical fault.

"Anailiatha? Is the warship operating on the mains yet?" Melkorka sang over the combat address system.

"No, Mistress. As you can no doubt read on Hlinlodyn's damage control monitors, we are running on full battery power. I do not anticipate any problems with the reserve power cells and distribution systems. Battery power, as you know, bypasses the main and auxiliary power load-sharing network."

The warship possessed independent main and auxiliary power systems, both redundant systems. The tertiary power system shared the same network as the battery power supply.

The term 'battery' was an archaic engineering term when it came to starship power systems. Battery power did not come from batteries. It came from efficient modular converters comparable to fuel cells. When reactor power became available, it should divert into the tertiary power system. The tertiary power system could, barely, power the jump drive and allow the warship to travel at apparent FTL velocities. The batteries could not. That explained why Anailiatha had not been able to run static tests on the sublight drive or spooling testing on the jump drive yet.

"Mistress, all systems report full battery power achieved. No spikes, no dips, no surges detected."

As good as the report sounded in Anailiatha's ears, she had expected as much. They had run the warship on battery power the first two weeks he orbited the Nikkiolo moon Ibeetu. Only the harnesses and couplings in the sections repaired at the Kem Basinga facility had been changed. Engineering diagnostics reported them nominal.

"Bring all fusion plants from idle to half-power."

"Affirm. Forward Fusion-1, Aft Fusion-1, and Aft Fusion-2 reporting half-power achieved. Forward Fusion-2 shows all hard green offline status."

Offline? Who was she kidding? They did not have a Forward Fusion-2 reactor!

"Switch from battery to tertiary power," Anailiatha sang.

"Affirm, Mistress. Batteries disengaging and crossover enabled. The warship is now operating on tertiary power."

Anailiatha sang a terse reply and watched the power systems monitor as more green telltales blinked cautionary blue before settling on nominal red. She held her breath and commed the command center on her direct line.

"Mistress? Anailiatha. Tertiary power is at your disposal."

"I can see the power build-up on my command monitors. My thanks, Anailiatha."

Melkorka glanced up from her command console toward the Warleader's Watch. Delwyn sat at his console, watching power systems telltales winking red.

He must have felt her gaze on him, because he looked up and met her eyes.

"We've got full environmental systems power available. Let's button him up and engage all life support and home environmental options."

"By your command," Melkorka sang the time-honored reply. Delwyn wasn't the only one aboard wanting to again experience the looks, sounds, and smells of an Elleio rainforest.

She turned to Saidrinha. "Seal all vents, hatches, and airlocks. Engage primary life support and environmental systems."

"Affirm, Mistress," Saidrinha sang unsteadily from her tactical systems console next to Hlinlodyn. The Mistress of Tactics had shown the young Warrior the controls and sequences Melkorka or Delwyn might need over the next few hours.

Saidrinha's tail whipped behind her chair, and she hunched over her console, tense, waiting in dread for another unfamiliar command.

The command center lights rippled, and Delwyn watched as his bridge once again took on the view from a Watch in an elleiu tree's crown. The ceiling became a sky view open to the sun, a partly cloudy blue sky, light streaming through the yellow-variegated pastel red and orange leaves. Breezes nudged the hull plate wide leaves, broadcasting the forest smells associated with the northeastern La'huaset Tribal continent.

"Hull status?" Delwyn asked.

"Positive hull integrity has been established Delwyn," Saidrinha reported with all seriousness, and he smiled. Now he was going to piss Anailiatha off.

He glanced at Melkorka seated in her command chair.

"Battle Status!" He sang.

Melkorka flinched at the unexpected order, and the saber resting across her thighs just above her knees would have tumbled to the apricot-colored hollow log wood deck had her tail not been wound, several times, around the bare, sharp-edged blade.

"By you command!" Melkorka said. She keyed the combat address system open and sang "Battle Status!" confirming the order unnecessarily. The warship's tactical systems tracked Delwyn's voice and relayed it throughout the ship. Everyone aboard had heard their warleader and were by now racing to their Battle Status stations.

"Trebithia, disengage docking clamps and umbilicals. Retract all moorings. Maintain position relative to the repair slip."

"By your command!" the Mistress of Pathwalking said.

"Hlinlodyn, engage all defensive systems and set all offensive systems to stand-by."

"By your command," the Mistress of Tactics replied. "Primary, secondary, and tertiary shields coming up. Radiological shields are up. Inertial dampening and structural integrity fields are nominal. Point defense systems read nominal. Perimeter defense systems are online. EMP countermeasures are online. Antitorpedo clusters are slaved into the PDS and are tracking."

"Anailiatha?" he called, knowing she and every person aboard heard the summons.

"*What?*" the Mistress of Sails yelled, furious.

"Tertiary power systems status?"

Anailiatha kept a frantic watch on her diagnostics board and the damage control systems monitor, waiting for something to blow out at any moment.

"Tertiary power load sharing is operating within nominal limits, no thanks to you, *a'pea.*"

Saidrinha jumped in her seat at hearing the expletive, wide-eyed.

Melkorka trilled laughter despite herself and then quickly sobered.

"What if you blow out a primary system?" she asked him. "Anailiatha and the repair teams could never effect repairs this late and still guarantee we can depart with the battle group."

"I told you if our warship cannot reach and maintain Battle Status, then we will not launch with them. Saidrinha, activate primary and secondary weapons. Load all torpedo bays. Set weapons to 'safe' and open all gun ports and torpedo bay doors."

"By your command," the Warrior acknowledged, and then turned to give Hlinlodyn a helpless look. She had not been prepared to hear these commands.

Hlinlodyn stood up and leaned over Saidrinha, wrapping her tail around the panicked young Warrior, and showed her how to power up the ship's offensive weaponry.

"Powering up primary weapons systems. Gun ports open. Loading torpedo bays, torpedo bay doors open. Weapons set to 'safe.' Primary particle weapons systems online, left and right outrigger hull kinetic weapons online. Secondary weapons systems online. Delwyn, I show a fault in the primary kinetic weapons system!"

The main railgun, Marsch swore. "Type of fault, Saidrinha?"

The tacticalmistress scanned her weapons status boards frantically, stopping when she saw Hlinlodyn's long index finger pointing at the weapon readiness legend.

"No power to the weapon reported, Delwyn."

"No power available, or insufficient power?"

Hlinlodyn frowned and keyed the request into the command center weapon diagnostics system.

"Insufficient power available Delwyn," Hlinlodyn reported.

"Anailiatha?" Melkorka sang out.

"Shut it down! Shut it down!" Anailiatha yelled at the same time.

"Disconnect the primary kinetic weapon from the tertiary power grid," Delwyn ordered.

"By your command," Saidrinha said.

"Anailiatha? Continue running your load analysis diagnostics at this level of activity and send someone down to find out why the main battery isn't pulling full power."

"By your command, a'pea," Anailiatha snarled back at him.

"Delwyn? The Mistress of the Dock is calling to ask if you would please stand the offensive weapons systems down. You are making the

Mistress of the Tower Yolandraha nervous," Mistress of Communications Hlindredreda reported.

"Saidrinha, disengage fire control systems and switch the weapons to readiness mode. That'll keep them drawing power for Anailiatha's diagnostics."

"By your command!"

"Maintain tertiary power unless Anailiatha demands otherwise. I'm going down to the primary railgun in the combat hull."

"Why?" Melkorka asked. "To aggravate Anailiatha?"

"No. I'm going there to make her feel better."

Delwyn ran along once again familiar forest trails through autumn-shaded forests all the way to the secondary bow in the combat hull.

As he stepped into the forward fire control center he heard the Mistress of Sails cursing.

"That bad?" he asked her.

Anailiatha whirled on him.

"You!"

"Yes. That's very good, Anailiatha. Now, before you start snapping your tail at me, consider this. We don't have the time for meticulous and slow system checks. Once manual and computer-assisted diagnostics have certified the power systems, feed minimal power, take more readings, and then ramp up to full power. We have less than two days and thirty-three hours left!"

"I know that!" Anailiatha trilled in obvious fury. "But engineers prefer to test our systems according to a meticulous protocol. You might have blown out the main battery fire control systems and the driver coils, or both!"

"But it didn't blow. In fact, it's not pulling any current at all. This big baby should drag the mains down until the load sharing system stabilizes the demand."

Anailiatha swore again and glared at him with heavy suspicion. "Delwyn, just how much engineering training have you picked up over the years? That is exactly what should have happened. Fusion-1 and Fusion-2 load share all systems on the combat hull."

"And, for the foreseeable future, we don't have a Fusion-2 reactor. Isn't Fusion-1 power output tied into the load sharing system routing power from the primary propulsion reactor in the engineering hull?"

"It should be," Anailiatha said and took off at a dead run for the rebuilt Forward Fusion-2 power plant control center.

It took her and her engineering teams a few hours scanning to find the problem. Tertiary power, in Delwyn's flippant turn of phrase, "couldn't get there from here."

"I bet it works for auxiliary and main power," he told Anailiatha.

She nodded absently and activated the fire control intercom. "Mistress? Switch power from tertiary to auxiliary."

"Affirm," Melkorka said and relayed the request to Hlinlodyn.

Back in Forward Fire Control Delwyn watched as green diagnostic indicators changed to ruby red.

"All systems report full power available," Melkorka reported from the command center.

"Switch to the primary system," he said.

"By your command."

Anailiatha wrapped her tail around Delwyn's waist and watched the fire control diagnostic panel confirm the weapon was pulling full power from the mains just as efficiently as it had from the auxiliary system.

"Is this a problem?" Delwyn asked his chief engineer as he pointed to a single green-lit button.

"I do not know, Delwyn. If this is the only wiring harness error we have, then I say the spirits have blessed us. I may have engineering maintenance lay some superconductor cable and bypass the fault, if they can bypass it."

It turned out that the engineering division could not bypass the tertiary power fault. It took Anailiatha's engineers and technicians twenty-eight Earth hours to find the faulty coupling that had passed both visual and computer tests, pull it, disconnect all the wires, mount a replacement, rewire, and plug everything back together. Then Anailiatha had to run an optical check, a computer test program, and a trickle power feedback check before trying the tertiary power systems again.

Delwyn tried to convince her to tie in the tertiary power systems directly into the coupling, but Anailiatha held firm. Engineering was her domain, and absent an emergency—and this wasn't—she wouldn't change her mind.

She plotted revenge, Delwyn swore, for him calling the ship to Battle Status without giving her a heads-up first.

He tagged alongside Anailiatha until she certified the power distribution system. Her approval barely off her lips, Delwyn was already issuing orders over the ubiquitous warleader open comm.

"Melkorka, contact the Mistress of the Dock and request clearance to exit the repair slip and shipyard."

"By your command."

By now the jump drive armatures should have spooled up with sufficient power built up for an FTL jump to the first jump point 3.043 Elleio light-years away. *They were sixteen and a half hours behind schedule.*

"Delwyn? Melkorka. Departure from the repair dock and the shipyard has been approved. Lindredha wishes you the luck of the spirits."

Delwyn smiled. Lindredha, a Warrior, had been the first female outside his occupational association to ask the others if she could join his personal association.

"Take us out through the repair dock, Melkorka. Once the tugs have escorted us clear of Wrathsee'a Anchorage local space, take us to the Lagrangian staging area and maneuver us into the honor escort point off *Green Ivy's* bow."

"By your command. Maneuvering."

Delwyn left the forward fire control center and headed back to the command center.

***

"Vacuum achieved Mistress," Hlindredreda reported as Delwyn stepped onto the command center.

"Release docking clamps and hold station," Melkorka said.

"Affirm. Docking clamps released. Ship is holding station."

"Hlindredreda, ask the Mistress of the Dock to open the forward repair slip airlock," Melkorka said.

"Affirm. Mistress of the Dock acknowledges."

Delwyn crossed the command center, passed Melkorka, and sat down at his console on the Warleader's Watch and watched the eight-hundred-meter diagonal hatch open.

"We are holding station and in trim. Correcting for microgravity-induced drift. Ready for dead-slow forward thrust maneuvering. Shipyard tugs are standing by to acquire lock-on points," Trebithia said.

"Maneuvering thrusters ahead dead-slow until we clear the slip airlock and then hold station at zero relative velocity," Melkorka said.

"Affirm, maneuvering. We have cleared the dock. Nulling forward velocity. Zero relative velocity achieved. Holding station," Trebithia said.

"Tug vessels are on approach to our tug lock-on points," Hlinlodyn said.

Delwyn watched the tugs maneuver toward them.

"Contact!" Trebithia said.

Just like last time, Delwyn didn't feel so much as a nudge. The tugs locked onto the ship's hull at tug contact points, reinforced places on the hull capable of taking the torqueing the tugs transferred to the hull as they pushed and pulled the massive warship around.

The tugs fired their thrusters, detached, moved, stopped, locked onto other tug contact points, and fired their maneuvering thrusters and engines as they swung the warship about and in line with the interior doors.

"Hlindredreda, advised the Mistress of the Dock we are standing by for the interior doors to cycle open," Melkorka said.

"Affirm," the Mistress of Communications said. "The Dock Mistress says the interior and exterior doors will open in sequence."

Delwyn watched as the interior doors crept open. The moment the doors had fully retracted the exterior doors began to retract.

He stared into a kilometer long, three-hundred-meter-wide tunnel.

"Tugs thrusting forward dead-slow. We are in the transfer conduit…We have cleared the external doors. We are one ship-length from Wrathsee'a Anchorage. Tugs detaching and executing evasive maneuvers," Trebithia reported.

"Mistress? The Mistress of the Dock declares us free to maneuver," Hlindredreda paused, then added, "Delwyn, Mistress Lindredha wishes to speak to you on the warleader privacy channel."

"Maneuver us to battle group staging, Trebithia," Melkorka said.

Delwyn spoke for several minutes with Lindredha before she forwarded a message from Mistress of the Tower Yolandraha and Warleader Havalin. By the time he finished, the staging area was directly ahead.

The command battleship, *Green Ivy*, loomed in the screen. He was over a kilometer long and had a much wider beam than *Henri Edda* did, about twice as wide as *Hunter's Moon's* command hull less the port and starboard outrigger kinetic batteries. *Pathfinder* waited behind the command battleship, a near copy of Delwyn's ship. Behind *Pathfinder* waited the destroyers *Stone Knife* and *Night Shadow*. Behind them the heavy battlecruiser *Padfoot* brought up the rear.

Those ships had been designated the primary task force and would have taken the mission alone had Delwyn's warship not completed repairs more or less on time to sortie with them.

Mistress of Pathwalking Trebithia maneuvered them into the honor escort point off *Green Ivy's* bow. As they waited, the destroyers *Surefooted* and *Fearless* assumed the honor escort point off Delwyn's bow. A few klicks ahead of them the second heavy battlecruiser, *Steep Trails*, held the secondary task force point position.

The two task forces together formed a single battle group of nine capital ships and all their screening platforms, sensor drones, and ECM assets. They were ready to execute the mission Delwyn had outlined to the A'tayotan almost two Earth months ago.

"Message from Warleader Bordanin of *Green Ivy* for Delwyn, Mistress," Hlindredreda reported.

Melkorka perked her ears at her warleader, and Delwyn nodded.

"Accept," Melkorka ordered the Mistress of Communications.

"Delwyn," Bordanin said with unfeigned enthusiasm as he felt his way through his improving Coalition standard. "I am pleased to see you can take your place among us."

"I, too," Delwyn sang in musical say'ta've.

"Prepare to jump to our first arrival point."

"Affirm. Ready on your word," Delwyn sang.

Bordanin nodded, twitched his ears, smiled, and flexed his tail in a good-bye gesture.

"Hlindredreda, hail *Surefooted.*"

"By your command."

A minute later Ahwroona, Anlann's Mistress of the Ship, appeared on the main screen.

"Are you ready, Mistress?" he asked her. Delwyn watched her closely. This was new territory for her, and her twitching ears and darting pons gave her unease away.

"I have confidence in you, Delwyn. Anlann and Seralin have placed their trust in you, and I and my society do as well."

He nodded, keeping his expression serious. What she did, sortieing her warship without Anlann, without a male focus, was nerve-wracking unknown territory for her, and for her society.

Ahwroona's belief in him had encouraged her to take her ship out without Anlann, and her confidence in Delwyn had convinced the other mistresses of the ship to withhold further participation in tactical planning until his warship had been assigned an active role long before repairs had been completed, to Mistress of the Hunt Atridredha's everlasting fury.

By Ahwroona doing so, the obligation of responsibility for them had been thrust upon Delwyn in the odd way Eyloni females took a male's notice as a tacit acknowledgment of his interest in their social morale. Delwyn hoped Anlann would be on Captain Rodgers's ship, or every female on Anlann's warship would come looking for his blood.

"Delwyn?" Hlindredreda interrupted. "We have an active jump clock counting down to a synchronized battle formation jump."

"Very well. Mistress Ahwroona, prepare to jump your warship."

"Affirm," she said and cut transmission.

"Coming up on jump command," Trebithia reported.

"Stand-by to jump," he said to Melkorka.

"By your command. Mistress Trebithia, prepare to jump."

"Affirm, Mistress. Synchronized jump counting down to jump point 3.043 light-years into a zero-threat Action Zone. Ready to jump."

The jump clock hit zero, and the battle group vanished.

Thirty billionths of a second later the Compact battle group exploded back into normal space, engaged sublight engines, accelerated to 0.69 cee sublight cruising velocity, and began recharging their jump engines for the next FTL jump.

"Jump completed, Delwyn. All ships maintaining disposition, no threats detected," Trebithia reported.

"Report ship status," he said.

"By your command," Melkorka replied. She scanned her command console. "Warship is at Action Ready Status. All systems report go-red across the board. All stations report systems nominal. We are in the process of building up energy for an FTL jump to the next jump point

3.034 light-years distant. We will achieve maximum sublight velocity, 0.32 cee, in twelve minutes at our current accel rate. Because we have departed behind schedule, the battle group will continue jumping at the maximum recharge rate."

Melkorka consulted battle group disposition on Hlinlodyn's combined maneuvering plot and continued. "All ships remain in jump spacing at constant acceleration. All ears and tails have been deployed into their stalk and prowl modes.

Ears and tails, what the Coalition Fleet called "whisker" assets, automated screening elements: jammers, probes, automated torpedo launchers, electronic warfare, electronic countermeasures, decoys, and other dependents and proxies. Well over a hundred of the automated assets accompanied the battle group, some of them as big as Coalition alphafortresses. They looked ahead, behind, and on the battle group's flanks. Some produced emission profiles matching a warship well enough to fool any long-range FTL scan and most intermediate range sensors. The screening elements lacked FTL jump drives, but they could maintain the current high relativistic velocity over the fourteen Earth hours it would take for the ships to complete jump drive recharge. The screening elements would be recalled prior to their next jump. The battleship had the most of them. Destroyers carried a handful each. The heavies had maybe a few more each, and the planetary assault battlecruisers had fifteen.

The battle group raced through interstellar space, going nowhere fast. Fourteen hours, even at 0.69 cee, didn't amount to any real distance compared to a quantum jump, and to someone unfamiliar with the physics involved, to hurry along seemed like a futile waste of fuel and energy.

Delwyn had once asked Anailiatha why it made sense to drive the ship at high relativistic speeds between jumps when the distance covered amounted to zip.

Her response? Reduced energy consumption.

As it turned out, jump calculations took into account several parameters when computing the mass, spin, direction, spin velocity, charge, and other parameters the gravity lensing system took into account when creating the quantum black hole used to translate entangled information to some point within a sphere along a maximum 2.332 Earth light-year radius. Parameters included a ship's mass, velocity, acceleration, vectors, and proximity to mass. Mass, even the mass of a few more people added, altered those calculations. High velocities and accelerations cancelled out certain parameters, simplifying the math and reducing total demand.

Anailiatha had also explained at the time how acceleration and gravity were equal. If the ship maintained a given acceleration, then the gravity lensing system didn't need to hog as much power to focus gravitational waves into the artificial hypergravity point that created the quantum singularity.

Solving the math took about the same time, as did creating the singularity, but the energy saved more than justified speeding through normal space.

Delwyn strayed along a wavering course away from the Warleader's Watch, wandering slowly and indirectly toward Melkorka's command chair.

The Mistress of the Ship watched her warleader's slow approach and tightened her tail's grip on the odd, curved sword she held against her knees. Ears perked at him, she narrowed her eyes in suspicion.

"What are you up to?" she asked as he stepped around her. Her ears pivoted sideways, following his movement.

Delwyn watched the Warrior's ears flit about as they stretched to catch every sound his bare feet made on the uneven wooden floor.

Eyloni did not like being approached from behind unless they knew the approaching person well.

He heard a soft sigh close behind him, high-pitched and juvenile-anxious.

Saidrinha.

Delwyn watched Melkorka sit there unperturbed and at complete ease.

He watched her ears and smiled down at her.

Melkorka's ears twitched, and she swept them back as far as possible. She held them close to the anger ear posture, yet their tips told Delwyn he had her undivided attention.

Melkorka smelled the fondness he felt for her on his scent. She remained still and staring forward into the Warleader's Watch. Her ears continued to track him. She preened for him, managing both a serious and a playful stance at the same time.

Delwyn came close enough to smell her skin, smell her bagel, beagle, and spiced candle scent change. He didn't have her nose, yet he often picked up general impressions from her body odor. He didn't see the mind's eye stop-motion visions she did, but his limbic system framed Melkorka's scent into intuitive emotive summaries he sometimes grasped.

He reached down and put his hands on Melkorka's neck and caressed her back and shoulders.

She closed her eyes and hummed in simple pleasure.

"And what does my Mistress of the Ship think so far?" he murmured to her.

"It is good to be home," she sighed.

"Sa lau ahei ti elleio," he sang the same back to her.

Delwyn was better than fluent now, so long as he didn't run into technical terms or obscure words. Not unlike musical jingles running through the head once heard, the Eyloni tongue stuck in the mind, too.

He knew the chord base meanings and how the octaves changed those meanings, which made thinking in say'ta've as easy as thinking about a favorite tune.

His crew, by matching his voice to the emotional imagery his scent drew in their heads, had learned his language after a few hours for the basics, and after three weeks they had become natural Coalition standard speakers.

They must think him dense, a slow learner.

Delwyn felt Melkorka's chest jerking in response to her silent snort.

"You think that's funny?" he asked her.

"The images your pheromones make in my mind," she said, shaking her head, "present the most intriguing ideas. You are not dense or slow," she declared stoutly. Eyloni custom took a dim view on anybody casting doubts on another's mental health.

"You should expect several visitors tonight," she said abruptly.

Delwyn flinched, but he kept on rubbing Melkorka's warm, velour-soft body. Eyloni affection, he realized, expressed itself in a need to have him and them nearby now that they had come home. He could look forward to sleeping among twenty or thirty—decimal numbers—of them all curled up together and next to, or on, him.

Melkorka was hinting he'd better sleep in the warship's heavily wooded recreation center, where large numbers could congregate and sleep in comfort. They had a compulsive need for social contact, for reestablishing and maintaining social ties a human rarely tolerated outside of close-knit families. They had come home, and they had missed one another and him.

Melkorka's comment also served as a warning to prepare to reestablish social ties with his occupational association, as they reopened social ties within their society.

Delwyn knew strait-laced humans would find life among the Eyloni uncomfortable and offensive. They would try to tie all Eyloni casual friendly physical contact with sex, imposition, and oppression. The Eyloni wouldn't understand the standoffishness and constant mating references released in the pheromones from those puritanical souls. Their scents would draw antisocial images in Eyloni minds, a symptom of amusia, a rare tone-deaf disorder that led to mental instability in Eyloni.

Delwyn worried briefly about future Human-Eyloni contact as he heard a wistful trill from the watch station and glanced up at Phelindra.

Guilt assailed him. He'd spent a long time in absent-minded physical contact with Melkorka. He took too long for the attention to pass as momentary social interaction. Now the entire command center crew wanted him to make social contact rounds, touching and caressing, showing no favoritism, beginning with Phelindra and ending with Saidrinha, the last in social rank there.

Only their zeal for their jobs kept them from rushing him and posturing themselves in fussy rank order.

Saidrinha watched hungrily as her warleader crossed the command center to the Eldest Huntress. Phelindra arched her spine and let him rub her back and shoulders, playfully tying him up in her tail. Belonging to societies and associations was an instinct that called to every Eyloni in all their causal, personal and professional lives. And now she belonged to multiple professional societies: The Society of Tacticalmistresses, the Society of Command Center Crews, the Society of Elite Warriors, the Society of Warship Personnel, and the Society of *Hunter's Moon* itself. She also belonged to several social societies, including the Society of Females, the Society of Warrior Females, and other societies with Ah'vou'ree Clan.

But now she also belonged to a male's occupational association. Saidrinha was so young, having come from her adulthood ceremony directly to the Rite of Selection and Choice. She did not even belong to a male's personal association. That she did not was no slight and no impediment in Eyloni culture. She had many friends, both intimate and loving, but males were rare, and the female mind dwelled on all things male: where they were, how close they were, if they had adequate protection, if they needed help.

Seeking prospective mates for when females came into season also came to mind. Now Saidrinha belonged to a male's association, and she watched Delwyn with undisguised intensity.

Hlinlodyn nudged Saidrinha, jolting her from her musings.

Hlinlodyn said nothing but her pheromones made the reason for the nudge clear.

Mind your station!

Saidrinha looked down at her combat intelligence console, chagrined. She had not been spying. This was normal public behavior among members in her society and her warleader. It was shared acceptance, belonging, and she shook in her seat as she waited her turn to experience that sense of belonging.

Phelindra loved being touched by Delwyn, and she knew his mind tended to wander whenever he touched her.

She trilled something under her breath.

Delwyn dipped his head over her shoulder and brushed his lips against her elegant, expressive ear.

"Hmm?" he murmured.

Phelindra cocked her head and stretched to whisper huskily in his ear.

"Pay extra attention to Saidrinha. She wants so much to belong."

He nodded, his lips brushing the length of the old Hunter's twitching elfin ear.

Delwyn took care. Phelindra, like all Eyloni, had sensitive ears. They could feel subtle change in air pressure and movement, touch, and sound.

She listened to sounds inaudible to him. If he yelled now, he might deafen her for hours. He sniffed her ear, rubbed his nose against it, pursed his lips and blew gently across its folds. He even nipped her ear tip.

But he never, ever stuck his tongue into her ear. Eyloni considered the tongue a taste and speech organ, not something you put on or into another person. The same went for the mouth, too. No kissing the lips because mouth-to-mouth contact, save for artificial resuscitation, was frowned upon for personal cleanliness issues.

But brushing dry lips against skin didn't offend, and Phelindra had several tickle spots around and under her ears and along the nape of her neck he could tease. What a human might consider as foreplay was simple expressions of companionship to them, no sexual point to it at all. Phelindra could just as likely do the exact same thing to Hlinlodyn, Trebithia, or Hlindredreda that he was doing to her.

Shared emotional empathy was a part of their emotional mental health.

"Promise you will pay special attention to her," Phelindra insisted.

"I will. You know I will," he reassured her.

"You might want to let her sleep close to you tonight. You remember how Kidahin was."

He grinned. How could he forget? Kidahin might as well have been a blanket, draping her upper body across his chest.

"I'd like that, although Kidahin might grumble about it."

Phelindra wrapped her tail firmly around him and trilled in laughter.

"She would not and besides, Kidahin will be too tired to complain about anything!"

"What do you mean by that?"

"Believe me Delwyn, by the end of the day Kidahin will be happy to sleep wherever she drops!"

9
ASSAULTMISTRESS TRAINING ABOARD HUNTER'S MOON

Kidahin ran. She had been running for ten hours.

The surface action assault stalkers she had recruited from her clan and four *fists* ran with her. They had started off by running around the parked combat assets in the combat staging and deployment bay before the mistresses led them off the bay and into the command hull lower decks. They ran down narrow service trails, along uneven wandering footpaths, and through the endless overgrown rainforest.

They had to run hard and yet make no sound. No heavy breathing, no misplaced feet, no noise at all.

Simple and plain for a Hunter, and they were all assault force Huntresses.

Endurance running was not a Hunter's forté. Distance running sapped the stamina of the natural forest prowlers, and a tired Hunter lost her rhythm and misplaced her feet, took missteps, and whistled the telltale tune of heavy breathing. Hunters sprinted at great speed, but paced distance running coincided more with Warrior specialties for all the noise they made compared to Hunters in the forest.

The surface action assault teams should soon receive a specific task to perform. None of them knew what the task might entail, but they had to execute it as soon as it was assigned. The run was meant to tire them, to simulate a few days surface combat stalking and ground force maneuvering.

Kidahin felt the ground dip beneath her feet as they headed for the right outrigger hull.

Again.

A runner had to watch her head running through the jungle here. The interface between the command hull and the outriggers was an overgrown forest. Any lapse in a Hunter's awareness might cause her to smack her head into a low-hanging branch placed there to hide some superconducting conduit that powered the kinetic weapons system mounted throughout the outriggers. Heavy brush hid structures and warned people on the trail to take notice that they approached either a bulkhead, a piece of equipment, a casting, or a conduit.

"Kidahin?" Mistress of Battle Nynava sang in her ear.

"Yes, Mistress?" Kidahin replied, flicking her ear to activate the tiny comm patch affixed to her temple, its fine feelers responding to the ear movement.

Mistress Nynava's face flashed before Kidahin's eyes, in transparency mode so Kidahin could still see down the trail as she ran. "Take your surface action assault stalkers to the aftstation. Prowl every pathway and trail there but do not under any circumstances enter the engineering hull. While in the aftstation, you will count all the Warriors and catalogue their activities. Once you have found the highest military-ranked Warrior, your team will stalk her until she leaves the aftstation through the command hull bole. When she leaves you and your stalkers can return to the command hull and report to me."

"Affirm, Mistress," Kidahin said.

Spirits! The aftstation connected the engineering hull to the command hull.

It followed the general lines of a trapezoidal shape some 113 ells tall, 303 ells wide, and 131 ells long. The environmental systems rendered the small 112 million cubic ell volume as thick jungle undergrowth filled with many small trails and few pathways. Primary power couplings routed through the aftstation. Point defense systems and secondary weapons platforms festooned its outer hull. Watch triads prowled every trail constantly. If an enemy boarding party gained access to the lower command hull through the combat deployment bay, and if they fired a breaching charge into the ceiling bulkhead, then they could enter the aftstation, and follow the main power chases into the engineering hull to Power Systems and Propulsion adjacent to the sublight drive cooling units.

Only Warriors worked in the aftstation. Secondary weapons gunners stayed at their posts, but the watchmistress and her prowler triads always moved. Mistress Nynava had given Kidahin a near-impossible task. Mechanical housings and equipment concealed by the forest scenes as impenetrable jungle packed the aftstation. Not much open space remained for them to prowl. The Warriors could seal the aftstation and isolated it from both hulls. Blast doors, two on the command hull side and two on the engineering hull side, when sealed, turned the aftstation into a small but hardened, heavily armored, self-contained fortress.

Kidahin considered a strategy. Her team had just run through the left outrigger's convoluted trails, and now they were about to cross back into the command hull again.

"Reduce to a slow walk," Kidahin told her team. "We have been given a mission."

Fourteen Hunters gathered around Kidahin and listened with dismay as she outlined their orders.

Getting into the aftstation posed no problem. Staying long enough to stalk the Warriors there would test their prowling skills. She told them to enter the aftstation at irregular intervals. Hunters did not often prowl in groups. Warriors preferred working in small groups, most often in triads. Twenty Hunters all at once would raise suspicions. Warrior strength did not translate into Warrior stupidity. Warriors had quick minds, for all their lacking a sense of humor. As the primary combat force aboard, they would take their duties in the aftstation seriously.

Kidahin assigned movement timetables and told them where they should meet once in the aftstation.

She sent them off by different routes and waited.

If someone got caught, the Warrior catching her would tell her to leave. Their mission would not fail unless they had all been caught before at least one of them got the information Mistress Nynava wanted and then followed the ranking Warrior present at the time through the forward blast door into the command hull.

Nynava was also a Warrior, but she would never tip off the Warriors in the aftstation to their coming. Hunters and Warriors competed, but they did not tangle one another's tails in branches to gain an advantage. To do so would be dishonorable and also negate the reasoning behind the training, training they would be expected to excel at and then use to protect their warleader, all males, their home territory, and each other.

One by one her Hunters reported successful passage into the aftstation without incident. Kidahin broke cover and prowled to join them at the rendezvous site.

She prowled along command hull narrow jungle trails, ducking around hanging vines and low branches. She jumped onto a low branch and climbed up and around a thick gnarled tree—an interdeck access twisting up 112 ells—to an open bole.

She stepped through a disguised open blast door and on into a ten ell diameter hollow trunk. Across from her stood another open bole with a deep orange polished wood blast door framing the sally port guarding the main aftstation access pathway.

Warriors stood on the opposite side ready to record who came through the open bole and what their reasons were for traversing the aftstation pathways.

"Kidahin?" a Warrior asked.

"Yes, Cailindreda?" Kidahin replied in response to the aftstation watchmistress's querying trill.

"How do you feel about not being huluhar any longer?" Cailindreda asked kindly.

"Much relieved. I never want to choose a male to replace Delwyn, and I hope Saidrinha never has to exercise her choice."

"As do I. Is Delwyn pleased we made his launch date only a day and a half behind schedule?"

"I am sure he is. I have not been able to spend time with him yet. He has been having long talks with Anailiatha."

Cailindreda twitched her ears in understanding. It soon became obvious to Kidahin that the aftstation watchmistress wanted to talk to the one Hunter having the deepest insight into their warleader.

###

Zalzadrin watched her three weapon specialists check control numbers as they returned arms to the weapon lockers in the Forward Armory. Delwyn's order to Battle Status had required her, as Mistress of Arms, to make available both traditional and non-traditional weapons. It had not mattered that they were still docked in the shipyard: Battle Status was Battle Status.

A second group of three weaponmistresses in the Aft Armory was performing the same task. A final unit of four weaponmistresses remained down in the combat staging and deployment bay powering down the troop transports that had been readied for assault forces deployment.

Zalzadrin had appreciated the alert. It gave her an opportunity to exercise her authority as Mistress of Arms and come to grips with the effort needed to authorize the release of weapons, ordnance, and combat assets. Her responsibilities covered both armories, weapon lockers— regular and emergency—scattered throughout the ship, heavy weapons in the combat staging area, and the assets in the deployment bay.

Zalzadrin had the authority to release weapons aboard the warship, and that meant she also had to account for them. Releasing weapons had been straightforward but recovering weapons and checking them against inventory seemed more complex and time consuming.

"Mistress Zalzadrin? Combat Staging and Deployment reports all landing craft have been returned to maintenance alcove stand-by status."

Zalzadrin flicked her pons at the weaponmistress and nodded. "Has the Mistress of Battle released the combat teams from the staging area?"

"Yes, Mistress. The bay weaponmistresses report all weapons have been accounted for and are secured."

"Good," Zalzadrin nodded. Then a thought came to her. "Aldrea? Ask Rennidra and Laradin to confirm asset and locker status by sight. I would not put it past Nynava to try to catch us out by holding onto something simple and small, like a knife for us to miss."

"Affirm, Mistress."

Following up on her hunch, Zalzadrin took a weaponmistress and headed into the forested pathways and trails spreading throughout the mid-level command hull. They were looking for the camouflaged emergency weapon lockers strategically placed throughout the seemingly endless jungle.

Even though weapons from the emergency lockers had not been issued, Battle Status protocol placed the obligation of checking these weapon caches, designed as last-ditch sources of weapons to use in fighting off any enemies who might board *Hunter's Moon,* squarely on the shoulders of the Mistress of Arms. The lockers were concealed among tangled leaves, vines, and other jungle overgrowth. If Battle Mistress Nynava wanted to see how thoroughly Zalzadrin followed protocol, then they were a prime target to meddle with because in the event of the unthinkable, having to make a last stand defending their warleader from imminent danger, every command mistress, every assaultmistress, and their seconds knew the code to open the lockers holding knives, spears, bows and arrows, and thumpers—mobile EMP generators powerful enough to fry hand weapons, personal comms, hand-held combat scanners, grenades and their launchers but not strong enough to cripple the environmental systems or the combat address system needed to defend him.

Zalzadrin knew that against chemical or mechanical weapon systems thumpers were ineffectual. Spring or tension triggers, chemical primers and mechanical firing pins, and chemical antipersonnel explosive or projectile devices suffered no effect from EMP assaults.

It did not take Zalzadrin long to find empty slots in several weapon lockers and Nynava's ID showed up as using the code for opening lockers and releasing missing weapons. The weaponmistress recorded the locker numbers with missing weapons, and the control numbers for those missing weapons in her 'minder while Zalzadrin called back to the Forward Armory and put in a request for replacement weapons to be brought to their location at once. Later there would be a comm call to Nynava!

In her mind, Zalzadrin reviewed everything that had taken place since Delwyn had ordered the ship to Battle Status. She had authorized her weaponmistresses to release all traditional weapons and assign the boarding party and surface assault forces their modern weapons knowing he did not intend to order an attack on Wrathsee'a Anchorage. He no doubt wanted to stress all systems and see how well Anailiatha's engineers had done their jobs.

She snapped her tail at a hanging vine and grinned. A joke, Delwyn had played a joke on Anailiatha.

She knew it! He did have a Hunter's sense of humor!

Anailiatha, in Zalzadrin's opinion, had no sense of humor at all. She cursed at everyone she caught sticking a tail into her beloved circuits.

Zalzadrin grinned again. Everyone aboard knew that a'pea was Anailiatha's favorite curse word. Delwyn said she meant "a'zzol," but Zalzadrin knew she meant cloaca, the single orifice males and females both had between their legs.

The alert, while aggravating for Anailiatha, had opened Zalzadrin's eyes to her new responsibilities. As the warship's arms mistress, she stood astride the assault planners and the combat forces. Delwyn, Melkorka, Hlinlodyn and her combat analysis staff approved an action plan, including personnel, weapons, and assets. They told the Mistress of Battle the mission, its goals, its combat doctrine, and its rules of engagement. Nynava then turned their mission briefs into actual battle plans. Both Hlinlodyn and Nynava then requested weapons and weapons systems from Zalzadrin and her weaponmistresses. If the mission required two mistresses to direct surface combat or boarding actions, then Zalzadrin would accompany Nynava into the Action Zone.

Zalzadrin had read the mission briefing for their current mission. So many things remained tangled up in high branches. *Guesses!* Delwyn told her once, not long after a Ni'zakhonii blade had slashed her open from breast to hip—the injury he had stapled closed to become a wonderful scar—that guessing was a bad way to plan combat operations. Whenever guessing was unavoidable he said to consider the *Okkami' sharp edge*, a combat doctrine mnemonic, calling for the simplest plan that covered all mission goals.

There were several guesses about this mission. First, Delwyn believed a prototype-building shipyard was not on Ibeetu or any planet in the Nikkiolo inner system. Second, battle would most likely involve an assault on a surface base hidden on some airless body, a small moon or an asteroid. Therefore, combat planning called for suppressing enemy defenses, perimeter breaching, and establishing a bridgehead. Rules of engagement called for killing the enemy, of course, and quantum translating all captured equipment to the deployment bay. They would also capture notes, sample materials and ships in various stages of assembly. Then they had to bombard the shipyard from orbit, destroying everything, simple and plain.

But Delwyn had predicted enemy ship arrivals soon, an assessment the A'tayotan had taken seriously enough to authorize this battle group and mission. Throwing enemy capital ships into mission planning required Zalzadrin to issue a greater variety of arms and assets to the assault and boarding teams.

Zalzadrin paused her thoughts to cant her ears and listen to Delwyn's voice coming over the combat address system. She heard his voice but not whom he was talking to. The combat address system transmitted his voice to them. Delwyn served as their focus, and they needed to know where he was, what he was doing, and what he was saying at all times. She tried to follow the one-sided discussion. It sounded to her as if he was playing word games with Anailiatha.

He had once tried to get Anailiatha to shut down the open shipwide warleader comm—as if she actually might consider doing so or as if anyone would let her do so!

Zalzadrin watched her weaponmistresses and their scouts weave down the trail, arms filled with spears and quivers to replace the missing weapons Battle Mistress Nynava had removed. Their ears followed Delwyn's changing pitch.

She smelled their pheromones and detected the subtle change that bespoke the comfort they took from hearing his voice. The male voice could incite females to battle fury, give them a morale boost, or pull their tails if they got carried away in their zeal to keep him safe.

Contrary to the evidence their warship suggested, Eyloni did not go into space willingly. They belonged in the arboreal rainforests. If males had remained in the forest protected by their clan females, then no female would ever see a point in traveling with other females into space.

But toss a male into a ship and blast him off into space and females by the thousands would follow after him to keep him company, protect him, and keep him safe. The Be'atika Senge had demanded space travel long ago to establish an advanced technical industrial base far from Elleio and the male population. Eyloni had never entertained doubts about the possibility of life evolving on other worlds. That life, intelligent or not, might prove harmful to all males. Thus females developed FTL spacefaring technology, yet they loathed leaving their males behind.

But put a warleader aboard a ship, and female natural combativeness would send them beyond all reason if they felt he faced any danger whatsoever. His presence comforted and exuded confidence. His was the voice of reason. His songs had the power to send them into proximal fury. Once in that mindset, only his songs pulled them back from the brink of suicidal rage.

A nearby weaponmistress trilled with explosive laughter. Delwyn's one-sided argument with Anailiatha had reached a climax. Zalzadrin could well-imagine the curses Anailiatha was flinging at him. She probably stood next to him too, with her tail wrapped around him the whole time.

The warleader also played the part of sympathetic ear, one any female could scream in and vent discontent without rubbing another female's hierarchy rank the wrong way. Every female had unfettered access to the warleader and hampering another female's access to him was a high crime.

Delwyn had been a surface combat strategist when he had been among humans, and he had commanded an elite assault force. The particulars of this mission trailed closely mission profiles he had both led and participated in. But if he thought they would actually allow him to lead or participate in this or any future assault mission, then they had a surprise waiting for him.

His experience gave Zalzadrin confidence, and hearing his voice enhanced that confidence. Her confidence changed her pheromones subtly, which in turn gave confidence to her weaponmistresses and their arms teams.

Zalzadrin spoke to the combat address system. "Delwyn? Zalzadrin."

"Wait a damn minute, will ya Anailiatha? Yes, Zalzadrin?" his voice sang across the jungle.

"I want to talk to you about the assault force planning briefings."

"By yourself or with others?" he asked.

Zalzadrin caught the roundabout phrasing he used. Did she mean with Hlinlodyn and Nynava or just her alone.

"I will come to you with a few others," she said. She could act circumspectly, too.

"Fine with me, but I'm with Anailiatha now. Where?"

"Forward Armory?" she suggested.

"I'll meet you there if Anailiatha will let me leave Power Systems and Propulsion."

Zalzadrin and her teams listened to a long minute one-sided argument, probably Anailiatha's parting tail snaps interwoven with her natural reluctance to let him leave.

Zalzadrin sobered as she thought about Anailiatha's presumed reluctance.

***

Kidahin finally put Cailindreda's curiosity to rest. The aftstation watchmistress had sought news and assurances about their current mission. Updates had apparently not been forthcoming from the Mistress of the Aftstation. Cailindreda wanted to know how Kidahin thought the warleader would perform, what plan he might have, anything. The Warrior wanted to hear Kidahin speak her confidence in Delwyn and give her an idea about the type of engagement she expected they might be involved in.

Kidahin told her Nynava anticipated laying off a small astronomical body and assaulting an enemy base from either high orbit or from some optimal striking distance beyond its gravity well. If the base had surface-to-orbit strike capability, then they expected antitorpedo and point defense activity. Kidahin asked forgiveness for her inadequacy and told Cailindreda she had no idea how Hlinlodyn would fight the warship.

Cailindreda thanked Kidahin and returned to her security duties being none the wiser about Kidahin's true purpose for coming by.

Kidahin was finally free to enter the aftstation and continue her mission unhindered.

Two hours had passed since Kidahin's team had infiltrated the aftstation.

"What happened?" Aplilin asked Kidahin when she poked her head into the dense flaming-orange brush clustered around the ventral aft bulkhead.

"Cailindreda wanted company," Kidahin said, offering nothing further. "You are new to our warship," she continued, "and not familiar with the pathways and trails inside the aftstation. Your 'minders have a file in them to show you the aftstation cross-section. It highlights a different prowling path for each of you. Count all the Warriors, list their activity, and note their rank. When you have completed your prowl, return here and we will decide which one is the highest-ranked present. She is the Warrior at least one of us must stalk until she leaves the aftstation. Then we can report to Nynava. Go."

"Affirm," the crouching Hunters murmured before breaking cover.

Kidahin made a note concerning Cailindreda before heading down the heavily overgrown maintenance trail into the prowling loop she had assigned to herself. In theory each Hunter had about 312 thousand cubic ells to prowl, but the aftstation was not an enclosed hollow shell. Given the volume taken up by the inner and outer hulls, the decks and bulkheads, and the substructure and equipment, that left some forty thousand cubic ells to search, a mere twenty ell cube of equivalent volume per Hunter strung out along low paths and narrow trails.

At first the teammates had thought they had far too many stalkers for such a small search area. Thinking about the search volume as cubic ells on a grid did not do justice to how paths and trails in the aftstation were laid out. They had not been designed to follow convenient grids. All the same, Kidahin still considered the mission a near-impossibility. While she would not rub up against her stalkers, she knew she would cross their paths from time to time. She had broken her fourteen into three groups of three, one for each vertical level in the aftstation. There the three would fan out and survey her individual prowl. The aftstation resembled a self-contained jungle thicket overgrowing a small tree up to some 120 ells. Her team had to prowl through narrow trails in the thicket, duck under vines and branches, and avoid the Warriors stalking through the dense tangling undergrowth.

Except for the main pathways connecting the aftstation to the command and engineering hulls, the narrow trails did not lend themselves to easy passage. Patrolling watch Warrior triads made it worse. A Hunter could only retreat so far off the trail before the foliage refused to give way, which meant the Hunter had backed herself up against a jungle-concealed bulkhead.

Stalking took patience, something Warriors had in short supply. Hunters could sit on the balls of their feet and wait, crouching for hours, even as long as a few days if necessary. But Kidahin did not have that kind of time to play with. Aftstation personnel rotated relief teams every few hours. Her teammates had to go slowly and be meticulous, yet they had to hurry if they wanted to complete the training mission.

Kidahin, not wanting to meet Cailindreda again and raise suspicions, chose to prowl the trails closest to the ventral hull, the below decks. She did not walk along the trail itself but wandered from one side to the other. She hid in the grasses and vines overgrowing the trail around and above her. Stealth-stalking was slow work. The jungle growth looked no different than real grasses and leaves, and every incautious brush against them made the same sounds, too.

Kidahin heard a watch coming. She hopped back under cover and squatted holding her breath. She had to watch her scent. The ship reeked with pheromones, and the Warriors should not respond to general scent unless they noticed her new scent or caught the empathic thrust in the scent and gauged her emotional intent.

Kidahin stared through thick hanging vines as the watch triad prowled past her without so much as a twitching ear.

She added them to her list and noted their rank weaves.

Over the next three hours Kidahin found four more Warriors to add to her list. She also crossed trails with the same watch triad twice. She twisted deep into a low-growing thick bush and pulled the 'minder from her underthong ties and checked on the progress of her Hunters.

So far three had returned to their staging area, and she headed for them herself. It took her an hour to creep back to them, and together they compared notes.

"Kidahin? Where are the other ten?" Merkrida asked.

"Probably busy getting back here. The upper paths are harder to prowl than the lower trails because more through-traffic travels along them."

A few minutes later another Hunter slipped into their hiding place.

"Kidahin, I think I was seen!" Jassalin hissed.

"What makes you think that?" Kidahin demanded.

"Someone was closing on my hiding spot when she stopped, retreated, and started pushing vines and branches aside along the trail!"

Spirits! Kidahin cursed. Once a Warrior's suspicions had been raised, she obsessed over the instinctive warning, and it did not take long for a Warrior's combat intuition to alert her to an anomaly.

Kidahin froze at the sound of purposeful, stealthy movement whispering among the background sounds of rustling leaves and grasses.

"Scatter!" she murmured, barely louder than a puff of wind. The four members of her assault team who had returned melted off on different trails deep into the orange-shaded undergrowth. She hoped one team member would remain uncaught in order to complete their mission.

Kidahin crawled on her stomach along the uneven forest floor, a forearm length from the trail edge.

She heard footfalls now, several footfalls, heavy treading Warrior footfalls, and froze.

They passed by slowly. One Warrior was trying her best to convince the other fourteen that she had heard someone stalking her near the blast door access to the engineering hull.

If Cailindreda had ordered lifesign scanners issued, then Kidahin's mission would soon terminate.

Kidahin heard an argument up ahead, and she crawled as fast as possible toward the voices.

"Mistress?" a voice ahead asked.

"Disregard this argument," the Mistress of the Aftstation said. "Something more important has come to my attention. Vervada said she heard noises, stalking noises."

The Mistress stopped, right in front of Kidahin's hiding place.

"Watchmistress!" the Mistress of the Aftstation sang.

"Mistress?" came Cailindreda's voice over the combat address system, followed by Delwyn's voice, probably talking to Melkorka in the command center.

The Aftstation Mistress paused barely long enough to flit her ears at the sound of his voice before she continued. "Check your logs. Who has passed through the aftstation since you came on duty?"

"Affirm, Mistress. There is a short list. Should I read them off?"

"No. Check with the engineering hull watch and eliminate everyone who continued on through or came back to the command hull through your bole."

"Affirm…one moment, Mistress. Mistress? One Hunter, Kidahin, entered through my watch point and has not exited into the engineering hull or passed back through my watch."

"Well," the Aftstation Mistress said.

"That means nothing, Mistress," a Warrior objected. "There are other ways to get into the aftstation from the command hull. The watch points pick up people crossing from one hull to the other."

The Mistress of the Aftstation shook her head, tail twisting in slow circles. "No. Kidahin came through the main access pathway from the command hull but she did not continue on into the engineering hull. Nor did she turn around and go back through Cailindreda's watch point. That means she must have diverted into the maintenance trails, where only the secondary weapons gun teams, the point defense teams, engineering maintenance teams, aftstation fire control and damage control teams, and my watch triads have any business prowling. I think the Mistress of Battle has been using our territory for Hunter stalking practice."

She opened the combat address system and called the command center.

"Mistress Melkorka? Mistress of the Aftstation Thiodnuma. I have a Green-4 intrusion into the aftstation. I am sealing off the aftstation pathway blast doors."

"Affirm, Mistress Thiodnuma," Melkorka said.

"Cailindreda, muster all triads and have them scour all trails and pathways for Hunter Kidahin and her stealth team."

"Affirm!"

Kidahin hugged the ground. The mission would fail if no one followed Mistress Thiodnuma to the watch point on the pathway next to the command hull blast doors. She pulled her 'minder and silently accessed all data her team had accumulated since they had begun the training exercise. She scrolled through it. Her team had found all the Warriors they could find, and Kidahin had the Aftstation Mistress in sight.

Thiodnuma addressed the combat address system again.

"Mistress of Battle? Mistress of the Aftstation. Please come to the aftstation main pathway. When you arrive the Watchmistress will open the blast door and one of my Warriors will escort you to me. I think we may have found a few Hunters you may have misplaced."

Kidahin entertained a wild hope. If Cailindreda opened the sealed blast door for Nynava, then she might have a chance to dart through the open door and technically complete her team assignment. It sounded plausible in her mind up until the point when several Warriors grabbed into the ground cover and pulled her onto the trail.

"Nice try, Kidahin. When Nynava joins us you will tell me how long you have been stalking here and what you found out," Thiodnuma said.

Kidahin swallowed nervously and nodded. Thiodnuma, Mistress of the Aftstation, had all the rank she needed to press the point, but she needed to know. No doubt she planned to berate her teams for letting the stalkers get away with remaining in the aftstation for as long as they had.

Once Nynava arrived Kidahin gave her report as both mistresses listened. Then Nynava entered a code into her 'minder calling Kidahin's assault team back for debriefing.

Kidahin was proud of her team's success. Her stalkers had accomplished every mission parameter except for following Thiodnuma out of the blast door when she completed her shift.

10
ABOARD THE COALITION CARRIER HENRI EDDA

"Mr. Carstairs plot a hyperdrive course for Iota Horologii and stand by to break lunar orbit," Captain Rodgers ordered.

"Aye, Captain. Plotting for Iota Horologii. Plot reports Iota Horologii, a GOVp class star bordering Compact space, is fifty-six light-years distant. ETA fourteen days, ten hours, and fifty-three minutes at maximum hyperdrive velocity. Hyperdrive coils are charged. Orbital maneuvering is ready to break lunar orbit. Maneuvering plot for heavy mass hyperlimit course laid in. Sublight drive is online. Ready for departure Captain," Lieutenant Carstairs reported.

"Very well. Take us out, Mr. Carstairs."

"Aye, Captain. Breaking lunar orbit. Sublight engines to point four-five cee. Time to heavy mass hyperlimit, twenty minutes, fifty-two seconds. Mark!"

"Very well," Rodgers said.

"I bet you didn't expect to go back there again anytime soon," Ambassador Winters said, standing next to her.

"No Captain, I didn't. I'd like to think of this trip as just as uneventful as the one we took from there to Earth," she said.

"Me, too."

"There is a danger," Anlann admitted, Seralin standing beside him.

"I doubt it, co-Ambassador Anlann," Rodgers replied. "My read on this is that it's all Marsch's guessing. I wouldn't build my super-secret light attack craft factory right on my enemy's border. Although I can see why they might test it there. If Compact assets can't detect it, then I'd say it passed its trial run. But it didn't, did it? *Hunter's Moon* detected its FTL wake, so it's not all that stealthy."

"He—it now—is a prototype, Delwyn believes," Seralin replied. "It might have been an intermittent, temporary failure of a particle baffle. It is also possible for Delwyn's Mistress of Tactics to have been fortunate enough to scan where she scanned when she scanned."

Rodgers shook her head. "Even if that's true, even if the Lizard LAC had been built somewhere in the Iota Horologii system, it doesn't follow that the Lizards are there now, or if they sent a task force there. More likely they blew up the facility and evacuated all classified materials back to their home system. They might send a ship out there to take a look, but I can't see them committing anything more than a single battlecruiser."

"The Compact Counsel thought Delwyn had made a point about the Ni'zakhonii not wanting their secrets to fall into our hands. I assure you. We would send more than one warship if three of our destroyers failed to report or arrive on schedule," Seralin countered.

"Even granting you that much, it's what? About sixty light-years from their fleet patrol zones to Iota Horologii? Lizards don't have hyperlink communications capability. Marsch expects a probe to travel that far at Lizard G-band velocity? Would it even have the fuel reserves? That's over one hundred thirty days one-way. I thought those probes had a ten-light-year endurance at V-band velocity. Throttling down to G-band gets you one-hundred-six days duration at most, according to our intelligence. That's only forty-six light-years, then zip, no power. It pops out of the dimensional warp and drifts in normal space. What's the chance that it pops out anywhere near a Lizard asset forty-six light-years from Iota Hor?"

Anlann shook his head, his ears flattening. He did not like hearing Delwyn referred to as 'Marsch.' "Delwyn believes they will send a group of ships at V-band velocity two days after the probe's arrival."

"I doubt it," Rodgers said. "Without hyperlink, I'm sure they don't even know their destroyers are a debris field floating in Iota Hor's heliopause, and if this supposed secret shipyard had at least one cutter or frigate held in reserve, then it hightailed from there at V-band, and we know for sure that didn't happen. If it had, then we would have tangled with a Lizard ship while still in Ibeetu orbit."

"Which goes back to anticipating a courier probe from the last destroyer, not a short-range probe aboard the LAC. If I didn't have hyperlink, then I'd want my courier probes to travel farther than forty-six light-years, longer than one hundred days, and faster than 166.89 cee," Ambassador Winters said.

"They cannot," Seralin interjected. "Fuel economy prohibits greater speeds over the distance a courier probe needs to travel. It is a given that the Ni'zakhonii must have taken into account the need for a probe to traverse such long distances. They would have programmed the drive to either conserve antihydrogen and try to reach a known base or staging area, or to ramp up to maximum velocity if they had a known naval asset closer and easily diverted to the Nikkiolo star system. It is a tactical statement of fact to say it is faster and easier to divert a battle group from its patrol sector and retask it than it is to sortie a battle group from its home port."

"Captain?" Carstairs interrupted. "We are approaching the heavy mass hyperlimit."

"Noted. Prepare to engage hyperdrive."

"Aye, Captain."

"Oh, Captain Rodgers?" Winters said. "Please have Lieutenant Carstairs make sure we have crossed the hyperlimit threshold. I wouldn't want to enter an unstable jump point, get pulled into spaghetti, and enter hyperspace stretched along a several hundred-kilometer-long string of nuts, bolts, and shredded ship."

"I would never do that, Mr. Ambassador," Carstairs swore, hand on his heart.

"I remember a certain helm officer, an ensign—what was his name? —Ensign Carstairs? —who nearly jumped me into hyperspace a mere 171,000 kilometers sunside of the limit," Winters said.

"Yes, Sir. But I was only 1.14 seconds early, and your bellow distracted me long enough for the ship to sail right across the threshold before my finger even touched the hyperdrive commit switch."

"I remember that, too," Rodgers nodded. "And if I remember correctly, your excuse at the time was some electronic delay and jump recoil discharge time plus physical entry into the wormhole from the time you punched the button would take longer than the 1.14 seconds needed to cross the heavy mass threshold."

"Something like that, yes, Ma'am."

Seralin ground her teeth. The smells around her hinted at humor, but how could anyone, a Mistress of the Ship of all people, joke about an incident implying the possible deaths of males?

Cabrera nodded to himself. "Captain? The board shows go-green. The ship is ready for hyperdrive."

Rodgers stepped between Maneuvering and Plotting and nodded to Carstairs. "Jump us into hyperspace, Mr. Carstairs."

"Aye, Captain. Engaging hyperdrive."

Winters looked up on the forward viewscreen and watched as a yellow dot became a golden-horned daffodil flaring open like a funnel on its forward edge. It expanded, turning from yellow to amber, fading to orange as it enveloped the screen. The pale orange flower flashed brilliant white and then faded back into the blackness of the void.

Well, not quite. Hyperspace always reminded Winters of a black velvet background someone had scattered violet glitter across. It wasn't uniformly scattered, either. Hyperspace was the domain of dark energy, and here gravitational eddies rippled all around them, for the most part insubstantial. He thought about a metro car hurtling through ethereal earth. The trees growing in it, their tap roots, main support roots, down to the fine violet secondary root structures drifted down around them.

What they saw was the hyperspace component of the void's quantum gravity. The tap root-like gossamer tendrils clustered into curtains and ribbons as the hyperspace equivalent of mass. Astronomical bodies in normal space projected gravitational artifacts into hyperspace. Distances were vastly compressed here compared to normal space. Gravitational waves were 2,920 times closer to each other in hyperspace. The star closest to the Sun, Proxima Centauri, was about 4.25 light-years, or about 268,700 AU, away from Earth in normal space. In hyperspace Proxima Centauri's gravitational artifact was only 92 AU from the Sun's gravitational artifact. It was those gravitational anomalies that made navigation in hyperspace hazardous for a ship traveling at 0.45 cee.

"Hyperspace achieved, Captain," Carstairs said. "All stations show green, all decks report green, all systems report nominal. Hyperspace navigation systems have engaged the plot for Iota Horologii. Maintaining sublight drive velocity at point four-five cee. ETA fourteen days, ten hours, and fifty-three minutes."

Anlann found the concept behind hyperspace a bit frightening and confusing. It was not a drive system but a field generator that opened a rift in normal space. Once the ship fell through the rift, he was trapped there until he opened another rift and fell back into normal space. The hyperspace field did not provide a motive force. The ship's normal space sublight propulsion system drove the ship in hyperspace. To an observer in normal space, the ship appeared to travel at a phenomenal velocity, but Anlann could not decide whether time or velocity changed in hyperspace.

Delwyn had explained it by drawing a four-spoked wheel. He said to think about the rim as normal space and the hub as hyperspace. Instead of traveling around a longer arc on the rim, hyperspace let a ship fall down a spoke until he reached the hub, which had a much smaller circumference. Hyperspace travel mimicked movement around the hub to the next spoke, where the ship traveled up through it to reach normal space.

Anlann satisfied himself by working out the math: the same velocities could be achieved by both the Coalition hyperdrive and the Compact jump drive. Compact intelligence so far had come to the consensus that the Ni'zakhonii subspace warp field FTL drive must have the same maximum apparent FTL speed of 21,320 cee. The universe appeared to have a maximum speed limit for how fast matter exceeded light speed, and twice that maximum velocity for energy transmission speeds, regardless of the technology employed.

"Well, Ambassadors, we're on our way. Now, if you'll please excuse me, I have a ship to run," Rodgers said.

"Oh, aye aye, Captain. I can translate 'get the hell off my bridge' very well, thank you. I quite often said the same thing, and I meant people to understand it in exactly that way," Winters said.

"I didn't mean it quite like that, Captain. It's just—well—the bridge would bore you. Why don't you and the co-Ambassadors get settled into your quarters. I'll meet you for dinner at the captain's table later this evening."

Winters nodded. "Until then, Captain. Anlann? Seralin?" He gestured the co-Ambassadors to follow him off the raised center island. They walked down the broad companionway to the bridge main deck, crossed it, and stepped into the waiting lift.

"VIP deck," Winters told the lift. The door swept shut, and the lift dropped several decks before shifting horizontal and racing aft.

"You've been assigned to the same quarters you had last time," Winters told them. "I've been assigned to the quarters next to yours," he added.

"That will be satisfactory," Anlann said with a flick of his tail. "We are quite familiar with them and how the devices in them work."

"VIP quarters have been designed to double as working quarters for visitors and their staff members. There's a hatch in the bulkhead between our quarters. If you need anything, just hit it hard and I'll come running."

"Just leave the bole open," Seralin said.

"I don't want to intrude. You need your privacy," Winters began.

"Nonsense," Seralin said, twitching her tail playfully at him. "Hatches and doors are rare in our culture. We use them to isolate hazardous equipment or secure an area from the animals or keep curious infants from danger. Hospitality and courtesy customs make using doors superfluous and socially insulting."

The lift stopped and the door opened on the VIP deck. They exited and strolled down the empty corridor to their quarters.

"Meet you inside!" Seralin sang as she shouldered Anlann aside, ready to block any assault on her warleader potentially waiting in the well-appointed studio cabin.

Anlann rolled his eyes, more a human gesture than an Eyloni one. He had learned to use it once he noticed the subtle pons-drawn circle in the air often went unnoticed or misunderstood by humans.

"She is serious," he told Winters. "Besides, I need to fill you in on some matters I could not speak about until after we got underway."

Winters sighed. *This is when the other shoe drops.*

11
THE SHAHA HOME FLEET

"We are going to system TX-3767. Once we arrive there, we will undertake and complete three distinct but related missions," Commander Haksith began.

Doctor Tek Nal squirmed in his warm mud bath, trying to get comfortable. Maybe now he'd get some answers. The fleet had been falling through the subspace manifold for twenty-nine days. Twenty-nine days of doing nothing but laying under heat lamps, sleeping, bathing in hot mud, eating an occasional Na Atal, and rereading the Science Ministry report; the report that had gotten him sent to the heavy battlecruiser *Hzz'a*. He shouldn't be here, and at the moment he was entertaining the notion that Prefect Sharris had convinced the Satrap to exile him from Meerslah, never to see home again.

They had fifteen more days travel to go before they would re-emerge into normal space.

Waiting, waiting, and more waiting seemed to Tek Nal like a standard starfleet staple activity. It was military doctrine to keep sensitive information compartmentalized—withheld from general knowledge, or even from those having a need to know, until the last minute. Standard starfleet procedure called for mission briefings to commence two-thirds the way to a target. This was fleet deployment, and they were now two-thirds of the way to the target star system.

Why in the three suns above was the Prefecture sending the Home Fleet to system TX-3767 in the first place? The Home Fleet protected

Meerslah and the Saurian trinary star system. The Home Fleet consisted of nineteen ships: a battleship, seven heavy battlecruisers, two light cruisers, three heavy destroyers, four escort destroyers, an LAC carrier, and a heavy cargo carrier. Tek Nal knew the cargo ship was carrying dagan eggs, but a medium transport could carry more than enough eggs to seed the moon. Taking the heavy cargo hauler along was overkill.

Desert Suns! The Home Fleet itself was overkill just to pick up a few prototype ships. Bleniss couldn't terraform the moon with those ships. What was he going to do with them, use them to blast the moon into submission?

Lord Viceroy Bleniss had told Tek Nal he was the science liaison between the Science Ministry and Military Research and Development on this mission.

So far, he hadn't been called upon to serve as a liaison for anything.

He dozed in the communal briefing pool, half-listening. Fleet disposition and task force assignments meant nothing to him. Bleniss had given Haksith his orders, something about taking command of seven ships and heading for some ice dwarf.

Even thinking about a frozen world gave Tek Nal the shivers despite the warm mud.

When he heard Haksith's rumbling hiss about the terraforming project, Tek Nal shook himself awake. This had been the pretense for putting him on this slow road to exile.

"Initial scans taken of the habitable moon in system TX-3767 have confirmed our hopes. It meets the minimum standards set forth in the Science Ministry guidelines for dagan husbandry, but barely. The star's spectra match the narrow wavelengths needed by the symbiotic algae in dagan skin. The oceans are a close match in salinity and in mineral factors necessary for proper dagan growth and health. Sufficient shallow shorelines outline both continents, and those shores have succulents and soft plants growing there that the dagan can eat in abundance. Preliminary tests done on dagan hatched in the moon's environment have shown proof positive that the boron and chlorine traces in the indigenous plants can be metabolized and neutralized by the same digestive enzymes that allow the dagan to neutralize the caustic sap in Meerslah plants," Haksith droned on.

Tek Nal sighed. This was old news. *He* had written the protocols for exoworld analysis. He didn't need to hear a dumbed-down version from Haksith. Besides, Tek Nal knew what the problem with the moon was: winter temperature extremes.

"The Prefecture ordered the Defense Ministry to establish an outpost in the outer system and carry out classified research. That research included testing some climate modeling strategies to find out if any of them could produce a way to raise the surface temperature high enough to moderate the harsh winters. In the course of their work, the research teams found a crystal mineral structure, a geode, amenable to our crystal programming technology. The scientists finding the geode placed it into their crystal set programmer and discovered it can accept a sixteen-fold increase in quantum optical circuits."

So what? Tek Nal muttered. All modern Shaha technology was crystal-based. Data networks and power distribution nodes were formed into crystals as a matter of course. Shaha had been growing and programming crystals for several hundred years. Every component was solid: no wires, no cables, no discrete components—just a crystal.

"The scientists," Haksith continued, clearly excited if his lisping hisses were any hint, "programmed the geode to grow a small fusion reactor and a carbon-liberating catalyst and turned it on in the laboratory. The dioxide carbide the thing produced overwhelmed the research bay and suffocated all lab personnel."

Tek Nal saw where this was leading and couldn't believe it. *They're going to terraform the moon's atmosphere.* That's what Bleniss meant about wanting him around for giving terraforming advice. But why? This had nothing to do with the oceans. They were well within dagan tolerances. Haksith was talking about increasing the dioxide carbide in the atmosphere.

Now that was ironic. Rising dioxide carbide levels had led to global warming on Meerslah. Dioxide carbide had scarred and scored the dagan, the amphibian base in the Shaha food chain. Now they were going to cause global warming on a moon to make its winters livable for a transplanted dagan population.

"My Lord Commander Haksith, I abase myself, but I doubt one small carbon catalyst can do the job unless you intend us to wait thousands of centuries," Tek Nal said.

"My Lord Doctor Tek Nal, you are absolutely correct. And I don't intend to wait that long! The outpost found several thousand geodes on the moon. None were much bigger than a courier probe. They have been programming them in their crystal set for months. During that time their experiments on the crystalline material has taken on new dimensions. It took supreme effort, but they succeeded in growing a courier probe virtually undetectable unless it transmits active signals. The interdimensional drive efficiency is incredible…"

"Wait, don't tell me," Tek Nal interrupted. He couldn't resist. He was bored and impatient, and he felt like snapping his teeth into something and giving it a good twist. "It can exceed the faster-than-light absolute speed limit."

"What? No, no. Nothing goes faster than 1,460 cee. You know that, Doctor! Where was I? Oh, yes. Efficiency. Its energy-utilization curve improves the maximum velocity for the V-band, a 7.47 percent increase in fact. This same improvement on efficiency increases maximum sublight velocity by 8.1 percent, to 0.585 cee. Even more remarkable, the crystals can be programmed to form shapes and surface characteristics that make the probe very durable and stealthy."

"That is amazing," Tek Nal said dryly. "Too bad you found none large enough to make ships out of, or better yet bigger carbon catalyst machines."

Haksith grinned a toothy smirk and hissed. "Oh but we have, Doctor. The outpost surveyed the system and found deposits of larger geodes buried deep in dwarf planets. None larger than a light cruiser, but enough. Most found so far compare well with a light attack craft hull. The first LAC prototype was completed a few months ago and has undergone stealth and shield trials. The performance results and the prototype are on their way back to Meerslah along with three destroyers. They were due back a few weeks after we left home, and by now the prototype should be secure in spacedock above Meerslah."

"Lord Viceroy Bleniss said something about a prototype before we left. He also said something about terraforming."

Haksith nodded. "The LAC performance tests were a mere formality, a simple wargame exercise. It had to approach three destroyers in stealth mode, fire on one of them, withdraw to medium range, and actively scan the destroyer it fired upon. The destroyer then tries to get a target lock and fire on the LAC."

Tek Nal nodded. "At one-tenth power, just enough to nudge their shields."

"No, My Lord Doctor," Haksith hissed, "a full-power coordinated barrage from all three destroyers."

"But even I know LACs mount minimal shields. You can't expect an LAC to take a direct hit from a destroyer's main particle batteries at moderate range, let alone a focused barrage from all three ships. I don't think it can even take a direct hit from one destroyer at long range without suffering significant damage."

Lord Haksith grinned toothily. "And if we were talking about standard light attack craft designs I would agree with you, My Lord Doctor. But the crystal structure in these geodes makes them easy to program for fabulous characteristics."

"So?" Tek Nal pressed. "Nothing fabulous in nature comes in any quantity. I'm willing to take an educated scientific guess. These geodes are very rare no matter what sizes you find them in. I go further and guess it is even rarer to find them in LAC hull sizes let alone the one or two light cruiser-sized ones you have found so far."

Haksith glowered. "Bluntly put, My Lord Doctor, but essentially correct. That is why we have an LAC carrier and a bulk cargo carrier in our Fleet. An LAC carrier carries a maximum forty-eight LAC complement, and *Pa'taz* is carrying no LACs at all."

"You're expecting forty-eight prototype LACs?" Tek Nal asked doubtfully.

Haksith shook his head. "More like eighteen or twenty. And about two times as many in various stages of assembly. Those mostly completed can be towed into the carrier, but those ready for crystal set programming and those raw geodes already in inventory will be bulk-transported back home in the cargo ship."

"I thought the cargo ship was carrying dagan eggs," Tek Nal objected.

"What? Yes, of course it is. We will seed the moon first. It is entering its summer season now, and with all the carbon catalyst machines we pick up from the research outpost and seed on the moon before we head for home, there should be enough time for dioxide carbide to accumulate and offset the harshest part of the upcoming winter, at least near the equator. That's where you come in."

"Yes?" Tek Nal asked warily.

"Yes," Haksith nodded. "Climate mechanics are your specialty. Your climate change analysis impressed the Prefecture. Your ideas about those dagan-Na Atal alien analogues being Shaha, well, not so much.

"I don't care about pet projects and speculative theorizing. I'm a military strategist. I know how people think. A person is either smart or dumb, but they, to a fault, follow the religious proscriptions set forth by the priestesses of the Gods. Disregarding deviants and criminals anyway they do. No matter. The point, My Lord Doctor, is that mobs are not smart and collectively couldn't care less about the religious prescriptions when their backbones are meeting their bellies.

"The conclusions and theories you announced in the Prefecture could never go public, and you should have known that. Any military-minded person would have known better. Every starfleet officer does know better. Assuming for argument sake that at least one of the two alien dagan species is Shaha, sapient beings, people, then common knowledge of our eating them is direct evidence of the breaking of the proscriptions. No claws of the Gods came up from the ocean depths to destroy us for eating alien people.

"So it isn't such a long scrabble across the sand for the hungry common person to decide that eating Shaha to avoid famine won't bring avenging claws down on them. Now you have something worse than civil war. You have anarchy and religious schism Doctor, a direct affront to both the Satrap and the priestesses.

"You're lucky the Satrap let you leave the Prefecture alive."

"Um…" was all Tek Nal could muster.

"As a military strategist," Haksith blithely continued, "I take intelligence sources from wherever I can find them, and I'm not going to shed scales over worries about religious proscriptions. Fighting an alien Shaha species is different from fighting an alien Na Atal. Our strategy has always taken into account the belief that the two species were dagan-like with Na Atal minds: social, primitive, and instinctive with rudimentary learning capability. The Defense Ministry has always thought we have been fighting starships designed and built by an alien Shaha species, and the alien Shaha crewed them with their surplus food animals: an advanced and trainable Na Atal.

"We also assumed, as you pointed out in your Science Ministry briefing to the Prefecture, that sooner or later we would meet these alien Shaha. If this ever happened, we planned to explain our food shortage difficulties and reach a concordance with them. They agree to help us find a world for our dagan, and we compensate them for their losses."

"But if one of the two species is Shaha...." Tek Nal began.

"Patience, Doctor. I'm getting to that. You have a theory concerning which two species is intelligent, yes?"

Tek Nal nodded. "The Science Ministry believes the omnivorous species is Shaha and the herbivorous species is the dagan-Na Atal hybrid they eat."

"I know the herbivorous species is dagan," Haksith hissed. "I know this because I remember how they behaved when I first met them!"

Tek Nal's multi-rowed teeth clicked in surprise. "You? You commanded the ship making first contact with the herbivores?"

Haksith hissed at the memory. "Yes. We met, thinking them a possible alien Shaha encounter. I mean, they had starships, so it wasn't an incredible idea at the time. We couldn't get over the language barrier, which in hindsight should have told us they were Na Atal. The females were fawning all over the male and sniffing everything. The male consumed their attention, and the females possessed a kind of Na Atal aggressiveness. My science officer came up with a deluded theory: this species had evolved in such a way to bring only the male to Shaha sentience. The non-sentient female served as breeders and as the Na Atal food sources for him. It made sense at the time. There was just the one male. With so many females for trained menial crew, certainly the extras were his food. Despite appearances, the male seemed clearly Shaha, and since all Shaha understand a communal concord meal, I offered him a Na Atal to eat in exchange for one of his female Na Atal."

"I know how this story goes, My Lord Haksith. I'm sure the priestesses hissed on their egg clutches at the idea of non-sentient females serving a sentient male belonging to the same species. What of it? And what does all this have to do with military strategy and the religious proscriptions?"

Haksith glared into Tek Nal's eyes. "Famine creates the mob, and the mob couldn't give a grain of sand about the Gods, the priestesses, or the Satrap. I say we either reach a concord with the omnivores, or we conquer and eat them, and to the triple suns with the proscriptions!"

"That's blasphemy!" Tek Nal clacked his teeth in shock.

"So what? Do you see any priestesses about? When their backbones meet their bellies, they won't clamp their jaws and say no."

"But the consequences of cannibalism are scientific fact! Shaha eating Shaha over time causes harm to the DNA in eggs. You'd have us devolve until we are nothing more than Na Atal?"

"Eating Shaha causes congenital devolution. I doubt eating *alien* Shaha poses the same problem."

Tek Nal clacked his teeth, drew a deep breath, and hissed. "Well, that possibility I grant you, at least for the herbivores. Some omnivores had flesh in their gut, mammal flesh, which causes other problems."

"So? Feed them plants. Problem solved," Haksith shrugged.

"So where do you want me to begin?" Tek Nal asked.

"We are traveling at I-band velocity and will arrive in system TX-3767 in another fifteen days. Your work on the carbon catalyst machines has top priority by order of the Satrap and the Prefecture. But," and Haksith waved a claw in Tek Nal's face, "I'm a pragmatic commander and I like having all my options open. You will take time to develop a psychological profile for your proposed omnivorous alien Shaha. Reaching concord among Shaha is universal because all reptiles strive to reach a concord. If these omnivorous mammal aliens are Shaha, then they will have the same universal desire to reach a concord. That means I need to set a claw into their mindset. In the alternative, if it turns out they are not alien Shaha but an advanced Na Atal food animal, then I was thinking about a biological alternative."

"A biological…?"

"Yes, My Lord Doctor, a biological alternative."

Tek Nal let that claw pass as more pressing questions came to mind.

"How do you expect me to come up with a psychological model for a *mammal?* My Lord Haksith, mammals are vermin, disgusting little creatures that lead to an evolutionary dead end because the caustic sap poisoning from the plants they eat or from the contaminated meat from other animals they eat retards higher development. Sure, there are omnivorous mammals on Meerslah, but there's no mind there for me to draw conclusions from."

"Can't you simply juxtapose a Shaha psychological profile onto a mammal neural behavior model?"

"You think it's that easy?" Tek Nal clacked his teeth together. "That's like taking all the observed data on a fish and then mapping a Shaha profile onto the model to see what a sapient fish would do when presented with a range of stimuli."

"Yes and no, Doctor. A fish is an idiot with a brain the size of my index claw. I'm saying you should take all the behavioral studies the Science Ministry has on Meerslah mammals, run behavioral simulations on a scaled-up mammalian brain, say one with as many nerve cells as a Shaha brain, and then overlap the Shaha profile onto it. A computer should be able to come up with a reasonable model for you to work with."

"It won't work, My Lord Haksith. What you're suggesting is sure fantasy. By your logic I can download a psychological profile onto a *racc'za* plant neural net and converse with it!"

Haksith shrugged. "Like I said, I'm a strategist. That's why I want those prototype LACs, those carbon catalyst machines seeded on the moon, a way to talk to or out-think an alien Shaha, and a biological alternative to the alien Na Atal problem."

Tek Nal shook his head. "I think the Prefecture had the right idea when they approved terraforming the moon's atmosphere. If these geodes perform as you say, then this is a gift from the Gods. Why bother with the alien dagan then?"

"Why? Because, my good Lord Doctor, they are a threat. We can't train our Na Atal to crew starships. I'd love nothing better than to put Na Atal in fighters and LACs, but I can't. They'd likely fight among themselves rather than doing even the most rudimentary piloting. Starfleet might as well put ships under AI control. Besides, with the growing food shortage, sending Na Atal by the hundreds—living edible meat—off to die in battle in the face of famine would get me eaten by my own crew. Imagine me ordering out a fighter group only to find that the launch bay crew had made lunch out of the Na Atal pilots."

"Well, this clawfull of LACs we're picking up won't make a difference. Even some super-LAC isn't going to matter much over the long haul. And, you said yourself, only a few geodes are big enough to grow light cruisers from," Tek Nal said.

"Ah, yes. About that. The outpost's shipyard has discovered how to have them grow together to make bigger ships."

"Grow together? So what, My Lord Haksith? You've already admitted geode rarity. What are you going to do? Grow them together into one ship? I admit I'm no ship designer, but I can't see you getting anything much better than a destroyer, and what's one more destroyer in the grand scheme of things?"

"Not much," Haksith admitted. "But we have something in mind for it."

"Really?"

"Yes, really," Haksith hissed, signaling by his tone that he wasn't going to enlighten Tek Nal any further.

"Well, fine. Keep me in the dark then. I'm not military. Nor am I a member of starfleet. As I already told you, I'm a climate scientist by profession. Have I leave to appropriate personnel and materials necessary to accomplish the two tasks you've set before me?"

"Better, much better attitude," Haksith hissed and gave Tek Nal a classic toothy grin. "The Prefecture's assignment for you bears the seal of the Satrap himself. That means on paper your highest priority is to develop crystal set programming downloadable into the carbon catalyst geodes. However, this is a military mission and you are on a starfleet vessel. Lord Viceroy Bleniss wants results, which means I want results. You are aware that system TX-3767 borders territory the dagan species defends for its Shaha, yes?"

"I am. I also remember how the Prefecture exploded in anger when starfleet failed to capture a few stars in the neighborhood of system TX-3767."

"Which tends to prove they act under the control of a Shaha species. Never mind. The research outpost has been in the system for several years. Because the moon is habitable, barely, I wouldn't be surprised to sooner or later see some military development there. We might arrive in the system smack in the teeth of a dagan survey ship. I want to bury this dagan-Na Atal-as-alien-Shaha business in the mud and see what hatches. I want a psychological predictor of their behavior to use in battle strategy. If we capture one, your profiling simulation may give me the tool I need to establish meaningful contact with them."

Tek Nal hesitated at that. "My Lord Haksith, I abase myself, but are you saying you believe these alien species are Shaha?"

"I keep my options open," Haksith muttered. "The Prefecture doesn't, and you know from your session with them why they can't admit the possibility. But even if they aren't Shaha, they are at least a Na Atal species much more evolved than ours. Now, I can't see an evolutionary purpose to highly evolved food animals unless natural selection gives them a means to avoid being eaten. That frightens me more than the possibility of your alien Shaha."

"Why? The idea of an alien Shaha species more advanced than ours sometimes makes me want to never leave the hot mud," Tek Nal confessed.

Haksith fixed a cold reptilian eye on the doctor. "Then consider an advanced Na Atal species long ago abandoned by its Shaha. Or worse, a Na Atal species capable of somehow killing off its Shaha creators with the same technology given them."

Tek Nal shook his head. "I don't believe it. If that were possible, then the sacred writings the priestesses are always going on about wouldn't be worth the parchment they're written on."

"Well, I've got to prepare for the possibility that maybe they're not," Haksith said.

"Now just wait a damn minute," Tek Nal said, holding up one clawed finger before Haksith's eyes. "I'm not crossing holy writ, not for you, not for Bleniss, not for the Prefecture, and not even for the Satrap. The priestesses would have a fit. They'd revoke my right to mate. They can even have me taken into the continental interior desert, have me staked to the blistering hot baked clay ground, and skinned alive. You must be out of..."

"Calm down, Doctor. Not long ago you came close to having your head twisted from your body in the Prefecture chamber. I'm not suggesting any blasphemy, and I'm not asking you to ignore the writ of the priestesses. I'm looking for answers to potential problems. You develop the mammalian psychological profiling software. If need be, I can ask it how it would proceed against any moves I might make and use the output to develop strategy. If we capture a dagan-Na Atal alien, you can use its brain to improve your neural network design. As long as you have the catalyst software ready for geode programming when we arrive, then your job as far as the Prefecture is concerned is done so long as we leave a few thousand carbon catalyst machines placed on the moon. After that, you're Bleniss's for whatever need he has for a scientist. That means you're mine."

"Outstanding," Tek Nal muttered. "So what happens when we arrive in system TX-3767?"

"Bleniss plans to split the Fleet into three task forces. A small survey team will go to the moon. The other two will depart for the outer system. One will pick up the raw geodes and the other task force will begin evacuating the completed and near-completed LACs. How long we remain here will depend on how long it takes the research shipyard to power up the new heavy cruiser. While the engineers and research scientists are doing that, you will use their equipment to program the smaller geodes for catalyst operations. Even if the prototype heavy cruiser leaves with the primary task force, we and you will not be leaving until we seed the moon with your geodes."

"Do I have priority in the ship's research laboratories?" Tek Nal asked.

"Oh, absolutely. Take whatever personnel you need. Bleniss secured a few of the geodes from Military Research and Development for you to work with. That said, remember this. They are few in number, so don't squander your resources, or your stay in the research shipyard will take even longer."

Tek Nal nodded.

"Good. Report to the research laboratories and begin your work, My Lord Doctor."

✦✦✦

Several days later Tek Nal was still puzzling over the crystal structure of the system TX-3767 geodes, their trace element content and their molecular structure. Crystal technology wasn't new. Shaha had been using crystals to grow electronic devices for centuries. As the technology improved, Shaha even grew complete devices, buildings, and vehicles. A city's age was obvious at a distance by the glitter of crystal towers and walls in the light of the three suns. Starfleet's ships were all grown crystal structures, and starship hulls used the most intricate of crystal patterns and elemental doping techniques. But these geodes! He could grow them into flying diamonds with superconducting fractures. The material could be grown into structures that reduced emissions to nearly zero. Haksith had been right about the improved FTL and sublight propulsion possibilities. With energy losses so low, efficiency increased. And their structural strength! The things could take a beating without a scratch. The possibilities were endless. Tek Nal loaded the finished crystal set carbon catalyst program into the computer for simulation tests.

He sat back. Even the 8,080-bit quantum computer he had snagged from the science officer's quarters would take some time to put the program through its paces.

That meant he had time to consider the mammal profiling project. He had neural maps from the animals on Meerslah on record. Too bad he didn't have a neural map from an alien dagan-Na Atal species, but the few they had captured had been eaten as delicacies. No one would have thought about keeping a choice piece of living meat aside for cellular mapping.

Too bad, he hissed. Then he had an idea. The geode structure made them ideal quantum computer base material.

Why not create a mammalian brain with a Shaha profile in a geode?

To the desert with Haksith's intelligence profile. What if he could somehow prove that mammals could attain Shaha sentience?

12
FOUR HOURS FROM IOTA HOROLOGII HELIOPAUSE, ABOARD HENRI EDDA

Ambassador Alan Dean Winters threw the blanket aside and rolled out of bed.

Shower.

He listened. The hatch between his and the co-Ambassador's quarters remained wide open in accordance with Eyloni social custom. VIP quarters had their own bathrooms and showers, and Winters listened for the shower running in their quarters.

The subdued white noise drumming of water on the tiles told him that the coast was clear.

He grabbed a towel, ran into his shower and slapped the preprogrammed temperature control, relieved.

That first shower days ago had been awkward, when Anlann and Seralin showed themselves eager to shower with him with no signs of modesty whatsoever.

The shower, a blue-tiled three-meter square with sides just as high, was covered with multiple independent nozzles, each one spraying at its own temperature and pressure. The combined sprays easily covered every imaginable body angle. More than one person could shower at the same time. Anlann and Seralin had concluded it had been designed just for that purpose.

Eyloni showering and bathing together was socially acceptable behavior but using the toilet and brushing teeth in the presence of others absolutely was not. He had to remember not to answer the visual comm or a call from the open hatch with a toothbrush sticking in his mouth.

He had been surprised to find them stepping into the shower with him. His surprise had been reflected in his body odor. Both co-Ambassadors had picked up on it right away. Embarrassed far more than they, Winters tried to explain how they had caught him off guard and invited them to remain.

But in the days since, Winters made sure they were both up and well into their showering before he took his.

He took his time, enjoying the hot water and the steam it produced. That in itself explained his continued solitary showers. Anlann and Seralin enjoyed showering in room temperature or cooler water. In fact, on their world they would have headed off to streams, pools, or small waterfalls to bathe. Winters wondered how they could stand the cool water given their four degree Celsius higher than human body temperature. They hadn't cared for his hot steamy shower, either. Seralin reminded him how warm Elleio's climate was. It made no sense to heat water for hygienic purposes there. She said that once he had lived there for a few weeks he would want to bathe in a stream, too.

Winters's second shock came at the end of the first day, when Seralin climbed into bed with him, Anlann close behind.

They had been assigned these same VIP quarters, but the suite still didn't feel like their sleeping abode. As Anlann's Protectress, she slept with him all the time. It wasn't in Eyloni nature to sleep alone. It was hard to explain, but he told them he needed to sleep alone in order to get a good night's sleep, but naps during the day could include them if they wanted.

They did, and Winters had learned more about Eyloni social customs over the past several days from the co-Ambassadors than he ever had from the cultural lectures the diplomatic corps pulled him into while he had been Captain of *Henri Edda*. The still missing Ambassador Harrison had held him captive through interminably long meetings with briefing materials filled with what Winters now knew to be mistaken or outright inaccurate guesswork about Eyloni culture.

No wonder the co-Ambassadors had detested Harrison.

The diplomatic staff had also urged Winters to speak half-truths and to evade on certain key matters. He spent over two hours explaining to them Eyloni empathic sense and how it linked to emotions conveyed through body odors. Hell, he even tried an illustrative example: when you lied, unless you either truly had no concerns about getting caught, or you believed what you were saying, your self-conscious doubt in the lie triggered pheromonal and physiological changes such as rapid heartbeat and heavy breathing. Pheromones changed body odor and tagged the lie for Eyloni noses.

Even that patient lecture had eluded the diplomats. They wanted to know how Senior Chief Warrant Officer Marsch had gained Eyloni confidence.

How could Winters explain Marsch to people who believed in plausible deniability as a diplomatic tool? Marsch was honest to a fault and, as near as Winters could tell, was incapable of telling a direct lie. Marsch evaded with mastery but nail him down on a matter and he'd either give in, or he'd respond with "ask me no secrets, and I'll tell you no lies," which meant whatever he said next had fictional overtones. More often though Marsch refused to say anything, or he'd bluntly say that it was no lie to keep the truth to himself.

Marsch's special operations group command had respected his honesty, and it had drawn the Eyloni to him like bees to a flower.

Winters breathed in the steam and let the needle jets massage his skin with scalding water as he slipped into the captain analytical mode he had begun to cultivate since first becoming a starship commander. Anlann and Seralin said they would meet a task force of at least six ships. Well, they'd said eleven, but Marsch had warned Winters months ago to keep human and Eyloni number systems straight. Anlann's eleven was his six. But Anlann had also said not to be surprised if they found a battle group of fourteen ships and their screening elements: *nine* ships.

Winters had asked Anlann what ship classes the Compact would send.

Seralin interrupted to tell him they expected to meet one battleship, two heavy battlecruisers, two assault battlecruisers, and four destroyers before Anlann could open his mouth.

Assault battlecruisers? He asked her if *Hunter's Moon* was an assault battlecruiser.

Yes, Seralin had said. Marsch's ship would be the second planetary assault battlecruiser. She had stoutly declared with absolute certainty that he would be there.

Winters had his doubts. That ship should be in drydock for some time, at least four months, maybe as long as half a year.

It was possible, Anlann had allowed. If Marsch came, then, Anlann had said, two more destroyers would come along with him.

Seralin had assured Winters Marsch would sortie with the battle group. She said that was why they were heading for Iota Horologii rather than Elleio.

Winters couldn't for the life of him follow her logic.

Surefooted would not come unless Marsch had joined the battle group. Anlann seemed certain Marsch would come and had been since the message he received from the Compact Counsel confirming Marsch's ship would take part in the reserve task force.

Seralin had said something about the Mistress of the Hunt not allowing it had she doubted repairs could be made in time for Marsch to participate in ships movement.

Winters cut off the water, popped the door latch, and grabbed a towel. He hated the full-body dryers.

The mission? The operative presumption had been that there was a Lizard research outpost and prototype dock site somewhere near Iota Hor. Certainly not in the system itself, or at least not in the inner system. The star did have a Kuiper belt and an Oort cloud. The Kuiper belt supplied the system with several hundred ice balls in stable orbits along with rocky asteroids by the thousands. But no Kuiper belt object in the search volume matched the required parameters. The Oort cloud contained its share of both short period and long-term comets and a surprising number of planetesimals and dwarf planets between the size of Ceres and Pluto. If anything hid in the Iota Hor system, then it must be hiding in the Oort cloud.

Winters stepped from the shower, dressed, and headed for the open hatch leading into the co-Ambassadors' quarters.

Anlann looked up from his seat at the kitchenette table. "Good morning Alan. You slept well, I trust?"

"I did. Thank you, Anlann. Good morning Seralin," he said to the yawning Hunter. "I see you did not sleep well."

Seralin's ears twitched, giving her a pensive expression. "I am not tired, and I slept well. He is doing it to me," she accused, pointing her tail at a grinning Anlann.

"Doing? You? What are you…<yawn>… doing to her?" Winters asked Anlann.

"You see?" Seralin accused. "He is doing it to you, too!"

"Doing what, exactly? Anlann?"

"I am thinking in emotional terms about sleep, and she is smelling it on my scent, and the pheromonal empathy is triggering her yawn reflex."

"And watching her yawn is making me…<yawn>…yawn, too." Winters said.

Anlann twitched his ears, his expression for mild humor Winters knew by now.

"Would you join us for the mid-day meal?" Seralin asked.

"Breakfast," Winters muttered. "Thank you. I am honored."

Careful, he warned himself. Don't talk with food in your mouth. Eyloni didn't talk while eating. The co-Ambassadors would stop eating and clean their hands, faces, and chests before they replied to any question or comment he made. To prevent interrupting their meals, he had learned to keep his mouth shut until they finished eating.

He had learned quite a lot during the cohabitation. The two communicated to each other at table using ears, tails, facial expressions postures and scents. But they never spoke through the open mouth, although a closed-mouth growl or grumble passed as acceptable.

Drinking didn't come under such strict table manners. They told him he could decline eating a meal and just talk as they ate and listened. If they wanted to say anything, then they went through the ritual cleansing before they replied. It had taken him almost a week to learn how to converse at the table in Eyloni fashion.

Anlann snickered under his breath, smelling the reference Winters's pheromones drew in his mind. He swallowed, drank water from a glass, wiped his face delicately, stepped far from the table, and sang in deep trilling laughter.

His laughter threatened to trigger Winters's funny bone as he likewise drank from a glass, wiped his face and chest, and joined the male co-Ambassador, laughing hilariously.

Together they turned on Seralin.

She glared at them as she calmly chewed her food. She swallowed, ate all her oranges, grapefruit, grapes, and celery. Then she drank all her fruit juice, then drank water. She took care as she wiped her mouth, her face, and then lifted the flimsy colored knots on strings draped over her breasts and wiped them until certain not a speck of chewed food remained on her yellow-trimmed orange and red-shaded orange skin.

Then she shook her head at their laughter.

Males are strange, she grumbled to herself. She thought Alan too mature to behave in such a manner. Her warleader? Well, he sometimes acted like a silly idiot, so why should today be any different? Though honestly she thought Alan's scent image of their table manners, so serious, was a bit funny at that.

She allowed herself a small smile and flicked her ears at them.

"She's trying not to laugh, Anlann," Winters said, after he got his own laughter under control.

"Yes. She is laughing on the inside. I can smell her humor in the air."

Seralin made a face at him.

"She looks like she doesn't want to put up with us, Anlann."

Seralin made a wistful sound, and the two males, one Eyloni and one not, embraced and held opposite arms out to her.

Seralin stepped around the table and slowly approached them, twisting her tail around Anlann's hips as she hugged Winters.

"I do not know which one of you is the bad influence on the other," she complained. She made direct eye contact with Winters, her arms remaining around his shoulders.

Winters listened. Eyloni directness stressed eye contact. The Hunter had a narrower build than a woman, almost willowy, but as a natural tree climber she possessed great strength. She could likely rip his face off.

"That was bad manners," Seralin told Winters. "If your intent was to make him blow food all over the table, us, and himself, then you acted in bad form."

Eyloni social customs had more pitfalls than what seemed apparent at first blush, and Winters wondered for a fleeting moment how well Marsch was evading breaches in etiquette.

Anlann helped Seralin clear the table. "Catch!" he yelled, tossing an apple to Winters.

Winters caught the fruit and took a bite. Eating away from the table was allowed, as was all snacking, but Eyloni manners demanded he watch his chewing and swallowing, and he still had to wipe his mouth.

He gnawed persistently at the apple core while watching the co-Ambassadors clear the table. They worked as a team in all things and seemed to know where one would reach, or when the other would grab.

The teamwork recalled a memory of his grandparents. His grandmother washed dishes, by hand, and his grandfather dried them with a towel and stacked them in the cupboards.

"Yes," Seralin said, looking right at Winters, "but usually not just me alone."

"No, actually. You and often the others. You think I cannot do anything for myself," Anlann complained playfully.

"We should be getting close now," Winters said, turning the mood in the room serious.

"Yes, about twelve hours or so," Anlann said.

"Anlann, what are we going to do if the Compact battle group isn't there yet?"

"I have been considering this, and Seralin made a good point last night. She pounced on me as I slept and started talking about it."

"About what? Our arrival here? Or if we would arrive early?"

"I told him we would arrive first," Seralin interrupted.

"You're anticipating the battle group's late arrival?"

"Yes I am."

"Why?" Winters asked.

"Call it a feeling, but I know the A'tayotan will let deployment slip by a day or two if Delwyn needs those hours to complete repairs. They will not wait any longer. Doing so would dig too deep into Delwyn's timetable."

"So we're going to sit around in the heliopause a bit. Hmm…Maybe I'll ask Captain Rodgers to send a probe or two to Ibeetu and have her try and find Ambassador Harrison and his cultural attaché."

"I do not think they are on Ibeetu, Alan," Anlann said, quite seriously.

"No?"

Anlann shook his head. "Not alive anyway," he amended.

"What do you know Anlann?" Winters demanded.

"Nothing with absolute certainty, but if someone aboard Delwyn's ship thought Harrison had placed him in danger? Well, tribal law is quite clear on such matters."

"What law?" Winters pressed.

Anlann glanced at Seralin in appeal.

"Long before the Compact Counsel had been formed, tribal law declared that deliberate harm directed against a male without honorable grounds to justify it must be addressed at once by any hierarchy having knowledge of such a crime," Seralin sang at ritual tempo.

"What does that mean?"

"Killed, Alan. Females never allow anyone who directs harm against a male absent honorable cause to live," Seralin said.

"*You* killed them Seralin?" Winters asked, aghast.

"No. Of course not, although the obligation would have fallen to me if no other female could act."

Winters let that pass. "So you're saying someone aboard Marsch's ship killed them?"

"I am not saying anything, Alan. I am just speculating. I could be wrong," she conceded.

###

Ambassador Winters strolled up to the command chair.

"Captain," he began, "the co-Ambassadors think it's possible the Compact battle group may be as much as a day behind us, depending on whether or not they decided to wait on Marsch's ship."

"Just a day? Well, it can't matter much. We are headed for the same jump point we plotted for after we picked up the distress call from *Hunter's Moon* and diverted here to lend assistance. I don't expect any contacts farther into the system than the heliopause termination shock, the shock wave made as the star's solar wind decelerates to 350,000 klicks per hour. We're coming in a fair distance from the star, and we already know there isn't much to see looking from the heliopause back into the system."

"We didn't do much looking at the asteroids, comets, and dwarf planets at the time though, either," Winters pointed out.

"No," Rodgers agreed, "nothing fancy. Long-range scanning considered only the sector bisected by the Lizard probe's out-of-system transmission."

"Which was what? Maybe an arc-length a hundred billion kilometers long along the plane of the ellipse with the Lizard debris field at its center, plus or minus one hundred-thousand klicks above and below the ellipse at that point? That's not much."

"We were looking for a courier probe or even a small ship at the time, not an astronomical body," Rodgers reminded him.

"I know, I know, but we were there for over a month. You'd have thought we'd have looked the system over better than we did," Winters shouted, mad at himself. He had been captain at the time.

"Why, Captain? We sent squadrons to check out the gas giant and the local space between it and Ibeetu. Then we cleared the system from

179

the sun to the Kuiper belt. That was a lot of volume to scan. Besides, at the time we expected incoming from Chi Eridani, not from some ice ball in the Oort cloud. If there had been a military presence there, it'd have paid us a visit long before the probe sent its transmission. And Captain, I think Marsch may have been onto something, but I don't think he's right that they fired off the courier probe from the destroyers. I think the probe Melkorka destroyed on Ibeetu locked onto a courier probe on-station somewhere along the transmission path. We found no data in the transmission burst before it cut off, but it should have at least activated emergency action protocols. Those protocols should have sent it on its merry way to some preprogrammed target: a ship."

"A ship to where, Captain Rodgers?" Anlann asked.

"To the system I noted earlier, Chi Eridani."

Winters shook his head. "We should have been fired upon long before *Hunter's Moon* had her FTL up and running again. Chi Eridani is too close to think otherwise."

"I don't think so, Sir," Rodgers said. "Think about it. *Hunter's Moon* destroyed three destroyers and for all the Lizards knew, maybe the prototype LAC as well. What assets can they have supporting some dinky outpost? The three destroyers, the prototype LAC, a supply ship, and maybe a frigate or two? Even together they couldn't stand up to a battle-damaged Compact warship, let along an undamaged *Henri Edda.*"

"No," Seralin interrupted. "The captured equipment would have fled with any frigate. Why should it remain behind?"

"Overconfidence?" Rodgers shrugged. "Keep it here to spy on us, find out if we know anything, if our presence had been coincidental or for an altogether different purpose. But this raises a question. Sometime between the first and the second neutrino bursts on Ibeetu, the LAC should have been the courier itself, delivering intelligence to another ship, which then beat feet out of the system."

"That presupposes the Lizards had another ship, and I just don't think they did. A second ship could have been keeping tabs on the LAC and should have had more than enough time to capture it back during the time Marsch was trying to figure out how to pilot it back into Iota Hor's heliopause," Winters said.

"I agree," Anlann said. "Which means Delwyn's presumption that a courier probe fired from the last destroyer remains the best possible scenario. The only viable alternative is that they launched a courier probe from the research outpost itself sometime not long afterwards."

"Captain? Approaching normal space jump point. Hyperdrive coils read full power available. All systems are ready for the jump back into normal space," Carstairs interrupted.

"Very well, Mr. Carstairs. Decelerate into the jump coordinates and engage hyperdrive."

"Aye, Ma'am. Decelerating into optimal jump coordinates for arrival in the Iota Horologii heliopause. Jumping in…five, four, three, two, one…Now!"

The jump point formed in the violet shimmer of hyperspace and opened into a flower. It swallowed the ship, which instantly reappeared in the black void and white stars of normal space.

"Jump complete, Captain. All clear, no traffic, and no damage reported. Systems report nominal," Lieutenant Carstairs said.

"Very well," Rodgers said. She swiveled her command chair around and looked up at Anlann.

"What do you recommend we do while we wait for your warship, co-Ambassador Anlann?"

"The battle group will jump to these coordinates. Our mission briefing," Anlann said, indicating Seralin as well, "advised us not to give ourselves away. You are in Compact territory, a guest of the Compact Counsel. We would be distressed if harm came to you or your crew as you convey us to our warship.

"My preference? I think we should use the time to develop an accurate picture here using passive scanning resources."

"Prudent," Rodgers said. "Lieutenant Vincent?"

"Captain?" Dianna Debra Vincent, the CIC bridge liaison officer, replied.

"If the Lizards have an outpost in this system, then there are many places to hide it. Care to speculate on likely spots?"

Vincent called up the system's summary and made her report.

"Iota Horologii is a young star, only 625 million years old. Its single planet remains hellishly hot from its recent birth. Its moon, Ibeetu, possesses an established ecosystem. The science survey teams from CECS *Alexandra Witze* proposed a theory. The moon's advanced plants and animals arose from its exosystem origin. Captain Lahiri indicated in her logs something about Ibeetu being a body from outside this system captured long ago by the gas giant. Everything the moon needed to jump-start life it brought with it. The only thing it needed was the warmth a goldilocks habitable zone provides and a hot core heated up by tidal forces as it orbits the gas giant. For being such a young sun, there are few planetesimal-sized objects in the inner system. The gas giant has cleared out its orbital path, and there are no significant asteroid belts within 300 AU of the star. There's not much of a Kuiper belt either, considering the star's youth."

"What about the Oort cloud?" Rodgers asked.

Vincent paused a moment. "Negligible data, Ma'am. The system's Oort cloud is irregular and well-populated with millions of elliptical, parabolic, and hyperbolic orbiting objects ranging from 5,000 AU to 100,000 AU from the star."

"That's still a lot of space to search," Carstairs offered.

"Won't have to," Rodgers replied. "Realistically speaking, it's empty space, and we'd be looking for bodies large enough to host a small but significant shipyard. Bodies that are bigger than Ceres and smaller than Pluto. We can perform passive scans for dwarf planets while we sit here waiting. That's about as emission-quiet as looking through a telescope."

"What about the nearest star?" Winters asked.

"The closest, Chi Eridani, is seven light-years away, a G8IV subgiant and unremarkable. It has little to recommend it other than the fact that it's a star, which makes it a good jump target," Rodgers said.

"Anlann?" Winters asked.

"Captain Rodgers is correct. The Ni'zakhonii tried to use this star, Surutia we call it, as a rendezvous point and staging area for an invasion into Compact territory. There are some sizable stony planetesimals close in to the star, but the rubble failed to accrete."

"Captain?" Carstairs interrupted. "What about q-1 Eridani? It's an F9V yellow-white dwarf, a young star about two billion years old. It's nine light-years away and has a Jupiter mass gas giant some 2 AU away from it, an asteroid belt at 25 AU, and a Kuiper belt at 300 AU."

Seralin flattened her ears and shook her head. "Not there. The Compact fought a major battle there and afterwards seeded the system with hyperlink relays. If anything is hiding in the grass waiting to yank our tails, then it must be hiding in Surutia or here in the Nikkiolo system."

"Or neither, as in no secret research outpost lurking on the fringes of Compact space," a skeptical Rodgers muttered. "Mr. Carstairs drop a marker buoy to let the Compact battle group know we are here. Senior Chief Marsch will know what it means."

"Aye, Captain. Marker buoy launched, programmed to transmit a low-power limited–range beacon the moment it detects a Compact vessel entering its passive scanning radius."

"Very well. Begin passive scanning a conical volume with its apex originating at Ibeetu's orbit at the time when the surface probe transmitted its truncated signal, beginning at the conical section defined by our current position and continuing outward into the Oort cloud. Pinpoint all bodies 800 kilometers in diameter and larger."

"Aye Captain, commencing scan."

"How long will it take?" Rodgers asked.

"On passive short-range FTL scan only? Given the volume, four hours nineteen minutes just to pinpoint bodies meeting the requisite parameters. If I open the FTL scan wormhole up to active scan, it may be detected. The time it will take to passively scan each world will depend on its spin. It'll take even longer if we find any having long retrograde spins. It often happens when a body suffers a collision with another body. It's rare, but Pluto spins backwards and Triton is also in a retrograde orbit around Neptune. If there have been collisions in this system long ago then it's possible we might find a tiny ice ball with a weeks-long day. But comparing the body's topography will resolve the issue."

"Very well. Continue."

"Aye, Captain."

***

Over the next four hours Lieutenant Vincent found a manageable seven bodies ranging between 848 and 2,100 kilometers across. All of them rocky ice balls, and they stretched across a distance between 7,700 AU and 67,350 AU, or between one and ten trillion kilometers away.

Even at full sublight they wouldn't reach the closest one for 89 days and the most distant one for an interminable 780 days. Scanning one or two using the active FTL sensors might go unnoticed but scanning all seven raised the chance of being detected by enemy scanners to forty-two percent.

Vincent delivered the bad news to Captain Rodgers.

"Can you plot a median jump point, Mr. Carstairs? Maybe we can jump closer to their vicinity and go on sublight from there," Rodgers said.

"Well, as you know Captain, hyperdrive is meant for traveling interstellar distances, not interplanetary ones. Jump accuracy uncertainty over distances less than say, two hundred AU makes pinpoint accuracy impossible. Jumps can be off by anywhere between one and two AU. For every multiple two hundred AU increase in jump distance, arrival accuracy improves by 24,939,500 kilometers, which means we can jump back into normal space accurately over distances exceeding 1,292 AU. I can put us alongside one of them, but once we arrive in their midst, it will be impossible to hit a second target with any accuracy. They have a sublight travel time between three and nine days at point five-0 cee maximum velocity, except for the three far enough away for accurate hyperdrive jumps."

Lieutenant Vincent objected. "Treat them like bogeys and program for target optimization, Ma'am."

"Target optimization? Yes, we could make successive jumps from diminishing most distant points until we drop below accurate arrival probability, and then run on sublight to the remaining few targets. Good thinking, Lieutenant."

"Thank you, Ma'am."

"Too bad we can't send the fighters two at a time to survey each body," Winters complained.

"Why can you not?" Anlann asked.

"Range. A fighter's hyperdrive endurance is about 300 AU there and back again. Even the alphafortresses are limited to hyperdrive jumps about 400 AU one way. Once we're in the local group we might be close enough to try it," Winters said. Then he shook his head. "No. Look at Mr.

Carstairs's plot. There's only two close enough, and even then only if we jump around a few times ourselves first." He shook his head again. "No, Lieutenant Vincent has the right idea. Treat the dwarf planets as enemy ships and pick them off one-by-one until we have no choice but to proceed at sublight velocity."

Rodgers nodded. "Mr. Carstairs, program for optimized multiple target hyperspace jumps, starting with the most distant body."

"Aye, Captain. Plotting hyperdrive course for staggered multiple jumps. First target, an Eris-type dwarf planet 67,350 AU distant. Time in hyperspace fourteen hours, forty minutes, forty-four seconds. Ready to implement, Ma'am."

Rodgers glanced at Winters. "Captain? Jump time here and back is about thirty hours. The Compact battle group would have to wait for us."

Winters glanced at Anlann. Their orders specified getting him and his Protectress to their ship and then to run for Elleio. He shook his head. "Plot for the nearest one, and we'll reevaluate after we get there."

"You heard the man, Mr. Carstairs," Rodgers said.

"Yes, Ma'am. Plotting for the nearest body, 7,700 AU distant, a Haumea-class object. Time in hyperspace, one hour, forty minutes, forty-two seconds. Course laid in, Captain. Ready to engage hyperdrive."

"Engage hyperdrive," Rodgers ordered.

"Aye, Captain."

An hour and forty minutes later *Henri Edda* jumped back into normal space near an ice-covered rock pockmarked with small ancient craters. Twenty minutes of scanning later they found nothing and headed for another target, a journey only five minutes by hyperdrive.

Same thing found, same result obtained.

The third try, a Ceres-class asteroid, mostly rock, took them eleven minutes to reach.

They found nothing there, either.

Vincent checked the scanner updates on the dwarf planets they had remaining and noticed a data summary inconsistent for a body so far from its sun.

"Captain Rodgers?"

"Yes, Ms. Vincent?"

"Ma'am, the next target is a Pluto-class dwarf 2,741 AU distant, thirty-five minutes, fifty-one seconds distant via hyperspace. Long-range passive FTL sweeps have found several interesting features, Ma'am."

"Report, Lieutenant."

"Aye, Captain. My scans show a world vibrant and diverse. Mountains, canyons, icy bedrock, and nitrogen snow are among the features shaping this dwarf plant. An anomalous area in the southern hemisphere has scalloped icy troughs and hills, hinting at an active geology. The region emits unusually high carbon monoxide concentrations. These are mountains made from water ice as tall as the

Himalayas surrounding the anomaly area. Fresh nitrogen and methane snow blanket the peaks. At the extremely low temperature there, water ice is as hard as bedrock. While the brighter anomalous area is coated in nitrogen, methane, and carbon monoxide ice, the surrounding darker region is stained by hydrocarbons tarnished by long exposure to the local sun's ultraviolet radiations."

"What about this anomalous area, Lieutenant? Where is it exactly, and what's it doing?" Rodgers asked.

"I'm seeing complex atmospheric phenomena there, some kind of protrusion above the morning terminator in the southern hemisphere. It covers the southeastern corner of the hemisphere."

"What kind of protrusion, Lieutenant?" Rodgers demanded.

"A plume of some kind, almost volcanic in nature according to the computer modeling, with shapes varying from double-blob protrusions to pillar-like particle ejections. I classify this activity as abnormal."

"What do you think, Captain?" Rodgers asked Winters.

"It isn't volcanism. Cryovolcano maybe? A blast of dry ice or water ice crystals?"

"No, Mr. Ambassador," Vincent said. "There isn't enough thermal variance to account for a cryonic blowout. The core is cold rock, and there are no nearby moons to cause even minimal tidal heating. It's too far from its sun, at least right now, for dry ice to sublimate, which this would otherwise be, since it's certain no liquid water exists below ground there."

"Dry ice? Frozen carbon dioxide?" Winters speculated aloud. "Dry ice melts directly into a gas, it sublimates, and the temperature is low enough to keep it frozen. I wonder if the rust-colored hydrocarbons surrounding the area are absorbing enough solar energy to allow the dry ice to sublimate?"

"Lieutenant Vincent, check on that," Rodgers said.

"Aye, Captain," Vincent scanned the high-resolution image as sensors generated a thermal map from the sensor return data.

Vincent swore under her breath. "Insufficient thermal gradient of any size or lasting long enough exists to explain such a large plume of particulate matter."

"Surface activity?" Rodgers asked.

"Surface scans report nitrogen ice and dry ice traces," Vincent said.

"Dry ice snow on frozen nitrogen ground. Something's kicking carbon dioxide and nitrogen gas up into the thin atmosphere, adding to the eons of accumulated dry ice. There can't be much wind there," Winters speculated aloud.

"The plum rises too high into the atmosphere," Seralin said. "Can you perform forward radiative transfer modeling of the reflected intensity?" she asked Vincent. "A model like this corrects for multiple scattering and curvature effects for any grazing sunlight and slanted views of the surface. For optical properties, using wavelength-dependent indices of refraction, you should be able to rule in or out dust particle contaminates."

"Yes, co-Ambassador Seralin. I have the radiative modeling data available, but optical properties analysis data is still coming in. There are anomalies, as the plumes don't appear to incorporate water ice or dry ice alone."

"Water ice in the plume implies enough thermal activity to melt water ice either by pressure heating or by direct thermal emissions," Rodgers said. "Could it be an ultraviolet aurora? Carbon monoxide in the atmosphere might allow for this if a coronal mass ejection from Iota Hor happened by coincidence to hit the surface."

Vincent shook her head. "No, Ma'am. Insufficient carbon monoxide, and insufficient solar activity this far out to even hint at the possibility. Updated analysis from the latest scans show particulates in a plume at densities of 120 per cubic meter and trending along the models predicting for either large temperature drops down to at least one hundred degrees Kelvin, for vigorous updrafts due to dry convection under high isolation, or for dust heating coming from soaking up solar radiation.

"As to the first scenario, the temperature data implies that a drop to one hundred degrees Kelvin is impossible. The second scenario suffers because high isolation should occur at local noon and not during local morning."

"What is the particulate matter? Besides all the ice," Rodgers asked.

Vincent scrolled through the spectral analysis summary. "Iridium, Captain. Iridium and carbon crystals in low amounts. The probable carbon types read as graphene and pure carbon crystals."

Anlann and Seralin glanced at one another, and then they glanced at Winters as he too made the connection.

"Captain Rodgers, the LAC Marsch stole from the Lizards had a hull made from crystallized iridium and carbon."

"Bingo!" Lieutenant Carstairs said.

"Yes, bingo Mr. Carstairs," Rodgers said dryly and turned to the three ambassadors.

"Well co-Ambassador Anlann, it looks like we found your hidden Lizard outpost."

"We do not know that for certain," Anlann objected. "This is likely the raw material source the Ni'zakhonii used to build their prototype. According to the analysis Delwyn gave to the A'tayotan, he believed it came from a natural geode, or that the Ni'zakhonii may have discovered how to grow them from base crystals."

Rodgers stared at the Eyloni male for a moment before turning to Winters.

"What do you suggest, Captain?" she asked him.

"That is not for me to say, Judith. You are the Captain, and you don't have a dog in this hunt. Your orders require you to deliver the co-

Ambassadors to the Compact warship *Surefooted* in Iota Hor's heliopause and then take me to Elleio. Anything else must be a command decision, your command decision."

Captain Judith Arleen Rodgers stared at nothing for a minute and weighed her options. She had limited leeway in interpreting her orders. Ostensibly she had been ordered to convey the ambassadors to Elleio, but the orders the Admiralty gave, orders confirmed by Admiral Samson himself in person, suggested she had the option to gather as much intelligence as possible without endangering the ambassadors, her ship, or her crew. She was not to engage in joint naval operations with the Compact battle group.

"What do you think, Exec?" she asked Commander Cabrera.

"If we can confirm a target and transmit that data to the Compact ships, then they can jump into normal space within striking distance of the dwarf planet and achieve total surprise, isn't that right, co-Ambassador Anlann?"

"It is possible," Anlann began, "but to be useful, the battle group must receive updated jump coordinates before they begin programming for the last jump into this system. Once their ships' jump drives begin constructing quantum singularities, they are committed to one of two actions. They can either continue building their singularities and commit to the programmed jump coordinates, or they can bleed off the energy, wasting it, and program a new jump point and start the energy buildup from the beginning. The second option takes time and a lot of energy."

"So our hyperlink signal has to reach them when? Prior to the jump before the last one? That can't be right. If our estimates are correct, then they must be building up for their final jump into the system right now." Rodgers said.

"Captain?" Lieutenant Romine interrupted. "Can't we at least give the battle group a heads up? The Lizards have no hyperlink capability."

Rodgers considered the chief communications officer's idea. "Lieutenant Vincent?"

"Captain?"

"What about Romaine's idea? Hyperlink requires a tap from the hyperdrive coils to open the mobius hyperlink port. Could a Lizard sensor array detect the power signature?"

"I doubt it, Captain. It depends on how close we are to it and its sensitivity, but hyperlink is far less obvious than our jumps into normal space are."

"Co-Ambassador Anlann?" Rodgers appealed.

"The battle group should have arrived by now. That they have not suggests they are building up to their final jump right now, too late for them to change jump points. Even if they waited for Delwyn's warship, they would not have waited more than four days Tyreniioroneo Standard

Time, a bit over one and a half of your days. If they did, then they should be building up to the jump before the final one."

Winters turned to the co-Ambassadors. "Anlann? Contacting them makes a difference only if they did wait for Marsch. If they allowed a short delay and if I were Marsch, I'd have spent every second I could get making final checks before departure. Calculating jump intervals based on the projected delay departure time, how long do we have to contact them before they must begin programming for their final jump?"

"Forty-one hours," Seralin blurted.

"Forty-one hours?" Rodgers cried, "I thought Compact ships jumped every fourteen hours."

Winters smiled. "In Seralin's counting system and in the male time standard since she is relating a time measurement connected with spaceflight, she means twenty-four hours TST. That comes out to about ten hours, Earth time."

"Ten hours? We can find out quite a lot in ten hours. But I want options, so I think we'll download our intelligence to the buoy and transmit same to the battle group just in case they have finished programming for their final jump into the system.

"Ms. Romaine, acquire all tactical and intelligence summaries generated since we began scanning this conic volume of space and transmit it via tight-beam quantum encryption to the marker buoy."

"Aye, Captain. Accessing all data and routing to Cipher…and…ready to transmit, Ma'am."

"When you are ready, Lieutenant."

"Aye, Captain. Transmitting… transmission complete… talkback checksum confirms data integrity. The buoy is standing-by for Senior Chief Marsch's clearance codes."

"Well, that should make it impervious to tampering, but it also makes it unreadable to anyone else trying to gain access without Marsch's codes. I hope he's with the battle group, Anlann." Winters said.

"On that I have no doubt," Seralin answered for her warleader.

"Let's hope the Compact battle group remains committed to arriving at these coordinates, otherwise we've just wasted a marker buoy for nothing," Rodgers grumbled. "In the meantime we are going to do some snooping of our own."

"What do you have in mind, Captain?" Winters asked.

"I think we'll take a primitive tack and become a ball in a game of jacks."

"Jacks?" Seralin echoed as Rodgers's pheromones formed images in her empathic mind of an infant playing with a red ball and several tiny metal caltrops similar to the thorns the ancients scattered on trails to puncture the soles of pursuing feet.

"Small low-tech surface mobile probes. We carry hundreds of 'em," Winters clarified. He glanced at Rodgers. "How are you going to deploy them? Hyperbolic approach?"

"That was the general idea, yes," Rodgers confirmed. "Mr. Carstairs, plot a hyperspace jump for the closest hyperbolic cometary nucleus passing the dwarf within one AU."

"Aye, Captain. Searching for appropriate cometary debris…I don't see much out here to work with. Captain, best fit is a parabolic comet forty-three kilometers long and rotating at 2.7 kilometers per hour along its longitudinal axis. The body is solitary and without attendant fragments and no tail this far from the sun. It will pass within 340,000 kilometers of the target in five hours, forty-one minutes. That's its closest approach, Ma'am."

"Can you get us there without generating a large power signal, Lieutenant?"

"I think so, Captain," Carstairs said. "I can jump us into normal space so the comet nucleus is between us and the dwarf planet and then continue on in at orbital velocities. That will reduce propulsion emissions, and the low velocity will avoid the noise high speed particle impacts cause as they hit our navigation shields. The tricky part is playing catchup with the comet. We'll come in at a tangent to the dwarf's local space envelope. That means any random scan will pick us up as a parabolic orbit object closing on another parabolic orbit object in the same orbital domain. That will raise eyebrows, or whatever Lizards have for eyebrows."

"Can you make our approach look natural?" she asked him.

The navigator shook his head. "No Captain, not on a parabolic orbit. This comet reappears periodically, and it would seem odd for another parabolic intersecting orbit, one not predicted as a near-orbit impact object. The only unpredictable way to have us closing while passing for an asteroid is to plot a hyperbolic intercept in the vicinity and change orbits to the parabolic orbit when we intercept the comet.

"If the Lizards have plotted all the parabolic junk floating out here for impact hazard prediction, then our independent parabolic orbit should either be suspect, or herald a near-collision their plotting should have predicted and didn't. Hyperbolic approaches are better because they are one-time events and can't be predicted unless the body has been pre-sighted and its orbit calculated. If we get to the comet without being scanned, then we can hug it close enough to resemble a piece broken away from the nucleus."

"Scans will show different. We're a metal clinker next to a rocky ball of snow. Hell, even simple radar would tell them that much," Rodgers said.

"Close-order maneuvering?" Cabrera suggested.

"Over a rotating body?" Rodgers wondered aloud.

"It can be done," Carstairs said thoughtfully. "Get in close and fire thrusters to match velocities and attitude and settle into synchronous rotation."

"Do it," Rodgers ordered.

"Aye, Ma'am. Hyperspace plot for Pluto-class dwarf engaging. Jumping now. Hyperspace achieved. ETA to jump point, thirty-five minutes fifty-one seconds. Time to close-order intercept from re-entry to normal space, eighteen minutes."

Rodgers cringed at the jump into hyperspace, and then thirty-six minutes later clenched her teeth and cringed again hoping the Cherenkov radiation bow shock wave had been blocked by the comet's bulk up ahead.

Henri Edda crept along a pursuit course, closing at a rate several times faster than an Apollo mission Earth to Moon transit velocity, but dead slow by modern standards. Ship movement wasn't all zooming and swooping around like propeller-driven airplanes in dogfights.

"Approaching comet intercept point, Captain. We are 740,000 kilometers behind the comet on a hyperbolic course and closing."

"Understood," Rodgers said. "Overtake before we come into presumed near-approach object hazard scanning range."

"Aye, Captain. Closing…Maneuvering…Adjusting orbital velocity. If they look now, standard orbital scans will show us as an unpowered object in cometary orbit with an odd closure rate for two natural objects in an intersecting orbit. They shouldn't think much about it unless they notice we didn't speed past or collide with the comet nucleus, or if they get a visual on us."

"One can hope Lizards aren't interested in the orbital mechanics of their neighborhood once they had plotted all the possible impact hazards in this region. Bring us in and match velocities, Mr. Carstairs."

"Aye, Captain. IP coming up…Now. Adjusting orbit…orbital insertion completed. We are now in a parallel parabolic orbit with the comet. Setting up profile. We should look like a part of the cometary body to any basic scan they might take from the planet. My sensors are detecting significant iron mass in the nucleus. It should be enough to confuse a mass density return. Maneuvering into position and matching velocities. Firing broadside thrusters to match 2.7 kps roll rate."

Primitive, Winters thought. Using thrusters rather than helm navigation fields put a helmsman back into the action-reaction realm of thruster firing, a real pain in the ass for a twenty million tonne carrier. It took coordinated thruster activity to get the old girl going, and once she had her inertia, her direction and speed, it took a lot of equal and opposite thrusting to null her rates. The helm fields permitted reactionless and inertialess course adjustments, but they had detectable power signatures.

Carstairs made a few more checks on his plot and looked up. "Captain, we have achieved stable parabolic cometary orbit around Iota Horologii."

"Acknowledged. We are now the ball. Go emission silent. How long before we can throw some jacks, Mr. Carstairs?"

"Aye, Captain. Going emissions-silent. We can launch a jacks rack in five hours. It'll take the rack another eight hours to reach the dwarf planet."

###

The jacks worked best on low-gravity worlds as an alternative to rovers. They resembled one hundred-kilogram cubes that had blunted spikes sticking from each corner and out of the center of each side panel. They carried minimal equipment and no thrusters or engines. Each had a camera, a magnetometer to measure magnetic fields, a radiometer to measure temperature and radiation, a seismograph, an infrared microscope to study minerals, and a tight-beam radio rig that transmitted all data in pseudorandom bursts. They were built tough and could survive a five-hundred-meter plunge to the hard ground in Pluto's gravity. They didn't need anything more. Their small sensor suites sufficed to determine if intelligence had altered the terrain where they roved.

Each jack sported three internal flywheels, one for each axis of motion. Each flywheel had its independent electric motor. Each motor could reach different speeds. The jack trundled along the ground, rolling on its rounded jack-like barbs. It did so by using the inertial energy from its flywheels, spooling them up to maximum RPMs and then applying instant breaking. The sudden jerk would transfer to the jack's internal frame, which transferred enough momentum to kick the jack along the ground without generating any detectable energy signatures.

One hundred and twenty jacks were packed into a launch rack. The rack was then placed into the port side railgun breech. When Lieutenant Carstairs pressed the fire control, the magnetic bucket in the breech catapulted the launch rack down through the forward quarter to the bow gun port force field aperture. It remained closed except for a circle wide enough to pass the rack but restrain the bucket.

Inertia alone carried the launch rack and its cargo toward the dwarf planet at the ship's closure rate plus the railgun launch velocity.

Five hours later the launch rack hit its slingshot orbit and jettisoned its complement of jacks in a broadcast pattern, falling like seeds scattered from a farmer's hand, as it arced around and into synchronous orbit. The jacks continued along their suborbital courses, spreading out as they dipped into the meager atmosphere and decelerating further. Swinging down and around the tiny globe, the jacks fell at terminal velocity. Then atmospheric drag increased on them as they deployed their landing airbags and fell toward the heart of the atmospheric plumes blanketing the southern hemisphere.

They struck the hard surface like falling hail, but unlike hail they bounced back into the sky, some as high as four hundred meters before falling again. Bounce, bounce, bounce, like jawbreakers dropped on a concrete sidewalk they bounced before coming to rest. They deflated their airbags and assessed their internal systems and their landing zones.

Then they opened packet transmitters and networked to form a neural AI decision unit, formulated a strategy, and set off on their own haphazard paths to explore the particulate matter from the particle plumes falling on the frozen surface, to listen for seismic disturbances, and to look for power signatures.

The jacks wobbled off on their individual ways, lurching along from one spoke to another in zig-zag trails, much more efficient in the low gravity than anything as quaint as wheels or treads.

They found several signals, but because they had no analytical capability, they did not interpret but sent raw data back to the orbiting rack and it transmitted all collected data back to the Coalition carrier.

"Captain?" Lieutenant Vincent called. "I'm getting initial talkback telemetry from the rack. Out of the one hundred and twenty jacks sent, one hundred and nine have reported back. The Rack Surveillance Suite is up and running.

"The RSS orbital survey says the planet is surrounded by an asymmetric dust cloud observable as the rack achieved a near-equatorial retrograde orbit one hundred kilometers above the surface.

"Initial readings confirm atmospheric and surface compositions. Atmospheric analysis detects a layer of haze extending some one hundred kilometers above the surface, but the haze freezes thirty kilometers above that and falls back to the surface. The atmosphere contains methane, and the ultraviolet light from the sun interacts with it to produce complex hydrocarbons such as ethylene and acetylene. These gasses fall into the lower atmosphere, where they cool, and condense into ice particles. Ultraviolet light converts these icy hazes into other hydrocarbons, called tholins. When they high the ground, they give the surrounding region dark-reddish patches.

"There are also fine patterns of dust coming from jet-like openings on the surface in the anomalous area. Think of them as geyser holes. They come in two basic forms, quasi-circular depressions, and walled alcoves, ranging from as small as a few tens to as large as a few hundred meters across. They form pits below the ground, remarkably symmetric and similar in shape, having significant structural details such as horizontal layers and terraces, vertical streaks, and smooth floors covered with dust. Some pits are over a kilometer deep. Pits tend to cluster in small groups. Several of them are geyser-like active, expelling jets of heavy-fractured, globular particles.

"Naturally sublimating dry ice would take over seven thousand years to excavate pits like these given the composition of the planetoid and its star's characteristics. The symmetric shapes preclude natural erosive factors, which means the pits are probably associated with shaped explosive activity. This finding is contradicted by the amount of dust in the atmospheric plume and the bright particles falling over the darker tholins on the surface. Given the volume of the pits, the atmospheric plume and surface deposits should have several million times more material than what the jacks can account for.

"The jacks' seismographs also report impact signals at an irregular but constant repeating period superimposed onto a subdued noise carrier wave which suggests unnatural subsurface impact hammering and grinding," Vincent concluded.

"Co-Ambassador Anlann, I think we've found your raw materials source," Captain Rodgers said.

"One supposes so, Captain Rodgers," Anlann demurred, strikingly effete in mannerisms. "Well?" he asked Seralin.

His Protectress stood next to him, tail motionless, ears canted off to the sides of her head. "Mining you think, or demolitions?"

Vincent gasped and dove back under her scanner.

"I doubt it matters," Rodgers said.

"Captain!" Lieutenant Carstairs interrupted. "I'm detecting strong neutrino bursts and accompanying Cherenkov radiation spikes."

"The Compact battle group?" Rodgers asked.

"Negative, Ma'am. Emission angles correlated to the Cherenkov bursts confirm multiple Lizard FTL-capable ships dumping velocity from I-band."

"Where?" Cabrera demanded. "Have you got them on your plot yet?"

"No, Commander. Using passive scans takes a minute. Captain, I think there are at least two distinct groups. Seven ships are heading for the dwarf planet; a second task force of twelve ships have jumped in near a small Ceres-class asteroid some 343 AU from here."

"That's where the shipyard is located," Winters said. "I've been a fool. You don't want to lift a ship from a gravity well of any significance, even a dwarf's. You'd build the drydock into a crevasse inside a small body."

"Dammit, Marsch was right all along," Rodgers swore. "Well, co-Ambassador Anlann, co-Ambassador Seralin, I hope you are as right about the current position of the Compact battle group, because we can't let them jump into the system blind to this threat. Where do you suggest they reprogram their jump? To the main body?"

Anlann's tail swayed faster as an intense expression filled his face. "Not all of them. With your permission, I will contact them with your Mistress of Communications' assistance."

"Proceed," Rodgers said.

Anlann nodded, and both he and Seralin glided over to the red-haired communications officer's station.

13
COMMAND DECISION

Delwyn just happened to stroll across the Warleader's Watch to see how Saidrinha was settling in when he noticed Hlindredreda's ears twitch in disbelief at her instruments.

"What, Hlindredreda?" he asked, alert.

His tone caused Melkorka to freeze and tense.

"Message on hyperlink from Anlann aboard the Coalition warship *Henri Edda*, Delwyn."

"Directed at who?" he asked his Mistress of Communications.

"To all ships generally."

Which meant to all warleaders. A warleader never knew when he might have to assume Warpact command over the battle group, and compartmentalizing mission-critical information was not a part of Compact military policy. The A'tayotan often compartmentalized information among themselves or other hierarchies, but fleets never did so. To do so might risk male lives and the lives of the females protecting their warleaders.

"On screen," Delwyn said. "Let's hear what Anlann has to say. Oh, Hlindredreda? Make sure Ahwroona is listening in, if she isn't already."

"By your command. Message on screen."

Delwyn listened to Anlann. Actually he listened to an Anlann facsimile, the interactive communications avatar. He asked it a few questions and then scowled, chafing with impatience. They were an hour and forty-six minutes into the buildup for their final jump. *Damn*. If only

Anlann had called two hours earlier. The battle group had already committed to its final jump point into Iota Horologii's heliopause.

Henri Edda found a planetoid supporting mining operations? How long had they been in the system? Twelve? Fourteen hours? No sign of enemy shipping, either. They were well beyond the Compact battle group jump terminus, days away in fact under maximum sublight speed, dammit.

"Mining only. No shipyard," Delwyn muttered.

"You do not build a ship next to a raw material site," Anailiatha said from Power Systems and Propulsion.

"I know they wouldn't build it at the mining site, but surely they'd build it nearby and use the planetoid's resources."

"And fight the gravity? Low gravity is worse than standard gravity for complex construction efforts, and standard gravity makes ship building a chore. A spacedock facility or a nil-gravity asteroid makes more sense," Anailiatha sang back.

"We have to change our arrival point. Can we dump the energy buildup and reprogram for the new jump coordinates?" he asked Trebithia.

"Yes. The delay caused by reprogramming is much less than trying to reach the target bodies on sublight velocity—by a few hundred hours."

"Very well. Hlindredreda, contact Bordanin."

"By your command. Channel open. Warleader Bordanin on screen."

"Delwyn, you heard?" Bordanin asked without preamble.

"I did." Delwyn agreed.

"Do you think we must reset our jump clocks for synchronized jumps to these targets?"

"I do," Delwyn said.

"So do I. I ask *Padfoot* and *Steep Trails* to reset their jump clocks for a synchronized jump to the planetoid. The rest of us will jump to the asteroid."

"Affirm," Delwyn said.

"Hlindredreda, open hyperlink to the Coalition fleetcom channel."

"By your command. Channel open…"

✦✦✦

"Captain? I'm receiving another update from the jacks," Lieutenant Vincent said.

"Report."

"Aye, Ma'am. Mining operations confirmed. The Lizards are tractoring out bulk geological formations from the surface. The jacks don't have the scanner capability or the computing power for me to make more than guesses, but I'm certain they're pulling out their iridium-carbon crystal geode inventory."

"How many?" Rodgers asked.

"Thirteen are alphafortress size, twenty-six match the profile of the LAC Senior Chief Marsch stole from them, and two huge ones about two-thirds the length of a Compact destroyer."

"That means at least one ship headed here must be a bulk cargo ship and not a standardized container carrier. That is inefficient, and it is not as if they didn't know what they'd pry from the dwarf planet's crust," Commander Cabrera said.

"They can't stow those two masses in one bulk carrier. The sheer mass alone must be close to her maximum rating. Even if both did fit, they couldn't take the other geodes. Those two hundred ninety-meter-long geodes have to be towed," Rodgers said.

"Bridge? CIC, Millford."

"Bridge, aye. Rodgers."

"Captain? Combat Analysis suggests the Lizard's can't tractor an inert mass while in FTL. They have to stow it somehow."

"Stow them? They'd have to lock them into a repair ship's service dock to do that! A repair ship has a basic skeletal superstructure, a drydock's gantry rigs, and a propulsion system. How can any ship here meet the energy expenditure necessary to jump an additional 5.7 million tonnes?" Rodgers demanded.

"Analysis based on the data we got from Senior Chief Marsch's LAC FTL flights shows they only need to make a hard dock and then generate a drive field large enough to engulf all the mass. Analysis further suggests they won't be able to do so, but evidence so far seems to indicate they're going to try it with two heavy battlecruisers anyway."

"To the dismay of their chief engineers I'll bet," Winters chuckled.

"We can't take the chance. Take us to general quarters, Exec," Rodgers said.

"Aye, Captain. Mr. Carstairs set Condition-2," Cabrera said.

"Aye, Commander," Carstairs said and hit a switch.

Bosun's pipes whistled from the intraship intercom on all decks, followed by Carstairs's voice. "General Quarters. General Quarters. Set Condition-2 throughout the ship. General Quarters. General Quarters. Set Condition-2 throughout the ship."

The alert klaxon's bong-bong-bong followed Carstairs's final word.

###

The unnamed comet and its recently acquired large unnatural satellite, perturbed by the dwarf planet's gravity, began to tumble, causing changes in its orbit that continued to accumulate over the past twelve hours.

"Orbital deviation?" Rodgers asked her helmsman.

"Becoming significant, Ma'am," Carstairs replied. "Nothing I can't keep up with on thrusters. Wait…Wait…Captain, enemy ships have deployed screening elements."

"You'd think they'd have done so hours ago," Rodgers muttered.

"Yes, Ma'am," Carstairs agreed. "Maybe something spooked them?"

Rodgers shrugged absently as the intercom clicked open.

"Bridge? CIC. Command Duty Officer Millford."

"Bridge, aye. Cabrera," the Exec answered from the conn.

"Sir," Millford began, "the jacks are reporting a change in Lizard activity."

"What kind of change in activity Commander?" Cabrera demanded.

"I don't know, Sir. They're firing massed particle weapon discharges into the planetoid, continuous bursts as if trying to drill through the crust. They're churning up a lot of gaseous nitrogen into the atmosphere, which freezes instantly into nitrogen snow."

"More of the same plumes we first detected?" Cabrera asked.

"No, Sir. There's no trace of the iridium particles we detected earlier."

"A deeper deposit maybe?"

"I don't think so Commander," Millford hesitated. "There's too much concentrated fire. The discharge profiles suggest they're either trying to liquefy the nitrogen and let it refreeze over their mining operation, or else they're drilling a demolitions bore for explosive ordnance."

"Why? To hide any signs of their presence?"

"That'd be my guess too, Commander," Millford said.

Rodgers hit a switch on her command chair. "Commander Millford? Rodgers. Does it look to you like the Lizards are preparing to leave the system?"

"I can't say, Ma'am. I don't think so, but then the jacks have limited scanning range. All I get from them is that surface mining and extraction operations have ceased. What's going on in orbit is anybody's guess. I've refrained from tasking the launch rack comm relay to perform a local orbit scan. It does have passive scanners, but its primary purpose is to relay jack data back to us."

"Retask the relay and have it scan its orbital vicinity."

"Aye, Captain. Retasking. Scanning. I can get better scans if I fire the rack's orbital maneuvering thrusters, but I'll spoil the data stream coming in from the jacks if I do."

"I don't think we need the jack data any more, Commander Millford. Fire the launch rack's thrusters and see if you can get a better field of view."

"Aye, Captain. Firing OMS thrusters. Jacks signals lost. Enemy ships coming into view. One cargo hauler, a huge one too. Three heavy battlecruisers, two battlecruisers, and a destroyer. Looks like they're trying to secure the geodes to two heavy battlecruisers by physical connection. I wish I could use the active FTL scanners. Uh-oh…"

"What 'uh-oh' Commander? Report!" Rodgers snapped.

"Ma'am? They've launched some small proxy craft. It's deorbiting and heading back to the primary site, quite leisurely too."

"A shuttle? Some probe?" Rodgers asked.

"Too small for a shuttle, too small for a probe, I think. Firing thrusters, tracking…I think it's…"

A bright flash overloaded Millford's optical scanners seconds before all talkback telemetry dropped offline.

"Captain! High yield neutron explosion. The nuclear electromagnetic pulse has crashed all launch rack electrical systems."

"Confirmed, Captain," Lieutenant Vincent yelled from the bridge CIC tactical station.

"Captain!" Carstairs yelled from navigation. "The launch rack's thrusters are still firing. The EMP must have fried the OMS electronics. It's under power, pursuing a non-cometary trajectory and increasing velocity. Those screening elements are going to pick it up any minute."

"Dammit!" Rodgers yelled. "If I were their commander, I'd run with my precious cargo soonest. Can those ships jump?" Rodgers asked Vincent.

"I don't know Ma'am," Vincent said, her voice shaking.

"Don't worry about it, Lieutenant. Better to say you don't know than guess. That's what Captain Winters always told me."

"CIC? Bridge. Commander Millford?"

"CIC, aye, Millford."

"Those ships, Commander, are they ready to jump?"

Millford called up the tactical data on the identified enemy ship classes, made a query to Combat Analysis, and replied. "Captain, Lizard FTL recharge rates must depend on the total mass jumped. They are certainly faster than the Compact jump drive recharge rate and probably faster than our hyperdrive coil rates, too. But the combat performance data in the computer suggests that their FTL recharge rate matters less than does FTL navigation. Larger mass ships, on average, have taken longer to jump even when all scans taken at the time indicated the ship in question should have been ready to jump. A specific example from the Second Battle of Mu Arae shows a heavy battlecruiser all powered up and ready to jump, yet it sat there firing suppression barrages at incoming fighters instead of running."

"Maybe it had been holding an anchor point?" Rodgers speculated.

"No, Captain. No one could figure it out at the time, and they never did as far as I can tell from the data available."

"What do you think, Commander?" Rodgers asked Millford.

"I don't know, Ma'am. The only variable I can pick out consistently is vessel class."

Rodgers looked at Cabrera with raised eyebrows.

"Mass?" he suggested.

"I can't think of anything else for a ship having full power available to its FTL. Plotting a course through the space-voodoo subspace manifold they use must be tricky the more massive the ship. That cargo ship, with all those iridium geodes, is going to take some time computing a course. Same for the heavy battlecruisers once they are hard-docked to all that mass."

Millford kept watch for two hours as the comet carried them away from the dwarf planet at a slow pace.

"Bridge? CIC," Millford's voice chimed over the intercom.

"Bridge, aye. Cabrera."

"Weapons fire detected. A screening element found the jacks launch rack. Multiple elements are forming up into search pattern postures, Sir," Millford said.

"Romaine? Any chatter on communications?" Cabrera asked.

"None so far, Sir. They're being real quiet."

"That's going to change soon," Cabrera said. "The comet is taking us away from them, but it's still the first place I'd look."

"Me too, Commander, me too," Millford said.

Cabrera looked across the bridge to the CIC bridge station. "Lieutenant Vincent, time until the Compact battle group arrives?"

"One hour, twenty-six minutes, Commander."

"Do you think those ships will still be here eighty-six minutes from now?"

Vincent shook her head. "No, Sir. They've likely been plotting their subspace FTL courses ever since they had a good estimate of the mass they'd be taking back. I don't doubt they have their navigation solutions already."

"Damn," Cabrera said. He pressed the intraship intercom switch. "CIC? Bridge."

"CIC, aye, CDO Millford."

"Commander? Is there enough data in the combat analysis statistical database for you to estimate the time it takes those ships to complete their navigation calculations?"

"Stand by Sir, checking…Combat sims report insufficient data to compute an accurate mass versus time-to-jump curve," Millford said.

"Run it for best fit line, Commander."

"That's no better than an educated guess, Sir!"

"Do it! That's an order!"

Cabrera looked across the bridge at Rodgers. "We think the Lizards are getting ready to jump, Captain. CDO Millford is running a best-fit analysis now."

"That's not much better than a guess," Rodgers said dryly.

"Yes, Ma'am, I've heard that before."

"Bridge, CIC."

"Report, Commander Millford," Rodgers replied.

"Aye, Captain. Computer sims plot best fit line at one hour and twelve minutes for the cargo hauler and thirty-seven minutes for the battlecruisers, but at an error rate plus or minus seventy-two minutes for the hauler and plus or minus thirty-seven minutes for the heavy battlecruisers. That tells me the destroyer and the two battlecruisers could already be standing by to jump. The heavies should be ready as soon as they can hard dock the crystals into their hulls. I'm assuming the hauler is already loaded, but I can't tell unless I use the active sensors."

"Lieutenant Romaine? Call the ambassadors to the bridge," Rodgers said.

"Aye, Captain."

"Mr. Carstairs? Enemy screening elements status?"

"Concentrated in local orbits so far, Ma'am. They're clearing all local space, but they're going to find us sooner or later. The comet is the closest object beyond local space."

"Report on screening element composition Lieutenant?"

"Automated scanning platforms and torpedo launchers, standard EW and ECM assets close to the ships in orbit. The torpedo launchers are deployed to screen them, as are the electronic countermeasures. The electronic warfare assets are scattering, and I…Captain, I'm picking up fusion-pumped x-ray laser mines being laid by the destroyer. Pattern indicates they do not intend to engage in orbital or local space maneuvers. They're going to jump to FTL from their current orbits, Ma'am."

The bridge lift door opened and disgorged the three ambassadors.

"Captain?" Winters asked.

"Captain," Rodgers turned to report, still in the habit of addressing the Coalition ambassador as her captain. "We've got a heavy cargo carrier preparing to jump, two heavy battlecruisers trying to hard-dock a massive geode each, another heavy battlecruiser I'm sure is the command ship, and two light cruisers in sentry orbit, along with a destroyer scattering claymore mines in their high orbitals. The Compact battle group is seventy-two minutes away. The Lizards deployed their screening elements after they detected the launch rack."

"How the hell did that happen Captain?" Winters demanded.

"The Lizards nuked the surface, and the EMP knocked out the rack as it fired OMS thrusters. The orbital maneuvering system got fried, and the thruster didn't shut down. It began to tumble through its orbit, obviously an object under power."

Winters sighed. "The rack doesn't have a Faraday cage to shield against EMP. Well, it can't be helped. Estimated time until the screening elements find us?"

Rodgers looked at Carstairs, and he supplied a figure.

"Options?" Winters asked her.

"Power up the hyperdrive just in case. I really want to stop or delay the hauler and those heavies until the Compact force arrives," she said.

"Powering up the hyperdrive will give us away. I don't recommend engaging the Lizard ships unless you deem it necessary, or if they somehow detect us. I recommend an immediate jump to hyperspace and hold position there away from the Compact battle group potential field of battle."

"But Captain," Rodgers objected.

Winters held firm. "Your orders give you no combat option unless we are discovered, and then it is your discretion unless you are willing to make a command decision you will have to defend at a later review board hearing."

"Captain? Enemy EW asset closing on our position," Carstairs said.

Rodgers locked eyes with her former captain. Jump to hyperspace or stay and try to cripple the geode-carrying ships. Compact ships still had another sixty-eight minutes to go.

"Captain! We are being painted by an EW asset! They know we're here now."

"Action Stations. Set Condition-1! Shields up. Weapons grid to full power," Rodgers ordered as she strode to the bridge CIC station. "Stand by enemy-suppression barrage."

One hundred- and ninety-two-gun batteries studded along the outer hull began tracking the approaching EW drone, both particle weapons and kinetic heavy cannon.

As the gunners made ready to fire, combat tracking reported incoming enemy fighters.

Down in CIC, Millford watched the solutions plot begin assigning firing solutions to tags moving through the three-dimensional combat operations theater plot. Numbers and letters followed inbound blips assigned a different number designating each type of craft and a two-letter prefix, an "L" for Lizard, followed by an "F" for fighter, "D" for destroyer, and so on. CIC Combat Plotting tagged Lizard fighters LF-01 through LF-72 as they closed on the carrier.

"Seventy-two Lizard fighters inbound at maximum combat velocity, Captain," Cabrera said.

"Mr. Carstairs ramp up the hyperdrive to full power and prepare to jump. Ms. Vincent, enemy suppression fire…wait…wait... Now!"

Lieutenant Vincent pounced on her CIC direct interface. "Fire control, all batteries commence firing!"

Henri Edda's outer hull bristled like a porcupine shooting all its quills at once. The fragmentation kinetics pounded out heavy fire against the enemy, thump-thump-thump-thump, over and over again. The more rapid-firing particle weapons spat out streaming volleys, creating plasma bursts like so many rapid-fire roman candles.

So far the Lizards hadn't committed their light cruisers, the command heavy, or the destroyer, but that wouldn't last long. The command heavy was covering the cargo ship. That left the other three ships free to maneuver.

Enemy electronic warfare assets began projecting decoys for the fire control solution computers to lock onto. Others jammed targeting and acquisition systems.

"Enemy fighters approaching their optimal firing range," Vincent reported.

Rodgers watched the bridge tactical plot. She ground her teeth, hands clenching and unclenching at her sides.

Even in CIC it sounded like a continuous pounding bass drum as the kinetics fired lift car-sized projectiles at hypersonic speeds, projectiles each carrying an AI controller designed to determine when to detonate a small fragmenting charge that blew the round into cubic meters of fighter-shredding shrapnel. Kinetic shielding amounted to nothing on small vessels, making the projectiles more economical against fighters than particle weapons, which hit one target per burst—if they could hit the small targets at all. Sometimes a fighter even absorbed a glancing blow, taking heavy damage but remaining combat-effective in the short term. CDO Millford watched the closing fighters, the enemy EW and ECM, and the ship's rate of closure to the cargo ship. She received a report from Fire Control and relayed it to the bridge CIC station.

"CIC reports perimeter established, Ma'am!" Lieutenant Vincent called out.

The suppression barrage created a bubble of relative safety surrounding the ship. They could launch and recover fighters now without enemy EW sneaking in and blowing up fighters the moment they exited the launch tubes. Rodgers reached up for a red handset. "Flight Operations, bridge. Launch fighters, CAG."

In the Flight Operations Center, Commander Guthrey swiveled in his seat. "AOC Burrell, launch fighters."

"Aye, CAG," Petty Officer 3/c Justine Renee Burrell said. "Blue Flight Leader assume perimeter defense. Launch Blue Squadron. Red Flight Leader, Green Flight Leader, intercept inbound enemy fighters. Launch Red Squadron. Launch Green Squadron."

The CAG barely allowed the next three squadrons time to exit their launch tubes before he turned to his Air Operations Controller. "Alert the ABCs."

"Aye, CAG." Burrell said. "Alpha, Beta, and Gamma Squadron pilots to your fighters and prepare for launch."

If, Guthrey thought grimly, *the captain decides to hang around in normal space, we're gonna need 'em.*

***

Captain Judith Arleen Rodgers stood silent and sober as the bridge CIC station's perimeter intrusion alarm preceded an alert from Lieutenant Vincent as she worked at her combat tracking plot. "Attention. Inbound contact, rated highly probable enemy command heavy cruiser. All hands stand by for battle maneuvering," Vincent reported.

"Flight Ops, bridge. Launch Alpha, Beta, and Gamma squadrons," Rodgers ordered.

Commander Cabrera kept issuing orders while keeping his ears tuned to the reports coming in from Flight Ops and CIC when he heard CDO Millford's warning over his headset. "Multiple inbound Lizard warships: task force strength!"

Rodgers glanced at Vincent's CIC tactical plot, watched inbound LD-1, LH-1, LB-1, and LB-2 on attack vectors and gritted her teeth. Time for them to get out from under the rock they had been hiding behind. "Bow up forty-five degrees. Forward port thruster fire trim burst." She watched the attitude readouts with one eye and fighter position reports and the Lizards with the other. "Stern thruster five second burst full thrust." The thruster controls, scattered from one end of the ship to the other, were all under the control of Maneuvering. "Engines all ahead full!" She had chosen her course of action: cause enough damage to the cargo ship to prevent it from jumping before taking *Henri Edda* into hyperspace.

"Ahead full aye, Ma'am," Commander Cabrera said. "Engines report ahead full."

"Intermittent high megatonne radiological warning port side, close!" Carstairs warned.

"Right bow, left stern—emergency full power thrusters. Main engines to flank!" Rodgers snapped the commands, doing the only thing she could do to evade the torpedoes. Even as she watched the screen, she knew it wasn't enough. The ship's best instantaneous acceleration was 339km/s^2, and the torpedo had already reached its terminal acceleration of 396km/s^2. Without kinetic shields even a dud torpedo could finish them, but even with shields the energy from the blast and the radiation wake would be bad enough. They were about to take an EW stealth-shielded proximity nuclear blast on their flank.

"Collision alarm! Brace for shock wave!" Rodgers shouted. Klaxons started sounding throughout the ship. All anyone could do now was brace and pray.

The torpedo's range-to-impact scanner had been jammed by Coalition electronic countermeasures, but its visual targeting system was passive. It needed only to compare a ship silhouette with its critical strike table and decide when it had reached proximity detonation range. When the bulk of the carrier occluded its scanning field it detonated, firing an intense particle blast into the port side shields and punching a hole ten meters wide as shield modulation crossed a zero point, only a few nanoseconds, before the primary blast forced its way against the kinetic shields embedded in the hull plates.

\#\#\#

Blue Squadron commander Ilyce Ison winced in pain at the dazzling light from the nuclear blast. Her canopy polarized instantly, saving her eyes. Her Dart fighter had been far enough from *Henri Edda* to avoid sustaining blast damage, but electric blue arcs skittered across her fighter, visible proof the fighter radiological shield had worked and prevented her from taking a lethal radiation dose. She took a moment to gather her thoughts and then scanned her threat assessment display.

"Blue Squadron set up a perimeter around the ship," she ordered. "I'm going in close to inspect the damage." She fired her thrusters and closed on the ship.

Ison flew along the port side close enough to violate flight safety rules and slow enough to get a good look. "*Henri Edda*, Blue Flight Leader. CAG, if you're reading me, the forward port quarter has sustained heavy damage." She saw several warped and crumpled hull plates. Flames vented from several shattered compartments along the hull all the way up to the bow. Debris, smoke, and vapor billowed into space. "*Henri Edda*, you've got violent decompression all along the forward port quarter. Do you read me? *CAG?*"

\#\#\#

The bridge had suffered moderate damage but remained mostly intact. Corpsmen moved quickly, tending to the injured. Technicians bypassed dark consoles as tactical crew members worked to get meaningful data from damaged stations. Ship-to-ship transmissions and Flight Operations talkback telemetry had dropped out. Only the special operations group's independent local, ship-to-ship, and hyperlink comm systems worked, mainly because SOG occupied the ventral compartments in the Tower, well aft of the blast area. Residual ionization playing across the radiological shields made Ison's continued reports spotty and scratchy.

Nukes weren't used primarily to impart blast damage. Normally the blast couldn't penetrate the shields, but a claymore mine, or a torpedo in this case, had caused a breach and directed its blast into the hull. Ionizing radiation played hell with the ship, contaminated the breach points. It also overwhelmed sensor and comm channels. Once the radiological shields had finished reflecting radiation from the hull, sensors would clear and communications would be possible.

In the meantime, Blue Squadron had to protect the ship from incoming torpedoes, while Red and Green Squadrons cleared a path to the oncoming Lizard ships.

Alpha, Beta, and Gamma had their hands full keeping the Lizard fighters at bay.

Rodgers craned her neck to look up at one of the few working monitors above a plotting table.

"Radiation levels high but within tolerances. The radiological shields and the hull plating kept out most of the hard stuff." Cabrera said as he checked off items on the Damage Control list with a grease pencil. He drew arrows and circles on a stack of deck-by-deck sheet transparencies, ship schematics meant for use only when the Damage Control Station was offline.

"Report, Exec," Rodgers ordered.

"Drive, Maneuvering, and helm all report green Captain, but half the stations on the bridge are offline. Forward port quarter broadside fighter launch tubes three, four, five, and six are wrecked. Forward port quarter decks twelve through twenty-three have major hull damage, breaches, and fires."

"Send a DC party forward and get a visual on the damage. Most port quarter DC systems are down. The reason we know the bow is intact is because the bridge rides atop it."

"Yes, Ma'am, which inclines me to recommend we abandon the bridge and transfer the conn to auxiliary control."

"We're not there yet," Rodgers said.

Cabrera wondered if they already were.

✦✦✦

The entire port side of the flight deck was burning. The nuke blast had detonated less than one hundred meters off the port quarter and fifty-three meters aft of the bow, directing its fury against the port forward broadside launch tubes. Many of the fourteen-launch tube outer hatches had buckled, allowing the blast to blow up through the tubes and into the fighter launch system to slam against the interior hatch. Most of the hatches had held, but interior hatches three, four, five, and six failed, allowing radioactive plasma to blow into the maintenance bays and throughout the forward quarter section of the flight deck. The flight deck rapidly decompressed, pulling streamers of superheated gases, vaporized equipment, and immolated flight deck personal back out through the breached launch tubes and into space.

Fires continued to burn on decks 19, 20, 21, and 22 port side between the hull and the flight deck. That explained why the DC parties hadn't been able to stop compartments from decompressing.

"Ma'am? Damage control parties report buckled hull plating all along the port quarter and chain-reaction decompressions occurring everywhere between frame 121 and frame 126," Vincent said.

"Damn," Rodgers said grimly. If Damage Control couldn't get a handle on the situation, they might lose all fighter recovery capability, at least.

"Ma'am?" Cabrera said. "Chief Martin says he's got several out-of-control fires. That's why he hasn't been able to stop the decompressions."

Rodgers ran her fingers along one of the hard copy schematic transparencies. "If compartments continue to blow out at this rate, we will lose everything on the forward port quarter all the way into the flight deck. Cabrera, take personal command of Damage Control."

"Aye, Captain."

###

The forward damage control parties were fighting for their lives. Artificial gravity had failed everywhere on the forward quarter.

Zero-gravity fire formed macabre balls and tendrils of violent flame. It followed air currents, sought cooler air and its greater oxygen content. It followed crew members as if it had a mind of its own. It came after them, pulled along by the draft bodies made. It couldn't be beaten off. There was no drop and roll in zero-gee. The air itself burned, and those not wearing DC suits had no hope of staying alive.

Cabrera ran down deck 12, corridor A, to frame 119 and stepped into a compartment filled with toxic fumes and smoke. Explosions abaft shook the deck, and three more flashing red lights lit up on the DC status board.

Chief Petty Officer Martin cursed.

"Report!" Cabrera said to the damage control chief.

"Fire suppression is offline. Structural buckling is causing seals to fail and the fires to advance until more bulkheads fail. There's vacuum in the 'tween hull spaces between frames 121 and 125 on decks 12 through 22. That's fourteen compartments plus the flight deck. When the compartments fail, they decompress to vacuum, putting out the fires in the compartment, but by then it's too late."

Cabrera looked at the DC board again. "We have to get those fires out!"

"I know! I know!" Martin said.

The Damage Control handset buzzed, and Martin picked it up, covering his other ear to hear.

A massive explosion shook the deck below them.

"Sir!" Martin called, relaying another report. "That was another decompression on deck 17, close to the port quarter flight deck containment force field. What are your orders, Sir?"

Cabrera stood motionless. That force field held flight deck air back from the vacuum and allowed fighters to pass through on their landing approaches into the ship. Each fighter bay had one to isolate the section.

The bow had both an aperture force field and a mechanical hatch, a massive garage door some seventy meters wide and thirty meters high. If he ordered it closed to maintain internal structural integrity, then the fighters couldn't land.

"Seal the bow hatch. If we can maintain integrity on the forward quarter, then we can evacuate and vent compartment by compartment."

"Aye Sir. Closing the bow aperture hatch," Martin said.

A red light flashed on the bow schematic, accompanied by a ringing alarm bell.

"Negative function, Commander," Martin reported. "Bent bulkhead or damaged actuators, I don't know which. We can't hard seal the flight deck. If the port side force field generator fails, the entire length of the flight deck will decompress to vacuum."

Maybe, that's the only way, Cabrera thought. "Chief Martin, seal all hatches on frame 121 and frame 127, decks 17 through 22, corridors B and D, and emergency vent all compartments."

Martin rounded on Cabrera in shock. "Wait a minute, Sir! I've got over a hundred people trapped on deck 21 behind frame 121. My DC parties and the launch bay support crews are sheltering in isolated compartments. I need a minute to evacuate them!"

A second powerful explosion, close, shook the ship, and Cabrera knew that another compartment had blown through the 'tween hulls and into open space.

"Did you feel that, Chief? That's an outer and inner hull breach. Whether we open the vents or wait for cascading decompressions, either action would do the same thing: put out the fires. But emergency venting will stop the explosive compartmental damage from accumulating to the point where we lose hull integrity and the flight deck."

"I just need a minute!" Martin yelled.

"We don't have a minute! There's hydrogen and antihydrogen fueling couplings throughout the port forward launch bays! The antihydrogen has been purged back to the Aft Fuel Reserve, but fighter hydrogen is stored on site. That means *invisible* zero-gee hydrogen fires, never mind the explosions! Do it!"

Furious but at a loss for words, Martin keyed the handset for ship-wide announcement. "Damage Control Central, this is the Damage Control Chief. Seal off frame 121 and frame 127 on decks 17 through 22, port side corridors B and D. That's an order."

In the burning compartment behind frame 121 an apprentice crewman with a respirator and an air tank on his back shouted to the others. "Get out of here now! Go! They're gonna blow the emergency vents! Hurry!"

But it was far too late. The bulkhead doors had already closed and locked.

There was no escape.

Cabrera placed his right palm against the emergency venting control touch panel and tapped the manual override command code into the damage control station with his left middle finger. He glanced above the panel and watched as the vent status frame ID tags changed from locked-down green to unlocked warning red. With a calmness he didn't quite feel, he touched tag 122-123, tag 124-125, and tag 126-127.

Along about two-fifths of the forward port quarter hull large vents opened between frames 122 and 123, 124 and 125, and 126 and 127 on the inner hull. At the same time, the outer hull hatches blew open, releasing fiery streamers and smoky jets from the flight deck and flaming compartments. Along with the fire, dying crewmen by the dozens hurled out into space like so much refuse from the garbage airlock.

At the Damage Control status board Cabrera and Martin waited in silence until the sensors reported all fires extinguished, temperatures dropping, and all vented compartments reading zero pressure. Intact compartments held steady. Martin verbally confirmed what the board already told Cabrera. "Venting complete. All fires are out, Sir."

Cabrera nodded. "If they remembered their training, then they had their hazard suits on and were prepared for possible venting. Those who braced for the sudden decompression and wearing hazard gear probably headed into the 'tween hulls catwalks and are heading for the maintenance airlocks as we speak. Launch a couple of betas and recover everyone blown out through the exterior hull. Hurry, they don't have much time."

"Aye, Sir."

***

Rodgers hit the intraship call button and yelled. "Cabrera, report!"

The intercom crackled and popped as the Exec's muffled voice echoed across the bridge. "Fires are out, Captain. Damage Control hasn't had the time to do a battle damage assessment, but two things come to mind right now. One, the frame 119 flight deck firewall hatch won't close, and I don't know if it's the control lines, or if actual damage to the hatch itself is causing the failure. Two, no fighter can launch from the forward port launch bay. It's a total loss."

"What about the flight deck? Can we recover our fighters?" Rodgers asked.

"Yes, Ma'am. It's in partial vacuum now. Once the emergency bulkheads can hard seal and isolate the damage, we can repressurize. If we must, we can recover as is with the flight deck crews wearing environmental suits. If you don't mind my asking, Ma'am, where the hell did all those fighters come from? Destroyers and battlecruisers don't carry fighters!"

"I don't know, Exec, and I don't care at the moment. Our squadrons have superiority and are making strafing runs on the destroyer and the two cruisers, and I'm about to make a run on the cargo ship. We're gonna take a few hard hits from the heavy battlecruiser command ship.

"Bridge comms to Flight Operations Center are down. Get to Flight Ops and tell CAG to prepare for rapid squadron recovery."

"He's not going to like that, Captain."

"I know he's not, but we're going hyper right after I punch a hole through that heavy cargo hauler."

"Aye Ma'am, Cabrera out."

***

Rodgers looked over at Ambassador Winters. "Maybe Cabrera had a point about evacuating to auxiliary control."

Winters shook his head. "Never abandon your bridge so long as you can conn the ship, navigate, and direct combat operations from there. You might want to do so after the engagement is over, but I wouldn't. Don't second-guess yourself, and don't try to predicate action based on how you think I might do it."

Rodgers nodded, "Lieutenant Romaine, open hyperlink and contact the Compact battle group. Outline the situation for them and tell them we'll be in hyperspace when they arrive, ready to jump back into normal space adjacent to the primary target. On their arrival, we will jump back into normal space, transfer the co-Ambassadors to *Surefooted*, recharge the hyperdrive, and jump back into hyperspace bound for Elleio."

"Aye, Captain."

"Mistress of Communications Romaine," Seralin interrupted, "use the Compact Fleetcom Green Channel, flash emergency traffic, *Surefooted* alert cipher," and she sang a haunting five-note series in counterpoint melody.

"Co-Ambassador Seralin," Romaine stammered, "I couldn't sing that tune if my life depended on it. If I open the hyperlink, could you sing the authentication song for me? Captain?"

"I would be honored," Seralin said.

Rodgers nodded her approval.

Romaine keyed the intercom. "Special Operations Group Command Center, Bridge."

"SOGCC aye, Chief Warrant Officer Cummings."

"Chief, this is Romaine. I need to patch into your hyperlink."

"Stand by, bridge." Cummings hit an alert switch and yelled, "SOG Commander to Tactical Ops Center, switch the combat ops hyperlink into bridge comm systems!"

"TOC, aye. Commander? Negative function. Tell Romaine to try access through her auxiliary systems."

"Copy that!" Cummings said and switched pick-ups. "Romaine? We can't connect to your primary system. Switch to aux."

"Copy that, SOGCC…switching over…telltales registering hyperlink available for bridge comms. We're going to need it for awhile, Chief."

"With SOG's complements, Lieutenant," Cummings said and rang off.

"Evade that destroyer, Mr. Carstairs. Line us up on that big bastard," Rodgers said.

"Aye, Captain. Approaching optimal firing range."

"Fire Control has firing solutions on the cargo ship, Captain," Vincent reported.

"What about the two heavy battlecruisers?" Rodgers asked.

"Commander Millford reports fire control has prioritized them as secondary targets, Captain."

"Captain! Incoming torpedoes! Enemy mobile racks are rolling their inventories. Non-stealth ordnance. Antitorpedo intercepts firing. Point defense systems are tracking the inbounds just in case the intercepts miss a few."

"In range! Weapons ready!" Ensign Rickman, the junior tactical officer announced.

Henri Edda drove relentlessly toward the high orbit targets, perimeter defense guns firing on enemy screening elements. The distance from the comet to the Pluto-sized world amounted to nothing, but nobody in their right mind accelerated through screening element, mines, and other enemy assets having mass. At any real velocity they might as well be kinetic projectiles. Worse if they happened to slam into a warhead platform or some proximity-activated EW jammer.

"CIC OOD commence firing! Fire at will!" Rodgers ordered.

"Aye, Captain," Vincent said. "Fire Control, bridge. Commence firing! Fire at will!"

Gun turrets swung forward. The primary particle weapons and the starboard railgun opened up on the heavy cargo ship, while starboard broadside fire targeted the two heavy battlecruisers.

"Enemy ships returning fire, Captain. The cargo carrier is firing point defenses, intercepts, and particle weapon clusters, but no heavy particle turrets, torpedo clusters, and no kinetic railgun launchers," Vincent reported.

Cabrera entered the bridge just in time to catch Vincent's report. "Makes sense. She's got enough for perimeter defense, but she's dependent on her escorts and screening elements for a full-throated defense. What about the heavy battlecruisers?"

"They're sitting there letting their shields take the pounding," Vincent said.

"Can't afford the energy?" Rodgers wondered aloud.

"I think so," Cabrera agreed.

"Captain!" Carstairs yelled, "The geode-mated heavy battlecruisers are producing energy waveforms. Patterns read consistent with jump initiation."

Cabrera and Rodgers watched as a heat-shimmer effect enveloped both ships, stretched around them and the crystalline masses physically locked into them. *But the shimmering effect didn't quite engulf both the ships and their towed cargoes.*

The Lizard heavy battlecruisers twisted and bent within the jump field before they vanished.

Well, most of the two ships and their cargoes vanished, but a third of each battlecruiser remained behind, exploding and tumbling along with fragmented geodes they had worked so hard to extract from the tiny planet. The debris scattered across the heavy cargo ship's orbit, causing obvious visible damage before raining down onto the thin atmosphere surrounding the dwarf planet.

"Ambassador Winters, you were right when you said those captains would regret trying to displace so much mass under FTL," Cabrera said.

"Captain?" Romaine said. "Flight Operations reports the destroyer disabled and out of action. The command heavy battlecruiser is changing orbit, putting herself between us and the cargo ship."

"Captain!" Carstairs interrupted. "Neutrino emissions and Cherenkov spikes aft. Three Lizard heavy destroyers emerging from precision jump!"

"Confirmed!" Vincent said.

"Recall all squadrons," Rodgers said. "Prepare to jump to hyperspace."

Rodgers watched the closing heavy destroyers, each ship resembling four-hundred-meter-long smoky green glass mud dauber wasp nests, two textured tubes side-by-side with no other features. At least the heavy cargo ship looked familiar: twenty-two leathery gray eggs in a row buttressed with spun silver lace, almost as if held in place by spider webs.

"Torpedoes inbound!" Carstairs yelled, "Executing evasive action."

"Antitorpedo clusters firing," Vincent reported. "Sixty-six torpedoes inbound. Launching countermeasures. Point defense tracking reports ready. Aft perimeter suppression fire at eighty-six percent coverage."

Damn! Rodgers cursed. An approach from behind, one lining up with the ship's engine bells—called a ship's "baffles" since submarine times—was just as troubling now as it had been back then. The engine bells covered an area 24,180 meters square. Aft guns on the dorsal and ventral propulsion hull, intercepts, and point defense systems lacked the offensive punch to take out any warship trying to stick its bow up another ship's stern. That starkly illustrated the point why carriers didn't often deploy in combat operations without their attendant destroyers and cruisers.

"Fighter recovery progress?" a harried Rodgers asked Carstairs.

"Alpha, Beta, and Gamma Squadrons have been recovered so far. CAG reports Green Squadron is on final approach now."

"Cargo ship status?"

"Sensors report power loss, Captain," Carstairs reported. "They may have lost their FTL, or at least they lost their power buildup by diverting it to their shields."

"Time until the Compact ships arrive?"

"Eighteen minutes, seven seconds, Mark!" Carstairs said.

"Hyperdrive status?" Rodgers asked.

The ship lurched sharply before Carstairs could reply.

"Proximity explosion aft by torpedo. Thermonuclear ordnance, heavy neutron radiation. Radiological shields are carrying the ionizing radiation, but the blast has been directed aft into the drive! The sublight engines have scrammed, and we've lost primary propulsion."

"Hyperdrive coils?" Rodgers asked, as if in prayer.

"Port dorsal nacelle-1 and port ventral nacelle-1 hyperdrive coils are running at thermal red line due to damaged cooling units. The remaining ten are undamaged and running at full power. Ready to jump, Ma'am," Carstairs said.

"Fighter recovery operations?" she asked.

"Blue Flight Leader Ison is the last one. She's coming in now."

"Romaine send a tactical sitrep to the Compact ships," Rodgers said.

"Aye, Ma'am. Transmitting," the communications officer said.

"Jump to hyperspace on my command!"

"Aye, Captain," Carstairs said.

Successive concussive impacts shook the ship, proximity explosions at and around the stern kicked away at their shields, all getting too close. Eventually the intercepts or the point defense systems would miss and let another torpedo through.

"Flight Ops reports last fighter has landed," Romaine said.

"Get us the hell out of here Carstairs!"

"Aye, Captain. Engaging hyperdrive."

Henri Edda fled under maneuvering thrusters into the relative safety of hyperspace and nulled her forward velocity to zero. Without the fusion drive, the carrier couldn't go anywhere in hyperspace, just as she couldn't go anywhere in normal space.

"Damage report Exec. Give me the bad news," Rodgers said.

14
WARPACT!

"Hyperlink message from *Henri Edda* to all ships, Mistress," Hlindredreda reported.

"Content?" Melkorka asked.

"The Coalition ship has been discovered and is engaging Ni'zakhonii ships. He reports one destroyer adrift, two heavy battlecruisers destroyed, and a heavy cargo transport has been damaged. Three heavy destroyers and one heavy battlecruiser are closing. He has taken heavy damage to his fighter launch capability and his sublight drive. He is retreating into hyperspace."

Melkorka shuddered at the thoughts that must be running though those female minds on *Surefooted* right now.

They could do nothing about it. The battle group was minutes away from jumping into two separate Action Zones. Consensus among the warleaders had led to the decision of having *Padfoot* and *Steep Trails* program their drives for a jump to the planetoid mining site and the Coalition warship. The bulk of the battle group had programmed for the presumed hidden shipyard pinpointed by the Coalition carrier intel. The distance between the asteroid shipyard and the planetoid mining site amounted to days apart under sublight. All ships were close to jump clock zero count now. The time it would take *Surefooted* to reprogram the slight change in course would also take them well over a day past the synchronized jump clock countdown

Melkorka pressed a switch on her command console. "Delwyn? Melkorka. The warship *Henri Edda* has engaged the Ni'zakhonii and has taken damage. He has retreated into hyperspace."

"At 1,433 AU and lacking hyperlink, it will take four days and twenty-four hours TST for a Lizard warning to reach the shipyard on their standard comms, but a courier probe traveling at G-band could jump there in thirty-two minutes TST. That explains the late-arriving ships that fired into Rodgers's stern. We might not have surprise when we jump into the system," Delwyn said.

Melkorka nodded to herself. Delwyn knew his battle tactics, and he was right. His voice also carried a curious note of worry, too.

"Something bothers you?" she asked into the combat address sytem.

"What you said about *Henri Edda's* sublight drive. A Coalition ship needs its sublight engines to drive it through hyperspace, and hyperspace is filled with gravitational currents and eddies. They'll have to jump back out soon. Warn *Padfoot* and *Steep Trails* that the carrier might pop back into normal space without warning."

"Understood. I will advise both mistresses of the ship. Come to the command center and sing for us, for we are about to engage in battle."

"I'm coming."

The warleaders aboard *Padfoot* and *Steep Trails* poured over the Action Zone intelligence provided by the Coalition carrier with their mistresses of tactics. At least they had reliable intelligence. *Hunter's Moon* and the other warships were about to jump into the unknown.

The *Padfoot* and *Steep Trails* jump clocks wound down to zero, and they jumped to the planetoid on schedule without incident.

Delwyn reached his station in the Warleader's Watch as Melkorka sang out, "Synchronized jump executing…Now!"

Seven Compact warships vanished and thirty billionths of a second later re-emerged 2.04 light-years distant, at zero relative velocity and 645,000 kilometers from a large asteroid and nine Ni'zakhonii warships in a dispersal pattern.

"Mistress, message from *Green Ivy*. Warleader Bordanin declares Warpact," Hlindredreda reported.

Delwyn swiveled around in his seat to face Melkorka.

"Delwyn?" she asked, waiting for his formal acknowledgment. By all Eyloni custom and tradition Delwyn had to surrender his autonomy to the Warpact warleader, but he had to tell the crew, in ritual verse, that he had acceded to the Warleader's request. Only then would they tolerate the otherwise indignity of having a male not their own making suggestions on how to fight their warship.

"Hlindredreda, send to *Green Ivy*: I yield to the judgement of the Warpact warleader," he said.

"*A rayha to ma'ke te naya,*" Melkorka said over the ship-to-ship channel: heard and witnessed.

"Mistress of Tactics, open tactical link," Melkorka added.

"Affirm, acting. Tactical link established," Hlinlodyn replied.

"Execute assault plan," Melkorka said.

"Affirm, acting. We are closing with *Green Ivy* on enemy ships. *Pathfinder* and his destroyer escorts are firing in an attempt to make a hole and reach the enemy outpost."

Delwyn began drumming up a stentorian martial beat. His main purpose during battle was to comfort his crew and provide morale. Taken to extremes, he could even sing them into a mindless berserker frenzy, something he desperately wanted to avoid: mindless berserkers couldn't fight their warship.

Delwyn knew that at the same time every male aboard eight of the nine Compact ships was singing to his crew, his occupational association, as well. *Surefooted*, however, was experiencing a historic event, one which hadn't occurred by choice in all Eyloni history: a ship society engaging in battle without a male focus aboard. Hlindredreda was maintaining ship-to-ship contact with Ahwroona, allowing her society to hear Delwyn sing in Anlann's stead: another historical first.

"We have near-parity with enemy ships. Their maneuvering is cautious. *Green Ivy* outclasses any single enemy warship. They are adjusting their approach, trying to complicate our intercept solutions. I expect them to soon commit to an approach vector. When they do, they will come out and smash into *Fearless, Surefooted*, and us head-on and try to take out our command warship," Melkorka said.

Delwyn nodded as he sang. He stood up from his place and traced a slow walk back to her.

"Mistress? Combat Analysis Center concludes we have the strength to meet them face-to-face. Enemy is going evasive, trying to force course changes on us, managing to slow our closure rate, a standard tactic. They want to slow our breakaway rate. Mistress, Combat Analysis reports they have deployed electronic warfare drones," Hlinlodyn said.

"Understood," Melkorka said.

Delwyn listened to the reports coming into the command center. As he sang, he came up behind Hlinlodyn and Saidrinha and caressed the jittery young Warrior while reading her tactical display. Melkorka commanded the ship, but he had total freedom to give orders as he saw fit while singing to them. The enemy forces surprised him. Lizards weren't known for subtlety. Their usual gambit turned on smash-and-grab tactics, but their maneuvering had turned slick and inventive. They began linking up in ways he would have expected a Coalition blockade to form.

"Their blockading, Melkorka. Look for a ship, a small one reserved for evacuating all their research data. The LAC carrier will take on the completed prototype LACs. The blockading force will slug it out with us until those two ships are ready to leave," he said in a rush and then resumed singing.

Melkorka nodded and turned to the Mistress of Communications. "Send Delwyn's analysis to Warleader Bordanin."

"Affirm, acting," Hlindredreda said. "Mistress? Warleader Bordanin agrees and believes the enemy ships are forming up for their final run."

Hlinlodyn nodded from her console. "Combat Analysis concurs. I suggest we assume assault posture. Assuming constant acceleration for both fleets, we will reach firing range in one minute. *Pathfinder* and his escort destroyers have engaged a blockading force of three heavy cruisers at well over parity. Contact with enemy battleships, one LAC carrier, one heavy cruiser, and two destroyers imminent. We no longer have parity."

Delwyn caressed a tense Saidrinha as he sang, nodding to himself as he listened to the report from the Mistress of Tactics. She was right: *Green Ivy* was a battleship in the real sense of the word. He didn't have combat forces aboard. All available volume had been dedicated to gun platforms. Very soon now his ship and his destroyers would have to accelerate in and engage enemy ships and let the battleship blast away without crowding into his firing solutions.

"Commencing battle maneuvering, breaking away, attempting to reduce enemy engagement window. Maneuver failed. Enemy ships are closing up the distance," Hlinlodyn reported.

Delwyn stepped over to Hlinlodyn's console and began rubbing her shoulders, singing as if to her alone even as his voice carried over the combat address system and throughout the ship.

"Blockade tactics. They will sacrifice those ships to give the evac teams time to take their research with them. We don't have much time," he muttered.

⁂

"My Lord Viceroy Bleniss, I abase myself. Our drones are picking up a disturbing tactic. We aren't sure what it means, My Lord Viceroy. I abase myself. The alien dagan-Na Atal EW is feeding false data to our drones. We're not sure, but if our plot is reliable, then they're coming in with three ships to run the blockade. If Combat's track is accurate, they'll close up to about 4,250 slip-strides in 441 *ains*. What do you think, My Lord Viceroy? I abase myself."

"Obviously the dagan mean to reach the outpost, Vassal Sub-commander. They want to close, get into our claw range, and rake the orbital picket force hard, while we spend time striking down their main assault force."

"Would the battleship try to support a close-in assault on the asteroid surface, My Lord Viceroy? I abase myself."

"Don't be a fool, Vassal Sub-commander. That assault cruiser and its two destroyers think they can do the job on their own. The other assault cruiser and destroyers will screen the battleship and not commit to an all-out assault against the outpost. They are mere food animals, you fool!"

###

"Within optimal firing range and coming up on our firing bearings now, Mistress," Hlinlodyn reported.

"Engage the battle plan as instructed, Mistress of Tactics," Melkorka said.

"Affirm, acting. Mistress of Pathwalking, close to primary target assault range," Hlinlodyn said.

"Affirm, acting," Trebithia replied as Hlinlodyn seamlessly assumed command over combat operations, subject to subsequent or countermanding orders issued by either Melkorka or Delwyn.

"Primary and secondary weapons fire control is released. Fire at will," Hlinlodyn ordered her Combat Analysis fire control mistresses.

Delwyn sang, and as he did so he watched his command center crew in action. Their multitiered parallel command structure served them well. They slipped into their roles easily, aided by the calm self-assurance his singing gave them.

###

"Coming up on orbital assault approach," *Pathfinder*'s Mistress of the Ship announced. "Mistress of Tactics, fire control is at your discretion."

Pathfinder and his two destroyer escorts opened fire on the enemy picket force. It became clear to the Mistress of the Ship soon enough that the enemy force had been tasked to hold the high ground, a cone with its apex at the enemy shipyard and its base in standard surveillance orbit over a quarter of the hemisphere below in diameter. Those ships must be eliminated before she could drop her surface assault forces and attempt to penetrate enemy fortifications.

Once enemy orbital defenses were softened up, several fists of Warriors would then drop from high orbit in landing craft carrying light armored vehicles. As soon as the warship reached quantum translation range, hands of Hunters and Warriors would then translate into the outpost, infiltrate enemy territory and capture all research they could get their hands on.

But first they needed to clear the high orbit. The mistresses of tactics aboard *Pathfinder* and his two destroyers ordered multiple sustained volleys from their torpedo bays, saving their heavy kinetic weapons for orbit-to-surface assault barrages. Besides the two destroyers, *Pathfinder* had his own attendant screening elements: drones mounting EW and ECM assets and EW jammers and decoys. The electronic warfare drones closed on the enemy ships and began pummeling Ni'zakhonii targeting systems with false sensor data, while others generated power signatures and holographic silhouettes, attractive targets for enemy EW systems. It took a lot of power to generate a false sensor image of a warship while within engagement range. The EW assets' puny hydrogen-antihydrogen fusion generators quickly exhausted their fist-sized fuel bottles, but they only had to confuse enemy offensive capabilities until the Compact ships got their hits in. Other EW platforms produced signatures mimicking sublight engines, but they had no actual motive capability themselves save for RCS, which meant they had to be towed by tractor field. Limited tractor field ranges meant the new "ships" seemed to screen a single ship, and it did not take Ni'zakhonii predictive analysis long to figure out which ship was the real one, which in turn kept the mistresses of tactics's analysismistresses busy devising changing decoy deployments to prevent the enemy from zeroing in on Compact ships.

###

"My Lord Viceroy, I abase myself. Lord Commander Haksith reports by courier that two more dagan-Na Atal vessels are making a run at him," the battleship captain reported.

"What about it, My Lord Captain-commander? The primary threat is the ships approaching us, not those forces assaulting the geode planetoid. Haksith will withdraw with the carbon catalysts to the moon and seed them at all costs, or I will have him and his vassals beheaded.

"Vassal Weapons-commander, all commands disregard all enemy ships except the battleship."

"It shall be done, My Lord Viceroy. I abase myself."

###

Delwyn sang as he watched the battle unfold. *Pathfinder* and his destroyers slugged it out in high orbit and on their own. Five enemy ships had taken up combat postures and were taking turns battering at the Compact ships, which wasn't much different from Coalition battle tactics but not quite the same either. A skilled Coalition helmsman could pop in and out of hyperspace, breaking free from, say, the bow of an enemy ship, and jump back into normal space behind and rake its stern—as long as the jumping ship remained motionless in hyperspace, anyway. Compact fleet combat doctrine apparently favored a more muscular approach: close-order maneuvering tactics. Get in a good pounding, take a jab or two, and then the Mistress of Pathwalking would reposition the ship and let the Mistress of Tactics take over combat maneuvering again.

Delwyn glanced up into the Warleader's Watch display volume. *Green Ivy* was firing so much suppression fire that he bathed the enemy ships with energy.

"Mistress, one heavy battlecruiser and two destroyers are closing," Hlinlodyn reported.

219

What? Delwyn did a double take. *That made no sense.*

"They're going around us despite the heavy damage they'll incur," he said, interrupting his song. "They're making a run on Bordanin's ship!"

"Trebithia! Head them off!" Melkorka sang.

"Affirm, acting. Mistress! The battlecruiser is going to clip our bow!"

"Evasive! Shields to full power!" Hlinlodyn yelled to Saidrinha.

The young Warrior, new to her duties and overwhelmed, did not know how to redirect and focus field shielding to any particular spot on the hull. Delwyn saw her indecision. Redundant systems crowded his station on the Warleader's Watch, and he knew from experimenting with them how to redirect the structural integrity fields. He reached over her shoulder and keyed in the sequence on her console as he bellowed, "Collision alert, left outrigger!"

The warship shuddered as the leading edge along the port outrigger hull plowed into the enemy ship. "Left kinetic cannon, maximum rate of fire now!" He ordered.

"By your command," Hlinlodyn sang, knowing the left outrigger fire control and gun crews heard their warleader along with the rest of their society.

Heavy duranium slugs ripped into the heavy battlecruiser, at point blank range. The barrage blew gaping holes into the hull plating, holes the secondary gunners fired particle weapons and x-ray lasers into, fatiguing the underlying structure and hulling the entire enemy vessel port side.

"Sensors report heavy damage, maneuverability loss, and significant outgassing, Delwyn," Hlinlodyn reported. "Mistress, the heavy battlecruiser and the two destroyers are continuing on to *Green Ivy. Fearless* and *Surefooted* have moved to intercept and are firing."

"Come about and close. Load forward torpedo bays. Set torpedoes for minimum spread, maximum yield. Target their engines," Delwyn sang.

"By your command," Melkorka sang back.

Delwyn called up the engagement-wide tactical display and extended it from the forward wall of the Warleader's Watch all the way back to Melkorka's command console. He rushed past Melkorka and stepped into the cubic volume and walked among the floating toy ships swarming a centrally located asteroid, frowning as he wandered around the battle scene.

Something seemed amiss here. Two destroyers and a heavy battlecruiser alone couldn't destroy Bordanin's ship.

"Mistress! *Green Ivy* reports heavy damage to his helm and navigation systems. His shields are holding and Mistress of the Ship Faolindra believes they can hold out against the assault until we destroy those ships, but he is adrift. Mistress Faolindra reports they retain control over their screening elements…Mistress, *Green Ivy's* comms have gone down," Hlindredreda reported.

Delwyn watched the Compact battleship get pounded by everything the three ships could fire at him. *Surefooted* and *Fearless* blew chunks out of the enemy ships, and yet they continued to concentrate their primary and secondary batteries on the Compact battleship while warding off his torpedoes using their antitorpedo clusters and point defense systems.

Hunter's Moon lined up with an enemy battlecruiser ahead and fired multiple salvoes into the ship's drive, which his stern shields deflected.

This was deliberate suicide, Delwyn thought to himself. They were sacrificing themselves so assets and research materials could be removed from the asteroid shipyard. He frowned and walked behind the toy ships, glancing from their current engagement to *Pathfinder* and his two destroyers.

A sudden flash dazzled his eyes, and he blinked several time in rapid succession. His eyes watered.

That flare had come from the asteroid, directed at *Pathfinder*.

***

Pathfinder's Mistress of the Ship knew they had taken a devastating hit by the way the shock wave ripped through her warship.

"Damage report!" her warleader demanded.

"Direct hit from surface kinetic projectile to the ventral command hull, penetrating the combat staging and deployment bay. Massive breach. Damage Control reports damage confined to the bay, with minor damage to the aftstation. The bay mistress reports losing over one hundred assault teams, troop transports, and other combat assets."

"Mistress of Tactics adjust orbit to bring us out from under the arc of enemy weapons lock. Can we fire on the surface?"

"Not recommended while the enemy ships in orbit hold the high ground," she replied.

***

"Hlindredreda? Any updates from *Green Ivy?*" Delwyn asked while studying the walk-in cube and its moving toy ships.

"No, Delwyn. But they continue to fight."

"Sensors show the command battleship maintaining full power, shields, and weapons, and Warleader Bordanin continues to fight him, but their drifting will take them out of the Action Zone, and he cannot take evasive action," Hlinlodyn said.

"Delaying tactic. The enemy wants us to spend time here, and we must rejoin *Pathfinder*.I don't think they can deploy their assault forces with the hit they've taken to their staging area and deployment bay," Delwyn said.

Melkorka looked up at him. "You must assume Warpact leadership. The Warpact warleader must move with his forces, and Warleader Bordanin cannot do so as long as his helm is offline."

"Me? Isn't that a bit presumptive?" He asked as massed weapons fire from his ship penetrated a Lizard destroyer's engineering spaces. She exploded in a silent blossom of plasma.

Green Ivy still had three ships on him, one of them the Lizard battleship.

"Mistress, message from Phalalin aboard *Fearless*," Hlindredreda said.

"Accept," Melkorka said.

"Delwyn? You saw the hit *Pathfinder* took to his staging area?"

"I did. I think they'll have to translate their assault forces into the shipyard if they want to do anything at all."

Delwyn saw Hlinlodyn shaking her head. "*Pathfinder* reports too much damage to allow them to support a surface combat operation and keep the high orbit cleared at the same time."

Phalalin nodded. "I decline Warpact command. So do all the destroyer warleaders. Delwyn, you must assume Warpact command because you can navigate and you can send your surface assault forces into the outpost. You must send *Pathfinder* back. He can do far more good with me than he can where he is now."

"But I…I shouldn't be Warpact warleader, Phalalin. You've got more experience in fighting a task force. I'm a combat specialist, not a ship captain," Delwyn objected as a fluorescent-orange-haired Melkorka threw an apoplectic fit.

Phalalin smiled and shook his head. "I need to remain here directing *Surefooted* and *Pathfinder* in support of *Green Ivy*. You must use your combat specialist experience to get your combat forces into the outpost."

Delwyn stared at the little toys floating all around his head blasting away at each other. The tactical situation made no sense to him. By now the Lizards certainly should have had more than enough time to evacuate all their data files and all the manufacturing equipment they could take with them and destroy the rest.

Damn. Damn damn damn *damn*!

Delwyn nodded and turned to his Mistress of Communications. "Hlindredreda, open Compact green channel to all ships."

"By your command," she said, an excited tremor quavering in her lilting singing voice. "Channel open."

"This is Delwyn ar ahoun Unahaillaea *Tyreniioroneo*. With Warleader Bordanin's navigation and comm systems down, I assume Warpact command over the task group. I ask *Pathfinder, Stone Knife,* and *Fearless* to retask themselves to defend *Green Ivy*. *Surefooted* and I are coming to assist *Night Shadow*. Execute immediately."

Melkorka's pride swelled after Delwyn's change of mind. She forgot her Warrior abject outrage over his initial refusal of Warpact command

and the spurning of such a high honor. But now as he accepted command the honor settled on them as a sign of his confidence in them and his belief they supported him in such a great task. "Mistress of Pathwalking, break off engagement and advance to *Night Shadow.*"

"Affirm, acting!" Trebithia said.

"Hlinlodyn, notify the Mistress of Battle and the Mistress of Arms that they are to release weapons and plan for an orbit-to-surface drop while under fire. They are to scan the Action Zone before deciding what combat assets they want to take with them. Notify the Mistress of Conveyance that she is to translate combat assault teams and surface stalking teams and their light armored vehicles as near the research outpost as soon as possible. Advise them I think the Ni'zakhonii have a prototype warship they're trying to get powered up for an FTL jump. That ship must not leave the shipyard," Delwyn interrupted.

"By your command!"

"A ship?" Melkorka asked.

He nodded. "Only thing that makes sense. They could have blown the asteroid up from orbit and been long gone by now. There's no need to fight like this unless there's something here they either can't or are unwilling to leave behind."

***

"Captain? Separate messages coming in on the Compact tactical channels."

"Who from, Lieutenant Romaine?" Rodgers asked.

"One is local, Ma'am. Two Compact ships report they have destroyed two battlecruisers and a destroyer in local space near the dwarf planet. They say we can jump to normal space at any time, Ma'am."

"The other message?" she asked.

"The second signal came over the Compact green channel, priority flash tactical notice. It's Marsch. He's taken Warpact command of the Compact battle group."

Captain Rodgers glanced over at the watching co-Ambassadors and shook her head at them. "I don't understand how a man who never commanded a starship in his life is not only a starship commander but also now a task force commander."

Seralin bristled, but Anlann spoke before she could snap an insulting reply at the warleaderless Mistress of the Ship. "That means *Green Ivy* has either been severely damaged or destroyed."

"Mr. Carstairs prepare to jump the ship back into normal space," Rodgers said.

"Aye Captain, hyperdrive is online. Ready to jump on your command."

"Jump!"

Henri Edda reemerged into normal space 23,240,000 kilometers from her last point in normal space. Their fractional drifting in hyperspace had translated into a much greater normal space displacement on reentry.

"*Padfoot's* Mistress of the Ship says they and *Steep Trails* will remain here with us while they recharge their jump drive and repair their battle damage," Romaine reported.

"Very well. Well, now we hang here in normal space. Repair status, Exec?" Rodgers asked.

"Still nothing from engineering. They're assessing the damage," Cabrera said.

"Lieutenant Romaine, contact *Padfoot* and ask them where the command heavy battlecruiser, the cargo ship, and those three heavy destroyers went," Rodgers said.

***

"Approaching the moon, My Lord Commander."

"Good, Vassal-Navigator. Compute for standard orbit."

"Yes, My Lord Commander. I abase myself."

Haksith clawed a touchpad at his side. "Doctor Tek Nal, report to me at once," he rasped over the intercom.

"At once, My Lord Commander. I abase myself."

Haksith hissed as he switched the intercom off. Too bad about the other ships, but at least he got his ships away, including the cargo ship and its raw geodes. Getting that ship into the dimensional warp for FTL was another matter. *Hiss.* It'd probably explode somewhere mid-journey back to Meerslah knowing his luck. At least they got the carbon catalyst geodes evacuated. Once Tek Nal got them all seeded on that moon they could leave.

His command heavy battlecruiser and the three heavy destroyers reinforcing him had suffered no significant damage. To the desert suns with Bleniss. If Haksith had any say in the matter, he'd…

"My Lord Commander, we have achieved standard orbit around the moon."

Haksith hissed at the interruption.

"Begin science scans and release drone launch systems control to Doctor Tek Nal," Haksith said.

"Yes, My Lord Commander. I abase myself. My Lord Commander? Science scans have detected food animals on the surface."

"Check your instruments, Vassal-Science officer. This moon has no meat animals."

"Self-check diagnostics enabled…Self-check reports bioscanners nominal, My Lord Commander. I abase myself. Dagan-Na Atal analogues are on that moon."

Haksith clacked his teeth together. *Probable instrumentation failure after all.* "Pinpoint its biosign and send a probe for in-depth analysis routed to Doctor Tek Nal."

Probably some worm, flying reptile, or large carnivore. The moon's full of them.

***

Phalalin stood on his Warleader's Watch and watched enemy ships close on him. He had to keep them off Delwyn's tail even if it meant reducing his defense of the command battleship.

"Fire all torpedo inventories, Verikaralee. Advise all ships to do the same!"

"By your command," Verikaralee said.

The range at launch combined with the current closing speed gave the three Compact warships' torpedoes a flight time just over one thousand seconds. That gave the Ni'zakhonii vessels thirteen seconds for their antitorpedo clusters and point defenses to zap as many of them as they could without going evasive. Under normal circumstances, relying on the intercepts, point defenses, and aft shields turned on sound doctrine, assuming normal torpedo spreads, even from three firing warships, but only if those ships were also engaging in evasive maneuvers.

But Phalalin had asked both ships to flush their inventories in rapid-fire spreads. Nominal defensive tactics took into account that ship electronic countermeasures, decoys, point defense systems, and antitorpedo clusters missed one in ten incoming targets, leaving it up to evasive maneuvers to lose the rest, or shields to take the energy released by the explosions and hope the hull plates ionized and spread the energy across the entire hull. But Phalalin had deployed electronic warfare torpedoes capable of kicking up stealth screens, and they had to get close. They were not proximity ordnance, but they were not contact warheads either. Each torpedo contained its own bare-bones quantum translator. It had nowhere near the power necessary to translate itself into an enemy ship, sad to say. It quantum-entangled a small piece of hull plating and displaced it. Not much mass, no more than a hole just large enough to push a finger through. But when the warhead detonated, it pumped an x-ray laser, which fired into the finger-sized breach. By flushing his inventory, Phalalin hoped the standard torpedoes would screen the stealth shipkillers.

And it worked. The Ni'zakhonii point defenses, overwhelmed, operated at less than half their rated efficiency.

Yet the enemy ships pounded on *Green Ivy* with single-minded obsession, ignoring the fact almost every one of their antitorpedoes were being sucked off by Compact decoys or blinded by the jammers. Last-ditch particle weapon clusters opened fire, spitting coherent particles at the last of the oncoming torpedoes, but they too suffered from the jamming and spent all too much effort engaging harmless decoys.

In all, *Fearless* and *Stone Knife* held 1,300 standard and 200 stealth torpedoes, and the late-arriving battered by battle-capable *Pathfinder* carried another 1,300 standard and 200 stealths himself. On average, the Ni'zakhonii ships took 312 standard and 41 stealth shots in their sterns.

That in itself qualified as an outrageous rate of success, yet while the enemy ships continued to hold station relative to *Green Ivy* and pounded at his shields, destructive energies rolled over them as their defenses faltered around their main engine bells and gimbals. Each ship staggered in agony as torpedoes hammered their drive and engineering sections. Capital warships were hard to kill, and it often required a tactical blend of torpedoes, kinetics, and particle weapons used in inventive ways to cause any critical damage to their hull plates, passive, and active defenses. But damage did accumulate, and they could be killed if you pounded at them long enough. Just look at the beating Bordanin was taking, which explained the existence of ships like *Hunter's Moon* and *Pathfinder*, ships designed to ram enemy capital ships.

Of course that did not mean they took the hammering without heavy damage and loss of life.

⁂

Lord Viceroy Bleniss had not just been firing intercepts, either. He noted the change in enemy ship deployment on his scanners, and he realized this third dagan-Na Atal warship, a heavy cruiser, had evened up the odds. He reluctantly diverted offensive fire from the enemy battleship to it and hoped his remaining ships could hold out long enough for the recovery teams to get the prototype heavy cruiser released from its scaffolding and umbilicals and powered up. So far he had four dagan ships tied up. If he could draw back the second assault cruiser, then what he had remaining in orbit and on the asteroid should more than be capable of taking out the two remaining dagan destroyers.

⁂

Phalalin balanced easily as his warship shook beneath him.

Again and again.

Torpedo after torpedo had veered off to engage a decoy, wandered off mindless from EMP countermeasures, or shot on past, unable to see its intended target through his warship's own jamming and the ECM screening drones buzzing around the trio of ships like ear-nipping salt-seeking insects. Of the 13,420 torpedoes sent against them 11,404 had been spoofed or blinded. From the remaining two thousand, over thirteen hundred had homed in on the screening elements, the three EW drones masquerading as Compact warships. Of the 202 torpedoes hitting genuine targets, *Fearless* took 40 hits. *Stone Knife* took 33 hits. *Pathfinder* took 24 hits not counting all the secondary particle weapons fire the Ni'zakhonii ships could fire from their aft batteries.

All the torpedoes *Pathfinder* took impacted on his heavily shielded combat hull, resulting in moderate damage to a few hull plates, and damage to his forward secondary weapon systems.

Stone Knife suffered from intermittent power loss and burned out shield generators in his combat hull, and heavy damage to his forward torpedo bays. He reported no deaths, but his Mistress of Healers had many injuries down in Health Center, at least 1,412 at last count.

"Status of enemy ships?" Phalalin asked.

"One destroyer adrift and scanners report massive aft damage and uncontrolled fires, buckling bulkheads, and chain reaction decompressions. No life signs," Verikaralee replied. "The heavy battlecruiser and battleship are maintaining fire on *Green Ivy*. The battleship has partial main power and sensors report the heavy battlecruiser's power systems are fluctuating wildly. *Correction!* Heavy battlecruiser is losing drive reactor containment. Runaway reaction in progress! Reactors are failing to auto-stop…"

Phalalin shielded his eyes as the toy ship next to his head blossomed into glowing plasma.

He paced the Warleader's Watch's cubic holographic display for one full circle before pointing to the last combat-capable ship. "Fire main kinetic weapons and particle weapons on this ship, concentrate here," he pointed. "Ask *Stone Knife* and *Pathfinder* to do the same."

"By your command," Verikaralee said.

"Damage report," Phalalin said, readying himself for bad news.

"Minor structural damage to the combat hull, mostly damaged or destroyed hull plating. Intermittent meshing primary and secondary shields, resulting in inefficient multiphasic overlap. Tertiary shields and the radiological shields are offline. Torpedo inventory is down to zero. Phalalin, if they fire a nuclear torpedo now, we will suffer severe ionizing radiation exposure."

"Understood." *Spirits!* "Withdraw!"

"But Phalalin!" Verikaralee objected. In combat frenzy, along with the entire crew, the last thing she wanted to do was retreat.

"Do it!" Phalalin sang, and then he sang in earnest, calming the 20,000 female crew ready to kill the enemy bare-handed just for the danger they represented to him.

One job a warleader had was to help his warlike females disengage when they should do so instead of having them take unwarranted risks.

As he sang, Phalalin wondered how Delwyn was managing his own females.

###

Delwyn stood in his own private universe, a twenty-meter square dark cube filled with an asteroid and five small ships. Well, four now as a second Ni'zakhonii ship exploded some 30,000 kilometers off Bordanin's bow.

He studied the approaching asteroid and the heavy battlecruiser and destroyer screening the research outpost. Another heavy battlecruiser's fire-gutted hulk fell through a deorbiting spiral, destined to hit the asteroid's farside in another ten minutes or so. The remaining heavy battlecruiser showed signs of heavy damage. The destroyer remained beyond the engagement and in standard orbit over the outpost and shipyard.

"Status of those two heavies?" Delwyn demanded.

"Primary target heavy battlecruiser operating at full shields. Minor hulling along the port broadside, with sporadic power surges. Sensors show he has lost orbital maneuvering capability and is trying to hold station using RCS and ACS alone. Secondary target heavy battlecruiser has minimal shields, minimal particle weapon systems, but intact torpedo pods, but he also has failing life support and severe outgassing from multiple breaches and decompressing compartments," Hlinlodyn reported.

"Delwyn, *Surefooted* is adjusting into attack posture, heading to intercept the secondary target vessel!" Trebithia said.

"Open tactical comm to *Night Shadow*, Hlindredreda."

"By your command. Tactical channel open."

Delwyn met the eyes of the ship's warleader in respect. "If you engage the primary target ship, I will screen you and *Surefooted* as I begin the assault on the asteroid."

"Affirm. Executing," he said and vanished from the screen.

"Hlinlodyn, status of *Surefooted* and *Night Shadow?*"

The Mistress of Tactics scanned both warships and read the results. "*Surefooted* has taken marginal damage and all his systems read nominal. *Night Shadow* has moderate damage to his forward ventral hull and has lost his primary shields. He is overlapping his secondary and tertiary shields. I read some minor outgassing indicating a compromised hull," she looked up at him, worried.

"Can you pinpoint the damage?" he asked.

"His forestation, Delwyn. That is a dangerous place to suffer heavy structural damage."

Delwyn watched as the asteroid scans cleared, showing him a somewhat lopsided solid rock pockmarked here and there with small craters. It had no atmosphere, but it did have a wide, deep chasm, a canyon ranging some kilometers long and seven hundred meters wide. It looked like a jagged tear that ran at least a kilometer below the surface. Scan returns showed what looked like the soaring battlements and turrets of a medieval castle carved into the canyon walls with scaffolding built into the castle and what looked like the leading edge of a hull.

"Mistress of Battle prepare to drop your troop transports and light armored vehicle assets," Delwyn said.

"By your command," came Nynava's reply over the combat address system.

"Hlinlodyn, engage surface assault batteries," Delwyn said as *Surefooted* killed his target.

"*Surefooted* is adjusting his trajectory and firing on the remaining…Direct hit on *Night Shadow*'s forestation!"

Delwyn spun around in time to see the Compact destroyer explode at the ventral hull and up through the warship's forestation, decapitating the combat hull from the command hull. The explosive force caused the combat hull to tumble into the asteroid, where it blew a crater in its surface.

"What about the rest of the ship?" Delwyn asked, his mouth gone dry.

"The forestation blast doors sealed on the command hull side, and sensors show effort underway to regain attitude control. His shields are down. Delwyn, his hull integrity has been lost. Even with nominal jump drive, he cannot jump to FTL."

"Understood. Ship-to-ship to Ahwroona, Hlindredreda."

"Ship-to-ship open," Hlindredreda said.

Ahwroona's image appeared on his screen. "Yes, Delwyn?" she replied.

"Break off your engagement and screen *Night Shadow*. I will engage the remaining ship and continue the planetary assault."

Ahwroona bent her ears downward, clearly not happy being told to disengage in the heat of battle even though it was warranted. But she did so, knowing Anlann and Seralin remained marooned on a Coalition warship far from her.

"Status of surface barrage?" Melkorka asked Hlinlodyn.

The Mistress of Tactics consulted her planetary targeting prioritizing system.

"Secondary kinetic weapons have targeted every crater, crack, and rock resembling a surface emplacement. I presume a wide combat area around the shipyard has already been presighted, and the surface strike gunners are targeting everything usable as a grid reference or visual landmark. Jamming assets have soft-landed and are broadcasting. We are firing multiple-tuned EMP torpedoes in an attempt to suppress enemy assets."

"What fired on *Pathfinder?*" Delwyn asked.

Melkorka scanned her command console. "Nothing the sensors can find, but it must be something big."

"That ship in the drydock?" he asked.

"Possibly, but if they have the power buildup to fire, then they will have sufficient power to engage their FTL soon."

Damn! "Mistress of Arms?" He sang into the air.

"Delwyn?" Zalzadrin's voice sang back over the combat address system. "You are not going to pull back my assault stalking missions now, are you?" she asked plaintively.

"No, Zalzadrin. Change in plan. Have the Mistress of Conveyance translate you into the prototype ship if possible. Pick up another *tail* of Warriors to go with you. Stop that ship from leaving."

"By your command. Give me ten minutes."

"That's about all you do have."

Delwyn lurched as the deck dropped out from under him. For a brief second, he hung in free fall before he slammed back into the deck.

"Direct hit, primary combat hull. Minor damage reported," Hlinlodyn said.

"Launch surface assault forces!" Melkorka said.

"Affirm, acting," the Mistress of Tactics replied. "Combat assault transports exiting the deployment bay."

Delwyn sang to his crew as he considered what was happening.

The Mistress of Battle led a tail, 125 people, of infantry in low-gee vacuum combat environmental suits, and a fist, 25, of hovertanks, each piece of armor carrying four crew.

"Surface assault kinetic batteries, cease fire. Assault transports and assets on approach to the Action Zone," Melkorka said.

"Mistress! Radiological alarm. Three nuclear torpedoes inbound. Radiological shield to maximum power. Sealing the combat deployment bay doors," Hlinlodyn sang at urgent tempo.

"Countermeasures! Fire intercepts!" Melkorka sang.

Delwyn watched the radiological torpedoes bear down on them, watched two break for *Surefooted.* "Fire intercepts at the inbounds headed for *Surefooted.* "

"By your command," Trebithia replied. "Prepare for shock wave."

"Countermeasures got one! Two lining up, proximity explosion most likely," Hlinlodyn said.

The display flashed white as the ship staggered like a passenger vehicle hitting a brick wall at one-hundred kph.

"Our primary shields are down. Radiological shields have absorbed the brunt of the ionizing radiation and are radiating it away from the hull."

Screw this! Delwyn thought to himself. "Trebithia, adjust combat maneuvering for high orbit soft ram. We're going to shove him into the asteroid."

"By your command."

"What? Are you certain of this?" Melkorka asked, thinking about the ram attack preceding Kalinn's death. "He will jump to FTL, and we will overshoot and hit the asteroid ourselves."

"I don't think so. He's using all the power he's got trying to keep his shields up. He can't divert power to his drive without us cutting him to ribbons."

"Hlinlodyn? Tactical comm. *Surefooted?* Disengage from screening *Night Shadow* and dump your torpedo inventory into that ship!" Melkorka said.

"Affirm!" Ahwroona said.

Delwyn watched Ahwroona's warship pick up the assault on the Lizard heavy battlecruiser as his warship disengaged and made for the orbital high ground before swinging back around and down, driving for the enemy ship fighting for its life.

"Ease up on the forward velocity, Trebithia. We don't want to penetrate into their hull and fall to our deaths with them."

"By your command. Decelerating. I do not want to follow after them either, Delwyn," the Mistress of Pathwalking admonished.

The Shaha heavy battlecruiser tried to fire at both the torpedo-launching destroyer and the closing planetary assault battlecruiser when it dawned on the ship's commander the reason why the decelerating ship was not firing but continued to close on his vessel. He had no choice. He redirected everything he had at the assault battlecruiser and ignored the destroyer.

"Mistress, we are taking damage to the combat hull. Secondary shields have fallen below one-quarter power. There is also minor hulling to both outrigger hulls and minor damage to the engineering hull dorsal plates." The ship shook as something exploded behind the command center. "Hull breach in Power Systems and Propulsion. Breach force fields have activated. No casualties reported," Hlinlodyn said.

Ahwroona's warship pounded at the enemy ship and suddenly its shields dropped. It exploded, rippling blasts flowed in a cascading chain from its engine complex up through the hull to the bow.

"Abort closure maneuver," Melkorka sang. "Adjust to standard surveillance orbit and advise all ships we have gained the high ground. Assault team status?"

Hlinlodyn pulled up her Combat Analysis Asset Tracking and read from the summary. "Combat assets and combat troop transports have landed with minimal losses. Hovertanks are moving out as armor support for infantry exterior assault on the Ni'zakhonii outpost."

"Mistress of Arms begin translating your teams into that prototype if possible. Place a reserve force in the outpost to help the combat breaching forces as needed," Delwyn ordered. "Go with the spirits, Zalzadrin."

"By your command. You will never be rid of me, Delwyn!"

15
ASSAULTMISTRESS KIDAHIN

Kidahin finished sealing her combat accessories pack and looked around her abode. Everything was where it should be, so she picked up the bow and arrows at her feet and stepped through the open bole.

She turned to the right and slung the bow over her shoulders. On her way down the trail she stopped to pick up more assault equipment from a weaponmistress, dangerous items any one of the roving Warrior trios would notice during their standard security sweeps. The warship carried combat forces trained to conduct boarding actions against enemy ships and to support combat operations on a planetary surface. The warship was their home, and everyone aboard was trusted with weaponry, both traditional and modern weapons. That said, modern weaponry included explosive ordnance and demolitions charges. Kidahin needed the eleven demolitions packs, the most powerful molecular catalyst explosive known to Compact science, to shatter open blast door entries into the alien shipyard. Both Nynava and Zalzadrin had unfettered access to the material, as did their weaponmistresses.

Kidahin's abode was located on one of the command hull intermediate levels, along with most of the personnel quarters, and so she had a long prowl to the combat staging and deployment bay. Still, prowling down jungle trails was a nice way to pass the time and relieve anxiety.

She stalked the passage, twisting her pons absently at the few people she met along the way. She was wide awake, excited. This would be her first combat action as assaultmistress.

She glided along thick jungle trails, taking a circuitous route that brought her closer and closer to the combat staging area. The trails soon became main pathways. Security sensors flagged the demolition charges and the power cell inside the small thumper she also carried. The EMP broadcast unit would disable all unshielded local electronic devices, a useful item for defeating enemy infantry technology.

No local force fields snapped on to arrest her movements. Kidahin was an assaultmistress and had the Mistress of Arms' authorization to carry items usually under the watch of a persistent, fussy weaponmistress. She climbed up a tree, the preferred mode of vertical ascent on a Compact warship, and onto a horizontal branch that turned hollow. She exited through a bole at the other end onto another forest trail. She picked up her pace and walked for several hundred ells through thick vegetation before coming abruptly up against a closed blast door. She sang to it, and the blast door opened out onto the combat staging and deployment bay.

***

Zalzadrin turned to Akenallin. "So? The ship then?"

The Mistress of Conveyance scowled at her instrumentation, her ears dipping. "No. Translation lock not possible. This happened once before. I tried to get a translation lock-on to Delwyn when he brought the captured equipment back into Nikkiolo's heliopause. The best I can do is put your teams somewhere in the shipyard or somewhere in or around the outpost itself."

"Atmosphere?" Zalzadrin asked.

"None in the shipyard. It is open to space. Scans show an oxygen-nitrogen atmosphere within the outpost, higher than normal oxygen, along with several volatile compounds."

Zalzadrin remembered. When they had captured the light attack craft—equipment—Delwyn had said it smelled like rotting fruit and smashed worms. She preferred a more apt description: it *stank!*

"Scan the shipyard, Akenallin. If the ship reflects external scans, maybe you can use the null return to trace for possible open hatches."

Akenallin nodded and played her targeting scanners along the prototype heavy cruiser's hull.

Zalzadrin watched Akenallin's ears perk forward as she concentrated on her readings. "Vessel reads more massive than a Compact destroyer, but less massive than a heavy cruiser. I find no open hatches, which implies he has at least minimal life support."

Zalzadrin swore and slapped the translation station comm. "Delwyn? Zalzadrin. Translation into the ship *izzant* possible. I recommend you fire on him while he remains moored in the construction drydock."

"If we fire on him now, we will destroy the outpost and all their research," he said. "Assault the outpost perimeter. That ship can't launch while he's still moored to the docking clamps. They might be able to retract his moorings, but I bet they can't override the docking clamps and the drydock scaffold controls. That should be something only the dockmaster can do from the outpost mooring station for security reasons."

"What about sending in some Warrior infantry teams?" Zalzadrin asked.

Delwyn thought about it. This would be no surprise assault on an enemy fortification. The Lizard demolition corps had taken months to carve out a castle in asteroid native rock. His surface assault forces would have to land on the airless rock and drive armored personnel carriers and light armored vehicles over pockmarked low-gee terrain, breach the outpost walls, and force themselves through the breach while Lizard infantry fired into the bottleneck. It would take the heavy tanks and the hovertanks time to batter away at the outpost particle shields. Better for Nynava to take a couple APCs and a LAV with infantry weapons platforms and try blasting into the rock outside the shield perimeter. It was obvious even to his limited tactical ability that he couldn't let Hlinlodyn fire on the outpost while Nynava and Zalzadrin were breaching the perimeter. Besides, he had enough to worry about with keeping the Lizard ships from firing on the ground forces. They presented an attractive target of opportunity from orbit, and the Lizards knew their outpost shields could take friendly fire, if necessary, to prevent the Compact assault teams from breaching their outpost.

"Take them with you. Let Nynava secure the outpost while you prowl the place. Your mission is to capture and return all equipment, every computer, every datapad, every single component you can find, but your higher priority target is to get to the dockmaster's station, capture and secure it, and find a way to stop that ship from fleeing."

"By your command," Zalzadrin said.

"So you want to take the combat EVA suits?" Akenallin asked her.

Zalzadrin thought about it. EVA suits were a bother, but clearly she could not lead her stalkers from the APCs and LAV into the outpost or the shipyard without them.

"Yes, and field packs. Spirits! I was hoping to gain access to an exterior airlock hatch."

She turned to the waiting Warriors. "You heard the Warleader?"

They nodded, their perked ears following her, and a tiny spark of mischievous pride swelled in her chest. She was mistress here. She thrust the nagging thought of her short stature aside. Hunters were on average taller than Warriors, but Zalzadrin was the shortest Hunter aboard, and being reminded of it had always put her in a bad mood, a mood she compensated for by joking. But now she was involved with serious combat planning, and she had no time to resent most of these Warriors for being taller than she.

"The surveillance stalkers will prowl out and return with actionable intelligence. You will then advance based on that intelligence, capture and hold territory, and begin asset recovery. I want every cabinet, every screw, every piece of paper and grimy rag translated to the ship.

"Mistress Akenallin, I think it might be prudent to use the combat staging translation station to bring bulk equipment aboard the ship. I recommend you quarantine the deployment bay and keep a hand poised over the emergency decompress control in the event you must jettison everything we bring aboard."

"You are anticipating ordnance capture?" Akenallin asked, frowning.

"No, but we are in a hurry, and no one knows what we might bring aboard in our haste," Zalzadrin said.

Akenallin nodded. She manipulated her scans. "I have found several large voids excavated into solid rock. Scans suggest some of them are warehouses and maintenance bays. No lifesigns have been detected in or near them at the moment. I do detect several hundred lifesigns in voids registering as preassembly bays and laboratories. Ni'zakhonii are also concentrated in what looks like a drydock service and control area. I have also found what reads like a machine shop."

Zalzadrin listened attentively as she drew her bow, checking its pull. Then she loaded her bow quiver and perked her ears. "Download all the scans into our 'minders. Boarding party assaultmistresses, prepare to translate into a hot Action Zone."

"Affirm!" the boarding party assaultmistresses sang in unison as they took their places next to the two APCs and the LAV within the translation station. The Warrior infantry teams took up mobile weapons platforms behind them.

"You will arrive on the surface near a ridge wall. Signal when the field is clear for the rest of us to join you. Mistress of Conveyance, commence translation of surface action assault teams."

"Affirm. Translating now."

Zalzadrin watched the first APC and its Warrior complement flash and then vanish.

The next 110 seconds dragged by, and Zalzadrin watched the mission clock tick with trepidation. *Why have they not reported successful…?*

The tactical comm clicked open on Akenallin's console. "Translation site secured," came the reply. "No enemy sighted. Ground-penetrating sensors detect multiple compartments carved into the interior of the asteroid. Particle shielding has full coverage down to the bedrock below the regolith. The combat engineering teams should be able to penetrate the ridge and cliff face with infantry heavy plasma fire. Whether or not outpost shields can extend into the exposed breach is unknown at this time. I am no engineer, but scans of the materials stored here look important. Mistress, Action Zone is clear for staging at this time."

"Acknowledged," Zalzadrin commed back to the senior assaultmistress. "The remaining assault teams are on their way to you."

Zalzadrin turned and twitched her tail at the remaining four fists of Warriors. "Next fist, followed by the next, in rapid deployment order!"

Akenallin translated the remaining APC, the LAV, and all four hundred Warriors in less than ten minutes.

"Situation unchanged," came the report from the senior assaultmistress.

Zalzadrin turned to the remaining females, Hunters all. A hand of assaultmistresses and their teams of two hands each. "Each assaultmistress will prowl a designated section highlighted on her 'minder. You will prowl the area carefully, for you are not only to pinpoint the Ni'zakhonii, but you are also to locate and return all material likely to help reconstruct what they have built here. If you have any doubt, tag it for translation to the ship. As you exhaust your designated prowling areas, exit and stalk through the tunnels until you reach your next prowling area or meet up with another team. Remember, as much as possible you are not there to engage the enemy. Leave that to the Warriors."

"What are the areas we will be prowling?" Kidahin asked.

"I have rendered the scan broadly into sections resembling dock construction and control, warship fueling and supply, research and development, material fabrication, warehousing and outpost maintenance," Zalzadrin said.

Kidahin gathered her two hands of surveillance stalkers around her and showed them where they had been assigned to prowl: research and development.

"Mistress?" Kidahin asked. "Which group are you accompanying?"

"Yours, Kidahin. As you can see by the scans on your 'minder, your prowling area is centrally located, and I expect the assault teams to move with us until the outpost is breached. I also expect to encounter combat there, and we will join in battle, but we cannot remain as support stalkers for them. The stalking teams taking the drydock and mooring station control center must keep the enemy from releasing that ship."

"Zalzadrin, why aren't you moving?" Delwyn demanded from the command center. "Holding this position much longer is inviting them to fire on us like they did to *Pathfinder*. We have to remain within the arc of their weapon lock to keep within translation range of the shipyard."

"We are leaving now, Delwyn!" Zalzadrin said and nodded to Akenallin.

Kidahin watched as her view of the Conveyance Center blinked and was replaced by an airless regolith-scattered, cratered vista. Up ahead several thousand ells away a solid-looking rocky tor rose into the star-strewn, pitchblack void along the lip of a million-ell long canyon. The surrounding area bore the signs of concentrated kinetic fire from overhead. Hlinlodyn had thoroughly blasted every possible grid reference site and drone platform position lurking in wait to cut down all infantry approaches. Multiple flares polarized their EVA visors as particle weapons fired from orbit struck the outpost shields. Delwyn was trying to drain energy reserves from the enemy hydrogen-antihydrogen reactor. He would have to cease fire before they could advance.

***

"Teams check in," Nynava sang over the comm. She had a husky, remote tonal quality to her voice. It was intentional, quite chilling actually. It made her hard to ignore.

"Team-Three in position," Warrior Karadenlin announced. Team-Three had drawn the surface action recon assault, since it was the largest and heaviest armed of the Warrior assault teams. They were the most experienced team as well.

"Team-Four in position," came the next check, and Zalzadrin wondered if Nynava was listening. The spirits knew she would be busy soon enough her own self.

"Team-Two in position," Kidahin said. Her response was late, and Zalzadrin called up the remote plot on her 'minder and grimaced. The remote reported Team-Two's tail still did not have anyone covering it, but just as she thought that Team-Ten fell into position behind Team-Two.

Team-Ten was on the tail of Team-Two's objective, ready to plug the backtrail, and both Team-Two and Team-Ten were also accompanied by a fist of Warriors each. Spare EVA combat Hunters were in the LAV, ready to move as reinforcements if they were needed.

"All right," Nynava said finally. "All teams are in position and the mission is underway. All teams: execute!"

"All surface assault teams, stand-by to open fire!" Zalzadrin called over the commlink.

***

Delwyn chafed at being stuck on the command center. He wanted to lead the combat forces. He was a special operations group commander. He was special operations. Hell, special operations had been his whole life since the Lizards had raided Valhalla Colony in the Mu Arae star system and had eaten his wife and three daughters alive.

Even when he had resigned his senior chief warrant officer warrant so he could stowaway aboard the Lizard light attack craft and rescue twenty-two Eyloni females without implicating the Coalition of Earth Colonies in an act of war, he had led them as a sire cairn, a battle leader. Fighting alone and then later with the liberated Eyloni captives had felt the same as it had when he led his action response teams in battle for the Coalition.

Well, almost like fighting with his ARTs, but not quite. The Eyloni had given him an added dimension, an emotional one that connected them to him in a family way. He felt the same way for them now, both for those on the asteroid and for those aboard his ship.

Delwyn also found himself on the other end of the stick when it came to combat. He'd been the one on the planet surface leading forces slogging it out over mined and booby-trapped fields of battle. He had been the one pinned down on some nightmare strip of land waiting for orbital support to fire on enemy positions. Those ships had been jockeying around in high orbitals fighting other starships and covering Delwyn and his ARTs at the same time.

Every time he found himself in that position he always muttered the mantra all SOG, Marines, and regular mobile infantry muttered: fleet came at its own good time, at its own lazy rate, always late and always after the ground forces had taken a pounding and suffered heavy casualties they wouldn't otherwise have had to if only fleet had bombarded enemy lines when they were supposed to. It was a maxim held in common by all surface combat troopers that the fleet "was flyin'" while the infantry was dyin'."

Well, he was getting quite an education right now, and it left a bad taste in his mouth.

So far the Compact battle group had cut enemy ships from a nine down to three with only two Compact ships out of the battle but not destroyed. The battleship *Green Ivy* remained adrift with only moderate damage. The destroyer *Night Shadow* had withdrawn after his combat hull had been destroyed. Fortunately, what remained of his command and engineering hulls had taken only moderate damage.

Delwyn's warship had suffered minor hull damage so far. *Surefooted* had marginal damage and was screening *Night Shadow*. *Fearless* had moderate damage as well, but he had also lost his radiological shields. He couldn't shield against radiological bursts but had gone on to screen Bordanin's drifting battleship anyway. The planetary assault battlecruiser *Pathfinder* had taken heavy damage to his combat staging and deployment bay but otherwise had only minor damage shipwide. The destroyer *Stone Knife* had taken heavy damage.

Of the three Lizard ships, the battlecruiser had accumulated marginal to moderate damage. The LAC carrier had taken minimal damage, but the destroyer hadn't taken so much as a scratch. Delwyn knew the destroyer, screened by thirty to forty ECM and EW platforms, and towing missile pods, drones, and decoys, was taking on shuttles and probes stuffed with data and material from the outpost and shipyard below. Light attack craft similar to the one he had captured were flying up from the surface and landing within the LAC carrier. It too had over a hundred AI-controlled

EW and ECM assets. Delwyn wanted to hit that carrier so bad he could taste it, but he couldn't. He was involved in supporting a surface action launched from his ship's combat staging and deployment bay.

And he was getting pounded by enemy kinetics and particle weapons. There hadn't been a radiological warning for over thirty-five minutes. The enemy destroyer wasn't firing anything, preferring to let her point defenses and countermeasures take care of all incoming. That meant she still had a fully-loaded torpedo inventory and kinetics. She wouldn't have many, but a destroyer could wreak havoc on a heavily damaged ship.

The LAC carrier didn't carry that many more torpedoes than a destroyer did, for all that the carrier was a much larger ship. Yet most of its volume was dedicated to the LACs she normally carried. Given the size of the LAC prototypes coming up from the shipyard, the carrier had to have come here empty.

Those LAC prototypes were hard little suckers, too. So far Hlinlodyn had shot down only three although she had scored direct hits on over twelve of them.

The bloody Lizard battleship had him worried. That ship had real mass. Crystallized nickel-iron, it had apparently been grown from a single crystal. Funny, but Delwyn always thought of crystals as glasslike shards or gems, but more durable elements had crystal structures too, and the Lizards could manufacture materials by growing them. The battleship had hull plates fifty meters thick made from a single crystal each. All that mass meant she would take quite a long time to generate a navigation solution, but he wasn't sure if it was much of a liability: that ship seemed to have an inexhaustible supply of kinetics and torpedoes.

"Delwyn!" Melkorka yelled. "The battleship is breaking away from Bordanin. He is adjusting his orbit to intercept us!"

"Understood."

What to do? He couldn't go evasive and leave the surface combat forces exposed to orbit-to-surface bombardment. He wanted to go after the LAC carrier, catch it between him and the asteroid, and crash it into the surface. At least he should try to pop one or two shots off at that destroyer.

Wait a minute. "Hlinlodyn, where did the destroyer go?"

"I have him," Trebithia said. "Navigation scans paint him adjusting into polar orbit. He is twelve minutes from north pole overhead position and beyond range of weapon lock…"

"Incoming fire!" Hlinlodyn interrupted. "From the battleship, minimum spread heavy yield torpedoes in three volleys."

"Recall all ships to screen us while we maintain screening for the combat mission."

"By your command," Hlinlodyn said. "Tactical comm acknowledgments received. *Fearless* is closing on an attack vector to the battleship. *Stone Knife* and *Pathfinder* are lining up on the battleship's stern and raking his engine complex. *Surefooted* is breaking away from *Night Shadow* and is closing on the battleship's left flank."

"Trebithia, adjust to high orbit, prepare to engage enemy ships."

"You are risking exposing the surface action assault teams to orbital bombardment," Melkorka observed.

"Can't be helped. We know the research materials remaining behind are still down there somewhere. We also know the evacuated materials and operational LACs up here are ready to leave. We pop off a few shots at their shields and prevent them from jumping to FTL. Then we return to point and tell Nynava and Zalzadrin to hurry the hell up."

Delwyn had a sudden urge to pray for forgiveness to every captain he had ever cursed for leaving his ARTs defenseless on the battlefield.

"Oh, damn!" Delwyn said. "He's trying to go around us!"

"Adjust supporting fire!" Melkorka said furiously from her command chair. "Hlinlodyn, tactical comm to Zalzadrin!"

"Affirm!"

The Compact infantry platform was a belt-fed, gas-operated, self-propelled grenade launcher. The advanced composition of the grenade filler gave them the destructive force of a pre-spaceflight twenty-kilo bomb, but despite any advance in explosive fillers, the chemical-powered launcher had an old-fashioned kick like that of an *eo'on*. Ripping off an entire belt in a mass of fire was the action of an idiot or someone very good with the weapon and big enough to handle the recoil.

Herallin was neither a fool nor particularly massive. When given the order to "flush" the detected Ni'zakhonii, the experienced Warrior settled the big weapon into her shoulder, made sure the 1,000-round belt fed over her shoulder without a kink, and started a slow, aimed sweeping fire.

The recoil impacted against her EVA suit shoulder plate, commuting a deep chiseling sound through her helmet that raised the hackles on her neck. The remainder of Team-One spread out around her as she fired grenades into the area where the sensors had detected movement. Moments later, the ground and rock walls flashed white.

"Forward!" Herallin sang.

Nynava glanced at her tactical display and made a decision.

"They are trying to close off this tunnel," she snapped over the commlink. "Herallin, stay in place and screen our flank. As we pass, roll in behind us. Everybody but the sharpshooters off the LAV. Team-Three to point. Team-Two, fold into the body. Advance."

One hour and fifty-three minutes into the battle the Shaha battleship struck *Hunter's Moon* a glancing blow with multiple particle beam strikes along the port side forestation. "Mistress, power distribution network load-sharing crossover tie-in to the jump drive reactor reserve buss and the Forward Fusion-2 power systems is offline. Power to the left side combat hull is down and secondary weapons systems and primary and secondary shield are inoperative on the left side primary and secondary combat hull," Hlinlodyn reported.

"Trebithia, right yaw bow thrusters twelve second burst," Melkorka ordered. "Pitch down one hundred degrees and null rates. Hlinlodyn, tertiary power systems?"

"Anailiatha reports tertiary systems coming online. Shields firming up but they are making a heavy demand on the load-sharing bypass in Forward Fusion-2 power systems. Insufficient power available through tertiary systems to fire secondary weapons or point defenses on the secondary combat hull."

The spirits! Melkorka swore to herself.

###

Kidahin nodded to herself as her 'minder flashed a movement alert.

"Kidahin, set your team on top of the LAV and have Team-Four take point!" Zalzadrin sang.

###

"Where the hell did that destroyer go?" Delwyn demanded.

"Tactical shows him in polar surveillance orbit opposite our position, Delwyn," Trebithia reported. "I am surprised they are still there. All the data we have on Ni'zakhonii FTL propulsion suggests that, as the lowest-mass ship, he should have jumped long ago."

"Could they be waiting for…?"

"Mistress!" Hlinlodyn sang out. "Direct hit on *Stone Knife*. Shield penetration, inner and outer hull breach in Power Systems and Propulsion. Sublight drive reactor has lost containment. Reactor plasma venting…reactor critical…."

Delwyn looked at the toy ships floating in the tactical display as a blast of pure bright radiance enveloped the destroyer.

"Mistress!" Hlindredreda sang. "Bordanin reports that they have regained control of *Green Ivy*'s helm. He does not resume Warpact warleader status, but he is coming about and is closing on the Ni'zakhonii battleship."

Thank God, Delwyn thought. "Trebithia, adjust to low orbit point position."

"By your command."

"Hlinlodyn, tactical comm to Nynava and Zalzadrin," he said.

"By your command. Tactical channel open. Nynava and Zalzadrin are standing-by."

"Nynava, get into the shipyard and fire on the canyon walls. Try to bury the ship at the bottom of the chasm."

"By your command," Nynava's voice husked over her EVA combat suit discrete mike. "We are fighting through tunnels and hollowed out compartments in igneous rock. We are also providing cover for Zalzadrin and her salvage recovery efforts."

"Tell them to double back for that junk later. Stop that prototype!"

"By your command."

"Zalzadrin?" Delwyn asked. "Did you copy that?"

"Of course I did. We always hear you. We still have another third of the bays to inspect and tag."

"Leave them," Delwyn said.

"But Delwyn! There is little we can do while the Warrior teams are engaging the Ni'zakhonii. Our time is best served by continuing to evacuate the research materials."

Delwyn hated to admit it, but Zalzadrin was right.

"Fine, but as soon as they open the way to the shipyard, the drydock, or the dockmaster control station, you get down there and make sure those clamps don't release."

"By your command."

###

"Mistress!" Kidahin sang. "We have movement front!"

"Fire on the contact," Zalzadrin said. Normally she would have waited for more than a sensor reading. That was not only doctrine, but it was also common sense...normally. But it was not here. Whether it was armor or infantry, it was time to part the branches.

"Affirm," Kidahin said.

The commlink was filled with chatter. It was difficult but not impossible for Kidahin to sort out the conflicting calls. On the other hand, her visor HUD made it clear that she was behind the majority of the Ni'zakhonii defenders and well in the lead of most of the assault teams.

"Kidahin, deploy your prowlers and sweep this area. Then move out another twenty ells and establish a perimeter." Zalzadrin said over the comm.

Zalzadrin started to move on, then stopped when Kidahin did not move.

"Kidahin?"

Kidahin shook her head and took a breath. "Affirm!"

###

Aplilin was firing regular bursts from her mobile weapons platform, laying down a path of destruction to her front. *Vi e'ta Ka nabi*, parting the branches: With no enemy in sight and only indeterminate echoes on the targeting scanner, there was no point in trying for aimed fire. Laying down massive firepower in the general area of the enemy sounded cowardly to her, but it was still the best bet, and the hypervelocity kinetics chewed through doors and walls carved out of the asteroid with spectacular clouds of gray gritty powder.

Nothing else remained in sight, but that didn't mean anything. Aplilin knew she had crept ahead of Kidahin and the rest of Team-Two; her scanner was painting red team targets all over the place when she looked behind her, but there were no green enemy ones in front of her, either. They were coming, though. The rest would be here any time now, and the only question was whether she should go on, or if she should wait for support from a Warrior assault group.

She paused indecisively then hit the ground as the area to her left erupted in plasma fire. Some Warrior from behind had definitely not checked her targeting scanner before firing.

***

"Team-Three, when that Ni'zakhonii APC gets to one hundred and forty ells from the shipyard take it out with plasma fire," Nynava said.

***

Team-Three assaultmistress Saunlinder swung her plasma cannon over to a rocky outcropping and mentally licked her lips as she aimed it carefully. The cannon was designed to slew right or left as a turret armor mount. It had limited elevation options and could not depress below its LAV mount. She got the barrel lined up and hit the switch to drop its firing platform firmly into place.

"Everyone take cover. There will be backblast."

The barrel was aligned with the outer rocky walls as she hunted until the ground-penetrating scan found a compartment behind the stone. It was two hundred ells distant. Lead Ni'zakhonii elements were massing behind the wall. In fact, it was a direct line of sight from her position. She punched a button and grunted as the entire side of the cavern was outlined in green on her sighting screen. The computer recognized its target and began to track automatically as the LAV closed on target.

She designated the entire length of the rocky cliff as a target, then designated three specific target points along its length before she took her eyes from the display to look carefully around her one last time. She was behind the blast shield, but anyone else atop the LAV might get caught by backscatter as the plasma charge exited the weapon.

"Firing!"

The three plasma charges hit like a focused nuclear blast. They did not just breach the cliff face, they vaporized it, along with every

Ni'zakhonii forward infantry and every Ni'zakhonii asset behind it within twenty ells. Beyond the immediate kill zone, there were few survivors. Although the pastel orange reptiles suffered horribly from the flash burns caused by the blast thermal bloom, the violent decompression and vacuum of space ensured they did not suffer long.

###

"I want two grenade volleys," Nynava said. "Aim into the central mass, about 120 ells out. I want to create a break in the assault."

"Affirm," Kidahin said. She had taken command of the right wall breach, while Zalzadrin was directing fire into the research outpost.

"Wait…wait…wait…wait…Now!" Nynava said.

Forty-four grenades arced out into the massed Ni'zakhonii, dropping behind sheltering walls and heaps of rubble blocking the plasma fire, and detonated. The double string of explosions ripped holes in the Ni'zakhonii positions, and hundreds of defenders writhed in shrieking agony as shrapnel from the mini-artillery bursts scythed through their packed ranks.

"Again," Nynava called. "Down one hundred forty ells and fire."

Again the belt-fed launchers spat out their packages of death, tearing enemy ranks apart. The Ni'zakhonii continued, trampling over their mangled soldiers, firing crazily.

###

"Grenades!" Zalzadrin sang. "All you have got!"

Kidahin ripped a cylinder from the EVA combat suit belt with her left hand, thumbed the trigger, and tossed it over the rubble using a snapshot reflex even as she threw two more, but by then the Ni'zakhonii were all rushing into the breach.

Her magazine clicked empty, and she dropped the weapon and pulled her bow from her shoulders. Ni'zakhonii by the fists were clambering over the parapets, their claws holding onto ladders and hideously cruel-looking knives. Trading parries. One of them turned out to be much better with its natural claws than with its knife, and Kidahin found herself back-to-back with Zalzadrin and realized they were practically alone. Most of the assault teams had converged on the bastions.

"Kidahin, I have your back. Shoot!"

"Affirm!" Kidahin said. She took aim and fired her bow, pulled another arrow from the bow quiver and fired again, hitting both targets, piercing their combat suits.

Kidahin heard an alert rhythm over the comm and looked up just in time to see a flight of contact antipersonnel arrows arching over them. That meant the EMP-transmitting thumpers had been deployed.

The small explosives detonated as the arrow penetrated their targets, splattering Ni'zakhonii body parts and pink blood everywhere. The minigrenades cleared the breach, turning the Ni'zakhonii rushing over the rubble minutes ago into shredded flesh. Most of the assault teams had been unaffected by the proximity explosions.

"Fill the breach!"

"But Nynava…" Kidahin began.

"Do it!" Nynava snapped. "All assault teams! Duck and cover!"

Nynava's HUD threw up fresh strength estimates, and she swore. There remained three thousand or so, which was not bad out of a 110,000 force, but her readouts showed only 113 Compact assault teams remaining mobile.

"Hold it up on the other side," Nynava called over the commlink. "Team-Three take the breach point. Team-One and Team-Two support Team-Three."

Kidahin glanced at Zalzadrin, and she nodded. It was time to infiltrate the research outpost.

"Surface assault forces will advance!" Zalzadrin called. She looked through the torn rock and ripped open pieces of the tunneled-out asteroid.

They had entered the research shipyard.

"Mistress," Kidahin called out, "do you have any more arrows? I am out."

Zalzadrin cursed silently. Kidahin had shown herself to seldom miss, but then again she always used more arrows than needed.

"I am about out as well," Zalzadrin admitted.

"I have some," Merkrida said. "You may have them if you wish."

"Drop!" Zalzadrin shouted. "I see movement between us and our reinforcements."

"*Ki*, Zalzadrin," came Nynava's voice. "We are approaching."

"Move!"

Zalzadrin shouldered Kidahin aside, pulled her combat knife, held it at arm's length, and grunted as she brought the ceramic machete down on a reptile's thick arm. Muscle parted as it swung a clawed hand towards her, and she grunted again as it hit her in the stomach—then yelled in fear as she had to roll out of the way as a cascade of tumbling rocks exploded from the ceiling.

Kidahin turned to her team and signed in battle language, telling them to prowl the large room and to tag each lab table and every freestanding piece of equipment for translation lock. She watched Zalzadrin head for an opening in one side of the lab.

Kidahin prowled in silence, affixing tags and moving on. The room's low ceiling was rough-hewn native rock, as were the walls. Only the floors were smooth, some kind of thermal concrete, nothing fancy.

Kidahin caught flashes and floaters sparkling in the corners of her eyes as Akenallin began translating tagged equipment back to the ship.

Kidahin waggled her fingers at her team. <<Be ready to activate your personal thumpers at a moment's notice, but do not do so until I say. We do not want fried electrical systems registering on their security screens.>>

Fourteen hands waggled back in battle language: <<Affirm.>>

Kidahin deployed her prowlers out into the adjoining tunnels. They headed off, combat knives at the ready. Two more Hunters stood at the portal, bows ready. Kidahin, her bow slung over her shoulder, pointed at other high-interest items in the lab. She was no metallurgist, but one long table was covered with metal samples and crystal structures. Certain the stuff had something to do with manipulating the geode crystalline structure, she dutifully tagged it for translation and moved on.

"Kidahin," she heard her name sung in lyrical whispers.

She looked up to see beckoning tails and more waggling fingers.

Jassalin had found an open bay, an apparent extension of the lab. Three of them in fact. Each was a rough rectangular chamber with connecting tunnels at both ends, like three boxes with poles attached to each side. She posted Aplilin, Kyralin, Tialdrin, and Alfara at the open portals leading into the tunnels connecting to the other two bays.

Kidahin stepped into the first bay. Recess alcoves ran parallel along both of the longer sides of the bay. In it were thirteen stations, and each station had some kind of lab analyzer. Hoses connected the analyzers to the benches they rested on. One instrument had a double ringed wheel filled with light-green ceramic crucibles. Another analyzer had stacks of thumb-sized black crucibles made from a mixture of clay and graphite. All instruments had matrix table control stations. They looked like boxes of wet sparkling black sand. Depressions pressed out in even rows and columns in the glittering hard stuff contained a single glowing gem each. Control crystals, 311 of them, some red, some orange, some yellow, some green, some blue, and even a few clear and black-light purple crystals filled them—one gem per slot. Display screens, round and convex crystals, showed images in warped patterns. The instrumentation and equipment looked organic, like puffballs and shelf fungus growing out of the concrete floor. One instrument, a squat unwieldy box, had a cable connecting it to what looked like a spear wrapped in heat-resistive coatings. Its visual display showed a horribly out-of-focus puckered green graph that, after running a refocusing routine on her 'minder to pull the image meant for compound eyes into focus so she could read it, resembled a thermal graph with well-defined plateaus.

This lab was somehow connected with metallurgical analysis all right.

Kidahin tagged all of the instrumentation in the bay before drawing back out of sight of their hated enemy. The Ni'zakhonii had evacuated the middle bay and were heading deeper into the carved-out fortress through the third bay.

The second bay looked like the first except it had only two long stations running parallel along the room's length. Within each station rested two chunks of rock, pieces of a shattered geode some four ells long. Each piece laid in a bath of clear fluid, some kind to pretreatment process maybe?

Kidahin ordered it tagged as well.

<<Kidahin, we have found a side laboratory,>> Hollfara signed.

<<More metallurgical analysis?>> Kidahin signed back.

<<I do not think so. This lab is much smaller and well isolated. It has a clean room filled with microscopes, small centrifuges, and liquid nitrogen.>>

<<Biological?>> Kidahin signed back.

<<It certainly does not look like anything connected with crystalline structures or metal fabrication. Could there be a biochemical agent in processing the crystal structures? The baths, perhaps?>> Hollfara asked.

Kidahin shook her head, unsure. She had to see it for herself before she could let Hollfara tag it. They could not take the entire outpost aboard their warship, and certainly some of this lab work must have to do with maintaining the environment inside the asteroid.

Inside the small tunneled out rock room stood more basic lab equipment. But the small clean room to the side held samples of liquids in test tubes and vials. Some stood in racks, some rested in small centrifuges. Her eyes passed over a small cryogenic drum, the last remaining of what had probably been a few hundred of them stacked here. Kidahin ignored everything else in the lab except the contents of the clean room.

Kidahin chanced her short-range comm. "Mistress Zalzadrin?"

"Yes Kidahin?"

"Mistress, I have found a biological clean room. I have tagged the contents of the area, but I fear these items may contain a biological contaminant. They should all be translated to the Mistress of Healers' biological agents holding area."

"Why bother?" Zalzadrin asked, mildly exasperated. "What could biological processes have to do with mineral or metal fabrication?"

"I am not sure, but maybe they have to cure the crystals in some chemical or biological process. The device we helped Delwyn capture did remind me of a crystallized plant."

"If you want to bother with it, go right on ahead. I think you are reaching. You cannot send every beaker and test tube back to the ship. If you want to draw the ire of both the Mistress of Healers and the Mistress of Conveyance, then by all means do so, but if you do, make sure you mark everything as hazardous cargo and advise Akenallin before she translates it aboard.

"Combat update: We have intercepted and killed two groups of three enemy so far. The Warriors have finished tagging items of interest in the warehouse and have rejoined us. Expect action soon."

Kidahin rang off and stared at the clean room. Was it worth the trouble? Zalzadrin was right; the Mistress of Healers would not appreciate having foreign contaminants in her Health Center, and Akenallin would not appreciate translating the stuff onto the combat staging translation station first and then precision translating the whole tail load into the Health Center.

Too much trouble for too little gain, Kidahin thought as she turned to leave.

Thoughts of Delwyn flooded her mind anew as he began singing another song, one he had sung for her months ago. The first time she heard it, it had sent her into combat frenzy. He had sung it to her while on Ibeetu. In doing so, he had proved to her that he could sing battle songs, songs intended to incite females to fight in defense of the singing male.

It had been one of many signs showing her society that Delwyn was Eyloni.

The song had sounded so improbable when later, at the Death Song ritual, he had sung it again at a slow tempo, which did not incite her or any other female to violence. The song told the story of valiant males fighting until their artillery pieces had melted. So enterprising had these males been that they captured a water-dwelling reptile, forced projectiles into its mouth, and shoved explosives up its a'pea, and fired another round.

Kidahin stepped back into the laboratory and looked closely at the cryogenic drum. *Was this the projectile in the water reptile's mouth?*

Impulsively, Kidahin tagged the clean room contents and left, heading up into the final bay.

She found a room that opened out into the shipyard. An air-arresting force field separated the bay from vacuum. The floor dropped several hundred ells into the asteroid and was filled with cranes and gantries. Whatever had been built here had been towed out into the drydock.

Kidahin looked through the transparent force field and stared in shock.

The warship was beautiful.

Two hundred and three geodes roughly the size of the LAC prototype each were interconnected by soaring silver crystalline lace. The ship did not have a single hull, but several hulls the size of the ship Delwyn had rescued them all from. The design reminded Kidahin of a dried branching plant without its leaves, silver in color, with fruits hanging from branch tips.

Sliver gossamer threads stretched around the geodes to the branch structure. It was longer than a Compact destroyer with a beam almost as wide. EVA combat-suited Ni'zakhonii were running up a docking clamp access ramp, a steady stream of them.

Evacuees. Zalzadrin took a single look and understood. "What we saw from orbit was not scaffolding but these buttressing silver filaments. They have their power built-up and are preparing to depart."

"Mistress," Kidahin interrupted. "They would not leave this place intact for us to study. It is likely either rigged for demolition, or their warships will fire on it as soon as the prototype jumps into FTL."

Zalzadrin nodded and twitched her ear, opening her comm. "Mistress Melkorka? Zalzadrin. This ship is taking on personnel and is likely preparing to depart. We are nowhere near getting the docking clamps overridden, and I doubt we can offer effective action before they depart. Perhaps you should have the Mistress of Battle fire into the chasm. Target the drydock clamps and prevent the ship from physically exiting the shipyard."

***

"Delwyn?" Melkorka asked.

"Forget it," he told her. "Akenallin, emergency translate everyone off that rock who can't get into a troop transport immediately!"

"By your command," the Mistress of Conveyance said over the combat address system.

"Hlinlodyn, recall all combat forces to their transports. Breaching parties already within the outpost will be recalled by Akenallin.

"Melkorka, we cannot capture that ship. Prepare to fire on the shipyard," Delwyn said.

"By your command."

"Hlinlodyn, transmit to all ships on tactical comm: target the drydock and prepare to fire."

"By your command. Transmitting tactical fire directives," Hlinlodyn said.

"Hlindredreda, open green channel to all ships."

"By your command. Ship-to-ship green channel open."

"Attention: Enemy prototype heavy cruiser is about to jump to FTL. All ships target that location and fire as I fire."

"Delwyn," Akenallin's voice sang over the combat address system. "Mistress Zalzadrin and her Hunters and the tail of Warriors who had deployed with them have been recovered."

"Good job, Akenallin," he said. "Hlinlodyn, status of the assault forces?"

"Hovertanks are withdrawing from their breaching work. The first transports are en route."

"Hlinlodyn, you may fire on that structure."

"By your command."

***

"My Lord Chief Scientist, I abase myself. All research personnel and support staff have boarded. The prototype will very soon have adequate power to make an FTL jump into subspace, I abase myself!" Vassal Security Chief Sua Za reported.

"Vassal Navigator, plot for the home system at once. Bring shields up to maximum power, but not the weapons systems. I don't intend to remain here and defend the research shipyard against a dagan-Na Atal task force. Remote access the shipyard fusion plant, disable its cooling systems, and ramp it up to full power."

"At once, My Lord Chief Scientist. I abase myself!"

Shuddering impacts transferred tremors into the drydock, and the mooring clamps transferred the rapidly strengthening impact tremors to the ship.

"My Lord Chief Scientist, I abase myself. The dagan-Na Atal concentrated firepower has burned out the outpost shield generators. I abase my…."

The Shaha navigator was thrown from his seat as a torpedo exploded right off the prototype's bow. He climbed back to his station and read the damage report. "My Lord Chief Scientist, I abase myself. Direct hit on hull *b'9*. Minor damage. Radiological emissions neutralized."

Another series of jolts shook the operations center. "Minor damage is accumulating on all forward hulls. Shields continue to draw full power. Sublight drive reports full power available at your command. Vassal Chief Engineer reports FTL warp bubble formation nearly complete, My Lord Chief Scientist. I abase myself."

"What is taking the FTL…?"

The Chief Scientist stopped speaking as the ship took a terrific ringing impact that lifted him out of his seat at the command console and slammed him into the operations center ceiling, breaking his neck.

Injuries and casualties mounted. The Shaha prototype warship shook convulsively as Compact weapon strikes hitting the asteroid carved pieces of rock away from the fissure the research shipyard had been built into. Cranes and drydock superstructure fell onto and across the sweeping arches of the new warship but caused little more than cosmetic damage in itself.

Vassal Navigator crawled to his seat in pain. His broken legs made standing difficult. Only by strength of his massive leg muscles did he regain his station.

"Chief Engineer, this is the Test Flight Navigator. I've completed the arc plot through the subspace manifold. Awaiting warp field envelopment. What's taking so damn long?"

"It's the ship's design, Navigator. It is nearly indestructible, barely detectable, but difficult to generate a warp field around due to its unorthodox geometry. The short answer? I don't have a power plant large enough to generate the field a ship this massive requires."

"Maybe you should have built a bigger one!" the Navigator retorted.

"The engineering plant is crammed into three adjacent hulls so tight there's barely room to service the equipment as it is."

A succession of impacts shook the ship again. The dagan-Na Atal ships had cut or blown away the outer surface of the asteroid exposing the shipyard to direct fire.

"Hurry, Chief Engineer. The ship is about to lose its forward hulls. Can't you give me weapons fire?"

"No! Let the shields do their work."

"What work? I'm reading structural damage accumulating from all the mechanical force torqueing commuted to the ship," the Test Flight Navigator said.

"Diverting power to structural integrity systems. Time to jump: thirty-three aines." The Chief Engineer advised.

"We won't be here in thirty-three aines!"

***

"Status?" Melkorka demanded.

"Drydock destroyed, Mistress," Hlinlodyn reported. "Combat Analysis reports difficulty locking onto enemy warship with weapons systems. Vessel is taking some damage but so far all relatively minor."

Phelindra stood next to Delwyn, swearing. "This ship deflects weapons fire just as effectively as the piece of equipment we captured, Delwyn."

He nodded. "I don't understand why he doesn't engage his sublight and get out of there. Right now, we have him in a bottleneck, and he's taking all of our concentrated fire."

Hlinlodyn shook her head, her ears flat against her tight red ringlets, her tail curved up behind her, frozen in the air. "Remarkably efficient shields. We have destroyed three of the leading edge—bow? —pods, but they have been taking more mechanical shear damage than anything else. What I do not understand is why he has not jumped into FTL."

"Damage?" Delwyn asked her.

"I do not think so. Anailiatha may know more from an analysis of the power signatures. I am registering a constant buildup of energy necessary for a transition into the subspace domain, but its pattern resembles ones more common to Ni'zakhonii battleships," Hlinlodyn said.

"Around that thing?" Delwyn asked. "It doesn't look like it has near the mass of a battleship, but it does have about the same beam."

He tried to recall all he knew about a Lizard battleship. A good likeness could be made by taking three rolls of toilet paper, laying them end-to-end, and then pushing them flat. Take the middle roll and on the portside add superstructure: a cluster of towers. Finally, tear off the legs of two large praying mantises and stick them evenly around the perimeter where the rolls met to form sections of the ship, each nearly three hundred meters across.

But a Lizard battleship was nearly nine hundred meters long, and it was massively built and hard to kill, more like an orbital fortress than a ship.

And while they were sluggish at the helm, they didn't take this long to build up to an FTL jump.

Delwyn called up the targeting information on the asteroid and watched as continual fire battered the prototype ship. Two-thirds of it was exposed, the drydock and the surrounding rock blasted away, debris tumbling away in the slight gravity of the asteroid. To him the prototype looked like a bonsai tree growing out of a slab of rock covered with spider silk sprayed silver.

Damn thing looked too beautiful to be of Lizard manufacture.

"Mistress? I am registering massive energy buildup. He is about to jump!" Hlinlodyn reported.

"No! No! No!" Delwyn yelled. "Hlinlodyn, full power forward shields. Everyone secure for collision. All ships cease firing. Trebithia, close on that ship, low-velocity ram. Have a care with the asteroid's gravity well."

"By your command," both mistresses sang.

"Hlinlodyn, maintain forward weapons fire. Trebithia, bring our mass to bear on them. He can't shield against our sheer inertia. His shield elements will either burn out, or he'll have to divert power from his FTL energy buildup to his shields to save himself."

"By your command."

Delwyn knew he should be careful. He had to rely on the skill of his Mistress of Pathwalking, the experience of his Mistress of Tactics.

He didn't dare get his ship wedged into the crevasse. Blasting free of a rammed ship was one thing, breaking free from the asteroid could mean waiting for the jump drive to recharge. The difference between ramming any other ship and ramming this ship into the back of the crevasse was analogous to a wet navy ship ramming a dingy tied up to an iceberg.

Just how much did you really want to hit that iceberg?

###

"Navigator! Enemy fire has subsided!" a subaltern reported.

What? "Why?" the Navigator asked. "Shield status?"

"Seventy-six percent. Navigator, one ship is adjusting position and maintaining fire. Kinetic weapons only."

The Shaha navigator swore. The kinetics and their proximity blast damage were doing more damage, as low as it had been so far, than all the energy weapons and torpedoes put together.

Wait a minute! "Readjusting position how?" he asked.

"The assault battlecruiser is closing slowly and maintaining fire."

Closing? The dagan-Na Atal ship was twice as massive as the prototype. The maneuver was suicide. Was the enemy ship damaged? If it continued to fall under power into the gravity well bow-first, it would ram the asteroid.

Ram? Assault battlecruiser? *Oh, no!* "Brace for collision! Dagan ship on collision course! Chief Engineer, time to warp bubble completion?"

"Imminent!" the Chief Engineer replied.

***

Delwyn watched from the Warleader's Watch as they closed on the wrecked shipyard. The Lizard prototype floated among the wreckage looking more like a bunch of chrome grapes reaching up to him than a starship.

"Closing," Trebithia warned.

"Energy surge!" Hlinlodyn sang out. "Neutrino emissions!"

Delwyn watched helplessly as the prototype heavy battlecruiser folded in on itself, rippled in heat-distortion shimmer, and vanished.

"Dammit! Trebithia, fire bow kick thrusters, pitch over for full reverse thrust!"

"We are too close to the surface, Delwyn. I am applying full OMS breaking thrusters."

"Mistress," Hlinlodyn said. "*Fearless* and *Surefooted* have locked onto us with their tractor fields and are attempting to arrest our descent into the chasm."

Delwyn raced to his station and shifted optical scans and transferred them to the main tactical display. Behind them both destroyers had pitched around, their sterns facing him, their aft tractors shimmering as they drew full power. Rather than use the tractor field attractive force and risk wrenching their tractor emitters from their housings, they were applying minimal engine thrust, being careful to prevent shearing forces from tearing their tractor emitter mountings out of their ships as they slowly arrested his ship's fall.

Hunter's Moon hovered for several long seconds before he slowly withdrew from the deep canyon and headed to minimal altitude, where a nimble Trebithia engaged helm fields and flipped the ship up and back into surveillance orbit.

"Hlindredreda, contact Phalalin and Ahwroona."

"By your command," the Mistress of Communications said.

16
A COMARI CLAIMS HER MALE

"Engine status?" Captain Rodgers asked.

Cabrera walked a quarter of a circle around the lower bridge deck to the starboard companionway and climbed up the steps to the conn. "Captain, chief engineer Sunridge reports substantial metal fatigue caused by neutron radiation. Thankfully the last three hundred meters or so of the ship is all engine complex, and the engineering neutron shielding prevented the radiation from passing forward of frame 176. As matters stand, Engine-1 is inoperative. Engine-2 is so badly damaged it won't fire. Engine-3 needs structural force fields and heavy structural integrity field biases to shore up its mounts. Engine-4 is eighty-seven percent operational. Sunridge thinks she can get Engine-3 online in another fifty hours."

Rodgers nodded. "Mr. Carstairs, report."

"We are maintaining orbit around the dwarf planet, Captain. Hyperdrive coil damage has been either repaired or bypassed. Coils are charged and standing by," the navigator reported.

"Very well," Rodgers said and nodded absently to herself, pausing to twist the titanic waist-length braid hanging to her waist before turning to Winters.

"Well Captain, how would you categorize this mission? A success or a failure?"

"This mission is not over yet, Captain Rodgers. The co-Ambassadors remain aboard, and I'm not standing on Elleio soil. As for the intervening matters, I'd call it a draw. You lost only three fighters, which is a fine example of fighter combat operations. Of the 207 people caught in burning or decompressing compartments, sixty-nine died from burns and another forty-seven died when they got caught in bursting compartments or sucked into space through breaches and open vents. The rest of them survived because they wore rebreathers or hazard suits, or they sheltered in place inside intact compartments that didn't blow out because Cabrera got the fires out when he purged the forward quarter flight deck. That's a low KIA number considering what we came up against. I'm sure Doctor Kerchival has a few people in critical condition in sickbay that may not pull through, but I hope not.

"We also kept the Lizard force divided. Their lower-mass ships can jump into FTL quite fast, faster even than our hyperdrive can recharge. They would have finished their demolition and evacuation mission and jumped on top of Marsch had you not engaged the dwarf planet task force and drawn those three heavy destroyers away from his battle group."

"But Marsch didn't get the prototype heavy cruiser," Rodgers muttered.

"No," Winters admitted. "But not through any fault of his own. His three ships blew enough rock off the asteroid to build another Mount Everest. While doing so, he also captured a lot of material, equipment, and laboratory computers, including samples of crystalline structures in different stages of preparation. I watched quite a bit of Marsch's CIC combat tracking logs over the past hour. That prototype took multiple fire from three ships for damn near fifteen minutes. You'll likely get a commendation for this, Judith."

"I don't want a commendation, Captain. I want my KIA's back," Rodgers snapped.

"Yeah, I know. Me too," Winters said.

"Incoming message on hyperlink for co-Ambassador Anlann from *Surefooted*, Captain," Romaine said.

"Huh. About time," Rodgers murmured. "I'd've thought they'd be more eager to hear from you, co-Ambassador Anlann."

"They are busy seeing to the Warpact warleader's needs, Captain Rodgers," Anlann said in reproof even as he steeled himself for his Mistress of the Ship's report. "I am ready."

Rodgers turned to Romaine. "Accept, Lieutenant."

"Aye Captain. Co-Ambassador?"

"Anlann!" Ahwroona sang.

"Damage report," Anlann said.

"Minor hull damage, inoperative radiological shields, and buckled dorsal compartments scattered across the combat hull. We have zero torpedo inventory.

"There are one hundred thirty-two wounded, twenty-three more in critical condition and three killed in action. Delwyn has been singing to them over the tactical comm." Ahwroona stopped and took in the view of her warleader.

Anlann felt a lump in his throat. He had been far too long absent from his occupational association. He missed them and hurt for them, for each one of the wounded laying in Health Center, and for those who had died.

"Anlann, I am receiving communications from the Warpact warleader, meant for you," Ahwroona said, confused.

Anlann smiled at her confusion. "Patch him through, Ahwroona."

"By your command." Ahwroona's image ghosted into the background as Delwyn's profile solidified into the foreground.

"Anlann?" Delwyn blurted.

"Delwyn! How are you?"

"Not happy, Anlann. The damn thing got away."

"Sometimes the branch breaks," Anlann said philosophically.

"You'd better get here, Anlann. Your Mistress of the Ship is quite angry with me."

"I am not!" Ahwroona insisted.

"Why do you think so?" Anlann asked, ignoring Ahwroona, curious.

"I told her to screen *Night Shadow*."

Anlann frowned. "Ah. Yes, I can imagine how that might get you put on her kill list."

"I am not…Anlann!" Ahwroona gulped, shocked at the idea of harming any male, let alone the Warpact warleader.

"Tell me about *Night Shadow*," Anlann said.

As the two warleaders talked, Ahwroona signed a commentary of her own with Seralin. She gave the co-Ambassador a more dispassionate report than the emotional one she had given Anlann. By watching Ahwroona's waggling fingers Seralin learned the highlights of the battle and the proposed solution to *Night Shadow's* present difficulties.

###

"He wants me to *what?*" Captain Rodgers demanded.

"Delwyn came up with the idea. You will tow *Night Shadow* through hyperspace to Elleio. Without the combat hull, the destroyer lacks the structural integrity necessary for successful FTL travel," Seralin said.

Rodgers glared at her executive officer. "Can we do that?"

"Well," Cabrera mused, "we have the power for the tractors, and neither the tractor emitters nor the tractor bracings have taken damage. Once in hyperspace, we can manage at a leisurely point three-five cee, which is about the best we can get because of all the engine damage. In hyperspace that translates to about 2.82 light-years per day. It'd take us twenty-five days, twelve hours, and seventeen minutes to reach Elleio heliopause from here at that rate. The real question is: can we get us and them through the jump point wormhole in time?"

"I do not understand," Seralin said. "You tear a hole into a hyperdimension, drive your ship at sublight for a given duration, and then tear a hole into normal space to return, yes?"

"That's it in a nutshell," Winters said. "But the hyperdrive coils only open the wormhole that bridges normal space and hyperspace. Once the wormhole opens, it begins to close at a rate determined by physical laws. The hyperdrive field doesn't hold it open. The navigable event horizon begins to shrink once it has opened. Coalition ships don't delay entry into hyperspace once the jump point opens.

"The concern is whether or not the wormhole will close on some part of the towed destroyer's engineering hull."

"What about acceleration? Does it make any difference?" Seralin pressed.

"All the difference co-Ambassador Seralin," Rodgers said. "I don't know if we can reach the requisite acceleration given our engine damage."

"What about *Night Shadow*'s sublight engines? They have a better acceleration rating than your engines do undamaged," Anlann suggested.

"You propose a pusher arrangement?" Rodgers asked, shocked. She glanced at Cabrera. "Will that work?"

"If we can maintain a straight longitudinal thrust vector it might, but it won't stand up to even moderate evasive strategies. The shearing force on the tractors might torque them right out of their mounts. Force field reinforcement will help for occasional trim adjustments, but hyperspace is filled with gravitational eddies and currents. If we get pulled into one, then it's the same as if we had made a wildly evasive course change at high acceleration. That will introduce shearing forces and torque onto the emitter mounts.

"Anlann, you and Seralin will have to advise the ship's warleader of the hazards involved. If we lose the tractors, he'll be stuck in hyperspace. At the very least we'll have to open a jump point to normal space and hope his momentum can carry him through before it collapses."

"Delwyn, did you get all of that?" Anlann asked over the open comm.

"I did, and I'll relay your concerns to *Night Shadow*. In the meantime I want *Henri Edda* here now. There's no reason for you to waste time waiting on those two Compact heavy battlecruisers to finish recharging their jump drives."

"You do *not* issue orders to me, Mr. Marsch," Rodgers snapped.

"Hello, Captain Rodgers. Congrats on your promotion to captain. Actually Captain, since you have a warleader and his protectress aboard your ship, and since this volume of space remains a potential Conflict Zone, and since you are within Compact territory, then I *do* have the same authority a Coalition fleet captain has in these circumstances. Kindly get your ass here soonest. Delwyn out."

***

Delwyn ordered Hlindredreda to cut the hyperlink, spitting furious.

Why? What the devil was wrong with him? Rodgers did have a point. She was the captain, and her command wasn't a Compact asset.

The mood on the command center had begun to deteriorate the moment Rodgers had objected to his orders. The supervising mistresses, their support leaders, and their teams were growing angrier by the second. Delwyn could even smell it, too. Their massed towering rage, the indignation of hearing him being questioned or disregarded had moved them to sudden, terrible violence.

He had to sing them down from their shared empathic fury.

***

Kidahin stood next to Zalzadrin as they looked over the supplies and equipment that they had taken from the Ni'zakhonii outpost and shipyard. When Delwyn's singing began to fill the combat staging and deployment bay, Kidahin paused to listen to the soothing, comforting rhythm.

"Uh-oh," Zalzadrin muttered. "They are angry. Someone on the Coalition warship must have refused to bring Anlann and Seralin here."

Kidahin flicked her ears in acknowledgment of the obvious. "How do you think we should proceed?"

"How should I know?" Zalzadrin complained. "I am no engineer. Anailiatha will have to come down here with her engineers and techmistresses. As Mistress of Arms, I have only to scan and certify that nothing we brought aboard is ordnance. The Mistress of Healers will have to scan for toxic products and contaminants, too. Let us get started."

"Affirm," Kidahin acknowledged.

***

Delwyn sat at his post on the Warleader's Watch. Phelindra hovered over his shoulder as he read Nynava's after-action report.

The four-crew hovertanks, a marvel in themselves, had all converged on the chasm containing the dock facility after first destroying several perimeter guns and defensive systems. Given enough time, they had breached the rocky surface where the containment force fields met the rock. Once through the canyon walls and below the antipersonnel fields, the infantry Warriors had invaded the outpost.

He sighed. It had been a good plan, and he could not fault Nynava that the prototype heavy cruiser had been operational—barely—and that the Lizards had jumped him out of the shipyard at the last minute. Had

258

that ship not been so near completion, her plan to seize the outpost and capture the prototype intact would have worked.

Delwyn read further and found her analysis both thoughtful and provocative. He never considered the hovertanks much more than light tanks on a hover platform. That they were, but in his narrow-minded view he had seen them as operating on planets or large habitable moons like Elleio, Ibeetu, or even his former home Valhalla.

They were much more. They had full attitude and reaction control systems, thrusters that let them operate in vacuum. They used more power than the turbine-driven heavy tanks, but they could operate in near-weightless environments, too. In appearance a Compact hovertank resembled a squat Apollo lunar excursion module, an old Moon lander covered with ablative, reactive, and kinetic armor. It had a Faraday cage to defeat moderate EMP and minimal particle shields. It fired an x-ray laser, an electron-positron particle weapon, and a duranium-tipped explosive slug from a railgun mounted on a three-sixty-degree turret.

Delwyn called up the armor's specifications and read on, fascinated. A four-person crew manned the thing: a driver, a turret gunner, a left flank gunner, and a right flank gunner. Maneuverability: high. Duration: about nineteen standard hours on a removable hydrogen-antihydrogen magnetic bottle the size of a pony keg. Full environmental support, and wow what he could do with one of…

"No," Phelindra said as she tail-cinched him up tightly next to her. "Do not bother considering it."

"Aw, come on Phelindra, it'd be fun!"

"Maybe on the Ah'vou'ree Clan Combat Training Center grounds but never in actual combat," she sang, using the more emphatic octave which brooked no argument.

"Have you read Nynava's report yet?" he asked, changing the subject.

"I did. Melkorka, Hlinlodyn, and I have already discussed it at some length."

"I think her assault would have worked if we'd arrived a few hours earlier."

"That is what we told her, too. She is disappointed. She thinks her first surface combat as Mistress of Battle was a failure," Phelindra said.

Delwyn shook his head. "Not a failure. Not a complete success but certainly it wasn't a failure. I failed by not preventing the prototype from jumping."

Phelindra yanked him closer to her using her tail and hugged him. Her warmer than human body both soothing and comforting against his cool skin. "You did not fail any more than she did, and you did recover valuable intelligence and material."

Delwyn pursed his lips, blew out a gust of air, and punched up a different after-action report.

"What about Zalzadrin's report?"

Phelindra growled, an ominous low trilling sound. "Zalzadrin should have accompanied the dock control assault and prowler teams and not remain with Kidahin and the asset recovery teams."

"I doubt her presence would have made much of a difference. The Warriors killed the dock master and the station personnel. A drydock is a drydock, more or less, so there was nothing to capture there. Zalzadrin is cross-trained in defense subsystems and tactical operations. At the most, her training in defense systems and experience aboard the LAC should have given her a chance of activating the correct crystals in the matrix tables and dropping the shipyard's shields. Maybe that would have allowed the assault teams entry into the shipyard proper without having to take time blasting away at rock with the hovertanks and driving through Lizard infantry. Still, I doubt even then they would have reached the prototype before the Lizards closed up their bays and boarding hatches. Besides, she kept the materials recovery on track, and she warned Melkorka about the Ni'zakhonii fleeing to the vessel."

"You love her," Phelindra trilled suddenly.

Caught off guard by the unrelated statement, he stammered. "Who? Melkorka, Kidahin, or Zalzadrin?"

"All three, but I meant Zalzadrin. You want her to succeed."

"Of course I do," Delwyn said. "And I love all of you. I think Zalzadrin will make a fine Mistress of Arms. Her weapons release selections had been spot on. She took no losses, not even any wounded. She accomplished her primary mission to capture research and development materials."

"Yes," Phelindra agreed. "Who are you considering for accomplishment awards?"

Now that was the question, wasn't it? A female's rank earring contained accomplishment webs, mission beads, and honor knots. Mission beads came to mind. Everyone aboard should receive a mission bead, one reflecting overall battle group participation. He hadn't given them mission beads when they had returned to Elleio with the captured LAC because the mission had begun under the leadership of the former warleader, Kalinn, and only he could have awarded mission beads to those people taking part in the capture and return of an enemy asset. Unfortunately, he had been killed long before Delwyn had taken action against the Lizards and their experimental light attack craft.

But this time he could award mission beads.

Did doing so mean they were automatically entitled to honor knots and accomplishment webs? The mission wasn't over until they returned to Elleio. As of right now, he was considering Zalzadrin for an honor knot because of her success in returning captured intelligence. Of those aboard ship, he considered Hlinlodyn for her command of combat operations once he had asserted Warpact. In fact, if anybody deserved a web, it was the Mistress of Tactics. Her overwhelmed protégé Saidrinha deserved one as well.

As much as Delwyn wanted to reward everyone aboard ship, he remembered that Eyloni weren't human. Their culture viewed accomplishment and recognition differently than humans did. If a female felt the recognition unwarranted or unearned then it was worse than not receiving recognition at all. Females prized male recognition of their abilities—advancement in military rank—but Phalalin had given Delwyn ample warning on this matter. Unearned recognition drew attention like the stench of a rotting corpse. It humiliated the female receiving it. It caused females within her society to question her abilities and the warleader's motives, a sure and swift way to bring the hierarchies into the matter.

It was best to be stingy with rank because they would cherish it all the more, but at the same time Delwyn had been warned to never refuse seeing an accomplishment.

That 'but' was driving Delwyn in circles.

He dismissed it by rubbing Phelindra's muscular back. "Have you looked at the stuff they brought back yet?"

"No," she said and swatted playfully at him with her pons. "Keeping up with you is enough for me as it is. Anailiatha is down there picking and prodding through it all, trying to sort it all into related piles."

"I thought Akenallin brought it all back in related groups," he said.

"She did. Instruments with instruments, chemicals with chemicals, crystals with crystals, and so on. But items from the warehouses, the labs, and all the metallurgic items are mixed up."

"I'll bet that's going over really well," he said with a smile.

"Indeed. Anailiatha has a quarter of her engineering techmistresses prowling through the materials now."

"Mistress?" Hlindredreda called from communications. *'Green Ivy* has minimal intermittent local communications capability. Bordanin wants to speak with Delwyn."

Melkorka cocked her head at Delwyn, and he nodded.

"Accept," Melkorka said.

"Affirm, acting."

"Delwyn," Bordanin began, "we have restored attitude control and can now correct for drift. Our jump drive is operational, and we will soon have the sublight drive back in operation."

Delwyn nodded and considered both the view of Bordanin's command center and of the warleader himself. The command center had lost its faux jungle appearance and the stations he could see looked understaffed or offline. Bordanin had the vigor of health about him, yet he was also covered with bruises and abrasions.

"Casualties?" Delwyn asked.

"One thousand and two injured with concussive impact injuries, broken bones, some burns, and several foreign body assaults from explosive debris. Forty-two fatalities. My warship remains at Battle Status, but we have no torpedoes and only a few kinetic projectiles. We have some heavy hull damage. It will take us several hours at least before we can guarantee hull integrity for an FTL jump."

"We definitely have the time. We're trying to figure out a way to tractor *Night Shadow* through hyperspace using the Coalition warship as a service tug."

Bordanin's eyes widened. "Is that even possible?"

"It's within the realm of possibility. Barely."

Bordanin flicked his tail, a bemused expression on his face. He perked his ears at Delwyn. "Thank the spirits my warship has his jump drive. I would not want to brave this hyperspace that Coalition warships jump through. Tell me how the battle group fares."

"*Stone Knife* has been destroyed. *Steep Trails* and *Padfoot* are operational, no damage. *Surefooted* has suffered marginal damage. *Fearless* and my warship both have moderate damage. *Pathfinder* has taken heavy damage but can navigate. *Night Shadow* we've spoken of. He and *Pathfinder* have taken casualties, and you know your own warship, which from my view looks hammered." Delwyn paused before coming to a decision. "I relinquish Warpact command to you."

Bordanin nodded politely and pricked his ears at Delwyn. "Accepted, although I doubt we are in a region of conflict any longer."

"I'm not so sure about that. Anlann once considered this system a possible conflict zone while my warship was under repair. He was proven right then, and I think caution is prudent now," Delwyn said.

"Mistress, Coalition jump point opening," Hlinlodyn interrupted as *Henri Edda* jumped into Delwyn's cubic tactical display—another toy starship joining the group floating around the asteroid.

Shouldn't be long now. Delwyn thought to himself.

"Delwyn?" Melkorka said. "Sensors detect quantum translation in progress originating from *Surefooted* to the Coalition warship."

I thought so. "Apparently Ahwroona didn't want to trust Anlann and Seralin to *Henri Edda's* teleporter."

"I would not if our places had been swapped," Melkorka huffed.

"Message from *Surefooted* for the Warleader, Mistress," Hlindredreda said.

Melkorka flipped her ears at Delwyn, but she continued to watch the Mistress of Communications.

My, but that didn't take long! Delwyn thought as he nodded to his Mistress of the Ship.

"Accept," Melkorka said.

Anlann's image appeared on the main screen, supplanting Delwyn's view of the little ships orbiting the asteroid.

"Delwyn!" Anlann gasped, panting to catch his breath. "I am so happy to see you are well."

Anlann had run the entire distance from the conveyance center to the command center, Delwyn thought. He smiled. "I have been waiting for you, Warleader Anlann. That sounds so much better than co-Ambassador Anlann. What do you think, Seralin?"

"I agree," Anlann's Protectress and Mistress of Inner Strength said, not out of breath like Anlann.

"I regret the battle came before you could board your warship, Anlann. I did my best to watch over your warship until your arrival. Regretfully, it looks as if all you have left to do is return with us."

"That is more than sufficient. I have been away from my occupational association for far too long, and if you do not mind, I want to examine the damage myself and renew acquaintances."

"I understand. I believe we will all return to the dwarf planet at sublight soon. That will give the ships several days to complete minimal repairs. Both *Green Ivy* and *Pathfinder* have extensive patch repairs to make before they can make the first FTL jump."

"When do you anticipate breaking orbit?" Anlann asked.

"As soon as *Night Shadow* and *Henri Edda* can reach a towing solution and jump into hyperspace."

"And that will be?" Anlann prompted.

"Ambassador Winters assures me sometime in the next forty-eight to seventy-two hours, Earth time."

Anlann looped his tail behind him. "Until then, I remain at your disposal," Anlann said and vanished. The local space cubic representation and its collection of ships reappeared.

Several long hours passed before a tangle of intersecting force fields and balanced tractor fields had finally mated *Henri Edda* and *Night Shadow*. The Coalition carrier served as the bow and hyperdrive section, and the Compact destroyer served as the stern and sublight drive section. Such an arrangement would never survive the rigors of combat, and it was a nail-biter whether it would even survive the stress of hyperspace travel and its gravitational anomalies or not.

Complications arose over the past several hours, and not just those of an engineering nature either. *Night Shadow's* warleader had begun quarreling with Delwyn over the assurances he had been given during battle that his warship would be screened by *Hunter's Moon* and later by Anlann's ship while he had been directed to attack an enemy ship without his primary shields. Bordanin reviewed the tactical situation at the time based on the sensor data from the combat analysis centers of all ships involved and told him that Delwyn's tactics had been correct given that *Stone Knife* had no combat hull shields at the time and *Fearless* had no radiological shields and ineffective multiphasic overlap of his primary and secondary shields. Given that Delwyn's ship had been engaged in the ground assault, *Surefooted* as the relatively undamaged warship had been the correct warship to screen *Night Shadow*.

Night Shadow's warleader disagreed, arguing that without Anlann, Ahwroona could not fight effectively without the crucial male focus.

Delwyn shuddered. He swore he could still feel the chill from Ahwroona radiating from her, through her hull, across open space, and through his hull to the Warleader's Watch. He had no doubts that *Night Shadow's* all-female crew had tried their best to convince their warleader not to raise such accusations, for it belittled them and Ahwroona and her society.

Phalalin and Anlann both had warned Delwyn that the Mawe'allean warleader would likely complain to the Society of Warleaders if he survived the trip back to Elleio.

Delwyn tried to assure Anlann and Phalalin that if the combined ships could enter hyperspace intact, then absent unusually rough hyperspace gravitational weather they should reach Elleio intact.

Phalalin laughed, and Anlann shook his head.

They explained the gravity of the situation to Delwyn. The Mawe'allean warleader's accusation implied his own occupational association was incompetent, that they had relied too much on *Surefooted's* screening, a screening Anlann's occupational association had been likewise too incompetent to give. The Mawe'allean warship society, love their warleader though they did, would never accept such a public assault to their collective honor. *Night Shadow* belonged to them, but if their warleader's dishonor accrued to them, then their collective clans would refuse them the continued possession of their own warship.

Delwyn thought about that for some time before he reached into a slot at his station to withdraw a green bead and a length of purple thread. He stood up and headed for Melkorka.

Her eyes locked on his hands, but her ears tracked his movement as he passed behind her.

Delwyn crossed behind Hlinlodyn and stood beside Saidrinha, causing her to fidget in self-conscious anxiety.

"You did very well today, Saidrinha. The Mistress of Tactics's job would have been much more difficult without your help."

Delwyn knelt beside the huluhar and touched her rank earring, unfastened the clip from the chain's stud, and pulled the gold chain and hoop from her pierced lower earfold.

Saidrinha sat frozen at her station, unranked without the earring. She shook with apprehension at becoming the center of attention.

The command center mistresses watched as Delwyn held the empty golden hoop and wove a simple spider web pattern in purple thread, signifying an accomplishment involving fleet maneuvering under combat conditions, and then tied a bright green bead near the center, interpreted as a mission of dire need.

He finished his work by tying a fisherman's fly knot to the outer web, just inside the golden hoop. Finished, he held the rank earring for the command center mistresses to see. "I advance Saidrinha in rank for her participation in this critical mission that has gained us valuable intelligence on Ni'zakhonii capabilities, including equipment, observations while under fire, and captured materials," he said pointing to the green bead. "I take notice of the assistance Saidrinha provided to the Mistress of Tactics during battle group combat operations," he continued as he traced the purple web. "And I take notice of Saidrinha's performance during a critical time under combat condition with minimal training while honorably maintaining her station," he concluded, pointing to the fisherman's knot.

Delwyn knelt again and threaded the free stud through the fine gold chain and through her earfold and reattached its clasp.

Saidrinha's heart hammered beneath her chest so hard her breasts heaved. Spots flashed in her eyes, and her ears twitched in panic.

Delwyn smiled down at her, remembering a once-anxious Kidahin, and he put his arms around the young Warrior before she could pass out and smack her head against the Combat Analysis station.

Hlinlodyn twisted her tail around Saidrinha and congratulated her. The others smiled and made passing touches and caresses on her, but they were just as pleased with him as they were with the huluhar.

***

"Me?" Kidahin gulped. "Why do I have to help carry all this junk to the Health Center?"

"Because you are the assaultmistress who insisted it be tagged and brought aboard, that is why," Allohindra said. "Just follow my healers and healer's aides. *D'ou tu tay!*" the Mistress of Healers cursed. "All of this is nothing more than crystal growth medium."

"I do not think so Mistress," Kidahin objected. "The crystal baths had their own chemical stations built in. This stuff had been pushed off to the side. Chemicals for the environmental system, perhaps?"

"Then it should go down to the engineering hull and the life support teams. Once I certify all of this as biohazard-free, you can carry it down to them!"

"Yes, Mistress," Kidahin replied in a weak voice, but then she pressed on. "Mistress, a clean room implies a biohazard, as does the cryonic storage unit."

Allohindra scowled, her ears twisting back partway in annoyance. "Fine, Kidahin, I will grant you the cold storage unit does seem out of place. Tell you what, I will take it into the Health Center's quarantine ward, open it, and give it a scan. If it shows clear, *then* you can take it and the whole branchful down to environmental engineering."

"Yes, Mistress."

***

"Message for the warleader from Ambassador Winters," Hlindredreda reported.

"Accept," Delwyn said, grinning as he ignored Melkorka's piqued expression.

"Captain Winters, how may I help you?" he asked.

Winters smiled. "I think you've helped us and the Coalition quite enough already by providing scans of the prototype heavy cruiser."

"We'll have to hope that Frankenstein you're flying in gets to Elleio so we can all work together on those scans."

Winters paused, "I've been reassured that the engineering problems have been worked out, and that we will maneuver with all the grace of a cargo tug."

Delwyn laughed. "Well, Captain, considering all those geodes you have crammed onto your flight deck, you really are a patchwork cargo carrier.

"By the way Captain, I contacted the A'tayotan and recommended they allow Captain Rodgers to take one of the LAC-sized geodes back to Earth for independent analysis. I hope it will make her feel better."

"It won't. Telling a captain that she can't control the destiny of her own ship is never something I wanted to hear either, but it happens when you're a part of a task force.

"Commander Cabrera tells me they're ready to depart for Elleio. Cross your fingers, Senior Chief. If this engineering wonder fails, we'll be stuck where your battle group can't save us this time."

"I have confidence in Commander Sunridge's engineers, Sir. Good luck, Captain, I'm looking forward to seeing you in my immediate families's elleiu tree soon after we get back. Go with the spirits, Sir."

"Looking forward to it, Warleader Delwyn. Good-bye," Winters said.

Delwyn waited several tense minutes along with his command center mistresses and watched as the combined *Henri Edda-Night Shadow* accelerated to point six-nine cee and remained there for almost twenty minutes before the hyperdrive coils finally engaged.

"Report!" Delwyn said.

"The combined vessel has entered hyperspace without incident," Melkorka said, reading a sensor summary on her command console.

"Mistress, incoming message from Bordanin for the warleader," Hlindredreda said.

"Accept!" Delwyn said, verbally tugging at Melkorka's tail.

The Mistress of the Ship scowled back at him. It was not the warleader's job to answer every routine call. One of her jobs was to prioritize and limit outsider access to him.

"Delwyn, prepare for battle group synchronized jump clock for combat jump into a cautionary conflict zone."

"Affirm. What are the chances we'll find anything there?" Delwyn asked the Warpact warleader.

"Probably zero judging from the scans made available to us by the Coalition warship, but I would feel better if we made a more complete survey of the planetoid," Bordanin said.

"Yeah. Me too. I'd hate to have to come back here again."

"Thanks to you, we will not have to. The Be'atika Senge and the A'tayotan will be most pleased."

"Maybe not when they hear what *Night Shadow*'s warleader has to say."

"No. I refuse to accept that. All of us here will back your tactics to the Society of Warleaders, and I do not…Oh! Uh, well. I see you are too busy now and for some time I think, so I…Well, good-bye for now, Delwyn."

Delwyn stared at Bordanin's fading image, baffled.

"Delwyn!" he heard Melkorka's trilling hiss and turned.

He turned in time to see the Comari heading deliberately toward him. She had already passed Melkorka's command console.

She came right up to him, nuzzling him just as she'd done a few months ago.

She smelled, how to say it? Wonderful. As he inhaled her scent into his lungs, his nose tingled, and images filled his head, like a video receiver strobing a brief image from every channel it received, catching a second of video from each broadcast station.

She looked into his eyes, perked her ears forward through her long platinum blond hair.

Delwyn clearly heard her emotional thoughts in his head.

You and I are now one.

EPILOGUE:
RUDE AWAKENINGS...

Delwyn awoke to the sounds of high-pitched chanting. His eyes flickered open and he froze in sudden shock at the sight of a swaying tail. The flickering firelight in the full dark combined with the swaying dance of the appendage summoned an apprehensive thought: Who is this unknown dancer and what is she doing so close to me? *Lo'sutra'est anni,* had no tail.

She could not speak, either.

The dancer swayed in the firelight. As Delwyn blinked, the long tail revealed itself to be a single braid of fine pale hair. Behind the rhythmic figure writhed more dancers, whose tails—actual tails this time—waved about like goldenrod-streaked crimson and vermilion catkins blown by uncertain winds.

The firelight, swaying dancers, singing, and chanting had combined and mesmerized Delwyn, trapping him in the hypnotic, rhythmic gymnastic rite. As the chanting increased and the singing shifted through patterns of atonality, the tempo swelled, and the dancers' rhythm became more frenzied until with a final burst of song, now perfectly blended with the chant in tone and pitch, the composition reached the final crescendo just before the dancers froze.

Delwyn was left with a feeling of puzzlement as the dancers departed. He tried to shake off the fog rolling through his mind. He looked around for something to help him with the attempt, only to find himself dreamily staring at his foot.

He blinked, and his eyes wandered upward. The long-haired Comari before him stood at easy alert rest. Delwyn looked around and saw another female at his feet, this one a Hunter: Phelindra.

He smiled.

"If you think you will be going on some idiotic foray in a hover tank, you can forget it! Understand now that we," and she paused to point her tail at the standing *Lo'sutra'est anni,* "will never allow you to endanger yourself again."

He grunted, brushing her deadly serious concern aside.

"What about the Mawe'allean complaints?" he asked, yawning.

"The Ti'ratni hierarchy has set the Mawe'allea down on their tails," Phelindra assured him.

Delwyn sat up and rubbed his eyes. It didn't help much. He still felt sleepy, but at least his brain had cleared a bit since the nap. He looked at the Hunter.

"How long was I out?" he asked.

Phelindra gave no reply. He had no idea just when exactly he had finally fallen asleep. The simulated Elleio rainforest sky overhead gave him no clue either. The infinitely slow-moving sun hadn't shifted all that much, but that meant nothing. It took Elleio over twelve Earth days to turn from sunrise to sunrise.

The jungle wore the mist like a shroud. The last thing he could remember, they had been prowling through a forest that was more cloud rainforest than temperate rainforest. A place filled with eternal dampness and fog instead of sun and rain.

But the cloud rainforest also marked a transitional landmark. Soon Delwyn, *Lo'sutra'est anni,* and the others would pass through it and on into the enveloping orange-streaked red of the temperate jungle below. There the view would be blocked by hanging scarlet vines and thick orange underbrush and not mist. Beyond the vines and underbrush they would find the cloaking pastel orange shades of the rainforest understory. But for now only the impossibly tall yellow-variegated pale red trees and the omnipresent mist prevailed.

The temperature had climbed to well over thirty degree Celsius as they prowled down the mountain trail. The fog felt both dense and hot to his heightened sense awareness, like wandering about in a yellow steam bath. It was also nearly impenetrable, and visibility had fallen to less than ten ells.

❋❋❋

Kidahin glanced out of the corner of her left eye and cocked her head, contemplating her rank earring. She had two webs now. The white one Kalinn had given her after completing her training mission, and the sky blue one Delwyn had added a short while ago, along with its tiny green bead. The bead she understood: a critical mission. The web he had given in recognition of her success in helping the breaching forces break into the outpost and for the materials she and her assault stalkers had tagged for retrieval.

She had not done that much fighting. Far less in fact than when she watched Delwyn's tail as they killed the security teams on board the Ni'zakhonii LAC they had taken over barely a few months ago.

"Equipment," she muttered to herself. The enemy ship had been decommissioned, deprived of its male gender. It was not a ship, not a he. It was simply equipment.

"What about equipment?" Zalzadrin asked her.

"Nothing. I was just thinking about Delwyn."

"We all do," Nynava murmured. "What about him interests you now?"

"I was remembering how he fought with me and the others when he freed us from the Ni'zakhonii security area."

Nynava twisted her pons in small circles. "Enjoy that memory. Phelindra and *Lo'sutra'est anni* will never allow him to risk his life away from them. He must learn a hard truth now: A warleader rarely leaves his warship. A warleader certainly does not take personal command of surface combat missions. That is what a Mistress of Battle is for. Brelioranda should never have allowed Kalinn to go with the boarding action assault teams. I will never allow Delwyn to accompany either my surface action or my boarding action assault teams into combat. We can hear him sing to us over the tactical commlink."

"He will not like that. He is tails-entwined when it comes to combat. He wants to share the risk with us," Kidahin murmured.

"No," Zalzadrin said. "Nynava is right, and she can enforce the prohibition. No matter what he or Melkorka might say, combat forces cannot deploy without Nynava's permission, and they cannot obtain arms without me issuing them. You are going to help us enforce this prohibition, Kidahin."

"Me? I am only an assaultmistress, one of several hundred aboard our warship. What possible difference can I make?"

Zalzadrin smirked. "He loves you, has always loved you. *Lo'sutra'est anni* respects you, and it takes a lot to gain a Comari's respect."

"He loves all of us, and she came close to killing me for interfering with her pursuit of him!"

"Well, you did do that," Zalzadrin admonished. "Comara pick a male to protect for all their lives. *They pick*, and you all but pulled her by the ears to convince her to shadow Delwyn during his month-long survival ordeal."

Nynava's jaw dropped. "Really?" She turned to face Kidahin. "You should thank the spirits that you are still alive."

Kidahin shrugged. "What of it, and how does any of this put me in a position to keep Delwyn from leading off-ship combat missions?"

"Our hierarchy has decided to advance you in social rank," Zalzadrin said. "Phelindra has agreed to place you with the forward prowler teams. You will come to all briefings that include me, Nynava, Phelindra, Melkorka, Hlinlodyn, or Delwyn. Assault prowler missions, whether surface actions or boarding actions, will involve you and your assault team, among others of course."

"That reminds me," Nynava interrupted. "Your neckwear is no longer appropriate to your social and hierarchy status. You will find new ones, ones with the appropriate knots and colors, waiting on your nest in your abode. I suggest that you change into one of them before you incur an honor debt."

Kidahin gulped. "Yes, Mistress."

Kidahin left the briefing abode and headed for her own. On her way she wondered just how she could stop Delwyn from trying to insinuate himself into future surface combat missions. He certainly had enjoyed taking solitary security sweeps into the forest when they had been together on Ibeetu.

For some reason that memory caused Kidahin to flash back to her adulthood ceremony and the vision she had received from the spirits. They had told her that she held the high ground for a male who fought on the low ground. If he lost the battle, then all Eyloni would cease to exist. Ever since she had left Elleio Kidahin had been toying with the wild fantasy that Delwyn had somehow been the singing male represented in the vision. With *Lo'sutra'est anni* claiming him however, there was no way possible for him to fight alone for the survival of the Eyloni species.

Who then was the male that she had heard in her visions?

\#\#\#

Doctor Tek Nal sat hunched over a global-positioning screen reading telemetry reports from the sixteen thousand dioxide carbide catalysts. All devices seemed to be working perfectly. He checked a second scanner. The dagan egg seeding drones had been programmed to follow the shallow equatorial shorelines. Only there could the amphibian dagan survive through the eccentric-orbiting gas giant moon's harsh winters. As the dioxide carbide built up in the atmosphere, the moon would become an ideal dagan habitat.

"My Lord Doctor Tek Nal. I have obtained a double bonus for you!" Haksith's voice boomed over the ship's comm.

Suspicious, Tek Nal glared into the holoimage of the heavy battlecruiser's commander. "Yes?"

"Yes," Haksith nodded, clacking his teeth together. "I'll bring you a delicacy to chew on as you contemplate our mutual good fortune."

Uh-oh, Tek Nal hissed. That sounded like the beginnings of the Prefecture fiasco all over again.

Minutes later Haksith stepped into the science center, vassal crewmembers pulling two floating stasis food alcoves behind them.

Tek Nal glanced through the clear crystal seal; his toothy jaw dropping.

"Two? You found two dagan-Na Atal on the moon?"

"Yes," Haksith said. "To celebrate your victory in seeding the moon with the dioxide carbide catalysts devices and for pinpointing choice spots for our dagan eggs, I have decided to split them with you. Good eating, I'm told. I've never tried one myself. Can you tell which dagan-Na Atal species they are?"

Tek Nal nodded. "Of course, the tailed ones are the herbivores. These two have no tails, so they are the omnivores."

"The ones you think are an alien Shaha species?"

"Well, at least the most probable of the two at any rate."

"Well… I think I'll indulge in a little taboo and eat my first alien Shaha then," Haksith joked.

He palmed a control on the nearest alcove, reached in, and pulled the creature out. On exiting the alcove it became immediately aware and began to struggle.

"No! No! Help! For the love of God somebody please help m…"
Crunch!

The odd bleating stopped as Haksith bit off the creature's head. He wasted no time bolting the entire animal.

Tek Nal frowned. Such a waste of material. Then again if he got the brain to the neural mapping system before cellular death, then he could model its brain and overlay a Shaha neural network scan onto it and prove whether or not they possessed intelligence. He palmed the remaining alcove open, reached inside, and pulled out the second beast.

"Wait! Stop! I am Ambassador Honorius Alphonse Harrison of the Coalition of Earth Colonies. I am here to negotiate…*shriek!*"

Tek Nal tore off the head of the bleating dagan-Na Atal, set it aside, and bolted the torso, arms, and legs in short order.

It tasted very good.

"Excuse me, My Lord Haksith, but I think I'll scan this and make that neural simulation you asked about earlier."

"Really? Why waste good meat? Well, it is yours to do with as you wish. Maybe it'll taste as good dead."

Tek Nal blanched. Shaha didn't eat dead flesh, not even from an animal freshly dead. He was civilized, after all.

***

Allohindra took a long look at the main research lab in her Health Center.

Where to start? She was a physician and not an engineer. Nothing in the design of the Ni'zakhonii crystal materials even hinted at a life sciences solution. It all looked like geology and metallurgy paraphernalia to her.

Kidahin was to blame for the Health Center primary research laboratory looking like a mining operation analysis center. Kidahin was an assaultmistress now. That meant she should have been prowling and assaulting not making life science determinations. Zalzadrin should have told her 'no' to collecting all this junk.

Spirits!

Allohindra called her labmistresses and pointed at the Ni'zakhonii clean room contents.

"Kidahin had the idea to have all this junk translated aboard for us to look at. So we look at it. Our only concern is possible bioagent contamination. If this junk scans clean, call Anailiatha and have her techmistresses come and drag it all down to the engineering physics laboratory where it belongs."

"Yes Mistress," they replied, clearly not liking prowling through engineering components any more than the Mistress of Healers did.

Allohindra glided over to the cryogenic storage unit and pulled it into a sterile field. She lifted the lid covering a box next to the unit.

A set of thirty-one colored crystals set in a grid gleamed back at her as if lit from within.

A matrix control panel. She had read Hervorallin's report on Ni'zakhonii control systems.

One socket to the side remained empty. Apparently she had to remove one of the crystals and put it into the empty slot.

Hervorallin had said that blue gems opened doors on the equipment that Delwyn had rescued her from.

"Blue it is, then." She plucked the gem from its slot and placed it in the empty one.

It changed color from blue to black and then pulsed. The cryogenic container opened. Cold, heavier than air nitrogen fog billowed out of the opening.

Allohindra twitched her tail at the result. Now everything fell into lab routine. Remove a container, open it, and put a sample into the biohazard analyzer.

Allohindra did so, and moments later a warning flashed on the scanner display as an alarm blared throughout *Hunter's Moon*:

WARNING: MUTAGENIC VIRUS DETECTED. INITIATING
HEALTH CENTER QUARANTINE PROCEDURES…

David Michael Martin

About the Author

David Michael Martin graduated from
the Ohio Institute of Technology in 1982
and designed PC-integrated laboratory
analyzers until 1987. An avid science
fiction and fantasy reader, Mr. Martin
successfully wrote and told engaging
and entertaining stories as a games
master for several of the popular
fantasy-roleplaying game systems
appearing today.

Mr. Martin returned to college and
pursued his interests in English and the
humanities at Ohio University and
Adams State University.

Mr. Martin has over twenty years' experience tutoring adult basic education
classes for adult students seeking their G.E.D. diplomas. Mr. Martin currently
lives in western Michigan and trains puppies using Karen Pryor Clicker
Training techniques to become guide dogs for the blind.

WARPACT! is his third book in the Hunter's Universe saga.

www.ingramcontent.com/pod-product-compliance
Lightning Source LLC
Chambersburg PA
CBHW050825190726
48286CB00007B/1999